Led by the Grey

Led by the Grey

Peter DeCosemo

© Peter DeCosemo 2009

Published by PAD Press 2009

Hardback: 978-0-9559221-1-4
Paperback: 978-0-9559221-2-1

A CIP catalogue record for this book is available from the British Library.

Cover design by Richard Ward
contact@richardwarddesign.com

Photograph of central trumpeter donated by
Evatt (Lez) Bullock
bulz@btopenworld.com

Prepared and printed by:

York Publishing Services Ltd
64 Hallfield Road
Layerthorpe
York YO31 7ZQ
Tel: 01904 431213

Website: www.yps-publishing.co.uk

Foreword

The idea that a groom will have led his horse somewhere is a simple concept easily understood by all, even those with no horse background. However, in this story Peter often reverses the role and will have the horse take the lead. Those familiar with horses may well remember times when they have allowed themselves to be led and have even encouraged the horse to take on this responsibility.

I first met Peter when he came to the Yorkshire Riding Centre to be an Instructor. He started training and riding with the Household Cavalry, but then he had to learn to teach others. He taught beginners as well as more experienced riders and the descriptions of riding and horsemanship in these chapters show he remembers clearly what it was like to be a learner. It was also fun for me in reading this book to recognize names, of both people and places, that I know come from his experiences here. I'm really chuffed that he shows such empathy for the horses. We are given an insight to the thoughts and conversations of the horses by using the medium of the ethereal Pegusinni and so the reader is being educated, perhaps unknowingly, in equine behavior and horsemanship.

Peter's description of Hyde Park, Rotten Row, the barracks, and the connections to Buckingham Palace gives a clear picture of the geography, as well as the formality and traditions of the Household Cavalry. So much that at times you might feel you should stand up and salute someone. He tells us about the daily routines, the appropriate dress and the drill, and many other correct procedures. All this was severely tested in the awful attack in July 1982, when the IRA let off a car bomb in Knightsbridge. Four 4 soldiers were killed. For many the incident, was more horrific because seven horses were also killed. I'm sure those in the Household Cavalry now will be rehearsing and repeating those same traditions, but with a much increased vigilance as a result of that attack. They will be as concerned for their horses as for themselves.

Peter has met so many different personalities. You will recognize some of the various different characters and those with names like Spartacus with his personable traits, you may feel you already know well as a soldier. Peter shows he certainly admires and respects Victoriana's Alpha leadership skills.

I hope you too enjoy being "Led by the Grey" as much as I did.

Jane Bartle-Wilson 2009

Introduction

One of the oldest remaining equine military bastions is the British Household Cavalry. The cavalry is made up of two mounted squadrons, *The Life Guards* and the *Blues and Royals* (formerly The Royal Horse Guards and First Dragoons) stationed in Knightsbridge Barracks, central London. (See map). The main entrance to the barracks leads directly into Hyde Park. Covering 140 hectares (approx 350acres), it is central London's largest park.

The old barracks were demolished in the 1960's and the new buildings were completed in 1970. The barracks houses over 200 horses for military service. For hundreds of years the Cavalry has supplied the Queen's Life Guard who ride from their barracks every day to Whitehall for a twenty-four hour guard duty.

On July 20, 1982, the I.R.A. launched a car bomb attack on the guard as they left Knightsbridge for Whitehall. Four men and seven horses were killed that day. This book opens in May 2007, twenty five years after the attack.

Peter D.
2009

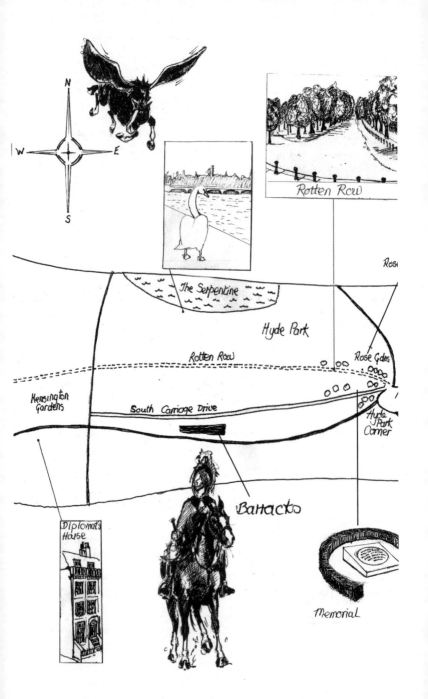

N

W   E

S

Rotten Row

The Serpentine

Hyde Park

Rose Gdns

Rotten Row

Kensington Gardens

South Carriage Drive

Hyde Park Corner

Barracks

Diplomat's House

Memorial

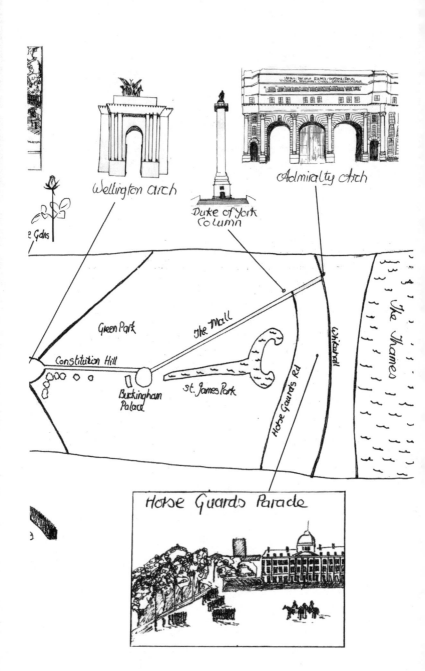

Wellington arch

Duke of York Column

Admiralty Arch

The Thames

Green Park

The Mall

Constitution Hill

Buckingham Palace

St. James Park

Horse Guards Rd

Whitehall

Horse Guards Parade

e Gdns

Chapter One

Victoriana was irritated. For two days she'd had a risen nail head on her front left hoof and her groom hadn't noticed it. This wasn't such a bad thing, but it was on the inside of the hoof which meant when she trotted the nail occasionally brushed against her right leg. Damned annoying. The groom would be around after morning feeding to clean her stall and groom her for exercise. Hopefully today he would notice and have it attended to. She had too many other things on her mind to be bothered by a risen clench.

From the darkness of her box stall she heard the clock above the barracks main entrance strike 5.a.m. She pulled absently at a stalk of rye grass in her hay as she mulled over the most recent goings on. The latest piece of news travelling through the barrack herd was that several Pegusinni had been noticed circling over Hyde Park. They had been spotted last week by Spartacus the regimental drum horse for the Blues and Royals when he was out on his morning constitutional.

There were two drum horses in the regiment, Spartacus in the Blues and Royals and Achilles in the Life Guards.

The drum horses were huge Shires, standing over 17 hands high and usually brown and white (skewbald). Spartacus and his groom had been on the south side of the Serpentine Lake in the park when he'd spotted half a dozen Pegusinni hovering high above. He watched as the Pegusinni, small winged horses about the size of a greyhound dog and invisible to the human eye, fluttered around and circled for several minutes before swooping lower and headed west in formation toward the Royal Albert Hall.

"Now then," wondered Spartacus as he watched them disappear from view, "what on earth could be of interest in Kensington to a bunch of Pegusinni?" He finished his walk and returned to barracks. The stable blocks for the two squadrons of horses are on a split level; Life Guards partially below ground level and Blues and Royals above them. Access for men, horses and vehicles are broad, gently sloped paved ramps. As his groom was dismounting and fiddling with tack, Spartacus spotted Victoriana walking elegantly as always up the ramp from the Life Guard's troop stables. She was leading her groom who Spartacus ignored as he lowered his neck in deference to the alpha mare. He towered above the thoroughbred and was probably twice her weight, but size and physical strength have nothing to do with the pecking order of equine. Victoriana was their leader and it was never doubted or questioned. He passed on his information to her; she nodded, thanked him and moved off ready for her own exercise. Had this news come from anyone else she may have doubted it's validity but Spartacus was a senior member of the Senate and had been with his regiment almost as long as she had. She took his words very seriously.

"Pegusinni over the park and then down to Kensington," she mused now as she ate her hay, "Could be serious or could be nothing."

Pegusinni were usually seen over the more rural and warmer parts of the planet enjoying the sunshine and freedom, so it was quite curious for them to be circling and busying over central London. Unless it meant the horses of the regiment were due for a visit from him.

Other business on her mind involved the two of the geldings on riding school duty who had been misbehaving, resulting in one trainee guardsman falling while practising riding in full ceremonial sate kit. Another had almost fallen but managed to stay on by holding tightly to the horse's neck strap, but his nerve and confidence had been badly shaken for the rest of the training ride. This report had come in from Agatha, a senior mare who had been on riding school duty for years. She kept Victoriana informed of the entire goings on in the trainee troop. Victoriana knew who the geldings were and would have their names brought up at the next Senate meeting. Years of experience had taught her that the cheeky geldings usually did things like this out of boredom and not malice, but it could not be tolerated. As equine they had a duty to perform and obey. A duty rarely questioned.

Then there was the intake of 22 new remounts recently arrived from Windsor. The initiations had gone well but there were still more lectures to be given. The remounts were the younger horses sent fresh from the bogs of Ireland to Combermere Barracks in Windsor where they started their training as cavalry mounts. After Combermere, the remounts were transferred to the Knightsbridge Barracks. Training of young horses and new recruits at Knightsbridge was done by the 'riding staff', a small elite group of men who had undergone specialist training.

Victoriana finished the remains of her hay, rinsed her mouth with some fresh water and retired to the corner of her box stall. She relaxed her neck muscles, lifted and

3

rested her right hind and shifted her weight to her stronger left leg, and dozed until her groom arrived.

As an officer's charger, carrying one of the Commissioned Officers while they were on duty was a prestigious and highly responsible position. Col. Peter Lindsay was the present commanding officer of the regiment. Victoriana carried Captain Johnson, the Riding Master, head of all riding staff for the whole regiment. While his rank was two places below that of a Colonel, because of his specialist position Captain Johnson had authority over more senior officers whenever it concerned mounted work. Indeed, any member of the riding staff, known as remount riders, could give instruction and direction to senior ranks if it concerned riding or training. Captain Johnson was known simply as 'Johno' throughout the barracks, except if someone was addressing him personally.

Johno had selected Victoriana as his mount out of dozens of prospects as she had plenty of natural talent and a sensible disposition. An officer's charger was generally of more thoroughbred breeding than the troop horses. Finer bone and perfectly straight mane and tail were charger requirements. Irish troop horses tended to be heavier set with coarse, wavy tail hair. Johno was a busy man and didn't ride every day so frequently Victoriana's exercise was conducted by Lance Corporal Christopher Webber, a younger and talented rider from the riding staff. Victoriana approved of this arrangement as Webber was a little lighter in weight, and naturally better balanced than Captain Johno.

As the duty trumpeter up on the parade square sounded reveille at 6.a.m., Victoriana opened her eyes, rocked back on her haunches and stretched out her fore limbs. She walked a couple of times around her box stall to loosen the rest of her muscles and then took a position by the door in anticipation of morning feed. Her stall was not in one of the four main troop barns but in a side wing used as the veterinary centre, also known as 'sick bay'. The few other stalls here were empty most of the time and she liked it that way. The noise coming from the main troops increased as the rest of the regiment also prepared for feeding and exercise. Two hundred troop horses yelling for their breakfast could make quite a racket.

A bleary-eyed trooper soon appeared and Victoriana stepped aside to allow him to drop her feed into the metal manger. More troopers could be heard chattering and calling to each other as they prepared the first string of troop horses for exercise, or 'watering order' as it was known in barracks. Sometime after morning feed her groom returned. He cleaned her stall and then she allowed him to fasten the rope from her head collar to a metal ring in the wall. This was done for safety to prevent a horse from walking out of an open stall door during grooming. A point which amused Victoriana as a closed door had never stopped her from leaving if she'd really wanted to.

At 9.a.m. Corporal Webber arrived carrying her tack; a simple snaffle bridle and a light weight civilian saddle. A status symbol for the riding staff was their work uniform which consisted of a dark blue tunic and breeches. The tunic had a high, rounded collar needing no tie. The breeches had a broad red stripe on the outside of the leg.. All other members of the regiment wore khaki clothing for day to day work. Corporal Webber swiftly had Victoriana ready and she proceeded to lead him out and up to the main parade square. Even though the groom had picked out and cleaned each of her hooves, he had failed to notice the risen clench on her left fore. She mildly cursed under her breath and decided to do something about it herself after exercise.

The parade square was a hive of activity, too early for the Queen's Life Guard to be lining up, but many horses and riders were coming and going from the park or across to the indoor riding arena at the West side of the square. As Webber put his foot into the left stirrup and swung himself lightly into her saddle, Victoriana saw a string of riding school horses leading their trainees back to the barns. The two geldings who had caused trouble the day before avoided her look. The others slightly lowered their necks as they passed her and she replied with an imperceptible opening of her nostrils. This was usually the only visible sign that equine were communicating.

"Hey, Webber!" another remount rider called from the upper walkway, "Hold up two minutes and I'll join you with my youngster."

"Sorry, mate, running late, catch you later," yelled back Webber. His legs brushed Victoriana's ribs and she set off a brisk walk toward the gate.

"Why on earth did humans talk so darn loudly?" she wondered as they paused at the gate, waiting for the duty M.P. to stop traffic and allow them to cross the road into the park.

Victoriana knew perfectly well why Webber had declined the offer of company but she didn't mind. They turned right onto the sand track that ran along the south edge of the park and headed east toward Hyde Park corner. Various civilian equine went by carrying their riders, most horses nodded to her, some looked a little intimidated. The track passed the outdoor manage on their left and continued on to the end of the park where it merged with the main riding trail known as 'Rotten Row', a broad, tree-lined sand surfaced avenue, once known as 'Ladies Mile.' A hundred years ago, this was a place for girls riding side-saddle to flirt with passing gentry.

The roar of the morning traffic grew louder as they approached Hyde Park corner. Rush hour. Black London taxis, red double decker buses, 18-wheeled lorries and private cars using five lanes and going at breakneck speed around one of the busiest traffic circles in Europe. Just before the end of the trail and the madness of the main road, Webber halted Victoriana by some large trees. She felt Webber look at his wrist watch as they waited. Presently a female civilian rider appeared riding a bay gelding, and from a short rope leading a grey Welsh mountain pony with a child on board.

"Morning, Clarissa," Victoriana heard Webber say.

"Why, good morning, Corporal Webber," said the female.

All three equine exchanged nods and tail gestures.

"You know, I don't tell many people I'm meeting my date on Rotten Row. And what a stupid damn name that is, eh?" said Webber.

The girl laughed. "Oh, you are such a peasant, Christopher; the name is a corruption of the expression *route de roi*, which means King's Road. It's quite a grand name. In its heyday this was a very posh place to be seen."

"You learned that at your finishing school then, along with flower arranging and deportment?"

She laughed again and then made a playful hitting gesture toward him with her riding crop.

"Oh good lord, I can't stand much more of this; let's get this show on the road," said Victoriana to the bay gelding.

With one accord, all three equine set off marching three abreast down the row. They zoned out the drone of the riders and had their own productive exchange.

"What's new in Civvy Street then, Mr. Nero?" asked Victoriana of the bay gelding walking in the centre of the three.

"Nothing much, same old stuff. Well, except for the arrival of this young thing," he gestured to the small grey mare being lead to his left.

"And what is your name, young lady?" enquired Victoriana.

"Florence," said a timid equine voice.

"Nice to meet you, Florence."

"And you too, Ma'am."

"Speak up, girl."

"Yes, ma'am," came the somewhat shaky reply.

Victoriana whipped her head and neck rapidly to her right shoulder to snap at an irritating fly. She watched it float away and turned back to her civilian companions.

"And I see you are carrying Sarah, Clarissa's younger sister."

"Yes, ma'am."

"And Sarah not being experienced will be why you are on the leading rein, correct?"

"Yes."

"Hmm, quite the responsibility, young lady," said the matriarch, "not to be taken frivolously."

The bay gelding stifled an equine snort, "Be kind to her. You were young and innocent at one time." After a brief pause, "So, what else is new behind the big walls?"

"Senate meeting day after tomorrow," she replied.

"Full moon already? Seems like just a week ago we had the last one."

"You need to keep up with the times, old man," she said with a wicked glint.

"Pwah!" was his only response.

The horses walked steadily forward as the humans above engaged in their typical inane and flirtatious banter. On their right the broad pavement separating the Row from the Serpentine Lake was busy with morning joggers, parents and nannies pushing strollers and child buggies or holding hands with other small children. A boy on a skate board wove in and out of the pedestrians, causing some to curse as he cut in too closely.

"I thought they'd banned those things," said Nero.

Before she could reply the adult riders gave simultaneous light tugs on the reins to bring the group to a halt. They had walked three quarters of the length of Rotten Row. Ahead of them to the west lay the end of the trail and the road crossing into Kensington gardens and the Prince Albert memorial. Clarissa spoke to Webber.

"Sarah's riding has improved so much this week she now has 5 minutes off the leading rein to show us what she can do on her own."

Webber made some sort of masculine grunt trying to sound kind and impressed at the same time. It didn't fool anyone. Clarissa leaned over and unclipped the leading rein from the pony's bridle. "Now, Sarah, you can go and do some riding on your own. Have a walk down there, practise your halts and walk transitions."

The girl and the young pony mare stepped off cautiously away from the group.

"I guess I have time for a quick smoke," said Webber pulling out his packet of cigarettes and lighter.

"You'll get into trouble if you're seen smoking again on duty," commented Clarissa.

He ignored her as he rolled his thumb over the wheel of the lighter. Simultaneously, a strong breeze came from overhead blew out the flame.

"Damn," he muttered and tried again.

Nero and Victoriana heard none of it as they stared upward at the four Pegusinni which had caused the breeze and were now flying toward the child rider and pony mare. The child had executed a halt and she and the pony were standing perfectly still facing a teenage boy holding his bicycle. The mane and tail of the pony mare started to shift in the draught caused by the circling Pegusinni. The boy appeared to be having a conversation with Sarah, and then suddenly he looked upward at the small winged horses. The child looked up too, and then shook her head. The Pegusinni dropped lower, wings beating frantically, causing dust and sand to blow up off the Row and the boy to shield his eyes.

By now the Webber and Clarissa had seen what was happening.

"Sarah! Come back right now!" called Clarissa.

Victoriana and Nero were transfixed. They had never seen anything like it. The pony and child were motionless, staring at the boy with the bicycle. The Pegusinni, increased in number now to fifteen, were going berserk overhead. Sand, dust and pieces of litter were caught up in a miniature whirlwind. Branches on the surrounding shrubbery swayed in the localised breeze. Pedestrians stopped to stare at the bizarre scene. The boy looked once more to the girl and pony and said something.

"Good grief," said Nero under his breath, "Pegusinni in the park?"

"Spartacus saw them last week," said Victoriana.

"And you didn't think to mention it?" he asked incredulously.

Victoriana was about to snap a reply but the words were trapped in her mind as the scene before them played out further. With no warning the grey pony mare let out a terrified squeal, spun on her haunches and bolted down the Row. In seconds she had flashed past the two standing horses and their riders. The child's left, foot had slipped from one of her stirrups and the young girl was partially dislodged from the saddle hanging precariously to the side of the pony's neck. This was no ordinary gallop. This was a death charge of a terrified creature fleeing for its life.

"Sarah!" yelled Clarissa, kicking the old gelding in the ribs to set chase. But Webber and Victoriana were already ahead of them. The pony was moving at a dangerous speed with the child rider screaming, the loose stirrup iron and leather flapping wildly out to the side, and the reins swinging precariously low around the pony's neck. Pedestrians crossing the Row leapt sideways out of the path of the galloping horses. Sand flew out behind the thundering hooves. Nero was elderly and unfit and Clarissa was young but not a bold rider so they had little chance of catching the crazed pony. Victoriana had already taken this into account and knew it was up to her and Webber to prevent further disaster. Webber flexed forward into a crouched position, parallel with Victoriana's neck. She didn't need urging as she connected with her thoroughbred heritage and flew across the sand.

Hooves pounded as they drew upside the petrified pony. Victoriana tried to connect to her. "It's ok, you're safe! You can stop, we're all with you!" To no avail. The pony was in flight and defence mode and her shut-down brain heard nothing.

"Hold on tight!" yelled Webber to the hysterical child, "I've nearly got you!" They were neck and neck, side by side as they flew down the Row. Webber was trying to grab the reins on the pony's bridle but they were beyond his reach. Victoriana clicked to her long distance vision and saw the end of the Row on the skyline.

"Oh mercy, Hyde Park Corner."

Taking the unusual step of partially ignoring Webber's commands to stay next to the pony, she summoned all her speed and kicked into equine overdrive. She flew past the pony, veered off sharply to the right; then when she was ahead, she swung brusquely back to the left and came to a sliding halt directly in the path of the runaway. With only a few metres to go before the corner, a look of recognition passed over the pony's eyes and she tried to slow. But not quite quickly enough. As the pony turned harshly to the left to avoid Victoriana, Sarah flew off the saddle to the right. She landed with a soft thud onto the sand, causing all the wind to be knocked from her lungs. She lay still, moaning and clutching her arm. The pony slowed to a trot, then walk, and finally halted. Her flanks heaving and sweat running, she turned to face Victoriana. The traffic less than a few metres away continued its incessant roar.

Webber jumped out of the saddle and began attending to the injured child. Nero lumbered up at his best speed and allowed Clarissa to vault off and join Webber. Clarissa opened her mobile telephone to call for help. Nero and Victoriana stood motionless in front of the pony; all three with sweat dripping from their sides and trying to recover their breath.

Victoriana regained her composure first. "You have some explaining to do," she said calmly and steadily to the pony.

Flanks double heaving, choking for air, the pony couldn't speak. Her eyeballs were still out on stalks and a little blood dripped from her mouth. In the panic of the bolt, she had accidentally bitten her tongue.

"That," said Nero to Victoriana, "has to be one of the strongest cases of IFR I've seen in many a day."

"Indeed," she replied, "and now we have to find out what caused it." She glanced downward. "Oh blast!"

"What?" asked the gelding.

"Cut my right fore on that damn risen clench."

Chapter Two

Freddy Hobbs was born in the small town of Stavely, North Derbyshire. His mother Jane had lived there all of her life. At the age of 18, she met a cheeky builder's assistant named Roger Hobbs who had come to her mother's house to work on a loft conversion. It was a popular thing to do to the small terraced houses in this area. The houses had no room to expand outwards so everyone built upwards to gain that elusive third bedroom or study. Roger was fit, told plenty of jokes and had a smile that made Jane melt. He wasted no time in asking her on a date and after the first date Jane knew this man was someone special. Within a year they were married and in their own small house which was characteristic to the area, but with a mortgage that stretched them to their limits.

Having a baby early in their marriage had definitely not been in their plans. They had been married only 18 months when Freddy (Frederick to his grandmother) arrived; a perfectly healthy, normal baby boy with his dad's natural dark blond hair and his mum's dimple on his left cheek. The Hobbs were a typical young family; tight financially but getting by. That is, until the day Roger fell off the roof of a three storey house and died before the ambulance could get him to the hospital. Freddy was three years old.

Unable to keep up the mortgage payments, even with the small insurance fee she'd been allocated from Roger's death, a devastated Jane found a two bedroom council-subsidised flat to rent. She'd always had a love of cooking and baking, so she took a part-time job at a local café four mornings a week while her mother looked after her son. When Freddy was 5 and ready to start school, she began to look for full time employment. She was determined to increase her earnings and get back on the property ladder. But the job market held thin pickings for a young single mother with few academic qualifications. One Monday morning in the café she was serving two older women who were enjoying a good gossip.

"Well, they're right up creek now that Enid's retired," said the thin one said, nibbling on her warm pastry.

"Aye, 15 years she'd been with them, ever since her Arthur passed away," replied the heavy red haired friend. "Gone to Skegness to live with her daughter now."

"They'll have a 'ard time finding someone to replace her cooking, cleaning and everything she did."

"They reckon they won't find anyone local so they're going to advertise nationally too. Right posh going on, eh?"

"Excuse me," said Jane returning to their table, "can I ask you who it is that's looking for help?"

"Aye lass, it's Professor Kinghorn and his Missus over in't Spinkhill; their Enid has buggered off to Skeggy!" the thin one giggled. "Left a week back and they still ant' got no replacement. Had to send their laundry out to be done."

"Eee, it's a hard life being a toff, eh?" said the red head as they both collapsed into laughter.

"Do you know exactly where in Spinkhill?" asked Jane.

"Of course, luv. Eh, I thought everyone knew their place. It's the old rectory across the road from church."

"Thanks," said Jane, "Very helpful." She turned to walk back to the kitchen.

"And one more thing, luv."

"Yes?" Jane paused and looked at the thin one.

"Two of them fresh cream éclairs, please."

Jane's shift at the café finished at 2.pm. giving her just an hour before Freddy was due to be collected from school. She went back to the flat, changed her clothes, fiddled with her hair and put on some fresh makeup. Then she ran outside and hammered on the door of Charlie, her neighbour. Thankfully he was home, having been on earlies at the building site that day.

"I need a huge favour," said Jane with her best smile fixed in place.

"Aye? Now what would that be, lass?" He scratched at his stomach through the red t-shirt. At 45, all the signs of middle age were showing.

"A lift to Spinkhill now, please."

"Well, you're always full of surprises, aint ya? What's the attraction there?"

"Possible job. Please Charlie, can you do it? I'll make you an extra pie when I make ours this week."

"Oh well, you always know how to persuade me, dontcha?" he laughed as he grabbed his coat from the peg, picked up his keys and closed the back door. They got into his old Ford Fiesta which smelled of yesterday's fish and chips and set off for the village a few miles away.

Spinkhill is a very small village in the far north of Derbyshire; a collection of old cottages and houses, several farms and a private school. The village sits on the side of one of the rolling hills that overlook the Peak District, one of Britain's most beautiful national parks.

Charlie pulled up and parked in front of the rectory. Three storeys high, the rectory was a huge house originally built for the parish priest several centuries back. Imposing bay windows bordered either side of the large arched front door.

"Blimey, who lives 'ere, luv, Cruella De Ville?"

"No, but I'm hoping my future employer."

"No way!"

"Way……dude," Jane said with a grin, "now hang on here and I'll see if they're home." She straightened her skirt and walked up the front path to the door.

Jane rang the bell and waited only a few moments before the door was opened by a tall, slim man. He pushed a hand back through his scraggly grey hair and looked at her quizzically. From the car Charlie could see him talking to Jane and after a few minutes she turned and signalled to Charlie that she was going inside for a while. He sighed, pulled an old newspaper off the back seat and prepared to wait. Within 5 minutes she was running down the path back toward the car. She leaned in the window.

"Ok, second favour. Can you pick up Freddy for me and keep him with you for an hour? Maybe give him a sandwich and a glass of milk."

"What? Taxi AND babysitting?"

"A pie and a Victoria sponge?"

"Deal. So what's going on in there?"

"I'm convincing them they can't live without me."

And that was the start of Jane's 11 years of employment with Professor Maurice Kinghorn and his wife Eleanor.

Maurice Kinghorn had met the recently widowed Eleanor Digby-Ovens at the local hunt ball. He was a heart surgeon, she a county magistrate. He was 29 and she was 49. A wonderfully ripe scandal then swept through the upper middle class circles of South Yorkshire and nearby counties. Paying no heed, they married and bought the rectory in the village of Spinkhill. When she retired from the judicial bench at 60, he was head of cardiology at Northern General Hospital in nearby Sheffield. Retired from employment but not retired from life, Eleanor immersed herself in hospital fund raising, animal charities, children's charities and local council affairs. The last thing she was was a domestic goddess.

When Jane had turned up for the unscheduled interview it was Eleanor who had seen the potential and possibilities. A tour of the house had inevitably led to the kitchen, in disarray with dirty dishes, frozen food cartons, open food packets on any available surface and laundry stacked in the corner. While Eleanor chatted vaguely about working hours and wages, Jane cleared counters, loaded the dishwasher and inspected the fridge and pantry for food. She asked Mrs Kinghorn what her favourite thing was to make for dinner. After a short pause Eleanor replied, "Reservations."

Mrs. Kinghorn put the large old kettle to boil on the Aga stove and got things ready to make tea. (This, she could manage). At the same time Jane looked in the fridge and pantry and put together a pasta, cheese and tomato casserole spiced up with few herbs she found lurking in old jars. As Eleanor poured the tea into faded china cups, Jane wrote down the heating instructions for the dish and explained this would be their dinner.

By the time Maurice joined them for tea around the kitchen table, Eleanor had hired Jane as their new full time cook/housekeeper. She let Maurice deal with that messy business about money. The main stumbling block was the distance between Jane's house in Stavely and the rectory. There wasn't any way Jane could afford a car at this point in her life.

Never one to allow disappointment to be part of his wife's life, Maurice asked if Jane had seen the entire house on her tour. She shook her head. He led her to a door across the kitchen which opened to a rear staircase. In the period the home had been built it was customary to have staff quarters on the upper floors at the rear of the house. Maurice and Jane walked up two flights of stairs to a well-appointed apartment on the top floor. Two good size bedrooms, a sitting room and separate bathroom; perfect for a single mother and her young son. The deal was done.

Maurice gave Jane a lift back home to Stavely and she collected Freddy, who was simultaneously eating a jam sandwich and bouncing on Charlie's beaten up couch. First thing in the morning after taking Freddy to school, she handed in her notice to the café. Then Eleanor drove in to collect her for her first full day at work. Over the next few weeks between being a full time and well paid housekeeper, Jane gave notice to the council for the rented flat and with help from family and neighbours moved her furniture and other possessions up to the rectory. The Kinghorns owned three vehicles, a small sporty one Maurice used for the hospital commute, a Range Rover they used for longer trips to London and Scotland, and a 'run about' shopping car. The latter quickly and unofficially became Jane's car.

Although he didn't have a dad, overall, Freddy Hobbs had a pretty good home life. A large bedroom all for himself, a big warm kitchen where his mum spent a lot of time cooking and doing laundry; but best of all, a truly gigantic walled garden to the rear of the house for a boy of five and three quarters to explore. The immense garden intimidated him, so to start with he didn't stray far from the back door without his mum or Gran when she visited. When he did go exploring alone he always kept the kitchen door in sight. Just in case. Huge trees broke up the expanse of the lawns and flower beds. The vegetable garden, green house and potting shed were toward the very bottom of the gardens. Mr. Scraggs, the gardener, came in three times a week to keep things in order. Mr. Scraggs was a bit scary in appearance but showed his soft side by allowing Freddy to sit on the steering wheel of the tractor-lawn mower when he cut the grass once a week during the summer. In the autumn Freddy helped rake and gather leaves and stood quite close to the bonfire the gardener lit. He'd go back to the house with his clothes smelling of smoke and burnt leaves, causing his mum to have a scene and march him upstairs to a hot bath.

Sometimes in the autumn evenings after the leaves had fallen, Freddy would look out of his bedroom window where the tall gnarled oak trees stood, looking like bogie men holding their long arms high above their heads, ready to walk toward his room. He'd shriek, his mum would come in and tell him it was only the trees and then tuck him in bed. The next morning Jane would take Freddy out into the garden and show him the trees. In the sunshine they didn't look scary at all. These were early lessons in how sometimes things aren't what they first appear to be.

Eleanor had a daughter, Caroline, from her first marriage. Caroline married a Canadian diplomat and now lived in Ottawa, Canada. Not having any children from their own marriage, Maurice and Eleanor were intrigued and enthused to have young Freddy running around bringing the place to life. As time moved along, Eleanor became a mentor and mother figure to Jane, and Maurice became a grandfather to Freddy. On weekends he'd take the boy and the two family dogs on long nature walks and point out all sorts of fun things about plants and wildlife. They frequently returned from such trips with arms full of flowers and branches which were then were displayed in the kitchen window. Freddy liked to spend hours staring from his bedroom window looking over the rear garden and the fields beyond. He liked watching the birds, the rabbits and the small winged horses that were regular visitors. Whenever he asked the grown ups what the horses were called, they smiled and complimented him on his great imagination.

When time permitted, Jane would accompany Eleanor on shopping trips to Leeds and Harrogate. This included visits to top hair stylists and clothing stores, gradually causing a change in the younger woman's appearance and outlook. The Kinghorns had guests to dinner at least once a week and while Eleanor was a disaster in the kitchen, she was a wealth of knowledge on foreign cuisine, wine and menu choices. She would discuss the plans for a social evening with Jane who would then create superb meals for the hosts and guests. On dinner party evenings, Jane would double as waitress to the table. This always resulted in a bonus in her pay check. All parties were very happy with the arrangement.

Freddy did well at school and was normally in the top ten of his class. He had plenty of friends and got along pretty well with all of his teachers. In one of his early biology classes the teacher explained about native wildlife in England and passed out text books with sections and photographs on small mammals such as rabbits, badgers, voles, water rats, and hares. But there was no mention of small winged horses. Freddy figured they must be a type of bird. But there was no reference to small winged horses in the lesson on birds, nor could he find them listed in the section on birds in his text book. In the end, he asked the teacher about winged horses. The teacher told Freddy he'd probably seen a large bird of prey. Freddy insisted it wasn't and explained that he'd seen winged animals with horse heads and small hooves. Eventually the teacher lost patience and told him to hush up. The rest of the class, seizing the opportunity, teased him ruthlessly for days afterwards. Freddy decided not to talk about the small winged horses any more until he could prove they were real.

His birthday was during the first week of December, far enough away from Christmas that he didn't have to suffer joint parties and presents. Each year through junior school he was allowed to have a birthday party at the rectory and his mum would make a great birthday tea for him and his friends in the kitchen. It was always too cold for outdoor games so after tea all the children went to the big drawing room at the front of the house. Mrs Kinghorn, wearing one of her very smart evening gowns, would play the baby grand piano for musical chairs and pass the parcel. Professor Kinghorn always wore a silly false red nose and did a conjuring act that got worse every year but also created whoops of laughter and jeers. Thankfully, the birthday party never coincided with the terrible Scottish invasion.

George and Effie Sinclair were long-time friends of Maurice and Eleanor's. Every year they would drive down from the Scottish highlands enroute to Cornwall and stay at the rectory for 3 or 4 days. The visit was usually the first week of August during their twin boys' school holiday. Hamish and Harold Sinclair were four years older than Freddy; both had dark red hair and faces covered with freckles. The freckles were the only way Freddy could tell them apart. Each summer when they arrived he would stare intently at the face of each twin, memorise the freckle pattern and then match it to their name.

For some reason adults always seem to think 15 year old boys will play well with an 11 year old, which, of course, is never the case at all. The twins found it a total bore to be expected to include an 11 year old in their plans and games. Freddy came to loathe their visit and, whenever he could, made excuses to visit friends for the day.

Every summer Jane prepared the extra bedrooms, did some mammoth size grocery shopping and prepared never-ending meals for the Scottish guests. Each year the twins brought their latest gadget or craze, driving Freddy mad with their showing off and cockiness. One year it was brand new skate boards, the next year new off-road mountain bikes and this year, it was bows and arrows. Not the toy sets for children, but genuine adult-size bows, quivers for holding the arrows, a dozen fierce looking metal pointed arrows, and strapped to the roof of their Range Rover, a full size round straw target and stand. On the second afternoon of their visit George Sinclair set up the target at the bottom end of the garden and then very strictly reminded the boys of the rules.

A white rope was laid in a straight line on the grass quite a few metres back from the target. This was the firing line. No one was ever allowed to step in front of the rope when someone else was even holding a bow, let alone firing arrows. If you had a bow and arrow in your hands, you were only allowed to face forward and never were you to turn away from the target while holding them. As soon as arrows were fired, the bow had to be pointed downwards or placed on the ground. And finally, archery was only allowed if a grown-up was present. The twins, keen to show off, agreed to all the rules and got ready to start their tournament. George, Effie, Maurice and Eleanor retired to the wicker chairs and wooden table on the patio to supervise and enjoy glasses of chilled wine and Pimms.

Freddy lay on his stomach, resting his chin in his hands, well back from the red headed twins who were making lots of noise and plenty of excuses as some of their arrows went well wide of the target. One arrow went so wide of the target it hit the branch of an oak tree with a loud twanging noise as it struck the wood. Freddy burst into giggles, and then covered his mouth with his fingers as both twins turned to glare at him.

"You think that's funny, do you?" asked Hamish.

"Think it's easy eh?" Harold followed up.

"Bet you think you're better, eh, Mr. Smarty-Pants?"

"He's the cook's dumb kid, bet he couldn't even figure out which way to hold the bow!"

"Probably kill a cow in the next field!"

By now the twins stood towering above Freddy lying on the grass. Hamish prodded him with the toe of his trainer.

"Come on, give us a laugh."

Hamish glanced up the garden to make sure the adults weren't watching, then bent down and got right into Freddy's face.

"You get 3 arrows. For each one that misses the target," he paused as a sick grin spread over his face, "we get to push your sweaty head down the toilet and flush it." This was followed by a sharper kick in the back by Harold.

"On your feet, Robin bloody Hoody. We could use a laugh."

Freddy knew there was no way out. If he refused they'd only make his life hell later so he might as well get on with the humiliation now. He slowly got to his feet and walked towards the archery equipment lying on the grass. He'd never even had a toy bow and arrow set, let alone picked up an adult-sized one.

Hamish was undoing the belt that held the holster quiver around his waist. The quiver was too big for Freddy and when they strapped it to him it hung loosely off his hips. Harold recovered the arrows from the target and shoved them into the quiver.

"Ok, I'm feeling generous," said Harold, "if any actually land anywhere on the target we'll consider that a hit. All the missed ones guarantee you will get a flushing, cook's boy."

Both twins stepped back and folded their arms, smirks fixed on their faces. Hamish sneaked another look over his shoulder to see if the adults were watching the shenanigans. Laughter and the chink of wine glasses came from the patio as a joke was shared. No adult was looking down into the garden.

Freddy bent down and picked up the bow. Holding it next to him, the full size long bow was almost as tall as the 11 year old boy. He looked down the length of the lawn and noticed for the first time that, unlike a dart board that had a red bull's eye, the archery target was a series of coloured concentric rings. Two white rings made up the perimeter, then two black rings, then two blue ones, two much smaller red ones and finally a golden centre ring. Freddy reached around and fumbled to get an arrow out of the quiver hanging from his waist. The twins snorted at his clumsiness. Freddy kept the bow and the arrow pointed downward as he placed the back of the arrow into the string. Still looking down he paused, totally still.

In one smooth movement he straightened up to full height, drew back the string to its maximum, levelled the bow and released the arrow. It looked as if he hadn't even paused to aim. The arrow flew straight into the centre of the gold ring.

A few silent seconds passed before Harold muttered, "Holy crap."

"Freakin' fluke," Hamish said, "watch where he lands the next sucker."

Freddy stared down the lawn, not quite sure what had just happened. Then, he fumbled for another arrow from the quiver. Looking down and pointing to the weapon to the ground, he loaded the bow, paused, and then again in one flowing movement, uncurled up to full height and released the string.

The second arrow hit several centimetres to the left of the first. Freddy was motionless. He was in a mild state of shock even he couldn't figure out what was going on.

"That can't be right," said a confused Harold, "two in a row?"

"He's figured out a way to bloody well cheat," hissed Hamish through clenched teeth.

Showing more confidence, Freddy reached for his third arrow and this time rapidly repeated his performance. The third arrow landed just to the right of the first.

"Hey! What on earth is going on down there?" yelled George from the patio. He was on his feet running, towards the group of boys.

"Are you two out of your minds? What the hell is Freddy doing holding that bow?"

Maurice and the women were striding down the lawn as well. The adults grouped around the boys and started to give the twins a terrible telling off. Neither boy spoke, but Hamish raised his arm and pointed to the target. There was silence, as everyone stared at the three arrows in the gold centre ring.

"Is this a joke?" asked their father.

"Nope, he did it," replied Hamish pointing to Freddy who was looking embarrassed and sheepish, ready to get into trouble too.

"Put down the bow and quiver, Freddy," directed George. Then the entire group walked down to the target for a closer inspection.

"Maurice looked down at Freddy. "Ok, Freddy, truth now, did you do this?" pointing to the three tightly grouped arrows.

Freddy looked at his shoes. "I did, Mr. Kinghorn."

Maurice put a hand on the boys shoulder. "Think you can do it again with all of us watching?"

"I dunno, I can give it a go."

George took the three arrows out of the target and everyone walked back up to the firing line. Eleanor leaned close to Effie and said quite loudly, "Personally I always knew he was a gifted child."

The twins chose to ignore her.

"If I have to do it again, can I do it without this bloody holster thing tied to me, please?" Freddie asked.

"Yes," said Maurice undoing the loose belt, "and don't swear in front of company."

Looking through the kitchen window, Jane noticed the group standing at the firing line; she dried her hands and went out to see what was going on. As she approached, she saw her son loading a lethal looking arrow into a long bow.

"Oh, my God! Are you people all crazy? Frederick, put that down at once!"

Maurice and Eleanor turned to her. "It's ok, let him do it, he's probably safer than all of us," said Maurice.

Jane looked to Eleanor who gave a small smile and nod of agreement. "Watch, you might get a surprise."

Freddy was holding the bow. "I'm only going to do this one more time, and then I'm done."

"Ok," said Maurice, "just take your time and let's see if it was a bit of luck, eh?"

"Mr. Kinghorn, would you pass the arrows to me please?"

"Of course, Freddy," he said, scooping up six arrows.

"He'll never do it again," said Harold loudly.

"Pure bloody beginner's luck," said Hamish.

"Oh shut up, you pair of whiners," said Eleanor and then smiled sweetly at Effie's glare.

Freddy took the first arrow from Maurice. He paused for a second, then bent down from the waist as he loaded the bow and pulled back the string to its maximum, straightened up and released. The whole group stared as the arrow hit the outer white circle at the very top of the target.

The twins snorted and slapped each other on the back. "See, total bloody crap. Nowhere near the bull's eye."

Everyone else remained quiet as Freddy took the second arrow from Maurice. It was the same process bend, load, draw back, straighten up, and release with no pause for aiming. The second arrow slammed into the black circle exactly 6inches below the arrow in the white circle.

"Oh," said Eleanor quietly, "I think he planned that."

Freddy now loaded arrow number three. It landed in the blue ring, immediately below arrow number two. Arrows four and five followed suit into the red ring and then the outer edge of the gold. No one spoke or moved as Freddy took the last arrow from Maurice. A short pause, and even quicker then before, in one flowing movement Freddie loaded the arrow, raised the bow and released. The arrow flew into the dead centre of the gold bull's eye. Six evenly spaced arrows formed a straight line from centre to outer perimeter. No one spoke as they stared at the target. Finally, Freddy broke the silence.

"Mum, can I have my tea now please?"

The three small winged horses who had been standing on the garden wall took flight to the south.

Chapter Three

Webber waited till medical help had arrived and then gave his version of events to the mounted police officer who had shown up at the scene. Victoriana was known to the gelding from the Metropolitan Mounted Division and after exchanging pleasantries she gave him her version of events. He was intrigued to hear of the Pegusinni and confused by the events that had followed.

"So the mare stood for a few minutes looking at the kid with the bike, the Pegusinni were directly over her head, and then she bolted?"

"Pretty much exactly that," Victoriana answered.

"What was this kid doing, farting flames?"

"Oh, typical of a Met Nag to lower the tone."

"Sorry, but when you go to as many football matches as we do you tend to pick up a few phrases."

"Leave them in the gutter where they belong."

"Sorry ma'am, I'll watch my language," the gelding said, knowing full well this dialogue would cause great entertainment back at base. Victoriana's reputation for no nonsense and discipline were well known across the city.

"I'll have the other lads keep an eye out for any Pegusinni and report back if we hear anything." He paused, and then lowered his voice further. "You're not expecting a visit from *him* are you?"

"Nothing scheduled."

Victoriana took to surveying the scene. Clarissa had called her family and they were there alongside the paramedic attending to the child's sprained wrist and bruising. Sarah's mother was thanking Webber for being a hero. Webber was modestly giving most of the credit to his horse. The pony mare was calmer but still not in a fit state to answer questions, so Victoriana and Nero quickly agreed that he would talk to the mare later back at their stables. He would give Victoriana his report when they met in the park the next day.

With the excitement over, Webber, exchanging a secret glance with Clarissa, mounted and hacked Victoriana slowly back to barracks. Neither of them noticed the boy with his bicycle standing well back, watching from behind the trees.

At precisely 10:28 am, Victoriana and Webber arrived at the main gate, the exact time each day the Queens Life Guard leaves barracks and rides to St. James Palace at Whitehall. Webber halted Victoriana as ten mounted troopers and two mounted non-commissioned officers from the Life Guards wheeled to the right and proceeded down the centre of the road. Tourists rushed to the side of the pavement, cameras clicking furiously as the guard went by. The soldiers in their red tunics and white plumed helmets stared steadfastly ahead, appearing to be unaware of the crowd. The black troop horses also seemed oblivious to the noise, though a few did take notice of a rather dishevelled-looking alpha mare waiting to enter the barracks.

As Webber and Victoriana walked through the main gate, Victoriana began to nod her head upwards as her left fore touched the ground. A farrier standing by the doors to the forge yelled to Webber, "That bleedin' mare is crippled lame, git 'er over 'ere right now!" Victoriana knew it was a touch melodramatic but she was determined to get that damn clench fixed once and for all.

Webber was shocked. "She was perfectly sound five metres ago, what the hell happened?" he said as he swung off her back.

"You lads in blue might be the best jockeys we've got, but yer' pretty crap when it comes hoof and leg care." the farrier said as he grabbed a leather head collar from a nearby peg, swiftly swapped it for Victoriana's bridle, and then tossed the end of the rope through the metal ring in the wall.

He passed the bridle to Webber who then undid the girth and pulled off the saddle and pad. Webber didn't voice his thoughts but he was concerned the wild gallop down the Row had caused tendon damage to the mare. He decided to wait on saying anything until the farrier had done his inspection and passed comment.

Like most of the regimental farriers, Lance Corporal of Horse Biggins was built like a bear and was almost as wide as he was tall. He ran his hand knowingly down the mare's leg, feeling for any heat or pain in the tendons and joints. His sausage-shaped fingers slid smoothly on down to the wall of the hoof and stopped abruptly. "Well there's one bloody problem, she's got a risen clench that I could hang my hat on."

"Yes, but it shouldn't have caused that amount of lameness. She was limping for England when I walked back in through the gate!" Webber did not like to look the fool in front of the farrier.

Victoriana assumed the stance of an innocent bystander as the men continued their discussion.

"You didn't find anything else then?" Webber asked.

Biggins ignored the question. "You got others to ride this morning?"

"Yes, three more," replied Webber. The farrier was now looking over his regimental record sheet.

"She's due in for a new set all round in a couple of days. May as well do it now."

"Can you fit her in straight away?"

"Yeah, had a cancellation from Two Troop. I was going to have a quick sandwich in the N.A.A.F.I., but my little tum can wait."

Webber glanced at the roll of flesh hanging over the farrier's belt but knew better than to make comment. Big mistake for a light-weight remount rider to irritate a farrier.

"Thanks, I really appreciate that; I'll let her groom know where she is." His arms loaded with tack, Webber turned on his heel and set off for his next ride of the day.

The regimental forge was a large airy covered area on the ground floor of the barracks adjacent to the top of the ramps leading to the stables. Large floor-to-ceiling sliding doors opened onto the main square. Anytime the forge was in use, the doors were pushed wide open to let in plenty of daylight and just as important, allow hot air to escape from the furnaces used to heat the metal shoes. It was a noisy place at the best of times with the continuous sound of roaring fans from the furnace and the symphony of steel hammers on anvils as shoes were adjusted to fit each individual hoof. Add to that the sound of a radio with a pop station playing and five or six loud farriers yelling to each other, the forge was overall a fairly rowdy place. This didn't matter at all to the equine communicating with each other because most of their speech is inaudible to human ear.

Novelists and Hollywood film directors usually have it wrong about how horses communicate. They portray it as endless neighs, whinnies and snorts with much hoof stamping. Only on rare occasions do equine use these coarse and rather vulgar methods. Background noise in the forge caused little problem as the equine simply sent their messages from mind to mind, augmented with slight facial expressions.

There is room for at least 6 horses to be worked on at any one time in the forge and replacing a full set of four shoes usually takes about an hour and fifteen minutes. For equine this makes the forge the equivalent of a trip to the coffee shop every six weeks, when they have their feet trimmed and new shoes fitted. Horses come and go, giving plenty of opportunity to swap news and catch up on what was going on around barracks.

Victoriana looked around at the four other horses being shod. Two troop mares from the Life Guards, one gelding from the Blues and Royals riding school troop, and Achilles, the drum horse for the Life Guards mounted band. As Farrier Biggins tied on his leather apron and gathered his tools around him, Victoriana nodded to the others and asked the gelding from riding school if he knew anything about the recent bucking episode. No, not a thing, he told her. He had been at the front of the ride and the incident had taken place behind him.

"Hmm," she thought, "a likely story." But she let it slide.

She adjusted her balance to three legs as Biggins picked up her left fore and started to loosen the clenches of the nails with hammer and buffer. The clatter of hooves at the door caused her to look over and see Venetia leading her groom into the building.

"Over there," yelled another farrier pointing to a spare tie-up point on the wall next to Victoriana, "she'll be done by 12.15."

"Fortuitous timing, indeed," Victoriana said to Venetia, "how are things with your squadron?"

Both black thoroughbred mares were the same age, and to the novice eye the two would have looked identical. Not a snip of white anywhere. Closer inspection showed the alpha mare had more rise and crest to the top of her neck and the angles of the joints in her haunches were more tightly closed, qualities which indicated greater strength and speed.

"Good, busy, but good," replied Venetia, "starting to brace ourselves for silly season as I'm sure you are too."

Venetia was leader for the Blues and Royals as Victoriana was for the Life Guards, but Victoriana, by nature, was the over-all alpha mare of the regiment and Venetia second in command. There was no rivalry or animosity between the two; both knew their place and never questioned it. Venetia was a valuable second in command to Victoriana and, as such, took over whenever the alpha mare was absent from barracks.

They spent a few minutes going over day to day housekeeping subjects, discussing the arrival of the new remounts and how their mentors were coping. Then they talked briefly about silly season, the busy time of the year which would include Trooping of the Colour, (two full dress rehearsals and then the actual event with royalty present), and several State visits. Thankfully there would be no royal weddings this year. With luck, the bachelor Princes would stay single until both mares retired from duty.

Victoriana flinched slightly as Biggins yanked downward and inward with the huge pincers and tore off the first of her old shoes. He tossed it onto a scrapheap of shoes in the corner and moved back to do the same on her left hind.

"Musical ride practice is going well, I hear."

"Yes," said Venetia, "been hearing good things about the routine this year. And they're all looking forward to getting out on the road with the show. They've quite a busy schedule."

The mares paused as the farrier attending to Venetia clicked his tongue and chivvied her into position to start his work. By now Biggins had all four of Victoriana's shoes off and she stood bare foot on the cold cobblestones of the forge floor. She revelled in the feeling of her soles in contact with the ground. She felt the light pulse in her hooves and vibrations from the floor flowing up her limbs. Steel shoes had been introduced to her when she was four years old, to protect her feet from the trauma of paved roads. These few minutes in the forge reminded Victoriana of her youth when she'd been bare foot with no cares.

"And you will be available for Senate later this week?" Victoriana asked Venetia.

"Yes, of course, can't see a problem," Venetia replied.

"Did Spartacus fill you in on what he saw in the park last Monday?"

"Yes, I spoke to him yesterday. What do you make of it?"

"Not a lot till this morning," Victoriana then relayed the morning's events in the park.

"So what do you think there is about the pony mare that caused all the fuss with the Pegusinni?"

"No idea. I'm hoping to get to the bottom of it tomorrow when I see Nero. He's going to talk to the little mare tonight."

They continued to discuss the situation while the farriers worked swiftly around their feet. As was a part of every shoeing routine for military horses, Biggins checked that Victoriana's regiment letters and army issue number were clearly visible on her hooves. The letters L.G., for Life

Guards, had been burned into the outer wall of her right fore hoof. Her army number, 129, had been burned into the wall of her left hoof. It was a painless process for equine, but important for the smooth running of the regiment. Should horses get loose, it was vital that any soldier could identify a horse at a glance. A military horse's career and medical history could all be traced through this one number. Just as with soldiers, horses had their own service numbers which they kept for life.

Biggins was soon done with Victoriana. He loosened the head-collar rope and walked with her outside the forge. It was customary to walk and then lightly jog a newly shod horse around the yard to check for signs of a hot nail. (A nail mistakenly driven into the sensitive structures of the hoof wall). Victoriana led Biggins anti-clockwise around the square, passing the open main gate. As they turned to jog back toward the forge, the duty M.P. walked out into the road to stop traffic and allow the returning guard to enter the barracks. The guard returning from St. James's palace were coming off their twenty-four hour duty, having been replaced by the troops Victoriana had seen leaving earlier. Biggins paused as the guards entered the gate. At that moment, the now all too familiar breeze started again.

Victoriana looked up to see the Pegusinni fly from the park like World War II fighter pilots in arrowhead formation. They dived and then in pairs flew under arch of the main gate, straight above the heads of the returning guard. The strong breeze from the Pegusinni's beating wings blew the red plumes crazily around the guards' helmets and wrapped the tails of the black troop horses around hind legs and haunches. As they flew over the barracks square, the soaring Pegusinni peeled off left and right, turning back to the park, then reversed and rocketed back under the main gate and over the square again.

Biggins stared at the mounted guard caught in the down draft.

"What the hell was that?" he said to no one but himself.

Victoriana watched the disappearing rears of the miniature winged horses as they flew back towards the park and then stared at the guard as they formed up. She was totally puzzled. What could it be about a small grey pony and now a troop of normal horses that had sent the Pegusinni into a spin twice in one day? She looked away from the guard and once more glanced through the open gates. Directly across the road was a teenage boy holding his bicycle.

Chapter Four

Freddy first heard voices three weeks after his sixteenth birthday. The birthday had been pretty good fun. No tea parties at this age but his mum had given him enough money for him and 8 friends to go to a Pizza joint to celebrate. Maurice and Eleanor gave him a sizeable cheque to put towards paying for driving lessons when he turned 17. The Kinghorns had always been thoughtful and generous whenever it was his birthday. Well, except when he was 12 and they'd given him a full-sized archery set. Freddy had never used it.

Professor Kinghorn had spent a long time trying to get Freddy to take up archery after the incident with the Sinclair twins. Maurice told Freddy he was very likely good enough to be on the county team and maybe even the national squad.

"I know you think I'm good, Mr Kinghorn, but really, I'm not interested. I reckon that whole business in the garden was just a bit of luck."

"You have an exceptional talent, Freddy; be a pity not to see you really develop it."

"A pity for who, Professor?"

Maurice Kinghorn had paused and given that question some thought. If the boy wasn't interested, was it really his place to push it? On the other hand if he didn't try, Freddy might grow up to regret it.

"Would you consider going with me just once to the archery club?"

"No thanks. Besides, I mean really, what good will it be to me in this day and age? Not going to help with my GCSE exams and A levels or get me a better job, is it?"

"No, but being talented is a good thing; it's such a pity not to see it develop."

"I'm *not* talented," said Freddy a little too loudly, "I just want to be normal like my mates." Deep down Freddy was still shocked at what had happened that afternoon in the garden. He had never picked up a bow before and yet he zapped off a bunch of arrows that flew into the target like programmed torpedoes. He walked away, hoping the professor wouldn't be mad at him. Maurice wasn't, but later that year in early December Freddy received the bow and arrow and all the gear to go with it. Maurice Kinghorn had a theory; if it was lying around, the boy would probably pick it up and build an interest. It hadn't happened.

Now it was four years later and early evening outside the village hall where a children's carol service was taking place. Some of the parents had brought sweet mince pies, Christmas cakes and hot chocolate. Eleanor, now over 80 and still active in village affairs, had arranged for a visit from Father Christmas. He would arrive at the hall in a small cart pulled by two Shetland ponies belonging to a friend's granddaughters. Mr. Grimshaw, who was to be dressed as an elf and help Santa hand out presents, had slipped on the ice outside the pub the night before and broken his ankle and the two bottles of cider he was carrying. Finding herself in need of an elf at the last minute, Eleanor asked

Freddy to play the part. He tried to protest but Eleanor cunningly asked him for the favour in front of Jane who had immediately given Freddy the "say no and you will lose your fingernails" look.

So there he was dressed as an elf, wearing red trousers, a green jacket, green hat and fake big ears, freezing his bum off waiting to throw parcels at ungrateful kids. Father Christmas, alias Mr. Scraggs the gardener, had gone into the village hall to scrounge a few mince pies and a hot drink. He left Freddy outside to watch the cart, presents and ponies. Freddy Hobbs prayed none of his mates from school were around.

"So, how did you get out of the pony club rally last week?"

"Abscess, right fore."

"For real? Or faked it?"

"Hey! It was real, you can't fake an abscess. They look for it, you know."

There was a short pause. "So, how was it?"

"The rally?"

"Yes."

"Usual mess. Trailer ride over there was like a death flight, they forgot part of my bridle, had to use string for reins, and in the lesson I got stuck following that Welsh cob from Barlborough."

"They one that farts like a machine gun?"

"The very same."

"Glad I had a sore foot."

There was no one on the street except Freddy. Muffled noises came from the village hall behind him, but not another person was in sight. Just Freddy, the cart with presents, and two Shetland ponies.

"You doing the Boxing Day meet?"

"Probably."

"Can be such a long darn day that one, eh?"

"Mine gets tired after about two hours; I'm usually home before lunch."

"If mine falls off again, I'll be back in twenty minutes!"

"Who the hell is there?" yelled Freddy looking up and down the street.

Nothing moved until the two Shetland ponies turned to stare at him.

He stared back.

Silence.

The doors of the village hall swung open and Mr Scraggs came out followed by several parents. "You ready for action, Mr. Elf Helper?" he asked.

"Yeah, yeah, ok," mumbled Freddy and went to stand next to the cart, ready for the torrent of kids.

Christmas came and went. Nothing more unusual happened; just the normal holiday visiting, the presents and the eating. He just about managed to block out the episode with the voices, the same way he tried not to see small winged horses in the garden. He never talked to anyone about those horses. Not since when he was seven and had dragged his mother into the garden to watch them nibbling on the short grass. She had taken him to the doctor the next day and the doctor had suggested a course of therapy and some anti-depressant pills. That's when Freddy laughed and told everyone he'd just made it all up for a bit of fun. Everyone believed him and no more was said. Later when he had his own computer, he'd searched for 'small winged horses' but all that came up was a bunch of stuff about some huge white horse back in the Greek times. Not a damn thing about small dark ones in a person's back garden.

In the week between Christmas and New Year he went with his best mate, Marty, to watch their favourite football team, Sheffield United. It was a freezing cold day and because of a glitch with the ticket machines they had to stand for ages outside in the crowd waiting to go into the stadium. Marty went off to get tea and hot dogs while Freddy kept their place in the queue. A line of portable steel barriers had been erected to guide the crowd in through the correct gates. Freddy was leaning on one of these; he pulled his scarf tighter up against his neck wishing Marty would hurry up.

"I thought there would be more than this for the first home game in a month."

"Probably a lot away for the week, visiting"

"Maybe. Wonder what the hold up is getting them in?"

"Problem with ticket machine, mine said"

"Don't want them waiting too long; always causes more bother when they get irritated."

"They're a lot better behaved since they know they have those CCTV cameras everywhere"

Freddy froze. Right in front of him were two police officers of the South Yorkshire mounted patrol, sitting on two very large police horses. The officer on the left was talking on his mobile phone. The one on the right was leaning over and talking to someone on the ground. Neither one of them said, "Yep, great thing that camera stuff, saves us a lot of work."

The two horses were looking directly toward Freddy. Only their nostrils moved slightly. "What's this one staring at?"

"Don't know, but he looks petrified."

"He's starting to look ill."

"If mine sees him, he'll call for an ambulance."

Freddy was shaking. All colour drained from his face. He took a couple of steps backwards and bumped directly into Marty who spilled the tea and dropped one of the hot dogs.

"Oh bloody marvellous," said Marty, "Cost me almost five quid!" He shook the tea off his hands, then looked back at Freddy. "You all right, mate? Look like you've seen a ghost."

Freddy was rock still, eyes locked on the two horses.

"Hey, lines moving, bugger the tea. We can get more inside. Come on, Fred, don't just stand there," Marty said, giving Freddy a shove.

Freddy didn't remember much about the game. There were too many images and thoughts flying around his head. And worse still, not the type of thing he could talk to anyone about. Twice now. Twice, he'd heard voices having the most bizarre conversations. These weren't voices talking to him. These were voices having their own conversations, unaware that he could hear them. Usually when you think about nutters who hear voices, the voices are telling them to commit mass murders or that Jesus is coming. The voices he heard talked about CCTV cameras and farting Welsh cobs.

During the first week of February, Eleanor became very ill. She was diagnosed with severe pneumonia, but much to everyone's frustration she refused to be taken into hospital. Maurice stopped arguing with her as it only made her more upset and distressed and drained what little strength she had. No matter what tasty and delicate small plates of food Jane prepared for Eleanor she hardly ate, and by the second week she was showing no signs of recovery. Maurice was distraught; at times, he would be short-tempered with everyone, and then immediately apologize. Eleanor had been ill for three weeks when Eleanor's daughter, Caroline, flew in from Canada with her husband, Paul Smith. The day after Caroline arrived, Eleanor Kinghorn passed away.

Paul Smith returned to Canada the day after the funeral, leaving his wife to share the sorrow of her mother's death with her stepfather. The rectory was a very quiet, sad place. Eleanor was a hugely popular and well-liked lady and the house was full of sympathy cards and flowers. Jane answered the constantly ringing phone and took messages to allow the family some peace. Maurice hardly spoke and when he was out of his room he spent his time with Caroline.

Several days after the funeral Maurice asked Jane to join him and Caroline for lunch in the main dining room. Jane usually had lunch with Freddy, but when she explained the situation to him, he said it was no bother. He would meet Marty at the café in Stavely. Freddy found life easier if he was out of the house and away from the sadness.

When the food had been passed around, Maurice spoke. "I'm afraid things are going to have to change."

"Will you stay here?" asked Jane.

"No, I can't now; it's too big for one old codger, and too many memories." He took his time explaining that, after a lot of thought, he had decided to sell the rectory and live with his younger sister and her husband until he decided where he wanted to settle.

"She lives abroad, doesn't she?" asked Jane.

"Oh yes, Austria, quite a few years now," Maurice paused and then went on, "beautiful place. Vienna will be a good distraction for me."

It turned into a lengthy lunch as Caroline and Maurice explained all of their plans.

Marty and Freddy sat in the café where his mum had worked years earlier. They were chomping down on burgers and pop when a teenage girl wearing riding breeches and leggings came in. She pulled off her hard helmet and walked to the counter.

"Who's she think she is?" muttered Marty, "Zara bloody Phillips?" Both boys sniggered.

"I'll have two cheese and ham sandwiches, two of those iced doughnuts and two cans of Pepsi please," she said to the lady behind the counter.

"That's a lot of food for a slim thing like you, young lady."

"Oh, there's two of us, my friend Katy is outside with the horses. She's spending the day riding with me. She rode over from Barlborough this morning."

Barlborough.

Freddy stood up and went to the door. He could see another girl outside holding two horses. He opened the door and stood on the step. The Welsh cob on the right let out a fart like a machine gun.

He cut his lunch with Marty short. With no bus for about an hour, he set off walking back to the rectory. He had now confirmed whose conversations he had been hearing, and it scared the crap out of him. He walked into the kitchen from the garden door as his mum walked in from the dining room. "Mum, do we have to live around here forever?"

"Funny you should ask that, sit down. We need to have a long talk."

Maurice had explained that he would be selling the rectory in the very near future. He would put all furniture, art works and valuables into storage while he was abroad. Obviously, this meant the end of employment and a place to live for Jane and Freddy. Jane, anticipating that their living situation would very likely be changing, had already been considering purchasing a small house in Stavely with the money she'd saved during her years with the Kinghorns. Then Caroline stepped into the conversation.

Her husband, Paul Smith the Canadian diplomat, was being transferred to a position at the Canadian embassy in London next month. They would be supplied with a good-sized home in Kensington with a small two bedroom annex apartment for staff. Caroline and Paul needed a cook/housekeeper, and who better to offer the job to than the person who had been groomed by Caroline's own mother for the past eleven years? Would Jane consider moving herself and Freddy to London to take the position? The embassy wages would be considerably higher than she was able to get anywhere around this area, and, of course, they would live rent free.

Jane had expressed concerns about Freddy's schooling. The move would be in the middle of a term with his 'GCSE' examinations coming up; a terrible time to change schools. Not a problem, they would have a private tutor for him for the remainder of the spring term and then after summer holidays he could join the local high school in Kensington.

"Wow, I know I said how about moving mum, but bloody London?" Freddy groaned.

"It will only be for a year or so; and you might be sixteen but don't swear in front of me."

"I'll be leaving all my mates."

"There are buses and trains, and it's only a few hours away."

Freddy considered the move. It would be pretty damn cool to be able to invite his mates down to London for weekends. He'd get to see every major thing in the city. And he'd get away from voices and little winged horses in his back yard.

Now, only six weeks after the talk with his mum in the kitchen at Spinkhill, Freddy was in Hyde Park holding his bicycle and staring through the main gates of the Household Cavalry barracks, eyes locked on one very curious alpha mare.

Chapter Five

Biggins pulled sharply on the head collar rope but Victoriana was rooted to her spot. All muscles in her neck had tightened and her ears locked like radar scanners onto the boy across the road in the park. She raised her head to use long distance vision in the lower part of her eye and renewed her focus. Should she know him? Why was he staring? Was this the same boy she had seen talking to the child on the grey pony before the crazed bolt? Victoriana couldn't be sure; she hadn't paid much attention to him at that time. And then she saw it. The boy lifted his head slightly and there was an imperceptible movement of his facial muscles. An insignificant opening of his nostril. A movement so small it would have been missed by human eye.

No.

No, she had to be mistaken.

Biggins rattled the rope sharply and raised his voice to her. "Hey, lady muck! Back to planet Earth, please!"

She dropped her gaze from the boy for a second to acknowledge Biggin's commands. She looked back to the gate, but now the boy's back was turned to her as he mounted his bicycle. He rode off toward Kensington and out of her sight. Victoriana pulled slightly toward the open gate hoping to influence Biggins in that direction but no luck. He was set on getting her back to her box stall and getting his lunch.

The returning Queen's Life Guard had formed rank and been dismissed by the guard N.C.O. Troopers in full ceremonial kit were dismounting and being led by their horses to the troop stables. Soldiers in working khaki clothing came out to assist the troops in full gear. None of the soldiers around the parade square saw the small winged horses standing high up on top of the brick walls of the barracks.

"Hey, guys, look! Pegusinni visiting!" called one of the black troop horses to his comrades.

"Wow, haven't seen any of them for ages," shouted back another.

"Quiet, all of you," called Victoriana as she went by, "everyone back to barns and less gossiping. Last thing we need is more rumours and speculation running through the place."

The troop horses dropped their necks slightly as she strode past leading Biggins.

"Yes, ma'am, no more gossip," said one of them.

She heard a smattering of stifled equine laughter behind her as she headed down the ramp to her quarters.

"I heard that!" as she glanced back over her shoulder. She wasn't really angry but order had to be kept with a large herd in such close confinement.

Biggins opened her stall door, undid the buckle on her head collar and allowed her to walk in. Her lunchtime feed had already been placed in the metal trough. Biggins closed and bolted the door, tossed the head collar onto a wall peg and strode off whistling, thinking about his own lunch.

Victoriana rested her right hind while she chewed thoughtfully on her grain feed. Quite the morning, she thought, as she tried to recall everything in sequence. She looked back to the moment when she and Nero had seen the pony standing rock still in front of the boy with the bicycle. At the time, they had been convinced that the child rider had stopped to talk, but that wouldn't explain the Pegusinni and the pony's bolting. Nero had been correct; it had been a particularly extreme case of I.F.R. Involuntary Flight Reflex.

All equine are programmed with I.F.R. Horses, ponies, donkeys, mules, even zebra have this built-in survival mechanism, a crucial part of life for equine in the wild who must be wary of predators. Flight is equine's main method of survival. Being prey and not predator, equine chose flight before fight. Fight is possible, but only in extreme situations when all avenues of flight had been exhausted. Defensive fight consists of bucking or a sharp kicking out of the hind limbs. Striking with forelegs and biting are aggressive actions usually limited to stallions battling for dominance over a band of mares. When I.F.R. is triggered, there is no pause for thought, only flight at the greatest speed possible. He who stops to look is often lunch for marauding predators. Run now, stop and ask what it was later, while you are still alive.

Through centuries of domestication and living in perfectly safe surroundings, most equine learn at a fairly early age to dominate their I.F.R. It will never go away completely, but the trained equine mind can reduce I.F.R. to a slight jump to one side and then regain control. Man knows this involuntary twitch or side jump as 'spooking'. With age and experience, equine usually managed to limit spooking to a minimum; although some highly strung, sensitive ones never learn how, which causes worry and frustration for themselves and their riders.

Victoriana paused from her chewing. It was becoming clear to her that the focal point of these strange events was not the pony, the child or the Pegusinni. It had to be the boy. If she had been allowed a split second longer on the parade square she could have confirmed her suspicions. She had not mistaken the facial movements of the teenager. Five or ten more seconds and she would have known for sure. Victoriana finished her grain and then rinsed her mouth with a fresh drink of water. Still lost in her own thoughts, she chewed steadily on the fresh hay put out for her lunch, wondering what information she would get from Nero the next day. The silence and her thoughts were broken by the sound of approaching hooves on cobble stones. She looked up through the metal bars of her stall to see Whimsy, a grey mare from Life Guard's Two Troop leading a groom into the building. The regiment had a small number of grey equine, ridden mainly by the duty trumpeters. Whimsy nodded as she walked into the large box stall across and further down the aisle. The groom closed and bolted the door, then jogged off out of the building.

"This is a pleasant surprise," said Victoriana, "or is it bad news?"

Generally equine were only brought to the sick bay quarters if there was a medical problem. Whimsy was in the box stall built with inward sloping walls and lined with thick mounds of shavings and sawdust.

"No, no, nothing so serious," sighed the grey mare.

Victoriana was thinking colic, a serious digestive disorder which was alarming because of the horrendous possibilities it brought.

"Just itchy withers," said the grey mare, "actually. I feel a bit embarrassed."

Victoriana nodded, now knowing what had transpired. "Well, don't be embarrassed, just enjoy the break. It will give us time to catch up."

Colic or acute digestive disorder is the number one killer of domesticated equine. Man has made great strides learning to give life-saving veterinary care for colic but it always starts with the intense pain in the stomach and intestine area from an impaction of food or a mammoth build up of gas. Desperate to alleviate the pain, equine will commonly drop to the floor and roll on his sides and back. Rolling and kicking gives temporary relief, but is dangerous for a horse in a box stall where he might easily hurt himself rolling and banging against the sides of the stall. The violence of the rolling can also cause serious damage to the delicate equine digestive tract. The sloping walls and thick shavings in the stall where Whimsy was standing were designed to prevent injury should a horse drop to the floor and roll. Around barracks it was known as 'the colic box'.

"Itchy withers, eh?" asked Victoriana with a twinkle in her eye; withers being the prominent bone where the top of the shoulders meet the base of the neck.

"Yes, got a new groom, he has no idea how much I need my withers scrubbed. It feels like he's doing light dusting with the brush instead of getting stuck in!" Whimsy was a somewhat highly strung mare, and her speech quickened as she spoke.

"And so after mid-day feed you decided to scratch them yourself by floor rolling?"

"Yes, then another one spotted me and started to scream about horses dying! You know how they panic when they see us down? It's all so humiliating. He had me on my feet and was dragging me down here before you could even say wheel barrow."

"Well, at least you had one who cares; nothing wrong with that now, is there?"

"No, I suppose not."

"Look, they'll be round again shortly; would you like to stay for the afternoon and then get back in time for evening feed?"

"Oh, that would be nice. I could use a break from all the troop group yabbering. They never stop, you know. Who saw what on guard today. Who said what to who. Who got their photo taken the most. Endless yakking!" Whimsy complained.

"Ok, when they return, you know the drill, right?"

"Yes, yes of course, do just enough to arouse doubt but not enough to need medications and all that. A bit of walking about and a bit of neck sweating should do it, correct?"

"Yes, that usually does it. Just no over-acting, ok?" Victoriana thought back to her own performance with the clench but quickly dismissed it.

Footsteps marked the return of the groom and a N.C.O. "I put her in the colic box, Corp.; then came straight up to get you. I hope she's ok."

"You did right, lad; now let's have a look at her." They stood quietly by the stall door and observed the grey mare walking unsteadily with light patches of damp sweat on her neck. "Don't look too serious yet; she just looks a bit uncomfortable. No point in calling the vet just now. You know how that goes, don't you?" asked the corporal looking at the young trooper.

"Er, no, Corp. I don't."

"If we call out the duty vet right now, when he walks through the door that horse will be on its feet, eating hay, cool as a cucumber, looking innocent like nuffin had happened. And Major Sanders, the duty vet today, will look at us like we are the biggest pair of plonkers on the planet."

"So......?"

"So, we keep an eye on her, and if she gets over it, you take her back to Two Troop. If she looks worse and really getting ill, then we call out the big guns. Do you still have tack to clean this afternoon?"

"Yes, Corp. I do."

"Right, go get started on that, come back and check on her every 15 or 20 minutes or so, ok?"

"Will do, Corp."

"Mind you, if she shows any signs of getting worse you get me and the vet, sharpish. Got it?"

"Got it, Corp."

"Right. Well, bugger off and get your tack started, we'll leave these two in peace for a bit." They both turned and left the sick bay area.

"So," asked Victoriana picking through her hay, "what's new with you?"

"Not a lot, same old things. Hardly any long guards recently, so haven't been up town for ages. But I am being tried out for the Musical Ride this year and hopefully won't mess it up like last time."

The traditional opening for a performance of the Musical Ride Display team is a drum roll and fanfare by the drummer riding the regimental drum horse and four mounted trumpeters, all riding greys. The drum horse leads the way with the four greys in tight formation behind. Last year Whimsy had been distracted by something in the crowd and didn't see the huge drum horse come to a full halt in front of her. She walked straight into his rear causing him to hump his back, break wind, and almost dislodge the drummer. The other greys teased her about it for weeks. Captain Johno, the Riding Master, deemed her unfit for the job and replaced her with a younger grey gelding from Three Troop. Whimsy was completely mortified.

"I believe we will be supplying several long guards fairly soon, so you should get out on one or two of those."

"Really?" asked Whimsy, "is she returning from Windsor? How long for?

"Sometime later this week I believe, just for a few days." Victoriana was referring to H.M. The Queen. She had been staying at Windsor castle for some time but was expected back at Buckingham Palace on a short stay for official business.

When the Queen was not in residence in London, the Cavalry supplied a 'short guard'; ten troopers and two N.C.O.s. However, when she was in town a full guard was required. A full guard was made up of ten troopers, two N.C.O.s, a Warrant officer to carry the Standard, a full commissioned officer, and a state trumpeter. All being well, Whimsy would carry the state trumpeter on several of the long guards.

The cavalry guard was mounted every day of the year at the gates to St. James's Palace. The palace was the official residence of the monarchy from 1698 until 1837 when Queen Victoria moved the official residence to Buckingham Palace.

The sound of rubber soled boots on cobbles announced the return of the anxious trooper. Both mares were quiet while he looked Whimsy over. She walked around the stall a little and generally looked unsettled but not in serious pain. After a minute the trooper nodded to himself, indicating all was well and walked away.

"Would you be interested in a short stint in trainee troop and doing riding school again for a while?" asked Victoriana.

"Could I? Even after the last disaster?"

"Well, we all make mistakes, and that was quite a while ago."

Whimsy cast her mind back to that fateful day last year in the indoor riding school. The trainee ride she was helping with had just finished their hour long session and was preparing to dismount. As was customary, the horses ending their ride were lined up down the centre of the school. The huge double doors to the arena had been opened and the next group of trainees and horses were lined up outside being inspected before their ride. The trainees were progressively starting to wear full ceremonial kit and today was their first day in the thigh-length jack boots, swan-neck spurs and the plumed, heavy brass helmets with chinstraps. They wore this with their customary khaki breeches and jackets and would gradually make the transition into white buckskin breeches, coloured tunics and breast plates. The instructor was having each trainee dismount individually today and as the man to the right of Whimsy landed, he locked his spurs behind his heels and promptly fell flat on his back.

As he hit the dirt, his helmet flew off and rolled between Whimsy's hind legs just as she was moving sideways to avoid stepping on him. Her own trainee was halfway dismounted when Whimsy felt the 'snake' around her right hind fetlock. (It was actually the chinstrap of the helmet, but to a wary equine it was a snake). As her trainee balanced on one stirrup in mid air, Whimsy's I.F.R. kicked in. Without a thought, she shot forward like something from a cannon. Her trainee flew through the air and ended up flat on his back too. Whimsy bolted straight for the open door with the brass helmet still hanging off her right hind leg. Chaos and general mayhem ensued in the arena as other horses squealed and jumped sideways and trainees fell like dominoes.

Within seconds the grey mare was outside the school, veering sharply to the right, directly in front of the waiting group of horses and trainees. She stopped dead in her tracks, dropped her head and neck down completely between her front legs and double barrelled both of her hind legs high into the air to kick off the attacking reptile. She succeeded and the brass, spiked helmet sailed high and far, landing on the rump of a horse in the waiting ranks. From a standing motionless position, the gelding shot his own rump into the air in defence and dropped his rider onto the tarmac. Two horses from the school ran out of the doors and were joined by the gelding who had just dumped his trainee. They flew up the concrete ramp hot on the heels of Whimsy, resulting in four loose horses in full tack careening across the parade square towards the safety of their barns.

It was on this bright and sunny day that a junior member of the Royal family (something like seventeenth in line to the throne) had chosen to make a formal visit to barracks and was being escorted by the Commanding Officer and the Adjutant to inspect the awaiting Queen's Life Guard formed up at the east end of the parade square. Paying no heed to formalities, the four equines burst through the ranks of the Life Guards. Two shot to the right up the ramp to the Blues and Royals barn, one veered left down the ramp to the Life Guards barn, while Whimsy crashed straight ahead through the wide open doors of the forge and tried to hide by the far wall. Sooty, one of the very senior guard horses, witnessing the whole pantomime, laughed, coughed and choked all at once, resulting in a huge sneeze that ejected a large piece of green mucus from his nostril. Which, unfortunately, landed directly on the side of the royal handbag.

The ten seconds of total silence that followed was eventually broken by the sound of the high heels of a lady attendant stepping forward and producing a packet of Kleenex to dab at the offending snot. Trainees came scurrying on foot from the riding school trying to find loose horses. Whimsy was led slowly from the forge by one of the farriers and taken shamefaced back to stables. Horses on the parade square lined themselves back up into correct ranks.

The junior Royal quickly finished the inspection and headed back to the waiting cars. She declined the invitation to see more activities in barracks and was whisked away. The Commanding Officer was heard to mutter, "I suppose that grey mare's too young to retire?"

Standing in the colic box, Whimsy reflected on the incident for a while and replied to Victoriana, "No, I should stick with the musical ride this year; it's just not fair on the trainees until I can totally control my nerves."

Victoriana had to agree with her. They spent the rest of the afternoon in general conversation and when Whimsy brought up the subject of all the recent sightings of so many Pegusinni, Victoriana made light of the subject and promised to inform everyone when she knew more. Just before four p.m., the trooper and N.C.O. returned to have a final look at Whimsy. Deciding she was better, they returned her to her troop barn. Shortly before six p.m. final hay for the day was brought around and the day shift did one last check-over before the night guard came on duty. As the lights turned off, Victoriana thought about the busy day tomorrow and looked forward to a quiet evening.

Not a chance.

Chapter Six

Freddy mounted his bike and slowly peddled away from the barrack gates. His head was in a total spin. He leaned his bike against a tree and plopped down on a park bench to think things through and try to make some sense of the insane goings-on. He had hoped the move from Spinkhill to central London would have changed all of the madness. Madness he just couldn't talk to anyone about. Last weekend had been pretty exciting when he and his mum had arrived in Kensington; they had unpacked their stuff in the comfortable sized flat to the rear of the main house. Jane quickly got involved in bringing the main house into order for her employers, making lists of things she was going to need for the kitchen and housekeeping.

The flat was furnished with larger items, sofas, chairs, and beds. Freddy went to work wiring up their TVs, DVD recorder, computer and unpacking books and personal items. He didn't have to start his private lessons with the tutor for another week so he made the most of the spare time and on Monday got his bicycle out and set off to explore Kensington gardens and Hyde Park. That was when he first saw the small dark winged horses high above the tree tops. He decided to ignore them as he knew they didn't really exist and, if they didn't exist then they could do him no harm. He cycled around the Royal Albert Hall, marvelling at the size of the place. Then he did a lap around the Prince Albert memorial, staring at the corner statues and wondered who on earth could have designed something so cheesy and gaudy?

It was after he crossed the road and entered Hyde Park that he had seen the huge brown and white Shire horse being ridden by a man in uniform. At the same time he saw the all too familiar flying horses come towards him and pass overhead. Once more Freddy chose to ignore them and cycled quickly home. He spent the next few days helping his mother with shopping and more unpacking. They took several trips on the underground train to get familiar with where it went and how it all worked and took the bus to see the school Freddy would attend next term. And then this morning he again ventured out on his bike to Hyde Park.

He had arrived at the end of the big sand covered lane when the little girl on the grey pony rode up to him. He leaned against his bike when she stopped with a smile and said, "Hello."

He'd given her a half smile back and a nod, and saw a soldier on a black horse and a girl on a brown one standing side by side further down the wide track.

"I'm Sarah and this is my pony Florence."

"Yeah, very nice," mumbled Freddy wishing the kid would shove off, but now looking up and to his left at the rapidly approaching group of small flying horses. "Oh bugger, here we go again."

"Why are you swearing?"

"Listen, kid, you'd be damn well swearing if you thought you were being haunted by little black flying horses."

"Oh, Pegusinni," said a third voice.

"Pegusinni, is that what they're called?" Freddy said, still staring and watching the winged horses come in lower.

"You heard me?" said the small voice.

Freddy looked at the girl, "Of course, I heard you, I'm not bloody deaf."

"Who are you talking to and why are you swearing at me now?" asked the girl.

"You! I'm talking to you. You're the one that just said they were called Peggi-somethings," Freddy said sharply.

The girl looked like she was about to start crying. "I didn't say anything and I don't know anyone called Peggy!" Her bottom lip was shaking.

"I said Pegusinni," said the small, quieter voice.

Fred locked eyes with the pony. "Oh no, please, not again."

"You can hear me?" asked a very shaky pony voice.

Freddy sighed, narrowed his eyes and without moving his mouth, "yes, yes, I can damn well hear you, but honest to God, I wish I couldn't!"

A few of the Pegusinni had dropped lower, their wings causing a down-draught that was kicking up sand and leaves.

"You can't! It's not possible, you can never hear us!"

"I've got news for you, little horse person, I can hear you loud and bloody clear!" He leaned toward the pony. "Boo!" he said loudly, but his mouth didn't open, only his nostrils moved slightly.

In one sharp movement the grey pony half stood on its hind legs, spun around and took off at a dead bolt down the wide sand track. Freddy saw the child rider swing dangerously to one side and almost fall off. The pony was now galloping flat out, the child was screaming and the soldier and the girl on the other horses chasing after them.

"Aww, bloody hell. Welcome to London, Fred," he said to himself.

He thought about heading home and just pretending none of this had happened but his conscience got the better of him. He hopped on the bike and set off in the direction of the galloping horses to see if there had been any damage done. The path had a slight downhill gradient and he gathered speed easily. Freddy knew the really big traffic roundabout was at the far end of the park and he hoped all the running horses had stopped before they got there. He had no idea the two bigger horses were actually galloping on purpose; he thought the whole lot had bolted. Fred was not a horseman; he'd hardly ever had any contact with horses. And now, all this weird stuff happened whenever he was near any of them. Freddy promised himself that once he'd checked out this whole bolting fiasco, he wouldn't go near another horse in his life.

It was a short-lived promise.

When he got to the end of the park, all the horses had stopped and the child rider was lying flat out in the sand, crying. Freddy stepped sideways behind a tree trying to stay out of sight as he watched. The soldier was off his horse and attending to the kid, his black horse standing directly in front of the sweating pony. It actually looked like she was guarding it and preventing it from moving. The girl on the other horse had reached the group and was acting like a typical girl, crying and shouting and generally making a fuss. Then a cop on a horse showed up and started asking the soldier guy questions. At the same time the large police horse started talking to the black mare. Freddy pretty much heard every word of the equine dialogue.

He wasn't as scared now as he had been the first few times he'd heard the voices. At least now he knew where the voices came from and had found out from the incident with the pony that they could hear him.

"Marvellous," he thought to himself, "just call me Dr. Freddy bloody Dolittle." He looked up at the distant Pegusinni flying overhead, "and you lot can bugger off as well!"

By now the action had calmed down, there was an ambulance and a few more people crowding around, and he saw the soldier step into his stirrup and lift himself into the saddle of the black horse. There was something different about this horse. Even to Freddy's novice eye he could see this one behaved differently than the others. She looked completely calm, aloof and moved with straight elegant steps. Freddy mounted his bike and followed the soldier and his horse from a safe distance. After a short ride they came to a set of huge walled buildings and he remembered his mother saying this was where the queen's guards lived. The soldier on the black horse paused on the park side of the road as a formation of soldiers wearing armour and riding black horses filed through the large gates of the barracks. The formation turned to the right and rode down the centre of the street. The soldier and black mare then crossed the road and went in through the gates. A soldier stood by the gate wearing M.P. arm band – Military Police. Freddy knew there was no point in trying to go any further.

Most of his friends had started smoking by his age and part of Freddy wished he had too. He decided he should stay calm and go get an ice cream from the café in the park. The fact that he had almost wet his pants a few times during the last hour was pushed to the back of his mind. After the ice cream he was tempted to go home and try to push it all out of his head, but he was far too psyched up for that. He peddled around the park and ended up again across the road from the barrack gates. The sound of hooves clattering on tarmac alerted him to more soldiers and horses but this group was returning to barracks. The soldiers wore blue tunics and their helmets were decorated with red plumes; different from the group he'd watch leave earlier. The earlier troop of soldiers wore red tunics with white plumes in their helmets. The soldiers stared straight ahead and did not speak as they rode down the centre of the street. However, Freddy could definitely hear someone chattering as the formation approached the gates.

"Glad to be back in my own barn tonight."

"Miss your home comforts, do you? Big softy," Someone said, followed by ribbing.

"This saddle is killing me; he put the blanket on with a big wrinkle in it!"

"Hey up, lads! Up over to the right, Pegusinni."

Some of the horses twisted their heads and necks to try look up. Freddy stepped back behind a tree as the small winged horses swooped down in formation and flew close above the heads of the returning troops going through the archway of the gate. As the last of the horses went through the gate and wheeled to the left, the view cleared across the parade square. There, rooted to the spot with eyes locked on Freddy, was the black mare he had seen in the park. Freddy stood immobile; his eyes locked on hers. A burly soldier was tugging on a rope attached to the mare's halter but she ignored him. The mare tilted her head and increased the intensity of her stare. Freddy tilted his head, vaguely moved his nostrils and was about to say, "Hello," when the soldier pulled more sharply on the rope and raised his voice. The mare broke her gaze with Freddy and turned her attention to the soldier.

Freddy mounted his bike and cycled away, muttering to himself about going bonkers and so missed the mare looking back out the gates toward him. He didn't slow down or stop until he was at the rear gate of his house. He jumped off the bike, kicked the wrought iron gate to the small yard open, chained his bicycle to the corner drainpipe and went straight indoors. Hot and sweating from the race home, he went upstairs to the small apartment, pulled off his clothes in his room and went to the shower. The water felt good pouring over him as he regained his breath and his pulse slowed. Dried and dressed, he flopped on his bed and stared at the ceiling. A possible conversation ran through his mind.

"Hi, kiddo, had a good day?"

"Hi, mum. Yes, pretty good."

"Anything interesting happen?"

"Not really, well, a couple of things I suppose."

"Going to tell me?"

"Sure. I went to the park on my bike, met a brat on a grey pony, a bunch of flying horses came in like 633 squadron, I talked to the pony, it talked back, then it peed itself in terror and bolted with the screaming kid. A soldier on a big black horse chased it, and then the black horse had a chat with a police horse and then I followed the black one back to the barracks, and later more flying horses came in and I heard the soldiers' horses talking about their saddles. Oh, and I had a staring match with the black mare and then I came home. Other than that it's been a quiet day."

Jane would think he was a couple of clowns short of a circus and have him on Prozac before you could say My Little Pony.

He'd forgotten about lunch and dug out some of yesterday's pizza and a coke from the fridge, went back to his room and turned on his computer. For the next few hours, he alternated between doing homework and searching the internet for information on flying horses, people who could talk to animals and talking horses. The only fascinating thing he came up with was a story about Hans the wonder horse in Germany. Apparently a gazillion years ago this horse had learned to count and could do basic arithmetic, but more curiously this horse could do his stuff even when his trainer was not present. Did Hans speak German, English or horse?

"You in your room, Fred?" his mother called from the kitchen.

"Yeah, just doing homework."

"Anything interesting happen today?"

"No, no, not really."

"Want to come down for something to eat before I go back to work?"

"Nah, I think I'll go out and have a look at Kensington and pick up something while I'm out."

"Ok, if that's what you want. I won't be late."

"'K."

The diplomat's house was located in a quiet street set back from Kensington Road, between Exhibition Road and Gloucester Road. There were quite a number of embassy buildings along Kensington Road, mainly for smaller, less well-known countries. Canada House was located at the top of Trafalgar Square which made for a short daily commute for Paul Smith. Freddy pulled on his jacket and set off east to walk along Kensington High Street. He definitely did not feel inspired to go west towards Knightsbridge and Hyde Park. Smart shops, fast food joints and trendy wine bars and restaurants all jostled for position in Kensington. After he got bored looking in shop windows at designer handbags and shoes, he ate some Kentucky fried chicken. Suddenly realizing how tired he was, Freddy set off back home. It started to rain lightly as he walked along the busy street. Every now and then he glanced back over his shoulder and then upwards, wary of spotting flying horses. Home, an hour of TV, then he crashed into bed, mentally drained from the games his head had been playing.

The rain became quite heavy and it rattled the glass of his bedroom window, waking him up at about 1.a.m. He sat up and became conscious of another noise accompanying the patter of the rain. It sounded as if someone wearing high heeled shoes was clicking around in the back yard. Freddy stepped tentatively over to the window, pulled back the blind and peered into the night. The neighbour's house had a garage to the rear and there, walking up and down in the rain on the flat roof, were two small winged horses. They stopped when they saw Freddy staring at them; then one of them opened its wings and glided over to the landing on the metal fire escape outside Freddy's window. The little horse was about 8 feet away from Freddy, not moving, just quietly looking at him. The teenager closed his eyes, counted to three, opened them and the horse was still there. Freddy sighed, leaned forward, unlatched the window and pushed the lower half upwards.

"It's time for you to come with us, Freddy." The voice was calm, quiet, masculine and clear. The boy said nothing, letting the rain hit his face and neck.

"You'll be fine, but you do need to come with us for a while."

"Why? Tell me why I should." Freddy asked.

"Everything will become clear soon, but please, for now, come with us."

"And if I don't?"

There was a short pause, then, "That could mean a lot of problems for all sorts of people. We need to introduce you to someone."

"And I'll get back home, O.K.?"

"Yes, of course, you have the assurance of all of us."

Fred looked beyond the horse and saw that quite a few more winged horses had arrived and were standing on the garage roof, the garden walls, and down in the small yard.

Choices. Life was full of choices. Ignore the little black imaginary horses, and go back to bed and crawl under the sheets? That was obviously the logical choice. He went back into his room, pulled on jeans, sweatshirt, jacket, trainers and a baseball cap.

"Could you come this way?" asked the voice outside, "better if no one knows you're gone."

He walked over to the window, climbed through and stepped onto the metal landing as the small horse fluttered back over to the garage.

"Are we going far?"

"Just to where you were this morning."

"I'll need my bike." He moved silently down the metal steps of the fire escape, pulled the cover sheet off his bike and unlocked it from the drain pipe. The small horses had disappeared. The old gate creaked noisily as he pushed it with his shoulder and wheeled his bike into the street. His jaw dropped when he saw what was waiting for him. In the middle of the road there were now more than a dozen small black horses standing in pairs and at the front one smaller grey horse who nodded to him in a friendly manner. They walked a few steps forward, tucked up their forelegs, opened their wings and took flight, arching up and over the houses and then back down again to Freddy. If he had been five years old he would have said it was the reindeer from Santa Claus's sleigh.

The rain eased to a light drizzle as he biked towards Kensington gardens, following his escort past the Prince Albert Memorial toward Hyde Park. Most of London's public parks are closed to traffic from midnight until five a.m. but this never stops pedestrians or cyclists from taking short cuts. The little group crossed Exhibition Road and entered Hyde Park, heading resolutely toward the barracks. Having seen South Carriage Drive busy with traffic in the day time, it was rather eerie to see it silent and empty now.

Once again Freddy was standing in the park across from the main gates of the barracks, only this time they were closed and bolted. The winged horses had landed and were clustered on the sand track, a few of them pulling mouthfuls of grass from the road edge. The same winged horse who had spoken outside his bedroom window stepped forward. This one was completely black except for greying hair around his eyes and nose.

"You have to go inside," he said to Freddy.

"Hah! Yeah, right, with about four hundred bloody soldiers running about and God knows what security? You're out of your little horsey mind, pal."

"No," said the horse evenly and calmly, "you need to go inside and meet someone tonight."

"Why don't I just go around to Knightsbridge Street and knock on the guardroom door then? I'm sure they'll let a sixteen year old in wet jeans come in for a walk-about."

Still calm, still patient, the little horse said, "No, they can't know you are here yet. Maybe later."

Freddy looked up at the huge locked gates and high brick walls. "So, anyone got a pass key?"

There were smiles and nods from the little horses.

"Leave your bicycle and come with us, we'll show you how to enter."

"News flash! Sixteen year old arrested on terrorist charges for trying to bust into army barracks! Read all about it! Death by firing squad, calls Home Secretary!" He paused for breath, and then more quietly, "I'll be taken away by the police if they see me."

"Exactly, which is why they won't see you? Now, leave your bike and cross the road."

With the sigh of a man going to his own funeral, Freddy tied up his bike and followed the horses across the empty road. They didn't stand in front of the big gates but more to the east, further along the towering walls.

"You will need to be very quiet until we are inside, particularly if we stop. Now, hold out your arms."

Freddy was staring up at the top of the twenty-foot high brick wall in front of him. He just knew this was a freaky dream and he would wake up shortly. He held out both arms parallel to the ground. "Am I going to fly in?" he asked with a laugh.

"No, but we are." With no further hesitation, two of the horses stepped up and put their strong necks under his arms. "Stay quiet and hold on."

Three incredibly powerful beats from the small wings and the two horses flew straight up to the top of the wall with Freddy between them.

"Holy crap!"

"Shhh....they can hear you when you talk with your mouth!"

Freddy and all of the small horses were now standing on top of the brick wall. It was no more than half a metre wide and Freddy swung unsteadily on his feet. "I am going to bloody well die!"

"Quiet, there's one coming, keep hold of us."

A lone soldier in khaki fatigues walked quietly up the ramp to the upper stables. His rubber soled boots made no noise on the wet concrete. Freddy was rigid with fear. He was standing on top of a twenty-foot high brick wall, lined up with a dozen or more miniature horses; all of them looking like targets at a shooting range.

"Night guard," said one of the small horses.

"You do know that I am not Harry Potter," Freddy hissed through clenched teeth.

"Keep still and keep quiet, he can't see you."

"I'm almost six feet bloody tall; of course he can see me!"

"No, not when you are holding one of us. You know of anyone else who has seen us other than you, Freddy?" said the horse with the greying face.

His mind flashed back to the garden at the Rectory and the other times when he had tried to get someone else to see the small horses.

"And when you are in contact with us, you can't be seen either. It's really quite simple."

"Could we continue this conversation when we are not wobbling on top of a brick wall in the rain, please?"

The soldier disappeared into one of the buildings. "Certainly," said the small horse, "hold on tight. Going down."

Once more the two horses he was holding stepped forward, tucked up their forelegs, opened their wings and glided to the ground at the base of the wall. Freddy was now illegally inside the Barracks of the Household Cavalry.

"Mr. Hobbs, would you prefer to be shot at dawn or dusk?" he asked himself, pretending to hold a microphone.

"This way, please, Freddy," said the horse with the greying face.

Again tucking forelegs and opening wings, the string of horses glided down the ramp toward the stables below. Freddy declined a ride and jogged on foot, following the horses who veered to the right through an open door into the stable. A low voltage night light dimly lit up the interior. Freddy could make out half a dozen box stalls, all of which were empty except one. Victoriana was now fully awake and looking at Freddy through the bars of her stall door. He said nothing but stared back.

Two of the small horses walked across the cobble stones to her door. One was the same grey-faced horse who had guided Freddy here; the other was also black but had tiny white socks above his hooves and a white stripe down his face.

"This is a surprise and honour," said Victoriana quietly, "It's been a long time, gentlemen. It's good to see you, Yeti," she paused, lowered her neck to both of them, "and you too, Sefton."

Chapter Seven

Freddy stood back, pressed as close to the wall of the passage way as he could. The small horses took turns going forward and speaking to the black mare in the box stall and then silently left the building. Only the two who had initially spoken remained. They moved closer to the stall door and talked very quietly with the her, a conversation that went on for several minutes before they turned and looked at him.

"We'll be leaving you for a while now, Freddy."

"What? You said you'd take me home!"

"We will, but you need to stay for a while and speak to Victoriana," the one called Yeti said, gesturing to the black mare.

"But you will take me home, right?"

"You have our word. But surely you must have a lot of questions you would like answers to?"

Freddy nodded in agreement. "Why do you have to leave? I feel sort of ok with you little guys around."

"Too much to do, we would only complicate things, you need time to talk one on one. Do you enjoy history at school, Freddy?"

"Not really, music, maths and computers are my gig."

"Well, time for a history lesson. Freddy, this is Victoriana, and Victoriana, please meet Freddy Hobbs." For the third time in twenty-four hours, the black mare and the teenage boy stared at each other.

"Hey, Ed, how do you know my name?"

The small horse looked up at him. "Ed? Who's Ed?"

"You know, Mr. Ed the talking horse, off the old telly programs."

"Freddy, horses can't talk. Not in that sense."

"So what are we doing?"

"Is your mouth moving?"

"No."

"Are ours?"

"No."

"So no one is talking, we are just communicating."

"If you say so."

"I do. Now, we'll be back shortly."

"One more thing, what did you say your name was?" asked Freddy.

"Yeti."

"You serious?"

"Perfectly."

"Wow, I thought Frederick was bad enough. Guess your mum didn't like you too much, eh?"

"It's my military name." He looked over to Victoriana, waiting patiently, "tell him about names as well, please."

"Of course," she replied. With that the two Pegusinni walked to the door. Sefton turned and looked at the boy.

"Don't worry, lad, you're being well looked after." They lowered their small haunches, raised their fore legs and silently took flight. Freddy turned and stared at the black mare behind the bars on the door. She stared back. "Well, Freddy, do you want to start with a question?"

"Yes. Why does this place smell so much?"

"I beg your pardon?"

"This whole place. It stinks of poo!"

"How dare you? These are probably some of the cleanest stables in the country!"

"Gawd, I'd hate to go to a dirty one then."

She chose to ignore these comments. "Tell me, do you prefer Frederick or Freddy?"

"Freddy. And you?"

"Me, what?"

"Do you prefer Vicky or Vics?"

She raised herself to full height, arched her neck, narrowed her eyes and leaned toward him.

"It is not Vicky, or Vics; it is Victoriana!" If an equine could speak through clenched teeth, she just did.

"'K, ok, don't get your pants in a bunch, just checking." There was a short silence between the two as they sized each other up. "Ok, so what's your job around here? Are you like a soldier horse and stand in front of Buckingham Palace?"

It was going to be a long night, Victoriana thought. "How much do you know about equine, Freddy?"

"Who's he?"

"Who's who?"

"This equiney guy?"

"Horses, how much do you know about horses?"

"Not a lot."

"How much riding have you done?"

"You're kidding me? None."

"None at all?" she looked incredulous.

"Nopes, never. Well, I stood close and held the reins of some ponies in a cart once, when I was an elf."

"You were an elf?"

"Long story. But then I heard the police horses talking at the footy match, and I know a farting Welsh cob in Barlborough."

There was another silence. Then Victoriana said, "Open the stall door please."

"What? If I did, you could escape."

"Escape? You think I'm held here against my will? This is not a prison, Freddy. Now, unbolt the door and pull it open."

"No way. If you come out, you could do me some serious damage. You're a big bugger! Not like the little quiet guys."

She let out a long slow sigh. "Freddy, if anyone was going to do you any harm we could have had it done years ago. Now, please, I will ask you one last time, politely. Unbolt the door."

"No," he said taking a step backwards, tightening his bottom lip.

"Very well, you leave me no choice." She stood directly behind the closed door, stretched her neck forward and a look of total concentration locked on to her face. Freddy pressed himself back against the wall of the passage. The mare closed her eyes and slowly raised her black muzzle upwards. There was a small creaking sound as the bolt shaft rotated, rose from its resting spot and became parallel with the ground. Eyes still closed, she drew her head slowly from right to left and the bolt slid open. She opened her eyes, stepped forward and nudged the door with her muzzle to swing it open.

"Oh, my God. You're a witch horse!"

With calm and elegant steps she walked from the stall until she was inches away from him. He felt the warm air from her nostrils on his cheek. She towered above him. Freddy waited, expecting at any moment to be bitten or kicked. Victoriana moved closer, her muzzle nearly touching his left ear.

"I am not a witch horse," the mare said in almost a whisper.

Freddie gave a trembled reply, "No, ma'am."

The black mare moved even closer until he could feel the fleshy part of her nostril against his ear and cheek. Once again he thought he was about to wet his pants.

"And the next time a lady asks you to open a door for her, do it!" Victoriana hissed. She took a step back, looked sweetly down at him and in a calm dignified voice said, "Now, we can do this the easy way, or the slower and more difficult way. Which would you prefer, Freddy?"

"Easy, please," Freddy begrudged, followed by a sniff.

"Good." Victoriana turned around and walked back into her box. She looked at him from the open door. "You too, please."

"Me too what?"

"In here."

"In there? We can chat with you there and me over here."

"Freddy, in about five or ten minutes the night guard trooper will be doing his rounds. Do you know what will happen to you if he finds you standing out there at two o'clock in the morning?"

Visions of screaming soldiers and military jail cells flashed through his mind. He walked slowly toward the open door and then stepped into the stall.

"Close the door, please."

He did.

"And bolt back in."

He did.

"Now, when the trooper comes around, it would be best if you drop down below the wood panel on the door where he can't see you, ok? He's only going to glance in, check that I am well and then he'll be gone. Until then make yourself comfortable. Please, sit down."

The floor was deeply bedded with softwood shavings and sawdust, so he pushed a heap together in a corner with his foot and plopped down on it.

"So how did you do it? The kinetic trick?

She looked puzzled.

"Moving the bolt." Freddy pointed at the stall door.

"Oh, that. Well, most creatures can do it to a greater or lesser degree."

"Even men?"

"Absolutely, but they are usually too busy doing other things with their minds, usually negative thoughts. Uses all the wrong energy."

"So could I do it?"

"Of course, you would just have to train your mind. If we have time I could help you at some point."

"Thanks." The two paused and then Freddy said, "I'm sorry."

"Sorry for what?"

"Acting like a prat."

"Prat? Is that like fool?"

"Yes, but worse."

"It's alright, you're young and probably just a bit scared."

"Yup."

"Want to try starting again?"

"O.K." Freddy paused, "why am I here?"

She thought for a minute, "I believe you're going to help us, Freddy."

"How? I'm actually bloody scared of horses."

"Yes, well, we need to get you past that for a start."

"How come I can hear you and the others, and you can hear me? It's really freaking me out."

"Someone else will explain all about that to you later. I think for now, we need to get you over your fears, and then give you some background."

"The little flying horses, the piggi-whats-it guys, what or who are they?"

"I'll get to that when we do a bit of history."

"And what is your job then? How come you're down here in this little place and not with all the others? There has to be hundreds in here."

"I believe you could say I'm the leader of the group."

"Like, the boss? Like the queen of 'em all?"

"That would be one way to put it."

"Gawd, no wonder you have an attitude! So, I'm chatting with the queen bee?"

Something distracted the mare before she could reply. She raised her neck and pricked both ears. "Night guard coming. Behind the door, please."

Freddy crawled on his hands and knees to the stall door just as footsteps stopped on the other side. He held his breath, not moving.

"You ok, then, you old battle axe?" asked a friendly masculine voice with a heavy Scottish accent. Victoriana was directly in front of the door, head drooping, ears flopped down, resting a hind leg. With only the mildest of interest, she moved an ear in the soldier's direction and then resumed her sleeping posture. The guard checked the door bolt and made his way back out. Victoriana stepped back and allowed Freddy to get to his feet.

"See," she said, "not a problem. Sit back down; I'll give you some history."

"Tell me about the names. Why are they so weird?"

"It's the military tradition and goes back to when the armies were recruiting thousands of horses each year. It's done in your alphabet, so you can tell how old a horse is at any time.

"How's that work, then?"

"Each year we have a new group of remounts or new recruits, if you will. Every horse coming in that year will be named with the same first letter. If it was the letter B one year then it will be C the next."

"Wow, just like our car licence plates?"

"Probably. So you can see that Venetia who is upstairs is the same age as me. Both V's. When they have to come up with about 25 names all starting with as the letter Y you get some pretty odd names."

"Such as Yeti?"

"Exactly. And this year our new intake of remounts is using H to start their names."

"Is that the history lesson?"

"No, not at all." She lowered her voice and told Freddy about events that occurred only a few hundred yards along the road from the barrack gates on 20th July 1982. She quietly explained how on that day in mid-summer, the Queen's Life Guard left as normal, just as he had seen them yesterday morning, and only minutes down the road they had been attacked by flames, gunpowder and flying hot nails.

"A bomb?" asked Freddy disbelievingly.

"Yes, that's what they called it."

"Some bugger blew up the horses?"

"Yes, and the soldiers."

Freddy sat with his mouth gaping. He was hearing her, but was not really comprehending what she was saying. Victoriana continued.

"Obviously, it was before I was here; in fact, none of the horses in the barracks now are old enough to have been there, but it will never be forgotten. The story is told very carefully by each generation now."

"I just can't believe it; some crazy bastard blew up a bunch of horses?"

"Yes," she said quietly.

"But why? What the hell reason could anyone have to kill horses that never did any harm?"

"We don't know, Freddy, and we probably will never understand it. I believe your people know who and why."

"Jesus, must be the biggest set of psyched out freaks on the planet!"

She was silent while he absorbed what she'd told him.

Then quietly he asked. "Did they, you know... did they all die?"

"Die?"

"Yes, die. Dead. Killed. You know, not living?"

"Oh, I see. Well, seven equine made their first transition that day. The others were hurt and injured but decided to stay for longer."

"Transition?"

She looked at him perplexed, as if he should know. "Yes, transitioned to Pegusinni."

He shot bolt upright. "You mean the little flying guys are the horses that were there?"

"Yes, all of the ones you've met today were there that day. Actually, I was quite surprised to see all of them here. I thought the seven would have made their second transition by now. It has been almost twenty-five years."

"You mean they're not dead?"

"No, not as you know it, Freddy. That doesn't happen to equine."

"You mean you don't die? Ever?"

"Not as I hear you think about it. Did the four soldiers not transition that day?"

"Which four soldiers?"

"The ones that wouldn't stand up again."

Freddy gave a long pause and then said, "Tell me about a transition."

She cocked her head to one side. "You don't know? How odd."

"Just tell me."

"When equine arrives into this galaxy, we're allotted so many moon changes or years as you say. If for some reason our time is cut short, for no fault of our own, we transition to Pegusinni and remain until we are ready for the next move."

"You are kidding me? I mean, joking, right?"

"No, not at all. So, eight of ours transitioned that day and the others chose to stay longer. What I don't understand is why the original eight are still here. As I said earlier, they should have made second transition by now."

"O.K., I'm following you, sort of. Now, what is second transition?"

"Transition to the next constellation, of course. Sagittarius."

"And now I am lost."

"After we have had sufficient time as Pegusinni we are escorted to Sagittarius. Why, where do you go?"

"God knows."

"Does he?"

"Yes. No. I mean, I don't really know anymore. Tell me more about becoming a Pegusinni."

"As I said, it's our choice if our original time is cut short."

"Such as a bloody bomb blowing you apart?"

"Yes, that or many other reasons."

"Tell me some."

"There are thousands of Pegusinni, many over a place called France. I've never been but we hear from the racehorses that come here for competitions."

"You're telling me there are thousands of Pegusinni all over France?"

"Yes."

"But why France?"

"Abattoirs."

He thought it through. Abattoirs were French slaughter houses. He'd read in a newspaper somewhere about how the French raise horses till they are four years old and then slaughter them for meat. In fact, he now remembered a posh girl from the school in Stavely talking about her family's camping holiday to Northern France and how they'd nearly eaten a horse steak by accident in a restaurant. She and her brother had started crying and the whole family was asked to leave.

"What about war?"

"Oh, yes, that was always a busy time. Thousands of Pegusinni are around for years after that."

"So all of you become Pegusinni?"

"Not always. It's a choice. If we feel we've been here a long time and are ready for a change we transition up and over. I know Yeti was here for thirty-six of your years, that's why I was surprised to see him. I heard he transitioned about three years ago."

"So, basically if a horse doesn't get to live out its full life expectancy, you get to hangout as little flying horses till you're ready to move on?"

"Well, allowing for mix ups between our two languages, I think that sounds right."

"Well, bloody hell. Who'd have known?"

"There is a much bigger question though, Freddy."

"What's that?"

"Why haven't all of those present on that day of fire transitioned? Every one of them is still here."

"Hell if I know."

"Even Gauntlet was here."

"Gauntlet?"

"Yes, the smaller grey horse. He was carrying the trumpeter at the front of the guard."

"Why didn't you ask them when they were here?"

"I tried to, but they were too busy and said everything would become clear soon."

"And this was the history lesson they wanted you to give me?"

"Part of it, but there is a lot more to come. I think they will be asking you to return tomorrow evening. Although, there is supposed to be a Senate meeting so I don't know."

"And a Senate meeting would be what?"

"When the herd leaders meet to make decisions."

"Where do you meet?"

"Here, unless the Regiment is on country leave, of course."

"Do the soldiers know about these meetings?"

"No, of course not."

"So how do you meet without them knowing?"

She remained quiet, tilted her head and winked.

"Don't tell me, more witchcraft, eh?" He thought for a moment, "What's this country leave?"

"Usually once a year, toward the end of the warm season we all travel to the country, near the coast, for fresh air and galloping."

"What about the soldiers?"

She laughed, "They take us."

They were both silent for a few minutes before Freddy spoke again.

"Am I going to meet everyone then? All of the horses here?"

"No, not for the time being, it will be best if you could keep quiet around the troops and, of course, civilian horses. Which reminds me, what did you say to the grey pony mare in the park yesterday morning?"

"Oh, that," Freddy looked sheepish, "er, I said, boo."

"Boo? What does that mean?"

"Nothing really, it was just for fun."

"Fun that caused her to bolt and put a child in serious danger?"

"Sorry 'bout that," he mumbled, "I'll try not to do it again."

"That would be good, in fact, even better if you don't speak to her again should you see her. Nero and I will think of some sort of story to cover it up."

"Tell me about me, about how I can do this, this horse talk stuff and why?"

"That's not my place, Freddy, but someone will soon."

They were disturbed by a light breeze signalling the return of Yeti, Sefton and the others. The Pegusinni glided quietly into the building and landed softly on the paved aisle way.

"Time to get you back, Freddy," said Sefton.

The boy looked at the black mare as he left the box stall, "Will you be in the park tomorrow?"

"Yes, probably."

"I'll try to see you there."

"O.K. but one thing."

"Yes?"

"No more boo, please."

"I promise."

"Boo?" asked Yeti.

"I'll tell you on the way home," said Freddy as the group quietly left the building and headed back to the park.

Chapter Eight

True to their word, the Pegusinni escorted Freddy up out of the stables and back to the park. The short flight over the wall wasn't quite so scary this time as he was starting to trust his new friends and, with no night guard in sight, they didn't pause on top. It was close to three a.m. when he flopped back into bed and much to his own surprise he fell straight to sleep. Waking around eight he heard his mother in the kitchen rattling pots about in the sink. Freddy went down to the kitchen and sat at the small table.

"Hi there, you're late." Jane said.

"Hi, mum. Yeah, woke up in the night for a while," he replied, trying to sound casual.

"Want a cuppa?"

"Yah, tea would be great."

"In the pot, not been made long," Jane continued washing dishes in the sink.

Freddy poured himself a mug of tea, had a few sips before speaking again, "Mum, did you know we're really close to the horse barracks along in Knightsbridge?"

"You mean the cavalry barracks, with all the black horses?"

"Yeah, but they're not all black. Some are grey and some big buggers are brown and white."

"And how would you know that?"

"Er, um, saw them exercising in the park."

"I didn't know they had grey ones too."

"Yep, for trumpeters."

"Oh, yes, of course, I've seen photos of them on calendars."

Freddy drained his mug and then refilled it, "Mum, did you know that some crazy buggers blew up the horses years ago?"

From the rear he saw his mother become still. She stared out of the window not saying anything and then turned to him, drying her hands on a towel. When she spoke it was in a much quieter tone.

"It must be over twenty years ago," she said sitting down across the table from him.

"Twenty-five, actually."

"It was in the early eighties."

"1982 was the year."

"Yes, probably, I was only about eleven or twelve years old when it happened."

"You remember it?"

"Oh God yes, it was one of those days that people say were like the day President Kennedy got shot."

"Kennedy, who's that guy?" Freddy asked.

"Oh, an American, years ago. But anyway, it was rather like that. You ask anyone in this country over the age of about thirty-five and they will all be able to tell you where they were when they heard the news."

"What was it like? What actually happened?"

Jane poured herself a mug of tea. "It was around the middle of July, we had just started school summer holidays. I was in the back garden playing with a girl from down our street, Phillipa, but we all called her Pip. She was big into gardening, odd thing for a kid that age. Anyway, she was always coming round to dig up our flower beds and plant odd flowers. Don't hear much about her now though; she's probably growing marijuana somewhere. She was a bit weird."

"Mum, go back to the horse story."

"Oh yes, anyway, it was late morning and I went into the house to get some pop and Mum, your Gran, was sitting in front of the telly crying. She had the news on."

Jane and Freddy were silent while they drank more tea; then Jane said, "I asked why she was crying and she just kept saying something about the poor boys."

"The boys?"

"Yes, the boys who had just been killed when the bomb went off."

"I thought it was the horses that died?"

"They did, at least six of them."

"Seven."

"Maybe, but there were also four soldiers killed too. Pip came in and sat with us while we watched the news, it was on for hours. It was really horrible. I remember we all cried"

"So what had actually happened?"

"If I remember it all correctly, they had only just left their barracks, the mounted guard that is, and were walking down the road to do the changing of the guard like they always did. Then someone detonated a car bomb parked at the side of the road."

"Jesus, they really were crazy buggers?"

"It was not a huge bomb, but it was a really evil one. They had packed it with six inch nails."

"No way!"

"The blast was so loud it shook and broke windows on buildings all around the park and in the barracks too. But worst of all the nails and metal bits were blasted into the soldiers and the horses."

"I think I'm going to be sick."

Jane paused, staring off into space, biting her bottom lip as she recalled the carnage. "Gran and all of her generation cried and prayed for the boys. We kids and younger people, we all cried for the horses."

"Mum, they were soldiers, not boys."

She put her mug down and stared at him from across the table. When she spoke it was very quietly. "Freddy, one of them was just nineteen, that's just over two years older than you. I think the others were twenty and about twenty one. One of them may have been thirty, but trust me, to your Gran and all the grown ups they were boys." Jane's eyes filled as she spoke. Freddy went to the shelf and got a box of Kleenex for her. She took a minute to blow her nose and clear her throat. "Sorry, it's a bit upsetting thinking back to it all. They were so helpless. Just unarmed ceremonial horses and soldiers taking part in tradition."

There was another long pause; Freddy figured it best to wait until she was ready to speak. Finally Jane began again, "they moved the soldiers very quickly, but the horses," she dabbed her eye again, "the horses were left for a long time, just laying there, huge, sad, dead, covered with plastic sheets and blood all over the road."

Freddy stood up and went to the sink to fill the kettle to make more tea. He left her lost in her memories for a while and then quietly he asked, "Who did it, Mum? Which insane buggers would do such a thing?"

"The I.R.A."

"What!"

"Yes, the Irish Republican Army, they claimed responsibility for it and were quite proud of it."

"But why? What the hell for?"

"Oh that wasn't the end of the day, not by a long chalk. They hadn't finished yet."

"There was more?"

"Yes, but not with horses. Just more unarmed young lads."

"The same day? But where, how?"

"Regents Park. There was a military band playing that afternoon, a free concert for tourists and retired folks who were enjoying a day out in the sun. They had put another bomb directly under the bandstand and blew it up while the lads were playing."

"This is like something from a horror movie." He paused, then said, "But if it was a flick, it would never get past the censor. It's bloody gruesome."

"Seven more boys were killed straight away. Others lost arms, legs or were maimed for life. All they were doing was trying to make people feel happy by playing nice show tunes. And then they were dead. Their trumpets and other instruments were blasted all over Regents Park."

"Same day as the cavalry got blasted then?"

"Yes, about two hours later."

He'd made more tea and now refilled their mugs. He sat down across from her before asking, "Why, mum? Why would they do such a thing?"

She looked up, "The I.R.A.? Because they had declared war on the British government is what we were told."

"But what was the war over?"

"What is any war over my lad? Men and religion, what else?"

"Men?"

"Sure, pretty much all wars are caused by men, not women, it's the men. Crazed buggers," she muttered.

"There must be some war that was to do with women?"

"Name me one."

He thought for a minute. "O.K. How about Margaret Thatcher? There's one."

She narrowed her eyes and looked at her son across the table. "Margaret Thatcher didn't *start* a war; she *finished* one that men had started."

He'd always known his mum was a bit of a feminist and believer in women's rights and equality so he steered the conversation away from this and back to the Hyde Park bombing.

"O.K., tell me exactly why the I.R.A. declared war on the British government?"

"Don't they teach you any of this at your school?"

"It's been mentioned in modern and recent history class, but no real detail."

"Well, I'm not a teacher but I believe it was when there was trouble and fighting in Northern Ireland between the Catholics and the Protestants. It got too much for the Irish police to handle and as Northern Ireland is part of the U.K., British troops were sent in to help the police and try to keep the peace. It didn't take long for them to become the enemy and they got attacked."

"And the I.R.A. decided to blow up horses and musicians here in England to scare everyone?"

"It didn't start with horses and musicians, they started years earlier by putting bombs under seats in pubs where soldiers would go to drink when off duty, and then they would blow up the pub." Jane stood up from the table. "Heck, look at the time. I need to get over to the main house and get cracking, but I must get a load of our laundry started before I go."

She left the room and Freddy made himself some toast. He could hear her moving around in the bedrooms. She came back into the kitchen carrying armfuls of clothes.

"Good grief! Where have you been in these?" she asked throwing his jeans onto the floor, "They stink like poo!"

"Oh, I guess I must have sat in something nasty in the park," Freddy said, avoiding her eye.

"Try falling into the rose bed next time. These stink like crap!"

Freddy left her loading the laundry into the machine, took his tea and toast to his bedroom and turned on his computer. He checked his e-mail, reading a couple of messages from old friends left behind in Derbyshire and then flicked the page to the Google search engine. He typed 'cavalry bombing Hyde Park' and hit 'search'.

"Whew," he whistled quietly at the number of hits he'd got and settled down to read.

By nine thirty Freddy was washed, dressed and getting his bike out of the back yard. It wasn't sunny but at least it was dry as he set off to the east toward Hyde Park and the barracks. He wove in and out of traffic, irritating some motorists but believing this was how to ride your bike in London as he had seen all the messengers and fitness freaks doing the same. He swung left-handed through the park gates and then right handed onto the quieter South Carriage Drive which ran between the park and the barracks. Freddy slowed down and took his time now, looking to the left, amazed at the number of joggers and runners around the park. It was never ending. All through the day into the evening he had seen them, running with intense faces, sweating, chugging at water bottles, looking at watches.

"They need a few weeks away from London," he thought, "where you have to walk a couple of miles to school and carry four grocery bags back from Tesco on your own. They wouldn't be so bloody keen on jogging then."

Further through the trees he could see Rotten Row, but no horses were on it. He kept riding slowly along the road, looking to his right at the walls of the barracks. It was only then he noticed the C.C.T.V. cameras mounted on the walls.

"Oh crap," thinking about his escapade into the barracks last night. But then he remembered what Yeti had said to him. Invisible to the human eye when he was in contact with the Pegusinni. He hoped Yeti was right. Freddy passed the barracks, some very old, very posh looking apartment buildings and one huge building that looked like it was a hotel. Now he slowed more, looking carefully to his left, seeing a sand riding trail, trees, grass and loads of flowers. Still further on, past the old buildings, not quite to the end of the park, he saw what he was looking for on the left hand side of the road.

He stopped his bike, dismounted and slowly walked toward the memorial. It wasn't a huge towering thing like a lot of them are; instead this memorial was a large round black stone, discreet, very close to the ground and edged three quarters of the way round by a neatly trimmed hedge. The hedge was shaped like a horse shoe and not even half a meter tall. Half a dozen weather-beaten small wreathes of poppies lay around the stone. He stood on the path at the open end of the hedge and read the stone's inscription. It told of the date and the event and the names of the four soldiers who had died here; Anthony Daly 23, Roy Bright 36, Jeffery Young 21 and Simon Tripper 19. This was it, Freddy thought. The place where it had actually happened. His mum, Victoriana, the Pegusinni and the Google search engine all had been right. In a few weeks time it would be twenty-five years to the day.

He pushed his bike along the path then crossed Rotten Row to get to the cycle path. On the far side of the path was a large garden with ornate shrubs and sculptured bushes and trees. A plaque on a neat wooden post indicated the place was the 'Rose Garden.' It looked very peaceful and calm but he couldn't go in as another large sign said '*Strictly no cycling*'. Just as he put his foot on the pedal of the bike, he felt a familiar breeze at his back. Looking over his shoulder he saw four Pegusinni coming in from the direction of Hyde Park corner and the Wellington Arch. They landed on the grass next to him. Freddy recognised three of them and smiled.

"Hello, Freddy, how are you this morning?"

"I'm fine thanks, Yeti, how's you guys?"

"Well, thank you."

"Morning, Sefton. Hello, Gauntlet," said Freddy to two of the others. They nodded and gave Pegusinni smiles. "I'm sorry, I don't know your name," to the fourth one standing slightly back.

The small black winged horse with a narrow white snip down the centre of his face lifted his neck and said, "Rochester, my name is Rochester, nice to see you again."

"You too," said Freddy, "you must have been with us last night, yes?"

"Indeed I was, to the rear."

"And you must be one year older than Sefton here, right?" asked Freddy with a cheeky look.

"My, someone has been doing their homework," said Yeti.

Freddy pointed his finger at Yeti and said, "And you're just a kid! Five years younger then him, eh?"

"Victoriana really did give you some lessons last night, then?"

"Yeah, and she also told me all about the day of fire and nails and burning," he said more quietly.

There was a short silence then Yeti spoke, "We've just been to St. James's Park and Horse Guards Parade, are you familiar with those places?"

"No, I've heard of them, but never been. Is it far?"

"No, indeed, not at all. Perhaps you could go there sometime soon, get familiar with the area. It will be useful."

"Why, what's going on?"

"It's not all totally clear yet," said Sefton, "but we should be able to explain a lot more to you very soon."

Freddy decided not to push the issue. So far everything they had told him had been true, or had come true. They would tell him when the time was right. He watched the grey horse, Gauntlet, nibbling at some short, sweet fresh grass.

After the talk with his mum and all the research he'd done on the internet he viewed these small, friendly little creatures with a new found respect.

"Before you go, I have a question."

"Yes?" asked Yeti.

"How do horses shake hands?"

"Well, we don't actually do that. I suppose the nearest thing would be mutual grooming."

"O.K. 'splain that to me."

"Because of our conformation, the way we are built, we have certain areas that are difficult to reach and scratch, so we help each other out. But only with close companions, not strangers."

"Show me."

Yeti and Sefton looked at each other, and then nodded. They stood side ways, facing each other, but slightly to one side. Then they both took a step forward and stopped.

Yeti's head lined up directly with Sefton's shoulder and vice versa. Simultaneously both horses lifted their heads, took the withers of the other horse in their teeth and started slowly biting.

"Oh my God! Doesn't that hurt?" asked Freddy.

"No, no, it actually feels really good. When we used to get groomed with brushes it was always difficult to tell them to do it harder. It's very relaxing for us."

"Hmm. O.K. so what about me? What if I wanted to say, you know, shake hands with you? As a person."

"Oh, easy!" said Rochester pushing to the front, "and me first please!"

Freddy looked down at the small black horse with the narrow snip of white down the middle of his face. "What do I do? Pat you on the nose?"

"Yuk!"

"No!"

Never!"

"Ugh!" all four protested.

"I thought horses liked their nose patted?"

"Freddy, only a plop would do that! It feels awful."

"A plop? What the hell is a plop?"

"You, you told it to Victoriana last night."

Freddy thought for a minute. "Oh! You mean a prat!"

"Exactly," said Yeti.

"So, no nose patting then?"

"No, it's terrible. Try poking you own nose and see how it feels."

He did. "Oh, got your point, not nice."

"Told you so."

"So, Rochester, you tell me, what do I do?"

The small black horse stepped a little closer and then said, "Behind and under the chin please."

"Really?" Freddy bent down and slowly reached forward and put his hand up and behind the little horses face.

"Now, in the wide gap, between the two bones, scratch please."

He curled his fingers upwards, dug his nails into the soft hair and flesh and began to scratch. The little horse shivered with pleasure.

"Wow! You really like that?"

"Oh yes. It's one of the few places we really can't reach. Even our companions can't help us there. But you can."

"Me next," said the smaller grey, Gauntlet, stepping forward.

"So, if you really want to say hello and shake hands as you say, that's the way to do it," finished Yeti.

"Gotcha."

"We have to go now, Freddy, but I believe we will see you this evening."

"O.K. I'll keep an eye out for you. But one more thing."

"Yes?"

"Is someone ever going to tell me how and why I can do horsey chat?"

"Soon, Freddy, very soon."

"Yeah, whatever." He watched as the four tucked their forelegs and took flight to the east.

Freddy climbed onto the bike and started to pedal slowly along the bike path in the same direction. He hadn't gone very far when movement ahead caught his attention. Two riders were coming down the Row; one soldier on a smart, black thoroughbred mare, and a girl on an older cob type horse. He smiled quietly to himself as he stopped the bike and leaned it against a tree. He stepped out onto the sand track as the riders approached.

"Hi, Mister!" he called to the soldier, "Nice horsey."

Webber slowed down and halted. Clarissa stopped next to him.

"Morning," said Lance Corporal Webber. All members of the regiment had been taught to be polite and pleasant to civilians in the park, no matter how annoying they might appear.

"Mister, can I stroke your horsey please?" He made sure to sound like a real plop as he stepped forward toward the soldier and the black mare.

Webber sighed to himself, "Ignorant little brat." Then out loud, "Yes, but slowly and be careful."

Freddy grinned again and stepped forward. Victoriana' eyes locked on him with a look that would have burned a hole into the side of a battle ship. He reached up and pretended to go to pat her nose. She flinched and tossed her head, but his hand changed course and slowly went up behind her jaw and gave a slow, deep scratch.

"Morning, you old battle axe," he said. But his mouth didn't move, only his nostrils, very slightly.

Chapter Nine

Yeti and Sefton escorted Freddy home and then returned to the barracks to discuss things with Victoriana. She told them about her conversation with Freddy and how he had reacted to the information. They all agreed that although young and at times cheeky, Freddy meant well and was coping with everything being thrown at him in a very mature way. All three thought it best to keep knowledge of Freddy and his talent at a very low profile for now. It could be a disaster if the troop horses heard about it and started yelling at him every time he was seen in public. The fewer who knew, the better. Then Yeti and Sefton told Victoriana something extremely disconcerting. In fact, it was beyond disconcerting, it was terrible. The Pegusinni would confirm everything in a day or two, but for now so as not to cause alarm, Victoriana was to keep quiet.

Four Pegusinni, Yeti, Sefton, Rochester and Gauntlet, would go to St. James's Park and Horse Guard's parade ground first thing in the morning to see if they could find out more. It was difficult to verify what they'd been hearing as the information was coming from others who were not the most reliable of sources.

A senate meeting was scheduled for tomorrow evening, as usual on the eve of a new moon. Victoriana, Venetia, Hercules and Agatha presently formed the senate. Normally, it was a brief affair where they discussed routine matters and occasionally decided on reprimands needed for poor behaviour. This time there was only the matter of the mentors for the fresh remounts and the issue of the two geldings bucking in the trainee ride.

Victoriana impatiently walked her stall, pausing only when she heard the Scottish night guard approaching. Finally, just before dawn, she moved to a corner, lowered her neck, allowed the check ligaments in her legs to click into place for support and dozed lightly.

The sound of reveille played by the trumpeter at six a.m. swiftly brought Victoriana fully awake. As always, the same routine feeding, stall cleaning, grooming and finally Lance Corporal Webber appearing with her tack. As Victoriana led Webber to the parade square she caught sight of Venetia on the ramp to the Blues and Royals.

"There may be a problem with the senate meeting tomorrow evening," she called, "I'll confirm as soon as I know. Would you get word to the others, please, while I'm out?"

"Yes, certainly," the other mare called back, "something serious come up?"

"No. No, not at all," Victoriana said just a little bit too quickly. "Hopefully I'll know one way or another by this afternoon." Webber now had her by the concrete mounting block, pulling the stirrup irons down on their leathers and preparing to mount.

"Also, see if you can find out from Agatha what excuse those two riding school geldings have come up with for their bucking."

"Will do," called Venetia as she disappeared from view into the barns.

Webber swung himself into the saddle, retrieved his white gloves from the pocket of his tunic and pulled them on.

"Yo! Webber! Hold up a minute," a voice shouted behind them.

Victoriana turned to look across the square to see Trooper Spike Yarrow, a junior officer's valet, running towards them. Webber looked down on the slightly dishevelled trooper with shoe polish stains on his fatigues and unruly hair. "That would be Corporal Webber to you, Yarrow."

"Yeah, whatever," said Yarrow, rubbing some sweat off his brow.

"Anyway, I got a message for you."

"And that would be….?"

"What would be?"

"The message. The bloody message, you thick bugger."

"Oh, right, that," then slightly quieter, Yarrow said, "got a spare ciggi, mate?"

Webber pulled himself up to full height. "Two things. One, I am not your mate, you scruffy, bloody piece of crap. And two, if I did have a spare cigarette," Webber paused, narrowing his eyes, "I'd probably rip your head off and stuff the ciggi down the hole in your neck! Now, what's the bloody message?"

"O.K. O.K. Keep your freaking wig on." Stuck up remount queen, Yarrow thought to himself.

Victoriana, bemused by this exchange, momentarily forgot all she'd been thinking about.

"The message is from Lieutenant Hewlett. He said to make sure you exercise that old nag really well today because he's taking her on Queen's Life Guard tomorrow."

"What?" said Webber, disbelieving what he'd just heard.

"What!" thought Victoriana, also in total disbelief.

"You're off your rocker," said Webber, "this mare doesn't do guard duty."

Victoriana vigorously agreed. "This mare does *not* do guard duty!"

Yarrow was enjoying his moment of glory. "Ha, well, she is now, mate. Johno's orders."

"You are such an ignorant piece of dirt, Yarrow. It's Captain Johnson to you!"

"Whatever," said the trooper, now picking his nose, "Anyway, you got the message. I did my bit."

"Wait a minute, you scumbag. What exactly did Captain Johnson say?"

Yarrow wiped something disgusting from his right nostril onto his trouser leg. "Webber, are you not aware that my boss, Lieutenant Hewlett, is the nephew of Brigadier Hewlett?"

Webber was silent, so Yarrow continued. "Yes, well apparently you aren't aware of that little detail. Anyways, the old boy, the Brigadier is an old chum of Johno's and it's Hewlett's first time on full guard duty tomorrow and his uncle asked Johno to make sure he had the best horse available."

"What about Hewlett's own horse? He should have his own charger."

"Not yet, mate. He's not been here long enough; hell, he's only just finished riding school training. Still figuring out which way to buckle his spurs on."

"And he's been told he can ride this mare?" asked Webber incredulously.

"Yes, *this* mare?" Victoriana was equally incredulous.

Yarrow attacked his left nostril with gusto. He then stared at something interesting on his finger and finally looked up at Webber. "I'm just the messenger, pal. Apparently the old dame is back in town tomorrow and we start sending out full guards for a few days till she's gone."

"I am well aware of when we do and when we don't send out full guards, Yarrow. Her Majesty the Queen is not to be referred to as 'the old dame' when you're wearing uniform." There was another pause, and then Webber glared, "A Yorkshire cretin like you shouldn't be allowed to wear uniform. You're a pathetic disgrace to the regiment."

Yarrow was now scratching at his rear and looking not the slightest bit bothered by the Corporal's remarks, which infuriated Webber even more.

"Now, do me a favour, Yarrow." Webber said through gritted teeth.

"What's that, matey?"

"Stick your head down a toilet and flush it."

The junior trooper pulled his hand away from his backside, grinned and wrinkled up his face as he strained. He could usually break wind on command; it was his party piece in the N.A.A.F.I. For some odd reason he didn't manage it, so he gave Webber a one-handed salute which was not in the military manual.

"'ave a nice day Cor-por-al." Yarrow chuckled and, marvelling at his own wit, he walked to the officers' mess quarters and back to cleaning duty.

A tight-lipped Webber wheeled Victoriana around and using more leg than was really necessary, rode her out of the gates. As they hit the broad sand track, he turned the mare left and went straight up into a brisk trot. It only took a few minutes for them to reach the top of the park where Exhibition Road divides Hyde Park from Kensington Gardens. So fluid was the design and landscaping, most visitors didn't realize Hyde Park and Kensington Gardens were actually two separate parks. Still trotting on the sand track, Webber and Victoriana were soon at the west end of Rotten Row where Clarissa and Nero were waiting.

"Keeping her waiting is not the best way to a girl's heart, or her apartment for that matter, Corporal."

"Sorry sweetie, I got held up by a peasant."

"Peasant?"

"Yes, some piece of Yorkshire riff-raff not fit to be in uniform."

"Trouble, darling?"

"No, no, not really, just bloody annoying. Anyway, how is Sarah and how is the pony?"

"Both are shaken and stirred. But, like wine, fine with time."

"Did you find out what spooked the pony?"

"Not really. Sarah remembers having a talk with some boy on a bike. She said he was odd, asking about some miniature horses or something. Then it was as if he started talking to someone else and the next minute the pony, Florence, was spinning around and bolting."

"Probably some park junkie. Tweaked out on pot or heroin."

"No, he was younger and she said she thought he was quite nice."

While the conversation went on above, another was going on below.

"You two are late."

"Don't even start with me, Nero; I've had the night and morning from hell."

"Wow, sorry, madam, shall we try this again? Good morning, Victoriana, how are you today?"

"Sorry," she muttered, "I've had better days."

"Sounds like somebody woke up on the wrong side of the wheelbarrow."

She chose to ignore his banter and got straight to the point, "The child, the pony, how are they?"

"From what I hear, the child will be fine, bruised, a bit knocked around but nothing seriously damaged except confidence."

"And the pony?" she asked cautiously, "any reason for such a violent I.F.R.?"

"Ah, well, now that's an interesting point."

"Go on." Victoriana was interested in hearing the pony mare's side of the story.

"Well, I waited 'till she had calmed down before I asked her. But then the little mare told me the strangest thing."

"What? What did she tell you?"

"She said that the boy with the bike could see Pegusinni."

"Really?"

"Yes, and she kept saying that they can't, can they? They can't see them, at all, can they?"

"And you said?"

"I said no, not usually."

"Usually, Nero?"

He looked at her, the wisdom of his years showing in his old eyes, "No, Victoriana, not usually."

"Is that all? Is that all she said?"

"No," he said slowly, "not at all, by any means."

"Go on."

"She said he talked to her." The older gelding gauged Victoriana's reaction carefully.

"The boy with the bike? He talked to her?" Victoriana asked guardedly.

"Yes, which is what set her into a blind panic. After all, she's been told her whole life that we and they can never talk. Completely freaked her out."

"Poor pony, quite a shock for her, then?"

"Indeed. But that's not what I find most curious."

"No? Well, what do you find curious?"

Nero paused and then quietly said, "What I find most curious is your lack of reaction."

It was decision time for Victoriana. Yeti and Sefton had both asked that she not disclose what had transpired in the past twenty-four hours. But Nero was a wise and trusted member of the community and he was not a troop horse. She had agreed not to tell troop horses just yet, but there had been no mention of Nero. Victoriana made her decision. As Webber and Clarissa directed their mounts into a walk down Rotten Row, Victoriana told Nero the outline of what had transpired in her stall last night. Nero remained quiet while she talked, something Victoriana found surprising.

"You don't seem to be alarmed or shocked?"

"No, not really. I've heard tales of this before, passed on from my great grandmare. She said it does happen but hasn't for many, many seasons. Something to do with timing of the Blue Moon and the White Moon passing either side of Earth's moon in the year of equine. If he was born at a precise moment in time, well, apparently it's possible."

Victoriana was looking ahead down the Row, "Well," she said, "here's your chance to verify it."

"What?"

"That's him, to the left with the bike." Victoriana watched as Freddy walked towards them.

Both horses halted as directed by their riders and listened to the dialogue between Freddy and Webber.

"Horsey? Bloody horsey? I thought you said this boy was clued up Victoriana?" Nero snorted. He watched as the boy approached the black mare. It looked as if Freddy was about to crassly pat her nose. Then Nero saw Freddy change his mind at the last minute and gave her a professional handshake.

"Hello, you old battle axe," said Freddy with a grin as he scratched between her jawbones.

"Freddy, do you see the size of my front hoof?" asked Victoriana

"I certainly do. No Cinderella, are ya?"

"One more comment like that and you'll be wearing this hoof on the back of your head!"

"O.K., O.K., just a little horsey humour there. Sorry to tick you off."

She peered down her nose at him and lightened her glare, "Freddy, I'd like you to meet Nero, a long time friend of mine."

"Hi, mate," said Freddy with a broad grin.

"Hello, young man, a real pleasure to meet you."

"Hmm, you don't know him too well yet, do you, Nero?" said the black mare.

At that point Webber spoke loudly to Freddy, "Alright, kid, enough patting the ponies, off you go on your bike, so to speak."

"Yeah, yeah, O.K, Mr. Soldier, see you around." Freddy put a foot on the pedal of his bike.

Victoriana lowered her neck and asked, "Freddy, can you be at a meeting this evening? About the same time?"

"Yeah, sure. But I'll need a 'lift' in."

"I'll get word to Sefton and Yeti," Victoriana said as the riders moved the horses on and the boy rode his bicycle away.

"So you have no idea why all fifteen of them are still here?" asked Nero, referring to the Pegusinni.

"I have some idea, but nothing positive. Apparently, we'll hear more tonight and tomorrow but that will be completely messed up if I'm gone on guard duty to Whitehall for twenty-four hours."

"I still can't believe they're pulling you down from the shelf and dusting you off for guard work," the old gelding chuckled.

Victoriana did what she did best. She ignored him.

When they reached the end of the Row near Hyde Park Corner, Webber told Clarissa about the guard duty the following day. As he needed to give Victoriana a full workout, they turned left across Serpentine Road and onto the narrower sand track which ran north, parallel with Park Lane. Both riders took a more forward, balanced position over the stirrups and set off into a strong hand canter. It didn't take them long to reach Speaker's Corner and the turn left to swing around the top of the park. When they reached the bridge over the Serpentine Lake, the horses were brought back to a walk. On the lake, a group of ducks were chivvied away by four swans showing their territorial dominance on the water.

Not as young or fit as Victoriana, Nero was sweating quite heavily,

"I need to cool this old boy down," said Clarissa, "you going round again?"

"Yep," replied Webber, "last thing I need to hear is that she didn't behave for the Brigadier's precious nephew. I'll call you later, darling."

"O.K. sweetie, my big soldier boy." She blew him a kiss.

Victoriana shuddered. As they parted company, Webber shortened his stirrups several more holes and this time really got into gallop position. Body streamlined with her neck, seat out behind, reins bridged. When they reached the top of Rotten Row, he told her to *go*.

They flew across the sand. Webber was taking a risk. Full gallop was actually not allowed in the park as there could be accidents with amateur riders or pedestrians, but neither one of this pair were amateurs. Ears pinned, nostrils wide open, Victoriana's forelegs extended forward to their maximum reach as her mane and tail flew horizontal in the wind they created. Webber and the horse were lost in their own world. This was different from the frenzied gallop of yesterday when they had chased the grey pony. This was powerful, fast and rhythmical. A truly good rider can accompany his horse in such a balanced way that the horse can almost forget he is there. This was when Victoriana really respected Webber. It felt like she was a yearling again, hurtling around a pasture, totally free as if she had no saddle, bridle, and certainly no rider. This was when she was allowed to behave like a horse.

As they reached the end of the Row for the second time that morning she heard him quietly saying, "O.K., steady now, let's come in to land, old girl." She reduced her length of stride, lost the intensity of the gallop and gradually slowed to a hand canter. He chuckled as he sat up, patted her damp neck and said, "Was it good for you?"

The return to barracks was uneventful. Later Victoriana was washed down, dried, groomed and had her mane and tail trimmed in preparation for duty the following day. She heard her groom, Trooper Cochrane, arguing with Yarrow about who would prepare her in the morning. Cochrane said there was no way he'd allow Yarrow near her. In fact, he wouldn't let Yarrow look after a hamster let alone a horse. Yarrow could clean the saddlery; Cochrane would deal with his charger. Victoriana sighed, let them argue, and tried to have a restful afternoon. She had a feeling it wasn't going to be a quiet night.

And she was right.

Chapter Ten

After meeting the Pegusinni and Victoriana, Freddy biked home to grab some lunch. Despite the strange goings on he felt remarkably calm. He thought things through as he made himself a sandwich. For so much of his life he'd thought he was a bit mad, this seeing little winged horses that no one else saw. Then pretending he couldn't see them, even though he could. It had been easier to believe they weren't there at all than to try and rationalise the situation. And there were the voices. The bloody weird, mysterious voices he'd been hearing over the past year. It wasn't him going crackers after all. They really were voices he was hearing, not from human beings, but instead from the minds of real and miniature horses. O.K. well, that part sounded like the thought of a crazy person. No, he definitely felt better, although it would be cool if he could actually get someone else to believe him which definitely would take some doing. For now he'd go on keeping it all to himself.

Freddy flicked on his computer while he ate his lunch and did a little bit more detailed search. This time when he hit 'Google' he entered names, not dates or places. The text and photographs that appeared on the screen made him feel like throwing his lunch back up. A photograph of a huge black horse called Sefton covered with scars and details of how his jugular vein had been blown open and six inch nails peppered his body. One had blasted through his bridle and into his head. Details of how he had only been given a fifty/fifty chance of survival. He read the list of the other injured horses and those horses who had died.

He was sickened as he read about the dying and injured soldiers, and now he felt his eyes fill, "No. I am sixteen and a half years old. I am not going to bloody well cry."

One report stated the queen had called from Buckingham palace twice that day; there were messages from all around the world, including one from the Pope and one from the President of the United States. This one seemed rather ironic as other reports showed a lot of the funding and support for the I.R.A. came from North America, in particular the big cities on the east coast, Boston, New York and Philadelphia. Freddy wondered if the Americans ever knew what their donations really funded.

He was lying on his bed staring at the ceiling, the room almost dark when he heard Jane come back to the flat several hours later.

"You home?" she called.

"Yeah, yes, mum, in my room."

She popped her head around the door. "Guess what?"

"Eh? I don't know what?"

"They are going out for dinner and I have the night off. And I am not going to cook! How good is that?"

"Pretty good, mum."

"You feel like going out to eat?"

"Not really, think I want to stay in for a bit."

"Oh, O.K. well, how about some take away food? Fish and chips? Or Chinese?"

"Chinese, definitely."

"Alright, off your bed. You go and get the food; I'll set the table and warm the plates."

"Yeah, alright," he said, getting to his feet.

"And go to the place next to the cinema, not the one by florists; the man in there creeps me out."

"Which man?"

"The one at the Chinese place next to the florists, he's a letch with tattooed ears, gave me sleazy looks and winks when I went in." Jane shuddered.

"Whatever you say, mum. So, what do you want?"

"Tangy beef with cashews and fried rice and you get what ever catches your fancy."

Freddy pulled on his shoes, picked up his jacket, took some cash from her and headed down the steps. One good thing about living in the middle of a big city, everything was always in walking distance. Up north, out in the sticks, you might have to go miles to find a restaurant or shop. When he returned, they set the cartons of food out on the table and sat down to eat; Jane with a glass of wine and Freddy with a coke.

"Look at that, I'm a monkey," she commented.

"Eh?" Freddy looked up from his plate.

"Year of the monkey." Jane was chewing and pointing down at the paper napkins that had come with the food. Around the perimeter, listed in red print, were the names of each year in the Chinese calendar. Twelve years in a cycle, each year named after an animal. "Lucky, I could have been a rat or a snake. What are you?"

Freddy ran his finger around the edge of his napkin, looking for the year he was born. He held his finger on 1990 and looked up at his mother. "Horse. Year of the horse, apparently." Freddy paused, "Why am I not surprised?"

"Don't know, but at least you're not a pig."

"Thanks, mum. Love you too."

After watching T.V. for a while he went to his room. He didn't bother getting undressed, just kicked off his shoes and lay on his bed dozing until his escort arrived. Promptly at one a.m. he heard the rattle on the fire escape, grabbed his jacket and shoes and went out to meet his new friends. Once again all fifteen were there, waiting in the street and lined up in pairs with Gauntlet at the front.

"Why do you guys nearly always go around in pairs?" he asked Yeti.

"Oh, you mean half sections?"

"Do I?" Freddy asked.

"A section is a line of four; a line of two is a half section. Force of habit, I guess, we go almost everywhere in half sections. Besides, we like the company. It's always good to have a friend next to you."

The trip to barracks was quicker this time as there was no explaining to do. Again Freddy tied his bike to a tree and he made sure he had a hand on Sefton's neck when they crossed the road and stood at the foot of the tall wall. He definitely didn't want to be picked up by a security camera.

"Ready?" asked Yeti.

Freddy nodded, held out both of his arms as they scooped him up and over the wall. Quickly and quietly they went down the ramp and were shortly all standing next to Victoriana's stall door. Everyone exchanged greetings and then it was straight to business.

"What's the news?" asked the alpha mare looking to Yeti and Sefton.

"We were down at St James's and Whitehall this morning and it looks like it will happen." There was silence as everyone digested this point.

Everyone except Freddy. "Scuse me, but what will happen?" he asked

"A thing, soon" said Yeti.

"A bad thing," said Sefton.

"A big, bad thing," said Rochester.

"A really big, bad thing," said Gauntlet nodding his head vigorously. The others all nodded agreement.

"Well, what is this really big bad thing?"

"We don't know," this from Yeti.

"Well, not yet, we don't know," from Sefton, "but we will soon."

"So there's going to be a big bad thing, happening soon, but you don't know what it is?" Freddy asked.

"Yes."

"No."

"Correct."

"O.K., that makes it easier," said Freddy. He tried again, "When? When will this thing happen?"

"Don't know," Sefton said.

"Not sure," Yeti added.

"But soon, we think," Gauntlet said.

"Any idea where this big bad thing might happen?" asked Freddy walking up and down the passageway.

"Not sure."

"Around here."

"Close."

"Terrific. A really big bad thing is going to happen, you don't know what it is, you don't know when and you don't know where? Have I got this correct?" Freddy was becoming slightly exasperated.

"Yes."

"Absolutely," various Pegusinni heads were nodding in agreement.

"Glad that's all cleared up then." Freddy said.

Victoriana moved forward in her stall. "Yeti, I thought you said there would be a message?"

"Oh, there will be, tomorrow morning."

"From who?" asked Freddy.

"Charles."

"Charles?" Freddy was confused again.

"Yes, Charles." There was more nodding from the group.

"Have I met Charles yet?" asked Freddy?

A collection of snorts and equine chuckles came with the reply. "Don't be silly."

"Of course not."

"So where is this damn Charles bloke?" Freddy asked, not just a little ready to tear his hair out.

"In the park."

"Where he always is."

"Where else would he be?"

"So, he's like a drunk, a wino guy, living on a bench?" asked the perplexed teenager.

More chuckles and head shaking from the Pegusinni. Victoriana looked at the boy.

"Freddy, Charles is an olor."

"What?"

"Er, large white bird, lives on the lake," she said helpfully.

"A swan?"

"Yes, Charles, he's a swan. Actually he's the head cob out there. But definitely a swan."

"And this bloody swan has a message to tell you about a really big bad thing, that you don't know what it is, when it will happen, or where it will happen?"

"Yes," said Yeti.

"Correct." The Pegusinni patiently nodded, pleased he was finally catching up.

Freddy pushed his hand back through his hair, "So, why don't you go out now and get the message?"

"Can't."

"Not yet."

"Why not?" Freddy asked.

"He hasn't got it yet."

"He's going to give you a message that he hasn't got yet?" Freddy was beyond confused now.

"Yes."

"And when do you think he will have the message?"

"Tonight."

"Should be."

"We hope."

Freddy walked up and down the stable aisle again trying to stay calm and patient. After all, it appeared he was the only one who didn't understand how things worked or what the heck was going on. He tried another angle.

"This message. This really important message, about the bad thing, who's it coming from? Who actually knows what the heck is going on?"

"Columbaceous," said Yeti, slightly perplexed by Freddy's confusion.

"Colum. Who?" Freddy had lost the battle with staying calm.

"Freddy, you're making us nervous, we don't like it when you shout," Rochester said, his eyes widening.

The boy took a slow, deep breath, closed his eyes for a minute, exhaled and tried again in a calmer voice, "Sorry, it's just I keep being confused. Now who is Colombo?"

"He's not a person, silly, he's a bird. Well, actually quite a few of them," Sefton explained.

"And its columbaceous, not colombo," said Yeti.

Victoriana joined in. "Freddy, you know the big concrete place in the city, with the fountains and statues?"

Freddy racked his brains.

"With the big tall stick with the man on top," she added.

He clicked his fingers. "Trafalgar Square? Nelson's Column?"

"I think that might be it, we never go there. But anyway, that's where the columbaceous are," said Yeti.

"Pigeons!" exclaimed the boy, "in Trafalgar Square!"

"Probably, could be. Small, grey, white. You call them pigeons then?"

"Yes, we call them pigeons."

"Very well, then we can too."

After a short silence Freddy asked, "So, a pigeon is going to give Charles the swan a message?"

The Pegusinni let off another round of laughter.

"Don't be silly!" said Gauntlet, "a pigeon can't talk to a swan!"

"Well excuse me for being thick," said Freddy, "but I thought Charlie the swan was getting a message tonight." Freddy paused, "if the pigeon can't talk to a swan, who's he telling?"

"Talpi," said Yeti.

This time Freddy remained calm. "And talpi would be?"

"In St. James's Park," said Sefton.

Still determined to stay calm, Freddy asked, "A clue please, so I can figure out who talpi might be?"

"Black."

"Furry."

"Digs lots of holes."

"A mole?" from the teenager.

"I think so," said Victoriana.

"So a pigeon can talk to a mole?"

"Yes."

"Of course."

"And how would that be?" Freddy asked.

"Similar thing in the heads," Gauntlet explained.

This needed some thought. Freddy knew that pigeons had some sort homing device or compass or, was it a sonar system like dolphins? He recalled from mammal biology something about moles having a system for knowing where they were in the dark and they had terrible eyesight. That must be it. The thing between the pigeon and the mole.

The sound of footsteps outside broke the silence. The night guard was coming.

"Oh crap!" There was no time to get into the box stall and hide behind Victoriana, so Freddy did the only thing he could think of and hoped it really worked. He grabbed hold of Rochester's neck with one hand and Yeti's with the other, pressed himself back against the wall and closed his eyes. A tall shadow fell across the doorway, and the guard walked into the dimly lit area. He glanced at the black mare sleepily resting a hind leg. He took a few more steps forward and looked down the wide passageway, totally unaware of a sweating teenager and a group of small winged horses less than a couple of metres to his right. Then without making a sound, the guard turned around and walked through the stable door out into the darkness.

Everyone relaxed

"How's about that then?" grinned Freddy, "I'm a regular Houdini, now you see me, and now you don't!"

Freddy and the winged horses moved forward again closer to Victoriana's stall door.

"And now," said Freddy, "I am going to make sense of this once and for all. I'll speak slowly, and clearly; let me know if I get it right."

The equine nodded hopefully.

"A big, bad thing is going to happen. We think the pigeons in Trafalgar Square know something about it. They have told a mole in St. James's Park to pass the message on. He's going to tell Charles the swan, who will tell us tomorrow. Do I have it correct?"

"Almost," Yeti said.

"Which bit don't I have?" asked Freddy.

"A mole can't talk to a swan."

"Well, who the hell can talk to a swan?" Freddy really had thought he'd gotten it right.

"You're shouting again."

"Sorry," Freddy apologized,

"I know! I know! I know the name for him," said an excited Gauntlet.

"You do?" asked Victoriana.

"Yep, because the musicians used to pretend their trumpets were guns and they would fire at them in the park. And they used their other name!" he said triumphantly.

"Which is?" They all stared at the little grey horse.

"Rabbits!" he said proudly.

"Well, I never did know that," said Sefton, "Iago are also rabbits. Who'd have known?"

Freddy got back into the conversation, trying to join the dots. "This rabbit person, he will pass the message on to Charles tonight?"

"Yes."

"And who will Charles tell tomorrow morning?"

"Victoriana," said Sefton.

"Why can't he just tell you?"

"Don't be silly, Freddy, a swan can't see or talk to Pegusinni. Sometimes you are such a plop."

"We have another problem then," said the alpha mare.

"What's that?" asked Yeti.

She paused and then quietly said, "I won't be in the park tomorrow. I will be on guard duty."

There was a stunned silence.

"*You* will be going on guard duty?" asked an amazed Sefton.

"That can't be right," said Yeti, "Squadron leader going on guard duty?"

"Wow," said Rochester, "I think I might just have to be around to see this tomorrow morning."

"It's not a freak show!" snapped Victoriana, "and I have done duty before."

"Yes, like a hundred moons ago," said Sefton.

"Guys, guys," said Freddy, "this is not going to help with our problem tomorrow. If Charlie Swan can't speak to Victoriana and he can't see Pegusinni, who the hell is going to take the message? And more importantly, get it right and tell us?"

"Nero," said the lead mare.

"Nero? He's not a troop horse, never done a day of duty in his life!" protested Yeti. "He's a civilian!"

"It doesn't matter; he's a long time and trusted friend. He'll collect the message and then pass it on to Freddy."

"Freddy?" asked Sefton, "he knows about Freddy?"

"Yes, I shared that with him this morning."

"I thought we agreed to keep quiet about the boy?" said Sefton.

"Excuse me, but the boy is standing here, listening to being talked about," said Freddy.

"It's the safest and best way," said Victoriana, "and that's my final word. Nero will take the message from Charles and pass it on to Freddy. You must visit Nero tonight and let him know what we need, Yeti."

The Pegusinni paused in thought and then all nodded in agreement.

"Freddy, you will need to be in the park first thing in the morning and assist Nero."

"Assist?" he queried.

"Yes, you may have to distract his rider, get her to stop or something so he can get the message."

Freddy nodded his head as he gave it some thought. "I have a couple of questions. How come a swan can talk to a horse?"

"Royal connections," said Sefton.

"Royal?"

"Yes, all swans are owned by the reigning monarch."

"Every one of them?"

"Every one in this country. I don't know about in other countries."

"And equine have served the monarchy for many centuries, actually since the very first monarch which gives us a foot in the door, so to speak."

"Another question. This rabbit, he's passing the message on tonight?" Freddy was starting to get a very unpleasant feeling.

"Yes, we believe so."

"And how and where are the rabbit and the swan meeting?"

"By the Serpentine Lake. Charles could never leave the lake area."

"No, no, never." There was group tutting and head shaking from the Pegusinni.

Freddy thought a bit and asked, "So this little rabbit guy, he's coming up from St James's Park tonight, all the way to Hyde Park?"

"Yes," said Victoriana, "it's not far."

"No," the others agreed, "Not far at all."

"Victoriana! You're a bloody horse! And you lot! You can all fly! No where is far to you! We're talking about a rabbit, for God's sakes!"

There was an uncomfortable silence while they all considered this detail. Freddy took a deep intake of breath.

"Right. You, you, you and you," he said pointing in turn to Yeti, Sefton, Rochester and Gauntlet, "we need to get going. Now!"

"Where to?"

"Well, call me thick sometimes, heck you can even call me a plop if you want, but answer me this. What chance do you think a rabbit has of crossing safely over Hyde Park Corner?"

"We hadn't thought of that," said Yeti.

"We always had an escort," said Gauntlet, "one that stopped the traffic."

"A police escort, actually," said Rochester.

"Well the Metropolitan police force is not going to send out a bunny escort at three in the freakin morning!" Freddy looked at the alpha mare, "we have to go, now. I'll try to see you in the morning."

"O.K. and do try to meet up with Nero or we might not get the message."

"If we don't get going now, some tramp in the park will be making bunny stew from a road kill and there will be no message. Come on, lads, let's move it!" Freddy started to walk out of the stables up the ramp.

"See," said Yeti to the others, "*he* said the boy would be good. And he is"

The rest agreed and after nodding to Victoriana, took flight behind the teenage boy who now appeared to be in charge.

"Have they actually met?" Sefton asked Yeti.

"No, tomorrow night, I believe. Eve of the new moon."

"That's another party I don't want to miss," said Rochester.

Chapter Eleven

They were soon out of barracks and back to where Freddy had left his bicycle. He unchained it, mounted and set off to the west.

"Er, Freddy, Green Park is the other way," said Sefton, "to the east from here."

"I know, but have you seen the height and size of the park gates and fence at that end? I'm going to cut through the small garden along here, the fence is much lower and fewer people about. I'll meet you at Hyde Park Corner." Freddy peddled off into the dark and the Pegusinni took flight to the east. He pushed his way through the low shrubs and bushes by the railings and glanced up and down the road devoid of pedestrians. He was now on the south side of the barracks where CCTV cameras were placed at various intervals. He biked down the road, close to the kerb, noting the strong smell of ammonia and manure wafting out into the Knightsbridge road. "I bet the posh neighbours love that," he thought. Black taxis and expensive cars brushed close by him as he cycled on past a big department store called Harvey Nichols and then up the slight hill toward Hyde Park Corner.

If they called New York the city that never sleeps, Freddy wondered, what London was called? The smaller side streets were relatively quiet but any through routes were busy, in particular with heavy goods vehicles driving at night across the city to avoid rush hour. Hyde Park Corner was a main junction for routes east to west and routes north to south. He stared at the carousel of traffic hurtling around the curves and thought, "Great, somewhere on the other side of this mayhem is a rabbit with no bus pass."

He stood on the kerb by the pedestrian crossing and noticed the steps down to the subway. Perfect! A rabbit would love a tunnel to go through. Freddy's joy was short lived. Metal gates were drawn across the entrances and would not be opened until the tube began running again at dawn. On the huge traffic island were various war memorial statues and in the centre a monstrous sized stone archway which reminded Freddy of the one in France, the Arc d'Triumph. There were large grass lawn areas as well as broad tarmac walk ways. As the lights on the crossing finally changed to red and the green man flashed for him to cross, he caught sight of four small winged horses grazing on the lawn. He was soon standing with them on the lawn as endless traffic circled the roundabout.

"Why are you here? I thought you said he was coming from Green Park?" Freddy asked them, "That's on the other side of the other road. We're only half way there."

They looked up and, rather sheepishly, Yeti said, "Well, we were waiting for you."

"And this lawn grass is much better than the rank stuff in the park," added Gauntlet, head back down and nibbling again.

"This is *not* a bloody picnic. Now, everyone, cross the next road and start to look for our friend." Freddy didn't mention that when he'd crossed the first half of the roundabout he'd looked for signs of splattered bunny on the road. Fortunately there were none and as he stepped onto the road at the second crossing he looked around again. Nothing he could see. Green Park is smaller and runs parallel to Constitution Hill, connecting Hyde Park to St James.

"So, where is he supposed to be?"

"Not sure, but he should be at this end of the park by now if he's going to make it before dawn," said Rochester.

"Damn, there are flower beds and bushes everywhere. He could be anywhere for all we know," said Freddy. He remained at the edge of the park while his companions commenced low flying searches of the area.

"How are we going to help if we find him?" asked Gauntlet.

"I'm going to pick him up and carry him across this darn road and put him in the other park."

"What?"

"No. Oh no."

"That will never work."

"Why not? You got any other ideas?" Freddy asked.

"He won't let you near him, let alone pick him up." Sefton stated.

"Probably have a heart attack and make a transition." Gauntlet warned.

"He'll be used to people from the park but not enough to let you hold him," said Yeti.

"Got any other ideas then?" Freddy was getting desperate.

"Wait!" said Yeti in an excited whisper, "Over there. By the fence!"

Sure enough, there by the fence was a small park bunny staring at the traffic. Freddy left the bike by some shrubs and walked over to the crossing. He stood perfectly still until the rabbit looked up at him. Very slowly and casually the boy gestured with his left arm, like a doorman saying, "This way, sir."

The rabbit hopped closer, stared at him and then came closer still until he was only a few metres away.

"Don't make any sudden or sharp moves," said a hovering Yeti to Freddy, "he'll be a bit nervous."

"Yes, I had figured that much out," said Freddy through clenched teeth.

The rabbit was now almost at the boy's feet and very close to the crossing. Freddy took a slow breath and pressed the button for the signal. The light changed immediately and the green man started to flash. All traffic momentarily halted. But the rabbit didn't move. Freddy gestured again knowing the light would be changing back again at any second. The rabbit made no move towards the crossing; instead he looked back over his shoulder to the shrubbery.

"What the heck is he doing?" hissed Freddy to Yeti. The light changed and the traffic started to roar again. "Bugger! Missed it."

"Mate," said Yeti.

"What?"

"He's waiting for his mate, she's still over there."

"He's brought his *wife* along?"

"Of course, you don't think he's going to try to get back from Hyde Park again, do you? He'll be setting up a new life on the other side."

"I've heard there are some pleasant burrows near the boat house," said Gauntlet, "nice views of the lake too."

"Terrific, we'll get them some Home Base gift vouchers as a house warming present." Freddy said through gritted teeth.

They watched as a rabbit came out of the shrubbery and greeted her mate. The two then moved towards the crossing together. Freddy once again went to the button. He waited until the two rabbits were almost at the kerb, then pressed and prayed. After what seemed like hours to Freddy, the lights changed and traffic stopped. Freddy gestured with his hand and the small animals hopped out into the road. They glanced up at him but kept moving cautiously forward. It seemed to take forever and the rabbits were only half way across when the light started to flash, signalling a change.

"Oh crap," cursed Freddy and limped out into the middle of the road dragging his right leg.

"Oy, you alright, cocker?" asked a cab driver from an open window.

"Yes, got kicked by a horse," said Freddy, trying not to look down at the hopping bunnies.

"A horse? At this time of day?" asked the cabbie.

"Yeah, call it a nightmare, mate." The lights changed to green and traffic started forward. Freddy stayed in the crossing, shielding the furry messengers. Horns beeped, but he held his ground till they all safely reached the traffic island. The four winged horses joined Freddy and they all stared as the rabbits veered off to the left.

"Oh good grief, where are they going now?"

"Ah," said Rochester, "I bet it's her feet."

"What?"

"She'll have sore feet, won't like the tarmac, likes the grass better."

The winged equine and Freddy tried to be patient as the messengers made their way slowly across the grass, taking the longest possible route to the second crossing. Fortunately the island was deserted; there were certain advantages to carrying out a mission at this hour. Eventually everyone arrived at the crossing; the rabbits had gained a second wind and were moving quicker. The same routine worked at the second light with Freddy putting in another performance as a lamed teen. When they saw the large gates to the park, the messengers picked up even more speed, squeezed themselves between the thick metal bars and made a dash for the grass and shrubbery.

"Let's hope they find Charles now," said Freddy eyeing the running rabbits.

"They will. And now we need to get over to where Nero is stabled and pass on the message from Victoriana."

"I have got to get back home," said Freddy.

"Want a ride?" asked Rochester and Gauntlet.

"No. No thanks, guys. I need to clear my head and think things through."

"O.K." they said.

Having got in at close to three a.m., he crashed and burned and didn't wake till almost eight o'clock. After a quick shower, fresh clothes, two mugs of tea at the kitchen table; Freddy cycled away from home with a piece of toast in one hand. London was in full swing with red double decker buses and black cabs careening everywhere and commuters clogging the pavements heading to wherever millions of commuters go. Freddy stood on his pedals and kicked it up a gear as he entered the park. He rode down the cycle path by the Serpentine Lake looking around for swans, horses or both. And saw nothing. He slowed his speed and started a gentle free-wheel down the full length of Rotten Row. It occurred to him that he had no idea where the meeting was to take place; that Nero could be anywhere in the huge park. Now Freddy was close to the end of the wide pathway near the rose garden and there was still no sign of what he was looking for.

"Freddy!" called a familiar voice. He looked up into the glow of the early morning sun to see Gauntlet and Rochester gliding down toward him.

"Any sign?" he asked the small horses.

"Yes, we just saw Nero and his rider at the top end of Rotten Row."

"Oh bummer again, and I just reached this end."

"We'll go ahead and let Nero know you are here. Have you seen Charles yet?"

"No, Gauntlet, I haven't. But then again how would I know one swan from another?"

"No matter, he won't be looking for you anyway. He'll be looking for Victoriana."

"She's not going to be here."

"This is why we have to make sure Nero sees Charles first and tells him. Catch us up when you can." And they set off to the east.

Freddy started the tedious bike ride back up the cycle path, going head to head with joggers and other cyclists. Three came straight at him with no intention of parting and letting him pass. He was forced to swerve onto the grass. His front wheel narrowly missed the rear end of a large swan tucked behind a litter bin.

"Strewth!" he muttered.

The swan squawked, leapt up and started to head back to the lake in the opposite direction of an approaching horse and rider on Rotten Row.

"Damn! Damn! Damn!" Freddy watched the swan marching in the opposite direction from the horse.

The Pegusinni circled and came in lower. "That's Charles! What did you do to him?"

"I accidentally hit him in the arse with my bike!" said Freddy.

"He probably thought you were going to kill him!"

"Well, go and stop him and tell him to get back here now!"

"We can't. He can't see Pegusinni, only equine."

Nero and his rider were close and were showing no signs of stopping.

"Hi there," called Freddy to Clarissa.

"Hello," replied the girl, slowing down and halting Nero.

"I saw you yesterday with the soldier. Nice horses."

"Thanks."

"Just you today?"

"Yes, he's on duty or something."

"Get over and talk to that swan," he muttered to the horse.

"With her?" asked Nero, rolling his eyes back at Clarissa.

Freddy slowly dropped to his knees, groaning and holding his stomach.

"Are you alright?" asked the girl, alarmed at what was happening to the boy.

"Pain," said Freddy, "huge pain in my side." He groaned and doubled up, nearly lying on the sand.

"Oh my God, do you need help?"

"Yes, yes, it's killing me. Might be my appendix," Freddy moaned.

Clarissa dismounted and reached in her pocket for her mobile phone. "I'm calling for help. Try to stay calm." And finally she let go of the reins as she dialled for help, leaving Nero free to jog off across the park.

"No! Wait. My horse!" Clarissa ran a few steps after Nero.

"Don't leave me," Freddy moaned again now rolling and thrashing like a beached dolphin. He had one eye on Nero's rump heading toward the swan and watched as the horse came to a dead stop.

"What's wrong with him?" called Freddy to Rochester. "Tell him to move it!"

"Grass." called back Rochester, "horses are not allowed on the grass."

"I'll pay the bloody fine! Now tell him to move!"

Moments later the old horse bravely stepped onto the forbidden turf and finally approached the waiting swan. Clarissa was kneeling by Freddy, talking on her mobile. "Yes, in Hyde Park on Rotten Row. He's really sick and my horse just ran off."

Freddy gave a few token moans and did some more stomach holding.

"No, no, you fool; it's not my horse that's sick! It's a boy," she yelled into the mobile. "His name's Nero," pause, then, "no, my horse is called Nero. I don't know the name of the boy!"

"Ah, thank heaven for blondes," thought Freddy lying in the sand. This could take some time.

"What's your name?" asked Clarissa.

"Charles," said Freddy, "Charles Swan." He was looking across the park at an old horse and a large swan facing each other. Several pedestrians attempted to catch the loose horse but were chased off by the viciously hissing swan attacking them with neck extended and full wing span open.

"I should call your parents," said Clarissa looking worried.

"Orphan. I'm an orphan, no parents," he replied.

"Oh, you poor dear! Foster parents? Where will they be?"

"No. None. I'm too old and too badly behaved, no one wants me." Freddy grimaced.

"Someone must want you!"

"No, not since I set fire to the last two foster homes."

"What?" Clarissa stood up.

"But I let the cats out first, they didn't burn."

"Dear god!" She backed slowly away from him.

Freddy couldn't stall her for much longer and he could hear the siren of an approaching ambulance. The old horse and the swan had ended their exchange so he jumped to his feet.

"Wow, look at that, I feel much better."

"Just like that?"

"Yep, must be a miracle. Let me help you get your horse."

"No! No! Stay away from him, you bloody little teenage pyromaniac!"

Freddy looked over to the horse now nibbling on the illegal grass and let out a low whistle to attract his attention. The horse looked up and came trotting back to Clarissa and Freddy. The swan was making his way towards the lake.

"Gotta run," called Freddy to the girl who was staring at him with her mouth open. "Thanks for your help!" And with that he was on the bike and moving as quickly as he could away from the direction of the approaching ambulance. Rochester and Gauntlet circled over Nero and the girl, ready to get the full message when they reached the private stables. But before that, Clarissa had some explaining to do with the N.H.S. paramedics.

Freddy biked across the park off Rotten Row to the South Carriage Drive. Out of breath he sat down on one of the old park benches. After a moment, he realised he was sitting behind the memorial for the 1982 bombing. A light breeze blew overhead, looking up he saw Yeti and Sefton gliding in.

"Where have you guys been?" Freddy asked.

"Across town. Did Nero get the message?" Yeti replied.

"As far as I could tell he did. It didn't exactly go smoothly. What were you doing across town?"

"Trying to find out if anyone else knows anything."

"More pigeons?"

"No, no, not at all. We were checking with all other equine."

"Can't be that many more in central London can there?" asked Freddy, stretching out his tired legs."

"Just the thirty at Buckingham Palace, carriage horses." Yeti said.

"And about another hundred over in St. John's Wood with the R.H.A.," said Sefton.

"R.H.A.?"

"Royal Horse Artillery, over a hundred horses there."

Freddy let out a low whistle. "Wow, who would have known?"

"Then there are about one hundred and twenty with the Met," chipped in Yeti.

"Met?" Freddy asked.

"Metropolitan mounted police force."

"And there are the private carriage horses kept for the tourist rides around town."

"Wow, so about another three hundred, not counting the Cavalry?" asked Freddy.

"Oh, and there are hippotigres at Regent's Park, but not many."

"Clues please?" Freddy knew to ask.

"Smaller."

"Stripes."

"Ah, zebra?" confirmed Freddy.

"Think so," said Yeti, "anyway, we checked with everyone we could and there are all sorts of stories and rumours going around. Something really bad."

"Let's hope Nero, and now Gauntlet and Rochester, really know what it's all about. Can't be that bad, eh?" asked Freddy.

The sound of approaching hooves along the road caught their attention. Freddy glanced at his watch, just gone ten-thirty. It was the Queen's Life Guard leaving barracks and heading to Whitehall for their twenty-four hour duty. They were approaching from the right, marching down the centre of the road. Escorted by mounted police, a single grey horse carrying a trumpeter in full state uniform led the formation.

"Is that what Gauntlet used to do?" he asked the Pegusinni.

"Yes, that's what we all did," replied Sefton looking at the black troop horses in half sections following the grey. In the centre of the group a soldier was carrying something that looked like an old flag, the Royal Standard. The standard bearer was flanked on one side by a Corporal and on the other by a young commissioned officer, carried by the alpha mare of the Household Cavalry.

"Wow, get a load of her in full drag," Freddy was about to stand up and call to her but was stopped by Yeti.

"Shhh, keep quiet."

Freddy stared at him. "Why, just going to say hello and tell her the news."

"Yes, but no one else knows about you. It could cause chaos in the troops if they find out while on duty."

"O.K., Gotcha"

"Carry swords!" screamed the guard commander from the rear of the group. All soldiers brought their swords from the slope position, (resting on their right shoulder), to the vertical as they rode along.

"Eyes left," the commander screamed from the back. All heads turned and appeared to stare at the teenage boy. Then Freddy realised what it was. A salute. A salute as the guard passed the memorial. A salute to those that who had been murdered by the I.R.A. almost twenty-five years earlier. He slowly got to his feet and removed his baseball cap. Yeti and Sefton stood next to him, silent.

"A really big bad thing is going to happen….." He heard the words ringing in his ears.

"Oh good lord, not this bad, please don't ever let it be this bad," he said to himself.

Chapter Twelve

With Freddy and the Pegusinni off to escort rabbits through Hyde Park Corner, Victoriana was left to think things through and make some decisions. She would definitely have to cancel or at least postpone the Senate meeting and leave instructions for Venetia to take charge while she was on guard duty. And now there was this new larger problem looming. There had to be a reason for Freddy's arrival and it looked like they were to find out very soon. The message system around London was never activated like this unless it was something extremely serious.

Shortly after the six a.m., trumpet call sounded reveille. Troopers for the day's Life Guard appeared to exercise horses in the riding school. The full guard does not assemble on the parade square until ten a.m. but work starts a long time before then. Wearing khaki fatigues, soldiers quickly put working bridles on the horses they would be taking on guard that day and then in the early dawn light, jogged over to the indoor arena. No saddles were worn, just a brown saddle blanket strapped on with a plain, flat surcingle rather like a bareback pad. There was no point in making saddlery dirty when it wasn't necessary. The walk to Whitehall from barracks only took thirty minutes so guard horses needed to be exercised beforehand. Webber arrived and saddled Victoriana in her exercise tack and joined the other ranks at the riding school. No blanket ride for these two. While the troop horses worked in file, nose to tail around the outside of the school and close to the walls, Webber rode his horse independently in the central area.

"Trot on!" yelled the duty guard Corporal to troop horses and riders. All horses moved up to a brisk trot, soldiers bobbing around on the blanket pads like corks at sea. A huge cloud of dust was kicked up as dozens of hooves pounded rhythmically along.

"Change rein!" came the next order and all troop horses fluently changed direction.

"Oh Gawd. No more trot, please!" called the troopers. "Can we move up a gear?"

"By the left. By the right. By the centre!
Close your legs, Squeeze your bum, prepare to canter!"

They all sang loudly and out of tune as they moved up into the next gait. Hoops and yells of laughter as some horses did small playful bucks, some troopers almost bounding off the pad. Webber was rather more dignified (also known by the troops as 'prissy') and moved Victoriana around in an elegant collected trot, occasionally executing half passes and travers.

"Woo hoo! Get a load of that old flashy ponce!" called one of the cheekier troopers.

"Anymore wise cracks from you," called back Webber, "and I'll have you doing rising trot without stirrups for an hour when you get back tomorrow."

Covered in dust but well exercised, all the horses were returned to stables for feeding. The soldiers ran up to the mess hall for their own breakfast. Then work began in earnest preparing for parade. The soldier's personal ceremonial kit would have been cleaned the evening before so now was the time for grooming, shampooing white socks, and wisping until black coats gleamed. Ceremonial state bridles were polished within an inch of their lives, brass buckles buffed till they sparkled. There was great motivation for the troops to present themselves for guard in the best possible manner. When they reached Whitehall, guard duty was broken down into several shifts, some mounted and some unmounted. The most prestigious duties were the four mounted places which only required duty of alternate one-hour shifts, ending at four p.m. The other less glamorous posts were two-hour shifts, on foot, and ended as late as eleven p.m. When the Adjutant and the Regimental Corporal Major inspected the guard every day, marks were given or discounted according to appearance and presentation. Soldiers with the highest marks were awarded the mounted guard positions. A speck of dust on a boot or a finger print on a buckle could mean the difference between a leisurely short guard duty and a tediously long one.

Victoriana and the commissioned officer she would be carrying were not subject to such inspections, but nevertheless their turnout and presentation had to equal that of the rest of the guard. Victoriana's black hooves had been scrubbed, then oiled and now glistened in the sunlight. Her groom, Trooper Cochrane, had worked until he was running sweat when the foul mouthed Yarrow arrived with her tack. Victoriana's ceremonial saddlery was similar to but more refined than that of the troop horses and even Cochrane had to admit Yarrow had done a good job. Between them, they saddled and bridled her and then she led them up to the parade square. An anxious Webber was there to give Lieutenant Hewlett, the duty officer, last minute advice and tips.

Whimsy, with the duty trumpeter on board, was already on the square and caught sight of Victoriana as she came up the ramp.

"Hello! I can't believe I get to go on guard duty with you! Oh my goodness, this is such an honour," gushed the grey mare.

"Whimsy, for once, just shut up." Victoriana snapped.

"Yes, well, just being sociable," Whimsy sniffed.

All the troops mounted when Lieutenant Hewlett appeared, walking uneasily in his unfamiliar state kit and looking ungainly in his thigh-length jack-boots. Webber held Victoriana while he mounted. Hewlett landed heavily on the saddle and teetered to the right causing the knowledgeable mare to swing her weight in the same direction to adjust his balance.

When all inspections were over, the guard formed half sections and with the single grey horse at the front, headed out the gates to Whitehall. Lieutenant Hewlett rode to the right of the Corporal Major who was carrying the standard. As the guard moved along the South Carriage Drive, Victoriana noticed Freddy, Sefton and Yeti by the memorial. After the salute, the two Pegusinni took flight and cruised above on her right.

"Did Nero get the message?" she asked them as the guard continued its way along the road.

"Yes, think so. Rochester and Gauntlet have gone back with him to collect it."

"So everything went smoothly last night and this morning?" she asked anxiously.

"Er, um, let's say we got the job done in the end," said Sefton.

"Do I want to know the details?" Victoriana asked.

Both Pegusinni looked at each other and simultaneously said, "No. No not at all."

She gave them a stern look, "I'll expect to see all four of you at Whitehall to go over the message."

"When should we tell Freddy?"

"As soon as you can. He can be working out what to do."

The two Pegusinni peeled away and returned to Freddy who was sitting on the park bench.

"We're going to go over and catch up with Rochester and Gauntlet to see what Nero has to say. Can you wait here for a while?" asked Yeti.

"Sure, but I might wander around this side of the park."

"No problem, we'll find you." The two Pegusinni took off.

Bored with dodging joggers, dog walkers and other cyclists, Freddy decided to push his bike. He went across the grass to the edge of the Serpentine Lake, an area he hadn't really explored before. Close to the edge was a prim Knightsbridge nanny with her two small charges who were gleefully feeding bread to a large crowd of ducks. The young nanny looked over and gave him a cheery smile. He smiled, half waved and walked closer.

"Looks like this is good fun," he said to her.

"Oh yes, we come most mornings. Olivia and Rupert love the ducks. Want to join in?"

"Sure, why not." He laid the bike down and took a handful of crumbs from the bag she offered.

"You have to throw them waaaaaay out into the water," said the small boy with an intense look. He obviously took duck feeding as serious business.

"O.K., will do," Freddy said as he took another step forward and tossed the bread toward the lake. All the birds immediately stopped feeding and looked up at him, momentarily frozen. Then with ear piercing screeches, the birds took flight, wings moving as if on turbo charge, squawking and flapping their way over the water. Other small birds feeding around the water's edge joined in. Even the large swans moved quickly away.

Everyone stared at Freddy. Olivia, the little girl, started to cry, "You," she said, pointing to Freddy, "you scared them all away!"

"They're our friends," said the boy, close to tears too.

"I never saw them do anything like that before," said the nanny, "how bizarre."

Freddy was staring at the disappearing birds and commented, "Well, you know, I get on better with horses." He walked away shaking his head.

"Freddy, meet us by the rose gardens," called Sefton from above, "we think we have the message."

"On my way," Freddy said, hopping on the bike and heading toward them.

Three black and one grey Pegusinni were waiting by the park bench.

"O.K. guys, finally, let's hear it," Freddy said as he sat down and looked at them assembled on the grass in front of him.

Rochester spoke first, "Nero did manage to get the message from Charles, but Charles was pretty angry, and the message was a bit mixed up"

"Why? What can a swan have to be angry about?"

"He was cross because no one told him a hunter would be here. It really shocked him."

"Yes," agreed the others, nodding together as they nearly always did, "he was shocked," said Gauntlet.

"What hunter?" asked Freddy.

"You, of course," said Sefton looking up at him.

"Me!" Me? I'm not a flipping hunter!" He paused for a moment, gave it a thought, then said, "O.K. I did accidentally hit him on the bum with the bike wheel, but I wasn't hunting."

"Well, you are. He could sense it and smell it. He said the worst and deadliest kind."

"What was going on with all of those ducks on the lake as we arrived?" asked Yeti.

"I went to feed them with some kids and they went crazy and took off."

The four small elderly horses nodded knowingly. "So, they knew, as well, did they?" asked Rochester.

"Look, I am not a damn hunter. I don't know what is spooking all these birds so let's get back to the plot. Tell me about the message."

Yeti started to explain. "Well, the birds in the square have been overhearing some really bad and strange things; some odd meetings between men have been taking place. Men have been meeting in the square once or twice a week for about a month. They appear separately, meet and talk and then leave in different directions."

"Do we know what these guys have been talking about? Or what they're going to do?"

"We think the important part is the numbers, but we don't know what they mean yet. And there are a few words that keep coming up. Really odd words."

"Do you remember the numbers?" asked Freddy.

"Oh yes," said Gauntlet, "we knew they would be important."

"160607," said Rochester.

"That's it?"

"Well, six numbers is quite a lot, isn't it?" asked Gauntlet.

"Yes, I suppose, but did they say what the numbers mean?" Freddy asked.

"No."

"Not really."

"Not any meaning, just the numbers."

"But we knew you would know what they meant," said Gauntlet nodding and smiling.

"Me? How would I know what they mean?"

"We thought that's why you're here," said Yeti, "to help us."

"You guys really do have it in your heads that I'm like some Harry Potter plonker or something, don't you?"

"What's that?" asked Sefton.

"A plonker is like a prat." Freddy said.

"No, a Harry Potter."

"Some guy in a book, he was a witch or a wizard or something, could fly on a broomstick."

The Pegusinni all thought about this for a minute.

"A broom that could fly?" asked Yeti.

"Yep."

They all rocked with laughter. "Now that is silly!" said Gauntlet.

Then Rochester asked, "Could he talk to equine?"

"Don't know. Don't think so. It wasn't in any of the stories."

"So, he wasn't as smart as you," said Gauntlet.

"And it was just stories? Not real then?" asked Sefton.

"No, not real, "said Freddy.

"Well, if he was real, you would be smarter than him," said Rochester.

The others all nodded together again.

"Tell me the numbers again." Freddy asked.

"160607."

"And you said there were some words, what were the words?"

"Me. I remember the words," said Rochester. Everyone looked toward him.

"*Sewers to the side*," he said triumphantly.

"And the other word, don't forget the other word," Gauntlet prompted him.

"Yes, the other word, there was another word."

"*Toilets*," said Gauntlet helping out.

"Yes, right, definitely toilets," confirmed Rochester.

Freddy was staring, waiting for more. The Pegusinni all stared back, nodding and smiling.

"What? What are you waiting for?" Freddy asked.

"For you to tell us what it means," said Sefton. More group nodding.

"You give me six numbers, something about sewers and toilets and I'm supposed to tell you what it means?"

"Yes."

"Of course."

"Why not?"

Freddy put his hands on his head, "Why not? Why not? I'll tell you why not. Because I haven't got a bloody clue what you're on about!"

"Freddy," said Sefton.

"What now?"

"You're shouting again."

"We hate shouting," said Rochester.

"Sorry, sorry about the shouting. But guys, you're asking me something I have no clue about."

"No clue at all?"

"Do you guys have any idea what it means?"

They all looked at each other and then back to him.

"O.K. let's go over what we know." Freddy stood up and paced slowly as he spoke. "We know that the pigeons saw some strange or weird guys meeting in the square. We know they got a really bad vibe from them. The men met several times and definitely did not look or act like locals or normal tourists. They talked about something really bad going to happen."

"Something really big and bad," said Yeti.

Freddy continued his pacing. "Then the pigeons heard some numbers and a few odd words."

"No, wait," said Rochester, "the numbers were on a paper. That's why they know the numbers were right for sure."

"So the six numbers were right, then they heard things about sewers and toilets. And that, gentlemen, is pretty much all we have to go on. Not much is it?"

"No, not a lot."

"And, don't you think for a minute, that the message that went from a pigeon, to a mole, to a rabbit, to an angry swan and finally to you might possibly have got mixed up along the way?"

"There's more," said Sefton quietly.

"More? What more? I thought you said that's all they heard?"

"It was. But they got the feeling. The knowing."

"The knowing? 'Splain that one."

"The knowing, knowing that they were really bad, evil men. They knew."

No one said anything.

"You guys really believe that stuff, don't you?"

"Yes."

"Yes, of course we do."

"How do you think we survive?"

"How do you think we can know right from wrong.?"

"How would we know if a man did a bad thing as a mistake or if he did a bad thing because he's bad. An evil man?"

"You can tell that?"

"Yes, of course we can."

"Men hurt us all the time when they are trying to train us and ride, but mostly it's mistakes, so we forgive them." Rochester lowered his voice. "But we never forget evil."

This line of conversation had a very sobering effect on Freddy. He thought about the years of service this small group of horses had given to men. How they never complained and just got on with it, mostly forgiving any wrongs. But then came the evil ones. The ones who blew them up on that sunny July day. And now these equine were convinced there was more evil about. There wasn't a mean thought in any of their minds. This wasn't about revenge, nor was it vindictive. This was something bad they truly believed was going to happen. And they looked at him.

Freddy reached into his back pocket and took out the stub of a pencil. There was an empty cigarette packet on the ground which he tore open and pressed out flat. "Now, one more time, give me the numbers and the words again. Slowly please." They did and he wrote it all on the inside of the packet. "Now, you said the numbers were written down, right?"

"Yes."

"Definitely."

"And the words, were the words written down?"

"Don't know."

"Not sure."

"Wouldn't matter if they were. We can't read, you know."

"Hang on, you guys can count and know numbers but you can't read?" Freddy asked.

"Yes."

"Correct."

"How did you learn to count?"

"Clocks."

"All day, clocks."

"Our lives revolved around clocks in the regiment."

"Morning trumpet at six."

"On guard parade at ten"

"Leave barracks at exactly half past."

"Arrive at Whitehall on eleven bongs."

"Except on the calm day."

"Calm?" asked Freddy.

"Less traffic, less noise day."

"Must have been Sunday, was it?" asked Freddy

"Probably, happened every seven days."

"On that day, guard parade was at nine."

"Arrive at Whitehall at ten."

"Change guard every four bongs of the clock."

"You mean every hour?"

"Yes. It would bong four times during guard shift and then we would change."

"Live like that for over twenty years and it's easy to learn to count," said Rochester.

"So the words, no one saw the words written down. Just heard them?" asked Freddy.

"Yes, that's correct."

"O.K. I'm going back home to think about this and try to make some sense for you. If I need you this afternoon how will I find you?"

"Just come to the park, one of us will see you."

"Will do. Give me a bit of time. See you soon."

All four small winged horses looked optimistically and hopefully at him.

"And I can do without that type of pressure," Freddy told them as he biked toward home.

Back at the small apartment he got some of the left-over Chinese food from the fridge, nuked it and then turned on his computer. Maybe the World Wide Web could offer some help. He shovelled a fork full of fried rice into his mouth as the machine booted up.

"Okie dokie, let's see what our friends at Google make of this." First he typed in the numbers and hit search. All sorts of seemingly unrelated things came up. Golf tournaments. Football matches. Film titles. Rugby match, the list looked endless. "So what do all you have in common with 160607?" he asked himself. Then he rocked back on his chair and slapped his forehead. "Oh well bloody duh! How thick am I? It's a date. A damn date. Sixteenth of June 2007!"

The thing now was to find out why this date was relevant. It was already near the end of May, so it wasn't far away. This time he typed in the date fully and hit search. Once more, masses of unrelated items and events. Racing in Edinburgh. National Badger Day. Football match in Liverpool. Nothing that made any sense. Then he had another thought, went back to the Google home page, typed in the date but added London, U.K. at the end. The he hit search. Again, many events, functions, even weddings. It could be any one of them. Then, on the third page of his search he saw it. Staring back at him. Almost like a neon sign, glowing and flashing.

"16th. June 2007. Her Majesty Queen Elizabeth's official birthday parade. The Trooping of the Colour. Over one thousand foot soldiers from the guard's regiments, and two hundred horses from the Household Cavalry will be on parade for this celebration. In attendance, the royal family, the Prime Minister, visiting foreign dignitaries. Thousands of spectators are expected."

"Holy crap. Some crazed bugger is going to try to blow up the freaking Trooping of the Colour." Freddy was speechless. This couldn't happen. Not really. Not here in London, not while he was here. Then thoughts of the attacks on America on 9/11 went through his mind. In this day of madness and crazies, anything was possible.

The words. Freddy thought of the words so carefully remembered by Rochester and Gauntlet.

"Sewers to the side."

"Toilets."

No way. Not possible. Someone was going to put something in the sewers and the toilets? At the Trooping of the Colour? There had to be security that took care of all of that. No way anyone could get away with it.

No way.

Not ever.

Chapter Thirteen

Freddy looked at his watch. It was almost one o'clock. He grabbed his jacket and the pocket guide to London his mum had bought when they had first arrived. He rode straight back over to Hyde Park and stood at the top of Rotten Row, hand shielding his eyes from the sun as he scanned the skies and trees. Not a Pegusinni in sight.

"Damn."

He biked the full length of the Row, but still no luck. Not one horse, rider or flying horse anywhere to be seen. Freddy made a decision. He needed to scope out this place they called Whitehall and Horse Guard's Parade. He'd never been before, but it couldn't be that far because the guard horses walked there every day. Looking at the map in the guide book he saw it was at the other side of Hyde Park corner and down a long, straight road called 'The Mall'. This time he crossed Hyde Park corner with no drama and no acting and got straight into the west end of Green Park.

According to the guide book, Green Park, St. James's Park, Hyde Park, Kensington Gardens and Regents Park had at one time all been open and joined together as the hunting grounds for whoever was king at the time. Wild boars, deer and all sorts of game had been hunted here. He biked down a road called Constitution Hill; on his left were the open spaces of Green Park and on the right was a tall, old brick wall. On top of the wall was four foot high black spiked railings capped with several feet of barbed wire.

"Wow, they really don't want anyone to get out of that place easily," Freddy thought. What he didn't know was that the queen held her garden parties on the other side of the wall and the fortifications were to keep people out, not in.

Constitution Hill merged with a very busy piece of road, packed with taxis, buses, and tourists. He glanced to his right to see what all the fuss was about.

"Bloody hell!" he said as he stood, momentarily speechless, only metres away from the front gates of Buckingham Palace. There was no mistaking it, having seen it on T.V. and in newspapers so many times, but none of those views gave the real proportions and the total magnitude of this historical gem. The crowds of tourists were three or four people deep all along the front fence line. Behind the tall wrought iron fences and gates was a vast expanse of open parade square which ended at the palace walls. Foot soldiers in red tunics and bearskin hats stood like clockwork toys in front of sentry boxes.

"Gee honey, ya would think it would take more than two or three dudes in furry hats to guard a place that size," commented an American tourist to his wife.

"Yeah, I guess England must be having cut backs," replied honey, "pretty 'lil flag they got flying way up there tho," as she pointed to the gold royal standard flapping high above the palace in the light breeze.

"Ya think she's home?"

"Yeah, she's probably out back, in her curlers, yelling at Philip to put the garbage out." They hooted and cackled with laughter.

Freddy wanted to run his bike over her foot. After he'd studied the buildings and the activity in front of the palace, he turned around to continue on his route. There facing him was a monstrous sized statue mounted on tiers of stone steps. At the very top were what looked like gold angels and cherubs. He slowly walked all the way around and on the side facing away from the palace was Queen Victoria in all of her glory.

"This old biddy didn't do things by halves," he thought to himself, thinking of the Albert memorial very close to his house.

Dodging traffic, he made his way to the bike track on the left side of The Mall which stretched out before him in a perfectly straight line. On the pavement was a tour guide, holding a yellow flag high in the air for all of his lemmings to follow. Freddy pushed his bike and tagged on at the rear, catching snatches of information regarding the Royal area. One of the first streets to the left led to another gated drive and building, apparently a place called Clarence House where more royals hung out. Interesting, but the tour was taking too long so he hopped on the bike and set off on the path along the Mall. Over to his right was the great expanse of St. James's Park, rolling manicured lawns, broad winding paths, flower beds, shrubberies everywhere and in the distance a large lake. "Now, that is a serious front garden." Freddy thought.

Directly ahead and marking the end of The Mall, Admiralty Arch spread completely across the road with three huge archways leading into Trafalgar Square. Almost at the end of The Mall, looking again to the right, Freddy caught his first sight of Horse Guard's Parade. He let out a low whistle between his teeth. The parade grounds were acres of open space and looked like a humongous car park, except the surface was a pale sand colour. On three sides were what appeared to be government buildings with St. James Park and war memorials bordering the fourth side. He free-wheeled slowly down the slight slope of the road that divided the square from the park and stopped in the centre, taking time to scope out the whole area. Behind him St. James's Park and in front, Horse Guard's Parade. He could see tourists pouring in and out of three small archways in a row of buildings that lined the far side of the parade grounds.

"Wonder what's through there then?" Freddy asked himself.

Over to his right, on a corner by the end of the square was a piece of fenced lawn with another statue inside. "Right, let's start over there and work around."

Dodging traffic he crossed over and headed toward the corner where he could see the back of a London policeman close to the fenced lawn. He was only a few metres away when the policeman turned around. He was in a navy uniform with a flat cap and what looked like a sub-machine gun slung across his front.

"Whoa," Freddy stopped in his tracks, "just looking, officer."

The cop smiled, obviously used to wandering tourists. "No problems. Need any help?"

"No. No, not really, just looking around the city. Moved here recently with my mum."

"So, not a tourist then?"

"Nope. We live here near Kensington Gardens."

"Nice area. So what brings you and your bike along here this afternoon?"

"Getting my bearings. Looking at things I've read about. Big place."

"You get used to it."

"Who's the stiff guy on the lawn?" pointing to the dark statue.

"Earl Mountbatten."

"Why's he fenced in?" asked Freddy pointing to the spiked black railings around the lawn. "Worried he'll run away?"

The cop smiled, lowered his voice, "It's actually to keep people out."

"Why? Most of the other statues aren't fenced?"

"No, they're not. That's because most of them don't back up to Number Ten Downing Street."

"Bloody hell, you mean that building right here by the parade square is where the Prime Minister is?"

"Yes, part of it is, the rear of it," the policeman gestured with the muzzle of the gun.

There was a short pause before Freddy asked, "I thought British police didn't carry guns?"

"Most don't. But special areas do. Anything else I can help you with?"

Sewers to the side. Toilets.

"Yeah, yeah there is. Is there a loo near here?"

"Your best bet is to go through to Whitehall and nip into a shop or restaurant if you're desperate."

"What? No loos? Not one crapper anywhere around? What about when they have parades here and loads of people?"

"Port-a-loos brought in for the day."

"Oh well, great," Freddy thought, "That makes it really easy to check out."

"O.K., thanks for your help, see you around," he waved as he walked away.

No damn toilets. He didn't actually need one right now but it would have been useful to know where they were. Moving anti-clockwise around the perimeter of the parade square he searched for drains, manhole covers and anything that might indicate a sewer entrance. Not much at all. Just more grey buildings behind fences, privet hedges, and a few more statues of dead guys. Then he came to the three archways he'd seen earlier. A sign said no riding bikes through the archway, so once more he got off and pushed his bike. He walked through the archway onto a fairly wide road about twenty metres long. The road ran under the building into another courtyard. The place was swarming with tourists, English, German, Chinese, Americans; it was like the League of Nations. A familiar smell of ammonia and manure drifted out toward him and then he saw a Household Calvary soldier in ceremonial kit at the front of courtyard. The soldier was on foot, no horse.

Tourists were crowding around the soldier to have their photographs taken. One rather pushy German man commandeered the area, carefully placed all five members of this family around the motionless soldier and stepped back to take his prized pictures. Just as he was about to snap the shot the soldier came to attention, did a swift about face, and marched off back through the archway, leaving all the Germans on their own looking foolish. As the soldier passed him, Freddy noticed a cheeky twinkle in his eye, although it was almost hidden by the heavy helmet. The soldier had obviously brightened up his own day a little.

"Yes, mate, I would have done the same thing," Freddy thought.

Freddy pushed his bike across the courtyard and through another archway with open wrought iron gates leading out to the main road. The crowds were even thicker here and it was soon apparent why. In two very large sentry boxes, flanking the great iron gates, were mounted soldiers. Their horses stood still, well-behaved but clearly enjoying all the fussing and petting from most of the crowd. He saw one woman go up and try to pat one of them directly on the nose, but the horse pulled his head away avoiding the tap.

"Bloody plop," thought Freddy smugly looking at the tourist. He walked over, waited for a gap in the group in front of the horse, then casually reached up and scratched him behind the chin. The horse immediately dropped his neck and stared at Freddy.

He backed away trying to keep a clear head with no horse thoughts or words, remembering he had agreed to be discreet.

"Hey, Beaufort! Did you see that kid?" called the first horse across to the other.

"Which one? There's loads of them," called back Beaufort.

"He's going back through the gates now with the bike. There's something weird about him."

"Looks like a normal one to me," said Beaufort turning to pose for the cameras.

"No, there was something different about that one."

"Ah, you've seen one scrawny teenager you've seen 'em all," called the black horse to the other, "sometimes I wonder how they tell each other apart."

Freddy pushed his bike back into the courtyard and saw to his right a more discreet archway leading into another building. Another foot soldier in full uniform and jack boots slowly marched the short distance under the arch. At the far end of the passage into the building, Freddy saw two horses getting ready to change shifts with the ones out on the main road. Obviously down there and off to the left were the stables for guard horses and the soldiers accommodations. And today they housed the alpha mare. Freddy knew there was absolutely no chance of walking down there with the soldier patrolling the entryway. Deciding there was not much more to see or do here, he walked back out to Horse Guards Parade. He almost missed a small sign and door to his right as he came out of the archway into the Parade.

'*Household Cavalry Museum,*' read the sign. A glass door led into what was obviously a building that had been used as a stable block in the past. Now there were glass counters, pictures, show cases and discreetly hung flat screen T.V. monitors playing lectures and video clips. The admission sign said £4.00 for children up to sixteen and £6.00 for adults. Not expensive; however, not open for someone like Freddy who had about £1.50 in his pocket. Two young ladies were busy with customers buying post cards and photos, but they were having problems with the credit card machine. While both girls huddled over the delinquent piece of electronics, Freddy casually strolled in and straight around the corner out of view.

Rows of ancient-looking standing stalls for horses were lit; each one containing museum artefacts. Monitors displayed videos of the armoured regiment of the Household Cavalry and their armoured fighting vehicles. The atmosphere was very calm and quiet. No other visitors were in this section. Wandering on and around other corners, he walked past glass cases with officers' uniforms, shiny ancient swords, fierce looking rowled silver spurs and soldiers' breast plates. He came to a halt directly in front of a free-standing well-lit glass display case. He stared at the exhibit. On the right side of the display case was a huge black ceremonial bridle from a troop horse. A plate underneath quietly stated that the bridle was from a horse named Sefton, survivor of a terrorist attack in 1982. Freddy thought of the faces of the Pegusinni, their eyes, large, dark, and calm, showing only trust, faith and forgiveness. To the left of the bridle, discreetly placed on a pedestal, was a brass helmet. The sign said this belonged to Trooper Simon Tripper who died on that day. There was no plume and a part of the helmet was blown away; the rest was bent at the side and rear. It looked small and sad.

"Excuse me, do you have a ticket?" asked one of the attendants as she approached him.

"Oh, no, sorry," Freddy said, hurriedly wiping his nose and eye with his sleeve.

The girl stood next to him and looked at the display. "It's very moving isn't it? A lot of people don't even come back here. It's too upsetting."

He just nodded and thought once more, "Damn, this should never, ever happen again."

"I'm sorry I don't have a ticket; actually I have no money, but I really wanted a peek in here. I'll leave right away."

"Do you want another minute here?" she asked kindly.

"No, no, I need to get going. Thanks for not being mad."

"Come on, no problem, I'll show you out," she said as they walked back to the front area.

"Thanks again," he called as he left through the glass door.

Freddy continued moving anticlockwise around the large parade ground and spotted the first drain cover at the third corner. The drain was about a metre in length, half a metre wide with black grating covering the gloom below. Checking over his shoulder before kneeling down, he peered through the grate into the dark. There was not really any smell. It could be a rain drain, not a sewer and it didn't look like it had been moved or opened recently. Standing up, he saw three more drains, evenly spaced down the side of the square. He thought it was weird how all the drains were on this side of the parade ground and none on the other. Weird till he studied the area more closely and realised that the ground had a slight slope in this direction. So definitely these were rain drains. Could someone, some crackpot think they were sewers anyway? The armed cop was still patrolling at the far side near to Earl Mountbatten. Should he go over and talk to him? He seemed like a nice guy, but what the heck should he tell him?

"I'm worried some nutter might have put a bomb in a drain over there."

Not really good, Freddy thought.

"I know of a pigeon that knows a mole that knows a rabbit that knows a swan that told a horse something really bad. Interested, officer?" And away they would take him in a little white van to a padded room.

Freddy took a last look at the drain covers, all on one side of the square, before cycling slowly away. "There's got to be something I can do. Problem is what?"

He reached the edge of The Mall and waited for a gap in the heavy traffic so he could cross. Looking up he realised he was staring at something he had missed when he first made his way along here. Set back up a broad stairway of stone steps was a huge narrow tower with yet another statue perched at the top. The tower looked like Nelson's Column but it couldn't be because that was in Trafalgar Square. It wasn't easy climbing the steps with a bike, but there was something about this thing that provoked his attention. Craning his neck back, he could see that at the very top, surrounding the statue was a metal railing, indicating there was a walk-way or viewing point. A person would be able to see for miles if they had the chance to be up there. A dark plaque stated this was a memorial for Frederick, Duke of York, once the commander-in-chief of the British army.

"Nice first name, mate," Freddy thought as he stared upward again. Before he turned to walk away, something else caught his attention; a door, a small wooden door, at the base of the tower. Not that odd in itself, but what was odd was that it looked like it had been burned and was quite heavily scorched. Black smoke and soot were on the concrete surrounding the door frame. It wasn't too badly damaged, and obviously still locked. But who would burn a door in the middle of the city that looked like it went nowhere except into a tower? Weird. Obviously vandals were the same all across the country; never a reason for damage, just the kick out of doing it.

He gave the statue at the top a little mock salute as he turned back toward The Mall. The trip back to Hyde Park only took a few minutes as he wasn't stopping to sightsee and gawk every few yards. He opted for biking back through the park and not along Knightsbridge.

"Freddy! Hey, Freddy, wait for a minute!" Coming in above and behind him were his four winged friends, calling and catching up with him.

"You guys are like buses!"

"What? Why, is that?" as they cruised in to land on the soft sand of Rotten Row.

"Never one around when I wanted one, then four of you all come along together."

"Freddy," said Gauntlet, the small grey, said with his head cocked to one side, "we don't have wheels, just wings."

"Never mind, just a figure of speech. Anyway, I think I might have some news for you."

"Really? Already?" asked Sefton.

Freddy walked over and sat on the park bench; they followed and gathered around him.

"The numbers you gave me. I might know what they mean. I think it's a date. Sixteenth of June, this year."

"Is that when something bad will happen?"

"Could be."

"And do you know what the bad thing is going to be?"

"I have an idea, but not sure."

They all remained silent and just looked optimistically at him.

"Well, I know you guys must have heard of The Trooping of the Colour, right?"

"Oh yes."

"Of course, we've all done it many times."

"Three times a year we do it," said Rochester.

"What? Did you say three times a year?" asked Freddy.

"Yes, three times," confirmed the small black horse.

"Actually, it would be four if you count khaki run-through too," added Yeti bending over and scratching his nostril on his fetlock.

"Oh, I hated those khaki ones, so darn early in the morning," said Gauntlet.

"Wait, wait a minute, you're confusing me yet again. The date I found for the trooping is same as the numbers you gave me. Now you're telling me there are more?" Freddy asked.

"Yes."

"Definitely." More group nodding.

"When? When are these extra troopings held?"

"Seven days before and seven days before that," the answer came from Sefton.

"So each Saturday for three in a row, you do a trooping?"

"Yes, and the early morning khaki one too, during the week."

"But that's very early to avoid traffic. So early when we start it's still dark." Gauntlet said.

Freddy gave this some more thought. "Would that first one be like a practice, a rehearsal?"

"Yes, for all the newbies, so they don't turn left instead of right in front of thousands of people."

"So, not many people at that one?"

"Hardly any, too early, too dark." This was followed by yet more group nodding as they all recalled those years before.

"And then you do *three* more, each on a Saturday? In all of your uniforms and all the carriages and everything?"

"Yes."

"People? Many people there at these?"

"Yes."

"Thousands and thousands, all down the streets. All around the parade ground."

"We get tired, but they don't. They put up lots of seats for everyone."

"Seats? Where are the seats?"

"All around the parade ground, all along all of the sides."

Sewers to the side. Toilets.

"Oh, bloody hell, they must put all the grandstands over the drains then?"

"Don't know, we were too busy keeping in line," said Rochester.

"And these three parades you do, they are all the same?"

"Yes."

"Identical?"

"Yes."

"All the same horses, all the same soldiers, all the same musicians, all in the same places," said Yeti.

"And all at the same time, exactly," added Gauntlet.

Freddy was slowly shaking his head. "So how do we know which parade it will be? If it is the trooping, now you've told me this."

Silence for a few moments, then Sefton spoke quietly. "There is one difference, don't you all remember?" looking to the other three. "At the last one, the third one, she's there.

She's not at the others. Someone else is in her carriage for those."

"She? She being who?" asked Freddy.

"Queen. The queen only shows up for the last one. That's the one that's called her birthday."

"So the queen only attends the very last one, the one this year to be held on the sixteenth of June?"

"Yes. Only the one."

"Oh bummer. We could have a really big problem, guys."

No one spoke for a few minutes; then Yeti stepped forward.

"Freddy, we need you to come to the park this evening after midnight, please."

"Again, tonight? Another group meeting?"

"No, Victoriana is still down at Horse Guards till tomorrow. But there will be someone else."

"And who's this?"

"It's the eve of the new moon, Freddy."

"He wants to meet you now."

"It's time."

And once again all four nodded slowly, knowingly.

Chapter Fourteen

Taking the bike to the park when it was closed had become a bit of a pain having to lift it up and over the railings each time, so Freddy decided to walk to Hyde Park; after all, it wasn't that far. His mother was working that evening over at the diplomat's house, cooking for one of their dinner parties. He'd dozed on his bed for a while, heard her come in fairly late and then heard her go to her own room for the night. He wondered if he would ever get to telling her all about his other life. Maybe, maybe one day, but not right now; it was too complicated.

The night was clear and dry with no moon; the sky was lit by the stars and city lights. Tonight was the eve of a new moon Yeti had said. Must have some significance, Freddy thought. He saw no one at the top of Rotten Row nor as he wandered across the vast open space of grass where he'd seen people playing football and other games during the daytime. Looking around, he saw the lights from the barracks further away across the road but nothing unusual. The Pegusinni had said to meet in the park, so no flying over walls would be required tonight.

A small movement by one of the old trees caught Freddy's attention. It was a Pegusinni grazing. He was just about to call out when he realised that he didn't actually recognise this one. It was smaller than the Pegusinni he knew; it had a brown body with black legs and black mane and tail. It moved casually over the short grass, occasionally looking up at the sky. It hadn't seen him and didn't notice as he discreetly stepped behind another tree to observe.

"Now, I wonder who you are? You definitely don't look like one of my military friends." Freddy thought to himself.

Another movement drew his attention to the arrival of a second Pegusinni, flying in from the west and landing softly close to the first. This one was small and light chestnut coloured.

"So, who might you be, my ginger chum?" he thought.

The second one moved over to join the first and after a minute they started mutual grooming, nibbling each others withers. A breeze from behind alerted Freddy to more activity, only this time it was a pair of dun coloured Pegusinni ponies landing from the east who wasted no time in joining the first two.

"Wow, quite the little convention commencing here." No sooner had that thought passed through his mind when another group, this time four greys, came into sight from the north. The branches above Freddy rustled as two shire horses, looking rather grey faced and elderly, slowly joined the group.

"Bloody hell, where are all these coming from?"

And then a silent craziness started. Winged Pegusinni came in from the night skies from every direction. Some solo, some in pairs, a few in small groups. Large, small, greys, bays, browns, a few blacks, ponies, more shires, some that looked thoroughbred; all landing softly and swarming across the acres of open grass. One in particular caught his attention, it was small, black and white striped, obviously a zebra on closer inspection. A few elderly looking donkeys showed up and some odd-looking spotted horses. All landing, folding their wings and then joining the increasing number of Pegusinni already there on the grass. And still they came, silently out of the night sky; show horses, jumpers, polo ponies, mustangs and Shetlands.

Freddy gave up counting as by now the Pegusinni numbered over a hundred and yet more came. All were quietly and calmly looking like they knew exactly what was going on.

"Hi, Freddy," said a familiar voice next to him.

"Sefton!" Freddy said in a stage whisper, "What the heck is going on? This is unbelievable!"

By now Gauntlet, Yeti and Rochester were close by too.

"I thought I mentioned it was the eve of the new moon," said Yeti.

"You did! But you didn't tell me what it meant! There's probably more than two hundred of them out there!"

"Should be closer to five hundred by the time they all get here," said Rochester looking across at the group.

"Isn't that one of the senior Met. equine?" said Gauntlet nodding toward a larger one on the edge of the group.

"I believe it is; looks like Echo," said Yeti, "haven't seen him for a long time."

"He escorted us on a lot of guard duties over the years," said Rochester to Freddy.

"Come along, we need to get over to the Row, not much time now," said Sefton.

The four military Pegusinni glided away with Freddy jogging behind. "Anyone going to tell me what's going on?"

All four were now lined up on the sand, perfectly straight of course, looking into the night sky to the east. The hundreds of grazing and playing Pegusinni took no notice. Freddy shrugged his shoulders, took a place behind his four small friends, then also looked up towards the sky and waited. He knew by now that they would explain when they were good and ready. The steady hum of the night traffic of London in the distance was the only sound he could hear.

And then, far off in the east, Freddy saw it. Only a flicker of light to start with but it gradually grew wider and stronger, slowly and silently coming closer. Movement in the large herd on the grass gradually ceased. The light became broader and brighter as it lowered toward the ground. If he'd been on his roof watching, he would have thought it was a small plane gliding into the park. Then he saw a vertical rise and fall of movement within the light. Wings. White wings moving effortlessly up and down. The wings made no noise, just fluid motion. Long, white wispy strands of light floated out and around the wings.

All Pegusinni were now motionless, their necks extended forward and upward to the east as they quietly watched the arrival. Then several hundred feet away, soaring in toward them above the sand of Rotten Row, the form in the light became recognizable. A colossal, white winged horse with a wing span of at least ten metres, the wispy strands now clear as a flowing mane and tail. Stardust fell from the feathers of the wings and huge black hooves glinted in the city lights. It had to be at least twice the size of the drum horse Freddy had seen in the park. Unlike the small winged horses, this one did not come in to land on all four feet. With wings fully extended, the giant equine's hind feet touched down first, its front hooves slowly pawed into the air, its mane swaying back and forth as it cascaded down over its shoulder. All five hundred Pegusinni in the park lowered their necks. Freddy lowered his jaw. His mouth was gaping; he was speechless.

Slowly and effortlessly the front hooves touched down and the great wings closed up tightly to the hugely muscled white body. Veins stood out in the equine's neck, vast dark eyes looking casually around. His white eyelashes were as long as Freddy's thumb. No one moved or spoke. The winged horse took a few steps forward, its white tail so long it trailed in the sand. Then, staring over the top of the four military Pegusinni, it looked directly at Freddy.

"So, you must be Frederick." It was not a question. The voice was deep and resonated through the darkness. It didn't quite echo and it was like no voice Freddy had heard before.

"Freddy!" hissed Yeti, "your manners please."

"Er... um... Hi," a feeble small hand wave from a shaking teenager was all he could manage.

The enormous white horse took a few more steps forward and the trembling teen took a few steps backwards.

"Freddy, you need to be polite," said Gauntlet, "now go and shake hands."

"What? Are you insane? I'm not going anywhere near that bloody thing! Gawd, I thought Victoriana was big but this is unbelievable!"

"Please, don't let us down," said Sefton.

By now, the several hundred Pegusinni on the grass were noticing the teenager for the first time. Gauntlet, Rochester, Yeti and Sefton separated to leave room for Freddy to walk forward but he stood still, just staring. The great white horse stared calmly back. Then Gauntlet, who had moved sneakily behind Freddy, gave him a nudge in his rear, sending him forward. Hesitantly, step by step, Freddy moved a little closer. Palms sweating, pulse racing, he stopped only a few metres in front of the white horse. The light was amazing, bright but not blinding, specks of star dust were still falling from the folded wings. Freddy could feel the warmth emitting from the huge body. This thing could step on him and squash him like a bug if it wanted to.

"Go on, he's waiting."

As the boy took another dubious step, the white horse slowly lowered his neck toward him. The warm breath from the wide nostrils wafted over Freddy's head and across his cheeks. One final step and then, shakily, he raised his arm and hand. The white horse obligingly dropped his neck even lower as trembling teenage fingers reached up to scratch behind the broad, strong jaw.

"And a pleasure to meet you too," said the calm, baritone voice.

Freddy dropped his arm, took a step back and looked up. "Hi, guess you must be the boss man?"

"Yes, in a manner of speaking, I suppose I am."

"I'm Frederick or Freddy," he said, slightly less shakily.

"Yes, I know. You prefer Freddy?"

"Yeah, it's my nick-name. It works."

"Then Freddy it will be."

"And you? What do you prefer?"

There was a momentary pause then, "I don't really have a human sounding name."

"So, er, what do I call you? Sir, maybe?"

"No, no, nothing so formal will be needed. Why don't you give me a name?"

"Me? Wow, that's kind of a big responsibility."

"It will only be temporary, just between us."

"Freddy scratched the back of his head. "How about Troy? You know like in the giant wooden horse thingy, way back."

"Yes, I seem to recall that fable from sometime ago."

"No, it wasn't a fable, it was history. We did it in school."

"Really? And have you heard of Apollo?"

"Oh sure, some guy from mythology, right?"

"So you think Troy was real, but Apollo was fiction?"

Several hundred small Pegusinni around them gave quiet equine chuckles and laughs.

"What's funny, guys?" asked Freddy looking at his four friends, "am I being a prat?"

"No, no, not at all. So for now, Troy I shall be," the white horse said.

Freddy looked up to the giant white horse standing calmly waiting, a wise twinkle glinting in his eyes.

"Well, nice to meet you, Troy, I think."

"We need to do some talking, some catching up, Freddy." With that, the large white winged horse, or Troy as he was to be known, walked purposefully across the sand to the grass area. Needing no signal, the gathered herd of Pegusinni parted to allow him to walk to the centre. Following in pairs were Gauntlet, Rochester, Yeti and Sefton. Freddy brought up the rear.

Troy paused and looked around, "This will be fine. Time to rest for a while."

The four cavalry Pegusinni shuffled around to form a circle facing inwards, with Troy at the top and Freddy directly opposite him. The surrounding herd formed similar circles around the central group. Each circle was bigger than the one in front and shortly there were about twenty circles, all evenly spaced, all facing in toward the centre. Troy looked around, gave a casual nod from his huge head and neck, and starting with the central ring, the Pegusinni folded and tucked their fore legs and dropped unhurriedly down into resting position. To Freddy it looked like rows of dominos going down in slow motion. Shortly, only the boy and the enormous horse were standing, facing each other across the circle. Troy nodded to Freddy who took the hint and slowly sat down, cross-legged on the grass. Finally, the white horse also lowered himself gracefully to the ground.

"Where would you like to start, Freddy?"

"Let's start with this," Freddy said, waving his hand around, "what the heck is all of this, hundreds of little horses. What's going on?"

"Freddy, I did mention to you that it was the eve of the new moon," said Sefton.

"Yes, but no one has told me what that means."

"Transition. Everyone here will make transition tonight."

"Where to?"

"Sagittarius, our constellation."

"So all of these little guys are leaving earth, to go to Sagittarius?"

"Yes, it's their time and I am their escort" said Troy.

"Why Sagittarius?"

"Because that's why it was created, when Zeus transformed Cheiron to relieve the pain of his wounds."

"And Cheiron, who's this guy?"

"Not a guy, or a man for that matter. A Centaur, probably the greatest and kindest Centaur there ever was."

"A Centaur?"

"To you he would appear as half man and half horse."

"Oh my god, I've seen pictures, drawings of them, but they were mythical, right? Not real?"

"They were history, Freddy. You can decide if they were real."

"The wounds, what wounds?"

"The wounds from the arrow that was fired by Hercules. It was an accident, but the wound was huge."

"So the guy called Zeus changed the guy called Cheiron into Sagittarius?"

"Yes. He was a great hunter, Cheiron, like yourself, Freddy."

Freddy's eyes were now wide open.

"Wait a minute here! What's with this about me being a damn hunter? That's at least three times in the last twenty-four hours!"

"But the Centaurs were great hunters, I thought you knew that?" commented the huge white horse. The surrounding Pegusinni all nodded in agreement.

"Yes, we all thought you knew, Freddy," said Yeti.

"Indeed, yes," agreed Gauntlet and Sefton with more nodding.

Freddy was now back on his feet. "No! No! No, I am not, I never killed a damn thing in my life!"

Troy looked over to him calmly. "Well, perhaps not in this life."

"I've only had one life! I'm not a bloody ghost, you know!"

The wise white horse continued to look calmly at the frustrated teenager.

"When were you born Freddy?"

"1990."

"And you know which year that was?"

He thought for a minute. Chinese food. Napkins. "Yes, the year of the horse."

"Precisely. And what month were you born?"

"December. December the 7th."

"Which makes your star sign?" Troy waited patiently for his answer.

"Sagittarius," he said very quietly.

"And Freddy, you have great hunting skills, yes? The Centaurs were great archers."

His mind was spinning. The Scottish twins. The rectory garden. The bow and arrows. All the direct hits. The

170

reaction of Charles the swan. The reaction of the ducks on the lake.

"Oh my god. I'm a bloody freak!" He slowly flopped back down onto the grass, shaking his head disbelievingly. "I'll be in the damn circus soon."

"Nonsense, it's just signs that things are reincarnating."

"You mean I'm going to turn into a Centaur? Grow hooves? All that stuff?"

"Not at all."

"Don't be silly, Freddy," said Gauntlet. The others were chuntering and shaking their heads.

"No, no, it simply means you have inherited several gifts and traits. I believe you were born at the time the Blue Moon and the White Moon passed either side of your earth moon. That always has repercussions."

"Like this horse talking stuff?" Freddy asked.

"Precisely. It's all very simple you know."

"Might be simple to you but I'm still trying to get my head around it."

"Actually, a word of caution. You may want to keep your gifts to yourself, at least for now. It can cause problems for some people."

"Problems? What sort of problems?"

"Well, the last time it happened, it was a female, many, many years ago. She told people about her gifts," he paused, "but it did cause her, let's say, some inconvenience."

"What sort of inconvenience?"

"People then thought she was a witch. She was burned at the stake."

"Yeah, I can see how that would be a bit inconvenient."

"Yes, it was very silly, as witches don't actually exist."

"Unlike flying giant talking horses? They're perfectly normal, right?"

"Exactly."

There were a few more moments of silence before Freddy asked another question.

"When I was little. Like really little. Like about 5 years old. I remember seeing small flying horses, even back then. What was that all about?"

"Apollo, he told us."

"Told you what?"

"He has many custodial charges, the defender of flocks and herds."

"And he told you about me?"

"Yes. After the tragedy that happened to the herd here twenty-five years ago, he was alerted. He consulted with Artemis and saw you would be needed to help us this year."

"You are kidding me?"

"Not at all, you've had friends watching you since you were born. And to some extent, taking care of you. Just making sure you came to no harm."

By now all five hundred resting Pegusinni were smiling and nodding, fully understanding what was being said.

"So, this bad thing, this really big bad thing, is what it's all about? I'm supposed to help all of you with this?"

"Yes," said Rochester, "that's why many of us have not made transition yet. We were waiting for you to help."

Freddy got to his feet once more and slowly looked around the huge area. Over five hundred pairs of kind, wise equine eyes looked back to him. Nodding, knowing.

"Great. So, no pressure, eh?"

Chapter Fifteen

The conversation continued for a few minutes more as Troy answered questions and cleared up any confusion that remained with Freddy.

"So all of you guys want me to keep quiet except to a few, like Victoriana? No more horses to know yet?" Freddy asked.

"It's better if you do. It would probably cause all sorts of chaos with the other ranks. If you think humans knowing what you can do would cause problems, wait till you see and hear the reaction of over two hundred cavalry horses. And, they won't keep quiet about it either. Word will be all around equine London within hours and then it will spread around the country like fire across a prairie."

"O.K., but why is that a problem?"

"Freddy," said Yeti, "you'll have every horse on the planet coming to you with all their aches, pains, complaints, expecting you to do something about it."

"My saddle keeps slipping," whined Gauntlet.

"He uses his legs too hard," moaned Rochester.

"I hate this hay they give me, have them change it!" complained Sefton.

"They drive the trailer too fast, makes me ill, tell them to go slower," this from Yeti.

"O.K., O.K., guys, I get it. I take your point." Freddy said.

"Good, because you need to be free to focus on the bigger issues," said Troy.

Once again everyone nodded agreement. The huge white horse then unhurriedly rose to his feet. Starting from the inner circle all Pegusinni stood too, the ripple effect moving outward as if someone had thrown a rock into a pool.

"Time for us to leave now, Freddy," said Troy as he walked across the grass toward the sand of Rotten Row, "do what you can and let me know if you need help."

"How will I get hold of you?"

"You know my name, yes?"

"Er, well, yeah, Troy, I guess."

"Then use that."

The hundreds of Pegusinni followed and were now close behind Troy. Freddy moved to the side and watched as the Pegusinni formed up behind the leader. Troy was walking down the centre of Rotten Row; miniature winged horses streaming behind him like a moving carpet. He paused, turned and very slowly gave Freddy an equine wink. Freddy raised his hand but said nothing.

Three or four strong canter strides, then the immense wings opened and with two beats, Troy was airborne over the sand track, heading to the east. His forelegs were tucked up close to his chest, mane and tail streaming. Row after row of Pegusinni took flight behind him as he soared higher and further into the distance. They weren't as organised as the cavalry horses; they sprawled and extended across the night sky like an unruly mass of migrating birds. Further and further away they flew, until they were almost out of sight. Then the white light at the front banked to the right, back over the park. As the throng spiralled overhead, Yeti, Sefton, Gauntlet and Rochester lowered their necks.

"Soon it will be our turn," said Yeti, "but not just yet. We still have business here."

Freddy craned his neck, watching the multitude of specks disappear into the night sky, "So what do we do next, guys?"

"Meeting with Victoriana to bring her up to date with everything."

"A meeting tonight?" asked Freddy.

"No, no, she's still down at Whitehall on guard duty, we'll meet tomorrow," said Yeti.

"That will give you some time to work out a plan too," said Sefton to Freddy.

"You mean this great plan I'm going to come up with to prevent some crazed buggers from blowing up the Trooping of the Colour?"

"Yes," the Pegusinni replied, followed by the usual group nodding.

"Then I need to get some sleep, I'll see you tomorrow night. Here, usual time?"

"Yes, please," said Rochester.

Freddy jogged home, let himself into his bedroom via the window on the fire escape and flopped on the bed. He was exhausted but not ready for sleep. His mind was too busy churning over the constantly changing events. What if all of this was just in his head? What if he had accidentally been taking some hallucinogenic drug in his breakfast cereal and none of it was real? Once more he imagined trying to explain what was going on to someone else and once more he realised how deranged he would sound. He'd heard about other kids who talked about invisible friends and Freddy pretty much thought they were nutters. Now he wondered. What if some other kid could talk to, say, pigs? Yeah, pigs, and that kid was sty-hopping around the country; problem solving like a caped pig crusader. The kid might become the patron saint of porkers. Were there little winged piggys flying around too? Was there a huge, white winged pig as their leader? Poor sod, Freddy thought, I'll stick with the horses.

At this point Freddy really didn't want to discuss it with anyone, the fall-out would be horrendous. They'd have him on the Jeremy Kyle or the Oprah show in no time. *Freak teen talks to invisible horses!*

On the other hand, there was one huge problem should there come a time when he did want to share it with someone. He didn't have one tangible piece of evidence or proof of what was happening. No matter how much he described them, no one else could see Pegusinni. No one could hear the equine dialogue. No one could hear him talking to them. So in fact, maybe it was a dream or nightmare and it wasn't at all real. He had no proof even to himself that it was real. Nothing that couldn't be put down to a fertile imagination. Closing his eyes, Freddy tried to sleep, thinking it might all go away in the morning.

Wait. Freddy sat bolt upright in his bed, staring across the dark bedroom. The smell. The smell on his jeans! His mother had commented that his jeans stunk of poo. She'd noticed the smell! The smell was real. It was all real. He really had been inside the barracks that evening. He really had talked to Victoriana. He really did know the Pegusinni. Freddy let out a huge sigh and fell dead asleep.

Jane was drinking coffee and reading the paper when he wandered into the kitchen the next morning.

"Hmm, decided to get up, did you?" she asked without really looking up.

"What time is it," Freddy asked, still rubbing his eyes.

"Almost quarter to ten."

"Bloody hell, I really did crash."

"Can't think why, you were in when I got home."

"Kept waking up," he mumbled, pouring a glass of orange juice, "Why aren't you at work, anyway?"

"They gave me the morning off for working late last night."

"Cool."

"Yes, and we have a few things to catch up on too. Want a coffee?"

"Yes, please," as he poured cereal into a bowl and sat down.

Jane got the coffee, pushed the mug over to him and looked back to her paper.

"What's new with the world?" he asked between mouthfuls of cornflakes.

"The big news is that pop singer Pete Doherty has been arrested on drugs charges."

"Think he'll go to prison?"

"No, of course not. They never send rich people to prison. He'll just get another warning." She folded the paper and took a sip of coffee. "Anyway, Rip van Winkle, we need to talk about your school work."

"Ah, yeah, GCSE exams and all that."

"Exactly. You've had a couple of weeks off and the exams are the end of this term, so time to hit the books, my lad."

"Yeah, I'll get to it."

"Oh, I know you'll get to it, starting Monday with your new tutor."

"What?"

"We discussed this before the move, Freddy. You're to work with a tutor until the exams, then after summer holidays join the local school for the last year."

"Yeah, yeah, I know I agreed, just thought I'd have more time to settle in."

"More time? You must be bored out of your brain by now with nothing to do. You don't even have any friends here yet."

"Yes, mum, I'm really bored," Freddy stared off, thinking of the last few days and nights.

"Don't take a sarcastic tone with me, my boy. You're not too old to be put on the naughty step."

"I'm really not bored and wouldn't mind waiting another couple of weeks or so. I'm serious," He took a sip of coffee and continued eating his cereal.

"Not going to happen. Study time starts Monday."

"What's his name?"

"She. It's a lady. Miss Dupree. Zahra Dupree."

He spluttered on the cornflakes, "You are kidding me!"

"No, I'm serious, she starts Monday morning."

"I mean kidding about the name!"

"Oh, that, yes, well I suppose it is a tad exotic. But she comes highly recommended."

"Exotic? Mum, she sounds like a French lap dancer!"

"And what would you know about lap dancers?"

"Mum, we used to record 'The Sopranos' and watch it together. Remember the name of the club? *Bada Bing*. It was a strip joint."

"Well, I don't think Miss Dupree has been to *Bada Bing* and she does start Monday."

He chewed on the last of the cornflakes, scraped out the small pile of sugar in the bottom of the bowl and thought about this announcement. "All day Monday? For how many days?"

"No, just half days, she's only coaching you, not you and the Coldstream Guards."

"Hey, I saw some of them yesterday."

"You? You saw the Coldstream Guards? Where on earth did you see them?

"Marching up and down outside of Buckingham Palace."

"You went to Buckingham Palace?"

"Yeah, it's not that far."

"Freddy, I thought you played in the park and stuck locally?"

"Mum, I'm nearly seventeen; I'm not going to play in the sand box in the park forever."

"No, but Buckingham Palace on your own?"

"It was broad daylight, masses of people around, police, tourists, everything."

"Exactly, that's when it's easy for muggers to do their thing." Quietly she was a little bit miffed he'd gone without her. She'd hoped they would do all the great sights together. "How did you get there?"

"On my bike."

"See! Far too dangerous. My God, you must have crossed Hyde Park Corner! It's crazy down there."

"Mum, it's not bad; they have crossing lights and everything. Even a rabbit could get across."

"What?"

"Nothing. Any more coffee?"

They each had another mug. "So mum, does the tutor lady have to be in the mornings? Couldn't we do afternoons?" He was thinking about all the early morning exercising that went on with the horses in the park. Afternoons seemed to be much quieter.

"Can't see why not, but I'll have to check with her. And Freddy, I really expect you to pull your finger out with this course work. Caroline and Paul are paying for it, so no messing about."

"O.K., I'll be as good as Harry Potter."

"Why him?"

"Just a topical joke, mum."

"I don't get it?"

"Never mind, I'm being a plop."

"Why are you talking in riddles? Too much sugar?"

"Forget it."

Jane let it slide. Teenagers, did anyone understand them? She thought for a few minutes before starting again. "I saved the really good stuff for last."

"Yeah? What's that? Actually, I really need to go and get in the shower."

"Wait just a minute, this is pretty good, even if I say so myself."

"You got a pay rise?"

"No."

"They bought you a car?"

"Here? In central London? Don't be silly."

"O.K., I give up."

She sat up straighter in her chair, then leaned forward across the table. "You know how Paul's a diplomat? Right?"

"Yes mum, that's why we live here."

"Shaddup, smart mouth, and listen."

He suppressed a grin and waited.

"You know how he and Caroline often get given tickets to movie premieres and opening nights of plays and fancy clubs?"

"Yeah, you've mentioned it; perk of his job, right?"

"It really is. Well, next month they both have to go back to Canada for a couple of weeks, so they won't be here."

"No, mum, they won't be here if they're in Canada."

She glared, but continued. "Well, get a load of this. He's given us the tickets for one of the poshest events of the summer."

"What's that, Wimbledon tennis?"

"No. Four tickets for central seats at The Trooping of The Colour."

"What!?"

"Yes, apparently they give them to a lot of diplomats; good P.R. for the foreign countries. We'll be sitting right up front, near all the politicians and junior royalty. It'll be a right posh day."

"No. No way. We're not going!"

"Freddy, calm down. This will be really fun. Something we would normally never get to see. At least, not close up."

"Mum, there is no way we are going to this thing. Nope. Not ever." Freddy was up, pacing around the small kitchen.

"I have no idea why you're reacting like this, but it's too late. I've already started to make arrangements."

"Arrangements? What arrangements?"

"They gave us four tickets, so I've called your Gran and your Aunt Sharon and they're coming to stay for the week end too."

"You are bloody kidding me?"

Jane was starting to get irritated with his irrational behaviour. "No, I am not kidding you. This is going to be a really fun and fancy weekend for the family and you will be going with us."

"O.K., let me just check now, you do mean the Trooping on the 16th of June, right?"

"Of course I do. Which other one would I mean?"

"It could be one on the 9th. Or the 2nd."

"Now you're being a prat. There's only one Trooping of the Colour. It's on the telly and everything."

"No mum, there are three. Two dress rehearsals and finally the third one. They sell tickets for all three."

"Since when did you become an expert on London pageants, Mister Smarty Pants?"

"Mum, I am not kidding. This is really, really serious. Is it the one on the 16th?"

"Yes, yes, Freddy, it is. Trooping of The Colour, on Saturday June the 16th. With her Majesty the Queen there too. Oh, and your Gran and Aunty Sharon, and you."

Freddy chewed his bottom lip and tried to stay calm as Jane glared at him. What the hell could he say? "We're not going cuz we all might die." Yep, that sounded calm and logical. He tried another approach.

"You know, Mum, there's like hundreds of thousands of people at this gig, maybe millions, and you know how Gran hates crowds? Right?"

"There will be a private car to take us there, and Paul said we would be escorted to our seats. We'll be out of the crowds."

"But it's probably really boring. Like, how interesting can it be to watch a bunch of soldiers faffing around a big parade and loads of horses probably pooing everywhere? How dull is that?"

"Your Gran and your Aunt Sharon are so excited about this, I can't even begin to tell you. I only talked to them yesterday, but your Gran has already told every member of her bingo club."

"I bet she has."

"And your Aunt Sharon, she's told everyone at Tesco's about it."

"Tesco's? Why Tesco's?"

"Because she just got a new job there, the twenty-four hour one in Clowne, on the checkouts, and she's told everyone."

"Bloody marvellous."

"Freddy, how many people can you think of from Stavely who would get an opportunity like this? It's part of history."

"Oh, it really could be part of history this time. No kidding."

"Look, you know how your Gran is about the royal family. She's got every commemorative tea cup, spoon and snow globe for every damn royal wedding, jubilee and funeral for the past fifty years! Hell, she's even got a Charles and Diana bedside clock!"

Freddy just glared.

"And you know she still doesn't believe Diana is dead? Gran's convinced it was a cover up so Diana could go into hiding with her boyfriend. Are you going to be the one to try to convince her she is now not going to the Trooping of the Colour and not seeing the queen?"

In the silence between them, Freddy thought about his Gran, tiny, wiry, still smoked twenty a day, bingo addict and staunch royalist. She'd be a tough one to convince.

"So, are you going to give me one good reason for your bloody-mindedness?" Freddy insisted.

Jane stood up, angry now. "You know, I don't claim to know how the teenage mind works; hell, I don't even know what food you like from one day to the next. But you are making no sense!" She pointed her finger and looked at him with narrowed eyes.

Freddy took a deep breath. Let it out slowly. And said nothing. Jane lowered her hand, thought for a minute and said, "And, I get to go shopping for a new outfit. You want to spoil that as well?"

They continued the stand off, glaring at each other across the table. Finally Jane got up and turned to the sink to start washing dishes.

"Mum, I'm not trying to be awkward, but I've got a really bad feeling about this."

Jane didn't turn, she just continued her work. "We're all going. No discussion. End of story. This is going to be a really big day. For all of us"

Yes, Mum, and you have no idea just how big it might be.

Chapter Sixteen

After his shower Freddy waited in his room until he heard Jane leave the apartment. Damn. Damn. Damn. What to do? O.K., first thing is, don't panic. No one ever thought of a good plan when they were panicking. They did a few dumb and stupid things but they never thought of clever things. He needed a plan that would stop the family trip to the event. But it had to be a plan that was so convincing, would work so well, that no one would ever know it had been a plan and no one would be upset about it. Not a cat in hell's chance of coming up with that plan, he thought. His Gran had probably already been out shopping and bought her new hat. Aunt Sharon was, well, not exactly backward in coming forward when it came to her taste in fashion. She'd probably show up in a Union Jack mini dress looking like an aging Spice Girl. Thank God there were only four tickets or she would have wanted to bring her latest dating conquest along as well.

It was past lunch time but with the late breakfast and more than a few things on his mind, he wasn't hungry. There was the meeting tonight with the Pegusinni and Victoriana, and he was supposed to be coming up with a strategy to present to them. The more he thought about it, the less he thought they could do anything. He had no plans for the afternoon but he needed a distraction; something completely separate from horses, terrorists, swans and visiting Grannies. So, he committed the act of a desperate teenager. He did his homework.

In the evening, Jane made dinner for the pair of them. Conversation was stilted, to say the least. More a series of polite grunts and nods than whole sentences. At the end of the meal, Jane spoke first. "Will you do the washing up, please, I'm going out tonight."

"Really? Where too? Who with? You know less people here than I do."

"Yes, well, that's what you think isn't it? I could have a date for all you know."

"You could, but you don't."

"And how would you know?"

"Because I've seen you on the day you have a date, you go all peculiar."

"I do not go peculiar!"

"Yeah? You call dancing with the Hoover normal?"

"That was only once! And you shouldn't have been watching."

"Come on, where are ya going?"

"If you must know, Cheryl, one of the secretaries who is often at the house, has invited me out for a drink with some of her girlfriends."

"Girlfriends? Bunch of single middle-aged women? Oh, that sounds like a barrel of laughs."

"It'll be fun. They usually get together on a Friday night over in Hammersmith somewhere."

"Karaoke? Hen night? Pole dancing?"

"Oh son of mine…you do have a warped mind." She put her tongue out at him then went to the bathroom to change. He threw the stuff in the sink, did the dishes and by the time he'd finished drying, she was ready to go.

"You know the rules? Keep the door locked. Don't answer it for anyone."

"Yeah, yeah."

"Keep your mobile phone on in case I have to ring you."

"Will do, what time will you be back?"

"Don't know, shouldn't be late though. If I don't see you tonight then I'll see you in the morning."

"K, bye," Freddy said as he flipped on the T.V. He looked at his watch. Half past seven. He could either go and nap or just stay awake until it was time to go to the park. On second thought, better to watch T.V. now and then go to his room. He didn't want to be in the sitting room when his mum got back. That could make slipping out a little tricky.

At about 11.45.pm, he climbed out of the window on to the fire escape and set off for the park. He must have been dozing when his mum returned as there was no noise around the flat when he left. It was cloudy and a wind had started; it might even rain. Should he go back for his jacket? Nope, no time and besides, he would be in the stables most of the time. Again he didn't bother with the bike and he managed to get into the park before midnight when the gates were locked. There were a few dubious characters lurking around but he ignored them and jogged on to the barracks. His four winged friends were waiting on the sand track across the road from the main gates.

"Hey, guys."

"Hello, Freddy, how did your day go today?"

"I've had better days, Sefton, had a bit of a set-to with my mother."

"What's a set of two?" asked Gauntlet.

"No, I mean an argument, I'll tell you about it when we're inside. But I have another question for you."

"What's that?"

"The first night we officially met there were loads of you; must have been over a dozen at least."

"Actually, fifteen," said Yeti.

"Was it that many?"

"Yes, fourteen blacks and one grey."

"I'm the grey," said Gauntlet.

Freddy grinned at the little white horse who was looking up at him very seriously. "Yes, Gauntlet, I can see you're the grey one. Are you always at the front?"

"Yes, on a Long Guard when we have the Standard, but not on short guards, I don't do those. My ancestors were often at the front too, when they went to battle, so the Generals could give orders to the trumpeters."

"So where are all the others? Haven't seen them these past few days."

"They're around," said Sefton, "but they're all out on search duty, trying to get more information on what's going to happen."

Yeti moved forward to add, "And we thought you might get a bit confused with fourteen black horses all around you. This is a better number."

"Well, I have you four figured out, but you're right, fourteen would be pushing it."

Rochester walked away from the group, quietly took flight and circled the wall to confirm no night guards were around. He flew back to the small group on the track and nodded to Sefton.

"Ready?" asked Sefton looking up to Freddy.

"Ready as ever," he replied walking across the road and holding out his arms. Yeti and Sefton positioned themselves and then smoothly elevated him up and over the twenty foot high wall. All three came down softly and quietly on the other side.

"We're getting pretty good at this, guys," whispered Freddy as they all headed down the ramp to the stables; none too soon as the rain started to fall. They moved quickly into the dimly lit passage way and stopped by Victoriana's stall.

"Good evening, everyone," she said from behind the gate across her stall door.

"Hey there, boss lady," said Freddy giving a little wave.

The Pegusinni all greeted her. "How was the guard?" asked Sefton.

"It doesn't change much, does it? It's been a while, well actually, a few years since I did it, but it never changes."

"Nothing new or exciting going on there then?" asked Rochester.

"No, not really. Wait, there was a little flurry of excitement with the troop horses yesterday afternoon."

"What was that?" asked Gauntlet.

"Apparently a very odd teenage boy approached the two horses on box duty. According to Beaufort and Algernon, this boy knew exactly how to shake hands and had a very strange look about him."

Freddy stared off at the ceiling, looking innocent.

"In fact, Algernon got a very strong feeling that the boy was about to talk to him."

All five equine looked at Freddy.

"Ok. Ok., I went for a little recce. Trip to Whitehall, thought it would be useful."

"Recce?" asked Victoriana.

"Recognisance, checked the place out, went ahead, you know? Heck, I thought army bods like you would know that one."

"We do know," she said, "but you did cause a bit of a stir."

"Yeah, Troy and the guys said last night I should keep shush about it."

"Troy?" asked the black mare.

"Yeah, last night, in the park."

"Ah yes, eve of the new moon. So, you met him?"

"Yeah, Troy. Well, that's what he said I could call him. Why, what do you call him?"

"Him."

"Oh well, I got to give him name. But wow, what a big bugger, eh?"

"I'm sure he'd be thrilled to hear you say that," Victoriana said dryly.

"He's pretty cool though, the way he took that crowd with him, kind of awesome."

"He's been doing that and other things for a very long time."

"Vics, can I open this door? I hate talking to you through bars."

"Yes, of course." So he did, sliding the bolt and swinging it open.

"Now bring me up to date with everything that went on while I was away," Victoriana said.

Between the five of them, they gave her the story about the rabbits, the message and the numbers and how Freddy had figured out it was a date, and that it was the date for the Trooping of The Colour.

"My, this is serious, very serious indeed if that's what it's about."

"It makes sense," said Freddy, "the more I've thought it through the more it has to be right."

"And what are they going to do?" she asked.

"That's the big question, isn't it, we don't know yet."

"When will you know, Freddy?" she asked.

"When will *I* know?" he replied, looking incredulously at her.

"Yes, you'll work it out, won't you?"

"I'm trying, I'm *really* trying, but we don't have much to go on."

"The message network is on full alert, trying to get more information."

"Yeah, well, anything would be a help. It would be easier to figure out what might happen if we knew who we're dealing with."

"Will it be the same ones as last time?" asked Rochester very quietly.

"No, no, mate, it won't. They've moved on to other things. Things where they're probably doing even more damage than before."

"What are they doing now?"

"Politics, they've gone very proper and political, pretending none of their bloody evil stuff ever happened."

"But we know when something will happen, and we know probably where something will happen, don't we?" asked Sefton, "That's two things we didn't know a couple of days ago."

"True, so if we think again about who, we should be able to come up with the what."

"The words, do they mean anything to you yet?" asked Victoriana.

Freddy stared back at her, not speaking. The Pegusinni all looked up at him, waiting. He didn't really want to tell them what had crossed his mind, but it looked like it would have to come out. Finally he started to tell them.

"The words, *sewers,* or *sewers to the side,* and *toilets,* I'm guessing they will be hiding places."

"Hiding places for people?"

"No, no, hiding places for…." He hesitated, not wanting to say it, knowing what these four little horses had already been through once before. "Hiding places for equipment."

Victoriana looked puzzled. "What sort of equipment?"

"Bad equipment."

"Bad?"

"Yes, really bad."

"Are you going to tell us?"

He sighed, then quietly said, "Possibly a bomb or two. If we're dealing with terrorists, it will probably be bombs."

"Bomb like before, when we went to guard?" asked Gauntlet nervously.

"Probably not like that, no."

"Oh, good."

"They'll be worse. They'll be bigger, more powerful, to do more damage."

"Damage to buildings?"

"Yes."

"Damage to people?"

"Probably."

"Damage to horses?"

"I don't know. Let's hope not."

There was a very long silence as the group digested this.

"Why do they do this?" asked Rochester.

"Why? God knows why. They're all mental, if you ask me."

"But why something like the Trooping?" asked Yeti, "it's not a war; it's all happy and peaceful."

"Because if they do what I think they might, it will be, well, spectacular to say the least."

"Oh."

"Think about it, blowing up a car or a train has limited effect. Blowing aeroplanes full of people out of the sky, that's spectacular, goes on T.V. all around the world."

"I see."

"But this? This would be beyond spectacular if they pull it off. Think about it, thousands of people, royalty, politicians, hundreds of soldiers and right behind Downing Street, and on live T.V. world wide."

"Oh my," said Victoriana, "I see what you mean."

"Wait a minute," said Yeti who had been quiet for sometime, "did you say they would put things into the sewers, the big drains below ground?"

"Yeah, probably. I had a look down at the parade ground yesterday, no toilets, but I found three or four pretty large flood drains for rain water."

"Did you look inside?" Yeti asked.

"Come on, Yeti, it was broad daylight and pitch dark down the hole. I could hardly do an inspection, could I?

"Then don't you think we could start by having them checked?"

"Checked? How the heck are we going to check them?"

"We're not, but we know someone who can."

"Oh yes," said Gauntlet, catching on.

"Yes, yes, indeed," said Sefton.

"Who? Who the hell can check that out?" asked Freddy.

"Talpi, talpi and lago can check. They'll have a look."

Freddy's brain had a flash back to the message system. "Moles? Moles and rabbits? They'll check?"

"Of course, we just have to ask them. They love darkness and tunnels."

"You know, guys, this is going to be a lot easier to figure out when I finally catch on to all of our resources. Of course, I should have known we can send a rabbit in, silly me!" He was grinning as he said it.

"Er, one problem," said Sefton, "how do we get the message to them in St James's Park?"

"Aww, no," said Freddy, "not more bunnies across Hyde Park Corner?"

"I have an idea; that foul mouthed Met nag," said Victoriana.

"Met nag?" Freddy asked.

"Sorry, police horse, Freddy; he'll be escorting tomorrow's guard to Whitehall, we'll have him pass a message on to Rupert."

"I know I'm going to regret asking this, but who would Rupert be?"

"Head swan at St James's Park, he'll get the message through."

"Who's going to talk to the Met Nag?" asked Freddy.

"We can. We can fly down next to the guard tomorrow morning and make sure he gets the question right," said Sefton.

Everyone thought this through and nodded; at least this way they would find out if there was anything already down in the drains. Freddy was just about to speak when footsteps caused them all to look to the door. Night guard. Night guard just around the corner. The Pegusinni and Freddy moved straight back against the far wall, Freddy with his hands on Yeti and Rochester. A shadow and then the guard entered the stable aisle way. And at the same time Freddy saw the open door of Victoriana's stall. "Uh, oh," he thought.

Seeing the stall door wide open, the guard turned on the overhead lights and walked toward the stall. The Pegusinni and Freddy remained silent, invisible against the wall. Victoriana turned in an Oscar winning performance of a horse dozing, hind leg resting, neck lowered, eyes half closed.

"Now how the bloody 'ell did your door get open, madam?"

He was reaching for the door when it happened. Freddy's mobile phone rang in his back pocket. The shrill, piercing ring tone resounded around the building.

"What the 'ell…?" said the guard, spinning around.

Freddy madly grabbed at his back pocket to get the phone and in the process lost connection with his two Pegusinni.

"Who the 'effing hell are you?" yelled the guard staring at the teenager crouching by the wall. The phone continued its shrill ringing spasms.

Freddy looked to the door, back to the guard but knew he had no chance of escape.

"Er, hi." he faked a nervous smile.

The guard grabbed Freddy by the shoulder and pinned him to the wall. "How in hell did you get in here? What are you doing here?" he yelled. He had his finger poked up under the boy's chin.

"Just stopped by to see the horses." Freddy replied. And finally the damn phone stopped ringing.

"My God," said the guard, "they get bloody younger every year!"

"Who get younger?"

"Terrorists! Sodding terrorists like you! That's why you're in here, isn't it? Trying to plant a bomb or something?"

"A bomb? I'm sixteen years old and don't even smoke! No, I don't have a bloody bomb!"

"Yeah? We'll let the Military Police and the terrorist squad deal with you." The guard still had an iron grip on Freddy's shoulder. "Come on, and don't try anything stupid you might regret." He spun Freddy around and held his arm tightly up into his back.

"That bloody hurts!" yelled Freddy. "Where are you taking me?"

"Guard room, my lad, nice little cell ready for the likes of you!"

"You can't arrest me! I'm a kid!"

"Yeah, a kid that got inside a military barracks in central London undetected at half past one in the 'effing morning! Doesn't that sound a bit suspicious to you?" The guard pushed Freddy to the open door and toward the ramp. The man was huge; Freddy struggled but it was pointless. He looked desperately back over his shoulder to the Pegusinni and Victoriana who stared back at him in shock.

"*Help me!*" he screamed silently to them. "If they lock me up, we have no plan!"

The guard pushed him roughly around the corner and toward the ramp up to the main square. Freddy tried to argue and struggle again but it was useless. He dragged his feet on the wet concrete, the rain splashing down on his terrified face.

"Oh my! Oh my," said Gauntlet, "he took Freddy!"

Victoriana sprang into action. With her stall door wide open, she strode out into the passageway. "Sefton, Rochester, down the troop aisles now! Wake them all! Tell anyone who can slip a head collar to do it! You other two, upstairs, go to the Blues, same message. I want the entire regiment on the parade square in less than thirty seconds! Go! Do it!"

The four Pegusinni took flight like launched rockets off on their mission. The black mare moved forward out of the barn and to the ramp. Rain poured and hit her ebony coat as she picked up a brisk trot. No head collar, no bridle, she was completely free. The guard holding Freddy had reached the top of the ramp when he heard her hooves rattling behind him.

"Oh bloody hell! I left your door open! Hobson! Hobson! Get down here and help me. Now!" he called to the night guard up in the Blues stables.

Hobson called back, "What are you playing at down there, Grimshaw?"

Victoriana reached them. Freddy stared wide mouthed, wondering if she was going to kill the guard. He struggled and twisted but the guard was determined not to let go of his prisoner. The black mare didn't stop; she simply trotted straight on past the two of them to the centre of the parade square. Hobson came running down the ramp toward the guard with the struggling teenager. The sound of hooves behind him made him stop. Three loose troop horses came trotting down the ramp, heading straight for the square.

"How did you three get loose?" Hobson desperately tried to block their path, waving his arms, attempting to get them to turn and go back up the ramp.

Meanwhile, the four Pegusinni were creating chaos in the troop barns, swooping up and down, yelling, screaming, "Everyone out! Now! Slip halters and out! Parade Square! Everyone! Emergency!"

Dozens of black horses were leaning backwards, twisting their heads to shake free of the halters. Those that didn't manage to slip from their halters simply pulled back hard enough to snap the leather and let the halters fall to the ground. A head collar could never hold a horse if the horse really wanted to be free.

Two hundred troop horses who normally lead very quiet lives with predictable routines seized the opportunity for adventure. It was as if someone had run into the dormitory of a boy's boarding school and screamed, "Pillow fight with the staff!" to a group of twelve year olds.

Clattering up the ramp from the lower stables signalled the arrival of more black horses. They were also pouring down the ramp from the Blues, and all were joining to swarm across the parade square.

Victoriana stood still in the centre of the square, watching the ensuing chaos. "Left handed! Everyone move left handed, hold to the trot! No canter till you get the order!"

Both guards were now in a state of shock, staggering across the square with huge black horses swarming all around on the concrete. The noise was becoming deafening. An alarm bell had been triggered. Lights were coming on in all of the barrack rooms. Soldiers were leaning out of windows to see what was happening. More and more loose horses flowed from the ramps to join the increasing herd. Five, in places six abreast, they were careening around the parade square.

Whimsy, the grey mare, was in a state of mild hysteria. "Is there a fire? Is it time to transition?" she called to any passing equine who would notice her.

Spartacus, having opened his own box stall door, was lumbering steadily down the ramp, looking around with interest. He didn't trot; he left that to the younger, lighter weights. "Well, Victoriana, aren't you the dark horse? You certainly know how to throw a party."

"Noise! Now!" called the alpha mare. And nearly two hundred horses started to shriek and whinny, screaming in high pitched equine voices.

"Outer ranks, canter!" she called from her position of command. Victoriana knew she was taking a risk commanding the equine to canter on concrete, but she had to push the boundaries of chaos. By now, the two guards and the dumbstruck teenager were trapped in a whirlpool of screaming and cantering horses. Complete and utter bedlam carefully choreographed by one very clever black mare. More soldiers, half dressed, were running out to try and help, the heavy rain pelting down onto them and the kaleidoscope of black equine. Then out from the barns came the four Pegusinni, circling low above the crazed throng. Victoriana saw the moment, the guard who was desperately trying to hang on to Freddy in all the chaos was only a couple of meters away. She looked up to Sefton and Yeti and nodded. She moved in closer, casually, innocently, and 'accidentally' stood on the guard's foot. As he screamed in shock, he released his hold on Freddy and the waiting Pegusinni dropped straight in to collect their prize a totally shell shocked teenager with his arms out. The winged horses scooped him up out of the centre of the throng, and to the guards watching, he vanished before their eyes.

"Hey! Guys! Look up!" called a troop horse to the others, "There's a kid getting a ride from Yeti and Sefton!"

They had almost made it over the wall before being spotted, but it was too late. Dozens of troop horses had seen the boy riding with the Pegusinni.

"Woo Hoo!"

"Go boys!"

"Yea! Who's the kid? Who's the kid?"

"Order now!" called Victoriana, "everyone walk! Silence Now!"

And the masses of loose horses slowed, gradually fell into a casual walk and finally halted, grinning, looking to each other to share the midnight adventure. What a jolly caper!

"When you are asked, you will all return to your stalls; and thank you for your help. I'll send a message around tomorrow that will explain everything."

Lights were on; soldiers were everywhere trying to catch loose horses. A police car siren sounded on the Knightsbridge side of the barracks. Troopers Grimshaw and Hobson, the two dumbfounded night guards, stood silently in the middle of the square trying desperately to think what they were going to tell the commanding officer when they got marched into his office first thing in the morning.

"Well," said Victoriana to herself, "and that concludes another quiet night in central London." She shook her neck to straighten her mane and with great poise, through the steady stream of rain, she took herself back to the stables.

Chapter Seventeen

They landed on the grass inside the park, the Pegusinni shaking the rain from their coats, Freddy choking for breath. "Oh, my god! Oh, my god! They nearly had me!"

Rochester and Gauntlet glided in to land near them, they too shaking rain and looking to see if Freddy was ok. He was leaning against a tree, still trying to catch his wind.

"Well, that was certainly lively," said Sefton.

"Lively? I was nearly arrested and possibly shot at dawn!"

"I do hope the night guard don't get into too much trouble," said Yeti, "they only mean well."

"Do you think Victoriana broke his foot?"

"Not the best way to end a meeting," said Rochester, "did we get the plan clear?"

"Yes," said Gauntlet, "tomorrow morning we fly with the Met nag to guard and have him get the message to Rupert in St. James's Park."

Freddy was still short of breath, "Look, you guys sort this out. I have to get home." He turned and started jogging to the west through the heavy rain.

"Bye, Freddy, see you tomorrow," called Yeti.

"Maybe," muttered the soaked teenager as he ran through the park. His socks got soggy as water seeped up through his thin trainers. With the park closed to traffic he didn't stop at the crossing into Kensington gardens, he just bolted straight across the road and then tripped on the kerb. He shot forward, put out his hands to break his fall, landed heavily, ripped his jeans and scraped the skin off his left knee. Both hands were jarred and scraped painfully on the gravel. Momentarily exhausted, he lay face down on the pavement allowing the rain to silently cover him, further drenching his jeans and thin shirt. Finally he got to his feet and made it to the end of the park. Mentally buzzed and physically drained he didn't make it cleanly over the fence and caught the front of his wet shirt on the railing spike, causing a large rip. Freddy ran through the dark, wet streets, into the garden and up the fire escape and was half way through the window when the lights in his room blazed on.

"So, look at who decided to come home finally," said his mother from the doorway.

Both stood frozen, silently looking at each other. "Oh, er, hi mum," Freddy said, water draining from him onto the carpet.

"Hi mum? Hi mum? It's gone two in the morning! I'm out of my mind with worry! And you say Hi mum?"

He was silent, staring down at the carpet.

"Into the sitting room. Now! We have some talking to do. No, wait, you will do the talking!"

He closed the bedroom window and then followed her into the sitting room. She was already sitting on the edge of the couch, wearing the clothes she'd put on for her evening out. He sidled by and took the single armchair.

"Don't even think of getting comfortable. Start talking," Jane said through clenched teeth, obviously making on effort to contain herself.

"Actually, could I get a towel, please, I'm really soaking."

She stood up, strode to the bathroom, returned and flung a towel at him.

"Sit on it; I don't want the furniture to get wet. Now, talk."

He shoved the towel under his seat and legs. "What do you want to hear?"

"Let's see now, how about your sad excuse for your behaviour and attitude recently?"

"How do you know it would be an excuse?"

"Well I'm looking forward to hearing a sane and sensible reason if you can muster one, but that's doubtful, so I'm expecting a pathetic excuse."

Freddy bit into his bottom lip and said nothing.

"Let's work backwards shall we? How about leaving the house in the middle of the night and trying to sneak back in? Obviously I was not supposed to know where you've been, or for that matter, who you've been with!"

"How do you know I've met anyone, I could have been on my own."

"Why didn't you answer your phone?"

"Oh, that was you?" he said without thinking.

"So you did hear it?"

No way could he back track now. "Yeah, yeah, I heard it ring."

"And, pray tell, why you refrained from answering?"

"It was, um, a bit, inconvenient at the time."

"A bit inconvenient? Oh, this just gets better."

He said nothing.

"I was calling from Hammersmith, to say I was going to be late and hoped you wouldn't be worried. Well, fat chance of that being the case. Damn it, you weren't even home!"

"I had to sort of go out for a bit."

"Out? Out?" She looked at her watch. "It's half past two in the morning and you had to step out? Through the bedroom window in the pouring rain?"

"Yeah, it was kind of like that."

"Let me guess. You sneaked out through the window because you thought I was home and I wasn't supposed to know about your little midnight jaunts. Right?"

"I wasn't sneaking! I just didn't want to disturb you if you had gone to bed."

"And then you come home, jeans ripped, knee bleeding, hands scraped, shirt ripped, soaking wet," she paused for effect, " and best of all you come in through the damn window!"

Not a lot a damp teen could say at this point.

"And, you stink again!" There was another short pause as Jane regained her composure. She pushed a hand back through her hair. Then quietly, "Don't think I don't know what you're up to, young man. It doesn't take a scientist to work this out."

He looked up, "What, what have I been up to?"

"It's obvious. Drugs."

"Drugs?" He jumped to his feet. "Bloody drugs? You're out of your mind, mum!"

"Sit down!"

He sat back down, making fists with his bruised knuckles.

Jane continued. "It's obvious. You have been sleeping till all hours. You have afternoon naps. You're moody, argumentative and have become totally disagreeable."

"Moody? Disagreeable? What? When have I been like that?"

"How about your reaction to the family day out I'm planning? Anyone would think I'd said I was going to take you to the Labour Party Conference!"

"Mum, it's not drugs."

"We've been in London for only a couple of weeks and already you are out of control! I thought this move would be good for us, but obviously I am wrong."

Freddy shook his head and flopped back into the chair.

"Look at the state of you. You've obviously been in a fight, a little gang action was it? Someone poaching on your patch, maybe?"

"I have not been in a fight, I tripped."

"Tripped? Where did you trip?"

"In the park, on the kerb."

"Oh marvellous, so your little crack den is in the park? Hyde Park? Meeting up with the local tweakers, junkies and smack heads are we?"

He closed his eyes and shook his head. "No mum, it's nothing like that."

"Stand up."

"What?"

"Stand up! And then empty your pockets."

"You are kidding me? You're going to search me?"

"Damn right I am! Now, last time, empty your pockets."

He stood up, and pulled out the contents of his pockets. There wasn't much; a handful of change, a crumpled packet of chewing gum and a broken pencil.

"Back pockets too."

He reached back, retrieved his phone and out with it fell the torn cigarette packet with the numbers on. She snatched it up.

"Contact number? Your dealer, eh?"

"Oh come on, mum, does it look like a phone number?"

"Could be. Could be in code. I know how devious smack head teenagers can get."

"You know? How do you know?"

She paused again, obviously making a decision and then said, "Sharon. Your Auntie Sharon. Why do you think we never moved back to my mum's when your Dad died?"

"I don't know. I never thought about it"

"She was at it from the age of fourteen. And let me tell you I know about the moods, and the lying, and the great excuses. She almost drove your Gran to an early grave!"

"Auntie Sharon is doing drugs?"

"No, no, not now, she's been clean for years. Why do you think she could never hold down a decent job or a boyfriend?"

"Wow, a tweaker auntie, it's kind of cool."

"What?"

"Well, I mean cool now that she's clean. Not because she was doing drugs," Freddy frantically back pedalled.

Jane sat herself further back on the couch, the signs of fatigue showing. "So, are you going to tell me what's been going on?"

There was a long silence between the two of them as he thought about it.

"Mum, you know how you've always taught me about helping people? About being nice and not a bully?"

"Yes, go on."

"Like, I mean, remember that kid at school, Alfred Eccles, the one with the red hair and played the trumpet, with the sticky out ears."

"His trumpet did not have ears."

"Oh lighten up, you know what I mean."

"Go on, what about him?"

"Remember how all the other lads used to regularly beat the crap out of him 'cuz he was a bit different?"

"Yes, I remember."

"And, what did you make me do?"

"Remind me."

"You told me to invite him over for tea, and to play in the garden with him, so he wouldn't be lonely and left out."

"OK, I remember."

"And do you remember the crap I had to put up with afterwards for being nice to the geek."

"Yes, you said the others weren't nice to you about it."

"Right, and that's an understatement."

"So what does Alfred Eccles and his trumpet have to do with all of this?"

"There are some people I met recently and they need help. That's where I've been."

"Are you giving me a line of B.S., Freddy?"

"No, no, mum, I'm not."

"Why do these new friends need help? What's their problem?"

"Well, they're small, and don't know about fighting. Actually, they don't have a mean bone in their body. They only see good in everyone. They are clueless about evil."

"And I'm to believe this?"

"Yes, please."

"And the fighting? You got into a fight because of these people?"

"No, no it wasn't a fight. Honest. I really did trip and fall flat on my face. Oh, and I caught my shirt on a railing."

"Who are they?"

"Who are who?"

"These people. These little people that you're so bravely helping at two in the morning? Fair question, eh? Who are they?"

"Ah, well, can't say right now."

"Can't or won't?"

"Can't, honest, I promised them I wouldn't."

"Where are they from? Around here?"

"Not originally. I think Ireland originally, but they've lived most of their lives around here."

"I'm supposed to believe this too?"

"Yes, or you can go on thinking I'm a smack head, which is totally bonkers."

"Tell me more about them. About the situation."

"Can't right now, honest."

"Can't or won't again?"

"Please, just give me a bit of time, ok?"

She stared directly at him. "Tell me you are not lying."

"I'm not lying, mum."

"And that you are going to tell me about this"

"Yeah, but not right now. Can we talk again in the morning?"

"You swear this is not drugs?"

"Swear, mum."

"And nothing illegal?"

"Nope, nothing illegal." OK, maybe a little glitch there with trespass, but it was a technicality.

She was silent again for a long time.

"Fred, I made a promise to myself a long time ago that I would not be like my own mother with you. I was going to be different, more liberal."

He nodded.

"But it's damn difficult when you are worried sick about your own kid's safety."

"I sort of understand."

"You're almost seventeen, you need to be having your own life and not having to tell mummy everything, but when it comes to safety, well, I worry like hell."

"Mum, there are no drugs involved, there are no gangs or knives or guns involved." The possibility of a bomb was another technicality he would have his lawyer argue on his behalf. "Please, just give me a bit of time. By the way, how was your night?"

She rolled her eyes. "Let's just say those secretary girls know how to party. I'll tell you in the morning. Now, go to bed, we have a damn sight more talking to do tomorrow."

"OK."

"And leave those bloody filthy clothes in the hall for washing."

Wow, seriously busted and caught twice in one night. What was worse? The military police or his mother? No contest. Jane, every time. Freddy didn't even remember his head touching the pillow. He was out like a light till almost eleven a.m. The apartment was quiet, Jane was already over at the house. His knees and knuckles were still sore. He took a good hot shower, pulled on shorts and sweat shirt and dug around in the kitchen for food. With a plate of cold stuff from the fridge, he flipped on the TV and tried to clear his mind as he ate. Saturday morning cartoons danced across the screen. Next thing Freddy knew he was waking up, a light tapping noise sounding in the back of his head. He sat up, caught the empty plate as it nearly slid off his lap and looked around. The TV was still on, no Jane; just a tapping sound. Then he realized it was coming from his room. Freddy went over to the window, pulled back the blind and saw two Pegusinni on the fire escape.

"We have a problem," said Rochester.

"Oh, well, tell me why I am not surprised to hear this news!" The rain had cleared, everything was damp but the sun shone. He lifted the window and sat on the sill. The two small black horses looked expectantly at him.

"So, go on, what little dilemma has this bright and sunny day brought?"

"A dilly what?" asked Sefton.

"Problem. What's today's problem."

"We went to guard with the police horse as we planned and gave him the message, but he didn't get all of the message properly over to Rupert."

"So we're not sure it's going to work," added Rochester.

"So we can't get the drains and sewers checked out?"

"Maybe not. Maybe we can."

Sefton leaned forward a little. "We went back to barracks and talked to Victoriana, she's come up with a great plan to fix things."

"That's great. How are you going to do it?"

"We? Oh no, not only us. You too, Freddy; she'll need you."

"Do you guys have any idea how much trouble I am already in? There is no way I can go back to barracks today!"

"There's no need to," said Sefton.

"Really?"

"Yes, we just need to meet you in the park by the rose garden, tonight."

"Tonight?"

"Yes, at about ten, by the rose garden."

"I'm not sure I can get out again so soon at night, guys."

"But we need you."

"And it is earlier."

"How long will it take?" Freddy asked.

"Not too long, not like last night."

Freddy thought about it. He could get away with saying he was going to see a film, then say he stopped for pizza on the way home. He could actually walk out through the front door for a change.

"OK, I'll give it a shot. Ten o'clock tonight, right?"

"Yes, down by the rose garden," said Sefton.

"Yes, I know about the rose garden."

"And you'll need to bring a couple of things with you," Rochester said.

"Things? What sort of things?"

"A head collar."

"And some cheese, please."

"What?"

"A head collar, you know, a halter, like we wear when we don't wear bridles."

"I meant about the cheese!"

"Oh, yes, very important. But any old stuff will do," said Sefton.

"And where am I going to find a head collar?"

"Well, they're always on the peg, at the end of the stall."

"Rochester, it may have escaped your notice, but I don't live in a stall."

"Oh."

"Yes, well, we hadn't thought of that."

"But this is London, Freddy; there must be lots about somewhere."

"You know, I'm not even going to ask why we need this stuff, I'm beyond guessing with you lads, but where am I going to get this head collar?"

"No problem with the cheese, then?"

"No, no problem with the cheese."

"Interesting," Sefton mused, "it would be the other way for us."

"Leave it with me," said Freddy, "I'll figure something out."

"OK, we'll see you tonight," said Rochester.

"At ten o'clock," said Sefton.

"By the rose garden," all three said together.

Chapter Eighteen

A head collar? In central London? OK, there had to be
some type of saddle shops about that sold this stuff.
Back to the computer. Google head collar, London. Bingo!
Plenty of shops selling them, places he'd never heard of,
let alone how to get to. And the prices! Some shops had
leather ones for over fifty quid! Where did he get that
kind of money? Further down on the second page Freddy
spotted a link to good old eBay. Over to eBay, search head
collar. Yikes. Over two hundred of them, all over the U.K.
and some were for *dogs*. Who knew dogs wore head collars?
Refine search to within ten miles of London. Two showed
up. One had a 'buy now' price of £1.99p and described it
as full size, webbing.

Freddy could scrape together the cash, figured that the
size wasn't too important, not sure about what 'webbing'
was but he couldn't be picky. He sent a message, included his
mobile phone number, said he would pay the asking price,
and then waited. At least it was Saturday and hopefully the
seller was the type who checked their eBay messages often.
Just over an hour later the phone rang.

"Hello?"

A female voice spoke, "Hi, you left a message. You wanted to buy my head collar?"

"Yeah, yes, I do. And you said it was full size?"

"Yep."

"Can I get it today?"

"Sure, I'm over near Oakwood."

"Where's that?"

"One stop before Cockfosters on the Piccadilly line. Or will you be driving?"

"No, no, definitely coming on the underground. Oakwood you said?"

"Yep. When are you coming?"

"I can leave now."

"OK," she sounded like she was chewing something, "where from?"

"Kensington."

"Wow, kind of posh eh?"

"No, not really, my mum works here."

"Gotcha." She gave him directions from the underground station to her place and hung up. Freddy scraped all his loose change out of pockets, drawers and the top of the desk, grabbed a jacket and headed out. The Smiths had supplied him and his mum with season passes for the bus and underground so that wouldn't cost anything. Even better that South Kensington station was on the Piccadilly line. The journey seemed to take ages, crossing directly across central London and then out to the north and east. Finally the train arrived at Oakwood; he got off and looked at the directions he'd written down on a piece of paper. As the woman said, her small apartment block with some garages below wasn't far from the station.

"Where the hell do you keep a horse in a block of flats?" he thought. Her apartment was on the second floor, number five. She flung the door open at his knock.

"Hiya. Becky," she said sticking out her hand.

"Hi, I'm Freddy."

She was quite tall, maybe forty something with rather unruly hair that hung vaguely between her ears and her shoulders. The baggy sweater and shoes she was wearing weren't in the first flush of youth.

"Come in, won't cha?"

Freddy followed her through to the apartment and like her, it wasn't exactly dirty, but it did remind him of a phrase he remembered Eleanor using, 'a little slovenly'.

"Here ya go," she said as she tossed a grocery bag to him.

Freddy pulled out the head collar and stared.

"It doesn't look like the others I've seen," he said, thinking about all the leather ones at the barracks.

"For £1.99p you can't be picky, mate, but I'll throw in the matching lead rope as well."

He hadn't even thought about the rope. Of course he would need that; it would be no good without it.

"Yeah, sure. You take care of it now. It belonged to my Princess."

"Princess?"

"Yeah, Princess Tallulah, my mare, got bad colic last year. She died."

"No, she didn't."

"Didn't what?"

"You know, die."

"Look, mate, I was there when the vet said she was a goner."

"Well, maybe she's at a better place now."

"Better place? I kept her at the poshest livery stable around here! She had a great life!"

"No, I mean, now that she's made a transition she'll be happy."

"Freddy, not sure what you're on, pal, but my mare is dead. Gone. And that's why I'm finally selling all her tack. Would you be interested in some travel boots too?"

"No, I have to get going." He rummaged for the change, put it down on the table and headed quickly for the door, clutching the grocery bag.

"Ok, bye. Hope it fits."

"Yep, bye," Freddy ran down the building steps and back to the tube station. When he finally got back to the flat in Kensington he carefully tucked the bag behind his bike under the cover in the rear yard. The last thing he needed was for Jane with her, "What's in the bag, kiddo?" questions. He'd pick it up later on the way out to the park.

It was close to six p.m. when Freddy walked back into the apartment. Jane was making spaghetti for their dinner. They hadn't spoken since the night before.

"Go and wash your hands and then get the salad stuff ready from the fridge," she directed.

OK, he could work with this. Bossy, but calm. Let's just tread carefully now, Freddy thought.

"Sure, no problem."

"Aren't you impressed that I'm not asking where you've been all afternoon?"

And here we go.

"You just did."

"No, not directly."

"And if I don't say, we'll have another fight, right?"

"Not necessarily."

"I've been out on the tube, mostly."

"The underground? What for?"

"I had some free time. And we have the season passes and I thought I'd look around, get familiar with places."

"Where? Where did you get familiar?"

"Oakwood actually." Jane looked surprised that he told her straight out.

"Really now? And where is Oakwood?"

"One stop before Cockfosters on the Piccadilly Line. Now, can we end the interview, please?"

This time it was her turn to bite her bottom lip.

"Yes, sure, why not?" she said brightly, turning around with a smile one size too large in place.

They kept the truce as she served and while they both ate dinner.

"You going out this evening?" he asked.

"After last night? You're kidding me. Nope, hot bath, feet up, glass of wine, bed. That's my night."

"OK."

"Why? Are you thinking you're going out?"

"Yeah, thought I might go to the flicks."

"Just to the cinema?"

He dodged the question, "I won't be late and I'll go in and out of the front door. Promise."

"I see." Obviously Jane was torn between wanting to pin him to the floor and interrogate him Gestapo style and being the cool, with-it modern parent. Her pride won. "That sounds fine. Which film are you seeing?"

"Er, just going to the multiplex, they have a choice of about ten going on, see what catches my fancy."

"I see." She finished eating, rose from the table and went to run her bath. When the door was closed she silently kicked the crap out of the side of the tub.

Knowing this truce could be short lived, Freddy got up, cleared away the table, washed all the dishes, boxed up leftovers and made the place as tidy as possible. Just when he thought he was done, he remembered the cheese. He found a good size packet of cheddar that had just been opened. That would do. He stuffed it into his jacket pocket. Lord knows what they wanted with cheese; he'd always thought horses liked sugar and oats.

He watched TV while Jane bathed. He jumped up when finally she came into the sitting room, wearing her robe and her hair wrapped up in a towel.

"Ok, I'll just grab my shower now, then."

"Two? Two showers in one day?"

"Yeah, I got kind of sweaty out today. It was humid after the rain."

"Two showers. Moody. Secretive…Hmm."

"Hmm what?"

"Oh, nothing," Jane grinned quietly.

Freddy went into the bathroom and locked the door. What on earth was she thinking now? He was only showering because he wanted to avoid being in the same room for too long. He was actually under the shower when it dawned on him. "Oh God, she thinks I'm dating!" But, this could work to his advantage if he played it right. He spent an extra long time washing and showering, put on loads of deodorant, gelled up his hair a bit, and splashed on way too much of the aftershave his Gran had given him last Christmas. Back in his room, he looked for some special clothes a snazzy shirt, his extra cool-dude jacket, new jeans and, instead of wet trainers, his best shoes. OK, that should do it. He glanced at his watch to see it was only eight o'clock. Better to leave early though, than suffer more grilling.

He bounced back into the sitting room. "Hey, well, I'm off now."

She looked up and suppressed another grin. "Ok. My, don't you look smart?" She was feeling good now that she had finally figured out what he was up to.

"Me?" He said, feigning innocence.

"Well, for just a regular night out at the cinema, that's very smart."

Summoning up all his acting skills, Freddy managed to blush red and look embarrassed at being found out. "No, just wanted to feel clean, ya know, after the last couple of days." Two could play at her game.

"Have fun," she said, swirling the red wine in her glass.

"Thanks. I shouldn't be too late. But don't wait up," and before she could say anything, "I'll call if I'm going to be late."

Phew, all bases covered and Freddy was out of the door. He stopped in the rear yard to pick up the bag and took the lump of cheese from his pocket and tossed that in too. No rain, but it was still rather humid. He set off walking toward Knightsbridge. Instead of going into the park he stayed on the main road and took his time strolling along the pavement. It was dusk with evening closing in. He walked all the way along Knightsbridge Road, passing the barracks on his left, avoiding looking toward the guard room gate, and then down toward the busy intersection at Hyde Corner. On his right he saw the huge building with the sign 'Harrods'. The place took up the whole of one block of the street; dozens and dozens of its windows were packed with glamorous displays of things at unbelievable prices. It was closed, but he spent almost an hour walking around the entire block investigating every window. He'd heard Caroline talking to his mum about some shrine the owner of the place had put up in honour of Princess Diana and the bloke she died with. Definitely a place for his Gran and Sharon to visit. Which brought his mind around to another train of thought -The Trooping of the Colour.

Because of all the craziness in the last twenty-four hours he'd almost lost track of what all this was about. He still had to figure out a way for him and his family to avoid the ceremony at all cost. Just in case.

By now it was almost dark and time to head over to the park. He weaved through traffic, then through the quiet and very expensive streets known as the mews. He crossed back over Knightsbridge Road and walked through the pedestrian access called Park Close. Once through the access, an immediate sense of quiet and calm was apparent. There was still some light traffic on the South Carriage Drive but nothing like the volume moving up and down behind him on the major roads. The Rose Garden, Freddy thought. They had been very clear about the Rose Garden. He walked across Rotten Row, went down the pathway to the east and was soon at the garden.

No one was there. The place was deserted. He sat down on a green park bench and waited. There weren't even any joggers this late in the day.

"Hey, Freddy, said Gauntlet gliding in from the north.

"Hi, Mr. Trumpet Horse, just you?"

"No, me too," said Yeti landing beside him.

"So, what's the plan, boys?"

"Just waiting for Rochester and Sefton, and of course," he paused, looking over to the thick shrubs surrounding the Rose garden, "ah, here she is too."

In the darkness Victoriana stepped out from behind the shrubbery.

"Good grief! You escaped!" Freddy stared, his jaw slack.

"Hush, don't make such noise," said Sefton stepping out with Rochester from behind the black mare.

"Good evening, Freddy," she said calmly.

"How? How in bloody hell did you get out? They'll be looking everywhere! Oh Lord, we've gone too far this time."

"For goodness sake, be quiet, stop the noise, please. Now, obviously we are going to have to explain, so please come into the garden out of sight."

The odd little group all scuttled back as she directed.

"Freddy," said Gauntlet quietly, "you really stink."

"Yes, it's very odd," Sefton said.

"Smells like the stuff they put down the drains at barracks," said Yeti.

"I do not smell like disinfectant!" Freddy said indignantly.

"What happened to your hair?" asked the black mare, "you look surprised. It's all on end."

"Enough! Enough about my appearance and smell. It's all part of my plan to keep this business low key. Besides, this is my rock star look."

Victoriana thought for a moment. "Rock star like Captain Blunt?"

"Captain Blunt?"

"Yes, he was with the Blues but now he's a rock star or singer or something."

"Captain Blunt? Wait, *James Blunt?*"

"Yes, that's his full name."

"James Blunt was in the cavalry?"

"Indeed, Venetia carried him to guard on many occasions."

"You are kidding? Besides, how would you know this now?"

"The polo ponies at Smith's Lawn, Windsor," replied the mare, "they have seen him attending parties and, I believe, singing there too."

"Well, I'll go to the foot of our stair!"

"Why would you go there, Freddy?" asked Gauntlet.

"No matter, another figure of our speech. Let's get back to today. Would you please explain how a huge black horse got out of the barracks and into Hyde Park on her own?"

"I walked."

"Oh now there's a concept. I could have guessed you flew with all that goes on around here! So, you just walked out through the main gate, and no one said dickey boo?"

"Who?"

"Forget it. How did you do it?"

She sighed, looked at him patiently and began to explain, "For a start, it's Saturday, you know the weekend?"

"Yes, I know it's the weekend."

"Well, by mid-day almost all the soldiers go away till Monday, there are just a few left behind for feeding and cleaning. When Webber and Cochrane, my groom, left I was where I should be."

"But you're not now!"

"No, obviously not. Later in the day the weekend shift arrives. They don't know who is on guard and who isn't, so, I let myself out and came over to the park before they closed the main gate. Simple really."

"I can understand you letting yourself out, I've seen you do it. But how does a huge horse walk out of the gates and not get lassoed and dragged back in?"

"Oh, I sat on her haunches," said Gauntlet.

"Yes, he's the lightest," said Sefton.

"You sat on her?"

"Well yes, just for a little while. While she walked up the ramp and across the yard. You remember what happens to you when you hold us?"

"Oh, right."

"Same thing, they didn't see her."

He looked toward the alpha mare. "But you're not there! Someone will notice an empty box stall!"

"Yes, they will, but no one wonders about an empty stall when the door is closed and bolted."

"Oh."

"Indeed, they would panic and search if the door was swinging open and no equine there."

"So you actually closed and bolted the door when you left?"

"Of course, and now weekend workers will simply think I am away on guard and I'll be back in before morning."

The smaller horses were all nodding, understanding fully, as if it were no big deal.

Freddy let out a large sigh. "So why? Why did you need to be out?"

"Ah well, that's about the mix up with this morning's plan. Rupert didn't get the message right and he needs it again. So, we need to know what they find in the drains, don't we?"

"Well yeah, but why are you here?"

"I thought we had explained this before," said Rochester, stepping forward, "a swan can't talk to a Pegusinni, and he certainly can't talk to you, so he'll talk to Victoriana."

"You are going to St. James's Park tonight?" asked Freddy looking at her.

"Yes, it was the quickest and easiest way. We certainly can't afford to waste any more time with useless Met nags. This requires military action."

"Get a load of you, G.I. Jane."

"Who?"

"Never mind. And how? How are you getting there?"

"We'll walk. It's not far."

"Excuse me? We'll walk?"

"Of course, that's why we needed you here. To act as escort."

"Me? I'm the escort?"

"Of course, I can't go on my own."

"Why not, you made it this far?"

"Freddy, that was out of barracks and across the park in almost darkness, with a Pegusinni. I can't get all the way to Whitehall like that!"

"No, indeed no," there was much group tutting and more group head shaking from the little guys.

"So I'm escorting you?"

"Yes, now, did you bring the head collar as asked?"

"Yeah, yes, it's here in the bag."

"Good, now please get it out and put it on me."

"Why do you need a head collar?"

"Because a loose horse walking through the streets of London at night would attract attention. It has to look like you are mine. As if I'm with you."

Freddy bent down, opened the bag and pulled out the head collar he had paid £1.99p for.

"Oh!"

"Good grief!"

"That's not like ours!"

"It's scary!"

"Hey! It was short notice! I did my best!" Freddy said somewhat defensively.

Victoriana stared at the piece of equipment. "Freddy, it's *pink!*"

"It's pink nylon!" said Yeti as though it were a conger eel with the plague.

"And a pink lead rope!"

"Yeah, it belonged to a Princess Tallulah, but she's gone now. Transitioned as you say."

"I'm not surprised she did if they made her wear that!" said Gauntlet rolling his eyes in horror and distain.

Victoriana regained her composure, "Very well, put it on me, please."

"Me?" Freddy asked.

"Well, I can't put it on myself. I can get them off, but equine can't put them on. Quickly now, we have to be done and back before midnight."

"Why?"

"Because the park closes and I don't wish to spend the rest of the night on Hyde Park corner!"

She lowered her head and he fumbled with the straps, then stood back and looked at it. The four Pegusinni failed to contain their amusement.

"Freddy, you have the nose band around my ear, and the buckle is in my eye. Could we try this again please?"

With more fumbling and some help thrown in from the Pegusinni, he managed to get the head collar looking reasonably correct.

"That feels about right now," she said, "so next step. Up you go."

"Up I go where?"

"On my back, of course."

"What?"

"Freddy you need to mount to ride me to Whitehall and we need to do it soon."

"Ride? Vicks, I can't ride! Never been on a horse in my whole life! Can't I just lead you? Do it that way?"

The equine group all looked perplexed and puzzled. The black mare spoke again. "Freddy, I already said I can't walk loose through the streets of London. I would be taken back to barracks immediately."

"I know, so I can lead you, right?"

"Wrong. Do you know how odd that would look? A boy leading a horse at night through the park to Whitehall?" Freddy just shook his head. She continued, "Now a boy riding a horse through the park is nothing unusual, happens all day everyday. Do you see my point?"

"Victoriana, I really can't ride," he said quietly.

"No worry, I can."

"Ride?"

"No, not ride but I've been carrying unbalanced people for years, you'll be fine. Just let me handle it."

"And no saddle? And no bridle?"

"We thought it would be hard for you to find those, besides, they probably would never have fit. So, up you go."

"What? Just climb on?"

Gauntlet peered outside of the Rose Garden. "Here, there's a bench, he can use that as a mounting block."

"Go and get on the bench," said Sefton, "we really need to get moving."

Freddy slowly walked toward the bench and then stood on it, shaking his head with doubt the whole time. Victoriana walked out and positioned herself directly next to him. "OK," she said, "one leg over and hop."

"Which leg?"

"It depends if you want to face forward or backward. Your choice."

"Forward, please."

"Very well, that one," she said as she tapped his right leg with her muzzle. "Hold a piece of my mane if you think it will help."

Tentatively he held the mare's short mane, leaned forward and lifted his right leg.

"Hop, now," shouted the Pegusinni.

"Come on, just jump!"

"One neat movement!"

As it turned out, it wasn't one neat movement; rather it was more a series of pulls, writhing, grunts and then an unexpected but welcome boost to his rear from the muzzle of a Pegusinni. But he was on.

"Oh my Gawd!"

"What?" asked Victoriana anxiously.

"You're all warm and furry!"

"I am not furry! That is the coat of a thoroughbred!"

"Wow, I can feel you breathing!"

"What did you expect, Freddy, a wheel barrow? How does he look?" she asked the others.

The other four all stood shaking their heads.

"Oh, dear."

"Not really."

"Quite bad, actually."

"He looks like a hoof pick," assessed Gauntlet.

"A hoof pick?" asked Freddy.

"Yes, all bent and crooked." Gauntlet said.

[It would have been good at this point if we could have said that *'from no where Freddy felt energy surging through his body; the feeling of a deep down, hidden equestrian talent being unleashed. A talent so strong, so natural, he knew he could ride and tame ANY horse on the planet. Needing no tuition, it all came coursing through his veins. He was ready to RIDE!'* Sadly, we can't say that.]

Freddy clung on; his body bent forward, his legs clamped like iron around the mare's side.

"Freddy?"

"Yes?"

Could you please let go of my mane, it's about to come out in your hand and it's hurting.

"Oh, sorry," Freddy said letting go.

"This could take some time," said Yeti slowly shaking his head.

"Aren't you the master of the understatement?" concluded Sefton.

Chapter Nineteen

"We only have a few minutes, then we really have to get going," Victoriana said, "we'll just walk a couple of large circles around on the sand."

Freddy made a sharp involuntary intake of breath as she stepped forward but to his own amazement he was still on her back a few minutes later when she stopped.

"Wow! I'm riding, I'm really riding."

"Hardly, but we won't debate the point. Now, let's get going." Victoriana looked to the Pegusinni as she stepped off again, "Give him some instruction as we go."

"Shoulders back!"

"Head up!"

"Back straight!"

"Heels down!"

"Stomach in!"

"Hands low!"

"Hey. Quite the bossy little crowd, aren't you?" Freddy said.

"Carry swords!" screamed Rochester.

"I don't have a sword!"

"Oh, sorry, got carried away there," said the slightly embarrassed Pegusinni.

"How do you know all this stuff? You're horses, not riders."

"After years of hearing the remount staff bawling at recruits, we've heard it hundreds of times," said Yeti.

Gauntlet came in closer. "We actually don't know what it means but we know all the words," he confided.

"My," said Rochester hovering by, "he does look better already."

"Could hardly have looked worse," commented Sefton.

"Does it occur to you guys that I can actually hear you when you talk about me?"

"Hush, all of you, we are almost at the first road crossing."

Freddy looked up as they approached the end of Rotten Row and the curve in the South Carriage Drive where they would cross to get to Hyde Park Corner. A couple of black cabs were the only traffic at this hour. He jolted forward and braced his hands on her neck as she came to a smart halt at the kerb.

"Balance, Freddy, you need better balance."

"A reality check is what I really need. And padded underwear."

The black mare walked confidently across the main road. The fair-haired teen perched less confidently on her back as they approached the huge wrought iron gates that ended Hyde Park. She headed knowledgeably to the central gateway which was still open and walked to the edge of the busy road. As usual, traffic flowed in an endless torrent from right to left.

"We're never going to get across," Freddy said to Victoriana. She stood calmly at the edge of the road, "Show him please, Yeti,"

The little old black horse hovered up near Freddy's shoulder. "Here, Freddy, the button. Just press the button."

He glanced up to his right. There on its own post, set about ten feet above the ground and above the reach of anyone on foot, was a small round button. Above it was a little light in the shape of the horse.

"You are kidding me? A special horsey crossing?"

"Of course, we use it every day when we go to guard."

He leaned and reached up and gave the button a poke. Immediately all lights changed to red, all traffic stopped and the little horsey light turned to green. "Well, would ya look at that?"

"No time to look," said the mare stepping briskly across the road to the central island, "we need to keep moving."

Freddy was getting just an ounce more confidence. He even looked down and smiled at the cabbies waiting at the red light, then gave a little mock salute of thanks. It was beginning to feel pretty cool up here, lording it over the lowly peasants. A guy could get used this. Having the women folk carry him around.

"What did you almost think there, Freddy?" asked Victoriana.

"Oh, nothing. Really nothing."

"Good, I hoped it was nothing." They went straight on, past the Wellington Arch to the next crossing where they used the horse button again. The group was at the top of Green Park with the high walls of Buckingham Palace gardens across the road to their right. Knowing exactly where she was going, Victoriana headed directly for a broad sand track that ran parallel between the road and the park. Freddy was getting used to the rhythmical swaying movement of the walk, his legs were more relaxed more and he lightly held the halter rope instead of clutching it.

"I've got a question while we're all on this jaunt."

"Yes, go ahead," said the voice below.

"I keep being surprised by who we can actually recruit or at least get to help us out. At first I thought it was just us, but now I'm realising we have a whole network at our finger tips."

"We do have some useful contacts, indeed."

"So, like, if we recruited every bird, rabbit, horse, cat and dog across the city we could beat this thing!"

Victoriana stopped abruptly. Pegusinni dropped in and down to the ground around them.

"Oh, no."

"No, no, not really."

"Can't do that."

"Why not? It could be the biggest urban army ever!" Freddy said.

Victoriana slightly twisted her neck to get him into her rear view vision. "Freddy, canine, feline and equine, not a good idea." There was much group tutting and agreeing from the Pegusinni.

"Why not?" You all have four legs and all that. You should work together."

"Predator and prey," she replied calmly.

"Eh?"

"One is predator, the other is prey," said Yeti.

"Eat or be eaten," confirmed Gauntlet.

"Oh, come on. A dog's not going to try to eat a horse, now is it?"

"Maybe not this week, not here in the park. But they have and they will if they need to."

"Fight or flight, Freddy."

"What?" Freddy asked.

"They choose to hunt and fight, we choose flight to live."

"Even in this day and age?" he asked.

They remained stationary. Victoriana lowered her voice, "Many miles away across the big water in the big place, really bad things still happen every day. The race horses that visit from there tell tales of it to equine at our race courses."

"America? What happens there?"

"Many equine roam free, living in open herds, not at all closed in. But they are exposed to great dangers. No protection like we have."

The Pegusinni were all gathered closely around, talking in whispers as though swapping ghost stories with him.

"There are packs of small wild canine there, quite small really, with little spots," said Yeti, "and teeth like buckle pins."

"They will follow a birthing mare," said Sefton.

"In a pack," said Rochester.

"Then eat the baby as it's being born!" said Gauntlet in a high pitched whisper.

"Coyotes? Coyotes do that? Oh Lord, that is disgusting," said Freddy reeling at the thought.

"Wait till you meet a one day old Pegusinni too!"

Freddy shuddered at the idea.

Victoriana straightened herself up and as she stepped forward again, she said, "Anyway, canine in particular can be exceptionally dumb on occasion. We'll manage without them, thank you."

"Total plops, just look at the way they chase sticks in the park," said Rochester, "where is the sense in that?"

"They can be real boinkers," said Gauntlet.

"Plonkers. That would be plonkers," advised Freddy.

"Oh right. Well, close enough," said the little grey.

The small procession had reached the end of Green Park with Buckingham Palace across the big road to the right. The black mare kept her course discreetly behind a large ornate wall as they rounded the bend and entered the Mall. Again she kept to the sandy track under the spring leaves of the trees lining each side of the road. An open-top sports car with two blonde girls inside slowed down.

"Hey! Hey, it's the Lone Ranger!" called the driver, collapsing in giggles behind the wheel.

"Can I be your Tonto, please?" called the girl in the passenger seat shrieking and laughing.

"You'd be a hot lookin' guy if it wasn't for the pink hat on the pony!" More shrieks and giggles came from the girls as the car accelerated away down the Mall.

Hmm, with a few adjustments there could be more to this riding lark than he first thought. Freddy had relaxed a lot and was almost enjoying the evening ride. He had no idea just how much his horse was contributing to his success. Similar to a woman in parts of Africa carrying a huge vase of water upon her head, Victoriana moved with the same posture and skill. As the woman feels even the slightest ripple wave across the top of the water, she adjusts her balance to immediately calm it. And so it was with the black mare. Every time the teenager wobbled even slightly to the left or right, she immediately adjusted her position underneath to straighten him up.

Victoriana halted almost at the end of the Mall, waited for a break in the light traffic and then crossed over to the approach road leading into Horse Guard's Parade. On the right hand side directly in front of St. James's Park was a large war memorial facing across the open spaces of the Parade Ground. She halted on the park grass next to it.

"Oh, good grief," said Freddy looking over to the parade square.

"What? What's the matter?"

"Look, seating! Hundreds of damn seats!"

"Well yes, they always have thousands of seats for the trooping."

"But they weren't here the other day, it was completely empty."

The black mare, the Pegusinni and Freddy all looked silently at row up on row of tiered seating running around three sides of the square.

"The flood drains," he said pointing, "are over there to the left hand corner. And now, they're underneath all those seats!"

"It may be ok; we anticipated this, which is why we have recruited extra help."

"Extra help?"

"Yes, they should be here soon."

"Rupert is on his way," called Yeti, hovering above the memorial and looking across the park in the darkness.

"Is everyone with him?" asked Victoriana.

"Looks like it, difficult to see the small ones in the dark."

"Everyone? Small ones?" asked Freddy, "so who do we have now?"

"Rattus Norvegicus," replied Victoriana.

Freddy thought for a moment. "Rats? We now have rats working on this?"

As he spoke, a large white swan walked slowly across the grass toward them, followed cautiously by a rabbit, a mole and a pair of rats.

"Anyone would think we were going to build an ark," muttered Freddy.

"I need to get down for a minute and stretch my legs; I'm not used to this heavy riding stuff."

"Well, get down slowly and quietly, no sudden sharp moves to frighten anyone," said Victoriana.

"Don't you think I should be the one who's a bit nervy?

I'm stood here at eleven o'clock at night in a park with a loose big horse, four flying ones, a huge swan, a rabbit, a mole, and now a pair of rats!" He drew his leg over the mare's back and slithered ungracefully to the ground. "Ugh, the inside of my jeans are all hairy."

The black mare ignored him, looked to the swan and started a dialogue. The swan nodded, looked to his right and spoke to the rabbit. The rabbit sat up, twitched his long whiskers and spoke to the mole. The bleary eyed mole slowly stroked his nose with his tiny claw, and then turned to the waiting rats. There was silent exchange for several minutes, then something that sounded like indignant squeaking from the rats and then a new message started to come back down the line. As they waited Freddy spoke, "Aren't rats predator?"

"Sort of," said the mare, "but they go both ways. Anything and everything, really. More like scavengers."

Finally the message reached Victoriana from the swan. Freddy and the Pegusinni waited expectantly for the news. She looked to Freddy who was now standing next to her, "They want half now and half when the job is done."

"Half? Half what?"

"The cheese. You did bring the cheese, didn't you?"

"The cheese is for them!" he said pointing at the rats in disbelief.

"Shhh, not so loud, you may upset them."

"They work for cheese? We're all trying to save mankind from God knows what type of disaster, and these little buggers want cheese?"

"They work for anyone, but only if they get paid."

"Do they go on to be lawyers after they've transitioned?"

"Enough, now, half of the cheese, please," Victoriana said briskly.

Freddy reached into his jacket pocket and got out the sweating packet of cheddar. He broke it in half and then slowly moved across the grass to the waiting rodents. They eyed him suspiciously but held their ground, having been assured by all the others assembled that this was a special human. He tossed half of it to the ground in front of them and immediately they scurried forward, got a good grip with their pointy teeth and dragged it off to a bush. Freddy walked back to the mare. "Why are we doing this?"

"I gave the matter some serious thought. If we want the drains to be properly searched we need the people who know them best, and will know if anything is out of the ordinary."

Freddy nodded at this.

"We were going to try with the mole or rabbit, but really our best chance is with them," she finished, nodding toward the returning rats. "And, they'll get under the seating and scaffold much easier than anyone."

"Can they be trusted?"

"Oh yes, they'll want that cheese again."

"What if they lie, just make up a bunch of stuff?"

"Rupert will deal with them if they do; he runs a very strict park here."

The rats were now sat back up on their haunches, front paws dangling, whiskers probing the night air, waiting for directions. Victoriana spoke to Rupert and the message went briskly down the line. The rats sat down, listened, questioned, listened again, then nodded and moved forward. They scurried to the edge of the grass, across the short pavement, looked around and then promptly disappeared down the small drain holes in the gutter at the road side. The remaining group lined up on the grass facing the Horse Guards Parade ground, Freddy on the left, then Victoriana, Sefton, Yeti, Rochester, Gauntlet, Rupert, the rabbit and on the end, the mole. No one spoke. Across the parade ground the clock above the archway chimed eleven fifteen, and everyone waited. Two minutes. Five minutes. Almost ten minutes had passed when the dark-coated rats popped back up from the drain hole. Water dripped from them as they scuttled back across the grass. They shook their coats and went to speak to the mole. The mole nodded, listened, asked them to repeat several things, nodded again and finally looked to the rabbit. The rabbit got wide-eyed as the mole spoke to him, then the rabbit turned to the swan. The swan leaned in closer, making sure he got every word. Then with more nodding, and what seemed to be a few questions asked to clarify things with the rabbit, Rupert looked to Victoriana. She lowered her neck and listened carefully.

"God, I can't stand this," said Freddy, "will someone tell me what is going on?" Victoriana pulled herself away from Rupert, straightened up and looked to Freddy and the four waiting Pegusinni.

"We had to be absolutely sure they had it right," she said. "The rats went down these drains and used the connecting tunnels to get over to where you said." Freddy nodded as she continued, "apart from all the usual mess and water, they did find something unusual; something they had not seen before."

"OK, and what was that?" he asked.

"Actually two things. A large metal box, and," she paused.

"And? And what?" Freddy asked.

"A very strange shaped shiny metal thing."

"Strange? What kind of strange shape?"

"They couldn't exactly describe it, but they gave us some clues."

"OK, clues, we can work with clues. What clues? What did it look like?"

She raised her head and neck and nodded to the skyline. "They said it looks like that, that big thing over there."

Everyone looked up and over to the night sky line. Freddy was puzzled, but then he saw it. The building that was known as 'The Gherkin', a skyscraper, oddly shaped, pointing to the stars. Some said it was shaped like a giant bullet. Or a bomb. The whole group stared silently. Then Freddy spoke to Victoriana again.

"Are they sure? Are they absolutely sure it looked like that?"

"Yes, they're quite sure, that shape and shiny and they have no reason to tell us anything different."

Another message was busily coming down the ranks and finally reached Victoriana from the swan. "Oh yes," she said, "right away."

"What? What now?"

"Payment. They want the rest of their payment now, please. And we need to get going, time is running out."

He grabbed the remaining cheese from his jacket and tossed it in the direction of the waiting rats.

"Freddy, you can use the steps by the memorial to mount again," said Rochester.

Victoriana was already positioning herself parallel to the steps to assist his second mount of the evening. She bent her knees slightly as he hauled himself back up, again helped by a boost from Gauntlet. The swan and other creatures walked back into the darkness of the park as the equine party moved forward to the Mall. Once they had crossed over the road and were again on the gravel and sand pathway heading back to Green Park, Freddy spoke. "This is really serious if they are really sure of what they saw."

"They were very sure," said Victoriana striding out briskly underneath him.

"What does it mean, Freddy?" asked Rochester who was gliding along with the others above him.

"It means some one has been down there and actually planted something. Something bad, by the sound of it." The group was silent for a moment.

Then Yeti said, "But you'll know how to fix it; right, Freddy?"

"I don't know mate, I've got to think about this. I'm not sure that there is anything we can do personally. I think I may have to call in the big guns."

"Big guns?"

"Police, bomb squad, terrorist guys."

"And they'll fix things?" asked Rochester.

"Hopefully. At least they'll know how to deal with it."

"And they'll think you're really clever, Freddy," said Gauntlet.

"God, no. They can't know it was me who found this stuff! They'll want to know how I know and they'll think I'm one of the bad guys." By this time they had reached the corner by Buckingham Palace and the end of the Mall. Again the black mare strode confidently on around behind the large wall, screening them from the road and traffic.

"'Ello, 'ello, now then, who do we have 'ere?" asked a broad cockney, masculine voice.

Victoriana stopped dead in her tracks as Freddy clutched her mane and the halter rope. Directly in front of them, blocking their path were two officers of the London mounted patrol on two very tall police horses. The police officers wore lime green high visibility jackets over their uniforms. Freddy gaped, grappling for words. None came.

"So," said the second officer, "looks like we found ourselves a regular midnight cowboy," as they eyed up and down the teenager with the spiky hair, sitting bareback on the black horse wearing a pink nylon halter and pink rope.

"Evening, sirs," mumbled Freddy.

"So, what are you up to, my lad?" asked the first one.

"Er, just, you know, riding my horse in the park, as you do," he said smiling.

"You see, this is where we're having a problem, young man. This is not exactly 'as you do'. You have no saddle, no bridle, no hard helmet and you're dressed to go to a night club. Not for riding in the park." The officers both nodded, smiled and waited for his explanation.

Meanwhile another conversation was going on.

"Good grief! Victoriana?" asked the chestnut police horse.

"Is that really you? In that head collar?" asked the fat grey.

"One word from either of you and I'll have you both on football match duty for the rest of your careers. I have a lot of clout across this town!"

"What on earth are you doing in the park at this hour," the grey said, pausing to gape at the teen, "with *that* on your back?"

"Freddy is part of an important military action we are currently involved with. Again, I remind you who is in charge here."

"Yes, ma'am," the two police horses both mumbled, trying not to stare and chuckle.

"So lad, some explaining please," said the officer on the chestnut.

Freddy's brain was in overdrive. Little flying horses couldn't help him now. They all just hovered and watched.

"You see, sir, it's like this. It's my girlfriend's birthday, and I wanted to surprise her."

"Really now?"

"Yes. You see she's always had this dream of a knight showing up on his horse and riding off with her, so I thought I would. For her birthday."

"And where does this girlfriend live, eh?"

"Knightsbridge. Just on my way there now, sir." Freddy beamed a huge smile, convinced his story was a good one.

"You see," said the one on the fat grey, "you don't exactly look like you can ride, let alone be in control of a large horse in just a head collar. That's what's worrying us."

"You could be a danger to yourself, and the people of London, lad."

"Oh, no, I'm fine. Really, I can manage."

"Freddy," said Victoriana to him quietly, "let me handle this. Just sit still and look confident."

"Eh, what the hell are you going to do?"

The black mare side stepped around the police horses and onto the grass of Green Park. She turned to face them, paused, took six very clean straight steps backwards, paused, and came back forward another six steps. Freddy smiled and waved to the police as she stopped. Without warning she then moved her entire body in a pirouette around her haunches, first 360 degrees to the right, then 360 back to the left. She finished with four side ways steps to the right, paused, and then four back to the left. The officers stared open mouthed.

"Ask them if they can do that with no saddles and no reins," she directed.

"So er, you wanted to see my controls, officer? Do the police do this with no reins?"

The officers were getting over the surprise of the dressage-talented, trendy teen and were now irritated by his bit of cockiness.

"Yes, well, very flash, but I think we will accompany you till you get home," said the one on the chestnut.

The Pegusinni flapped around overhead. "We can't have that!" said Gauntlet, "get rid of them, Freddy!"

"Me?" he hissed, "me get rid of two huge coppers?"

Victoriana once more did what she did best. She took control of matters. She looked to the two police horses, "When I say go I want you two to do a runner. Straight up there across the grass away from us. Don't stop till you are at the underground station."

"Are you serious?"

"From a standing halt to a flat out runner?"

"Totally serious. Freddy, get ready to hold on."

"Do you want us to drop them as well?" asked the chestnut.

"Good grief, no. No need for drama, just get them out of my way!"

The two officers were about to position themselves on either side of the boy on his horse when Victoriana gave the order. "Now! Go! And don't let them back onto this side of the park tonight!"

Without warning the two police horses spun on their haunches, came half way up into the air, let out a shrill equine squeal for dramatic effect and bolted across the grass.

"Bloody hell!" called one rider.

"Oh my god!" said the other, grappling to no effect with his reins as the two horses thundered into the dark across the turf and away from the little military group.

"Damn it, Vics, when you take control of a situation you really take control!"

"Quiet now, Freddy, we need to canter. It's close to midnight."

"Canter! I can just manage the walk!"

"It's ok, Freddy, we're all here for you in case you need us," said Sefton as the Pegusinni grouped around.

"Sit tall, hold the mane, and sit still!" called Victoriana.

And then the most amazing thing happened. She lowered her haunches, arched her neck and moved into a highly balanced collected canter underneath him. The sensation was mind blowing for a novice teenage rider. The controlled energy and power directly below him was staggering. The way she literally picked him up with her back and carried him easily forward gave him the sensation of floating or slow flying. She moved straight, swiftly and rhythmically down the sand track back toward Hyde Park Corner with Freddy, wide-eyed, not believing what was going on. In one way he was terrified but in another, the adrenalin rush was off the planet. As they reached Hyde Park corner, for once there was a short gap in the traffic and Victoriana saw her chance. She didn't hesitate. Adjusting the placement of her hooves for better balance, she rattled across the tarmac and onto the turf in the middle of the island. The Pegusinni, seeing Freddy was not in trouble, soared up and above, checking to see that the park gates were still open. The drivers on the second crossing side saw the boy, bareback on the cantering black mare, heading straight for the road. They screeched to a halt just as her hooves touched back onto the road, gaping out of their windscreens as the horse and the boy disappeared through the still open park gates. Victoriana slowed her canter across the road of the South Carriage Drive and returned to a walk as she touched the sand and safety of Rotten Row.

"Wow! Bloody Wow! Vics, that was amazing! Like too wild! I was really riding! Like really fast! I think I might be quite good at this!"

She said calmly, "Yes, Freddy, and I had nothing to do with it. Obviously you are very talented."

He leaned forward and patted her neck.

"What are you doing?"

"Oh sorry, got carried away. Forgot myself there." He thought for a minute, then with his fingers scratched hard into the top of her withers.

"Why, thank you," she said.

"Now we have you safely back in the park, can I ask a favour?"

"Certainly."

"Well, it's really late and I have to be home as quickly as possible. Any chance of a lift to Kensington Gardens?"

"Would you like to canter again?"

"Yes, yes, please, if that's ok?"

Victoriana didn't reply. She simply lowered her haunches, lifted her forehand and set off again in collected canter. Freddy sat as tall as he could, exhilarated again by the movement, speed and the wind across his face. And in the light of the pale moon, the Pegusinni took flight above them, silently soaring, gliding; enjoying the moment.

Chapter Twenty

After he left his equine friends Freddy hurried across Kensington Gardens, then over the fence into their yard and, as Jane knew he was out, in through the door, not the window.

"Late film?" Jane asked from her place on the couch as he entered the sitting room.

"Oh, hi, mum. Still up? Thought you were having an early night?"

"I was but half way through the glass of wine I fell asleep here. Just woke up a few minutes ago."

"I see."

"So?"

"So, what?"

"How was the film?"

"Good. Yeah, you know, good."

"It ran late?"

"Kind of, but met some people, hung out for a while."

She smirked. "Some people?"

Freddy knew he had to give her something or she would never let it end. In this mood she was like a terrier on the postman's leg.

"Yeah, ok, a girl."

"Really?"

"Yeah, what's so strange with that? I've met girls before."

"Name?"

"She has one."

Jane glared.

"OK, Vicki."

"Age?"

"About 17, I think."

"Blonde?"

"Dark."

"Long, short?"

"Er, pony tail. Can we leave this now? I'm home and it's not way late."

"Can't blame a mother for being curious. Where did you go with her?"

"We were out, then a walk in the park. And now I'm going to bed. End of interrogation, please."

"Ok, ok," said a smiling mother, "see you in the morning."

"Not if I can help it," he thought shutting the bedroom door.

He slept till almost eight. Jane was already out trying the Sunday morning Farmer's market at Notting Hill. Mug of tea in hand, Freddy flopped on to the couch, staring into space and wondering how to deal with last night's bit of news. Naturally he had to tell the police and let them deal with it. All he and the horses could do would be to sit back and wait to see what was found and if it was dealt with safely. How to give the police an anonymous tip-off was the next question. Not so long ago it would have been easy, simply walk up to a public pay phone somewhere, make the call and walk away. But now there were CCTV cameras all over the darn place, so he had to be sure he wasn't seen on camera as they would obviously trace the call and know which cam to check. If he went into a shop and used a pay phone, the staff could easily remember him if questioned. His mobile was out of the question as that could be traced. The thing was, the police needed to know now. The sooner the better so they could deal with it. He couldn't risk other people's safety just because he was worried he might be seen. He had to do it.

Fifteen minutes later, wearing his black 'Hoody' pullover and dark jeans, Freddy was walking down Kensington High Street looking for a pay phone. He saw a pub with a phone outside to his right down a side street. From his pocket he pulled out a pair of winter woolly gloves which was probably a bit paranoid but he didn't want to take any chances. Keeping the hood up and his head low he picked up the receiver and dialled nine, nine, nine.

"Emergency, which service, please?"

"Police, please." There was a short pause.

"Hello?"

"Yeah, I need to report a terrorist bomb."

"Your name, please?"

"Never mind that. It's been put in the drains under Horse Guard's Parade ground. On the north side. You need to send someone there."

"Let's have your name and where you are calling from."

"They're going to try and blow up the Trooping of The Colour and the soldiers and the horses and everything!" Freddy hung up, shaking. He stared at the phone for a moment, then tightened his hood and ran off down the street away from Kensington, zigzagging through side streets hoping to lose the damn CCTV cameras. He walked into a newsagent's, bought a paper, pulled off his black pullover, and wearing just his white t-shirt and baseball cap, walked back out. Hopefully that would make it impossible for him to be identified.

Back at home, he made the most of the empty apartment. He took a shower, tidied his room and eventually got text books ready for the start with the new tutor the next day. He figured if he was doing the school-boy-swot routine she might back off the questions about his social life.

Jane was back before lunch, loaded with bags of veggies and bits and bobs she'd picked up at the market. "You know, this is so unusual for both of us to be off and home on a Sunday," she said, dumping bags on the table, "I'm going to cook a proper Sunday roast just for us."

"Great, sounds good," Freddy's head was buried in a book.

"It should be ready for around five, so have a snack for now if you're hungry."

"Will do."

"You could be a bit more enthused."

"Sorry, getting stuck into the books here. Big day tomorrow."

She eyed him suspiciously as she started to pack away the shopping. "Hmm, yes, well, we'll see."

When she was done she flicked on the TV to watch while she prepared food. The mid-day news was just wrapping up.

"And this just in. Having received an anonymous tip this morning, there is a hive of police activity at Horse Guard's Parade ground right now"

Freddy dropped his pen, his eyes glued to the screen.

"The only information we have at the moment is the caller suggested a bomb threat. The police are treating this call seriously and we understand the bomb squad are there now investigating." The camera cut from the newscaster to a shot of the parade

ground. In the far corner there was a clutch of police and unmarked vehicles.

"We'll bring you more on this story as it develops. And now the weather…"

"Wow, they're right on it."

"On what?" Jane asked from the sink.

"Oh, just some police stuff going on in the city," he said, realising she had missed the gist of it, which was probably a good thing. The program changed to a Sunday afternoon antiques show which played in the back ground while they both worked; Freddy on the books, Jane on the food. Another hour went by and then the newscaster appeared on the screen again,

"We are interrupting this program to update you on the earlier breaking story." The camera cut to Horse Guard's Parade. Vehicles were being packed up and moved away. *"We have been told that police used video cameras to look into drains below the parade square. Two items were spotted, which were later retrieved."*

Freddy was frozen, waiting to hear about the horror of the near miss and how grateful the police were to the anonymous caller for saving so much loss of life.

"Police recovery experts found an empty metal sandwich box and a stainless steel thermos flask which had obviously been left behind by maintenance crews at some point. Nothing further was found.

"What! What?" Freddy couldn't believe it.

"Police are anxious to talk to the male teenager who made the call. And now back to your regular programming."

He was dumbfounded. A sandwich box? And a bloody thermos? This had to be wrong!

"What's up with you? Looks like you've seen a ghost," said his mum from across in the kitchen area.

"No, not a ghost. I wish it had been."

He wanted to go to St. James's Park and demand his cheese back. A damn thermos? OK, yes, it was sort of the shape of the Gherkin. And, to a rat, a metal sandwich box could appear quite large. "I need to go out," he said, picking up his books and heading to the bedroom.

"Out? Out where? Why?"

"Just too stuffy. Need some fresh air. Clear my head. Won't be long." He pulled on a denim jacket over his t-shirt as he went into the yard to grab his bike. He was needing to think. Needing fresh air. Needing exercise. Needing to figure out what the heck to do next. Without thinking where he was going, he cycled over to the park and wound his way toward the lake where he flopped onto the grass and stared out across the water.

"I'm useless. So bloody useless. Should have thought much more about this." It was all too easy. He'd just been relieved how relatively straightforward it had been to figure it out. But now, now they were back to square one. No darn clue. He lay flat on his back looking up at the sky and the scattered clouds, his mind empty.

"Hello, you're Freddy, right?"

He twisted his neck to the left. On the grass close by were two black Pegusinni, but not ones he recognised.

"Yes, that's me. Have we met?"

"Just the once, on the first night you went to barracks. We were all there."

"Yes, about twelve or so of you."

"Fifteen. I'm Cedric, this is Falcon."

Freddy sat fully upright and smiled at the two small horses. "Good to see you again. Do you know where the others are today?"

"The four you've been with this week were down at Horse Guard's most of the morning. They said something exciting was going on."

"Yes, well, it turned out not to be so exciting after all," said Freddy getting to his feet. "Could you get a message to them for me, today?"

"Certainly."

"We need a meeting. Tonight. Including Victoriana." Even though he dreaded the thought of going back in over the barrack walls, he knew they had to decide where to go from here. Maybe there was something they hadn't told him. Something lost in all the messages being passed backwards and forwards. "Tell them to meet me usual place, in front of barracks around midnight."

"Of course, do you need all of us?"

"No, I don't think so, not yet anyway."

"We'll go now and find them."

"Cheers. Thanks for your help." He watched as the two small horses took flight and disappeared over the tree tops. Then for the first time since he'd said goodbye last night he wondered about Victoriana. He still had the pink head collar in the grocery bag. She was going to spend the rest of Saturday night in the park and then return when the main gates were opened on Sunday morning. Was she ok? Had she managed it? The last thing they needed was more trouble to deal with.

His early dinner with Jane was calm and uneventful, except for a few casual questions from her trying for more information on the mystery girl. Vague and evasive was his tactic. Then Jane changed the subject.

"Talked to your Gran on the phone while you were out," she said.

"Yeah? How is she?"

"Beside herself with excitement, you know, their visit in a couple of weeks."

"Right, yeah, that."

"I hope you are not going to go all weird on me again about that weekend?"

"No, mum, I won't." Freddy had just over two weeks to get it sorted out. He'd hit the panic button if he hadn't managed it. "Where are they actually staying?"

"Here, of course. Sharon can share with me, Gran can have your room and you can sleep on the couch for a couple of nights."

"Wonderful, I get to share the bathroom with three women."

"You'll hardly know they're here. Now, help me clear up and do dishes."

As they tidied up she asked, "Out tonight?"

"Nope. No plans. How about you?"

"No, everything is back in full swing over at the house tomorrow, busy day coming up."

Later they watched TV together as she did some ironing and he flicked through school books. The usual dullness of Sunday night programming got them both off to their rooms early. There was no way he could have told her about his extra nocturnal outing so he had to be really careful this time. Deceiving his mother was not at all on the top of his 'to do' list, but sometimes a teenager had to take certain measures to get things done. Around half past eleven as he was ready to leave, he took the added precaution of using extra pillows and clothes stuffed under his blanket to create the look of a body. It was a sad and old trick but it might be enough if she only glanced around the door. He silently climbed out the window and down the fire escape, leaving the bike tied up as it was such a hassle getting it over fences when the park was closed. He took his time strolling slowly to the park, all the while trying to figure out how he was going to tell them they were no further forward. There had to be something missing from the information they had so far.

The Pegusinni were waiting for him on the grass across the road from the main gate.

"Hi, Freddy."

"Did you get home ok last night?"

"There were big things at Horse Guard's today!" Gauntlet said.

"Yes, I saw it on TV. But it's not all good."

"We couldn't really tell, just lots of vehicles and cameras and people," said Yeti.

"Is it all over now?" asked Rochester.

"No, guys, I don't think it is."

"But I thought they found the bad things," said Sefton.

"Let me explain when we're inside. Does she know we're coming tonight?"

"Oh yes, Cedric flew in earlier to tell her."

"I hate to say this but I need to get in over that darn wall again. You guys ready?"

"When you are, Freddy."

He had carefully made a point of turning off his phone and then leaving it in the bedroom. No way was there to be a repeat of that circus.

"Ok, let's do it," he said, holding out his arms to allow his escort to perform their part. Going over the wall and down the ramp he made a point of making connection with two of the Pegusinni to ensure he wasn't seen. Even so, he was soon running with nervous sweat. Realistically he figured the worst that could happen to him would be a short term in a young offender's prison.

"Good evening, gentlemen," said the familiar voice from behind the bars of the stall door.

"I'm afraid there is not too much good about it," said Freddy. "By the way, did you get back in OK? You know, on your own?"

"Yes, I had a pleasant evening grazing in the park, then returned when some civilian riders took out troop horses this morning. Gauntlet helped me back in."

"What's your news, Freddy?" asked Rochester.

He let out a slow breath and then started to explain slowly what had happened. When he'd finished they had questions.

"But I thought they removed from the drains what the rats found?" said Yeti.

"They did, but it wasn't what we thought. Not at all."

"So the bad thing, it could still happen?" Gauntlet asked.

"Yes, I'm afraid it could and probably will if we don't figure something out soon."

"This is terrible news, Freddy," said Victoriana, "What do you suggest we do now?"

"Ya know, I knew you were going to ask me that question, so I've prepared my answer."

As always they all looked to him expectantly.

"I haven't a bloody clue."

"Oh."

"I see."

"Well, that's clear then."

"Anyone else got any ideas?" he asked looking around the group.

"Do you still think it's to do with the drains and toilets?" asked Victoriana.

"I don't know what to think anymore, but probably we shouldn't give up on that."

"Very well, we can have Rupert arrange another search but with more contacts involved. A complete flush through the entire underground network."

"That might help, but I'm not hopeful," Freddy replied. "Can anyone think of any little thing that hasn't been done or said? Maybe part of the message? Anything?"

The group shook their heads. No, not a thing.

Then Freddy spoke again. "You know, there is something we're not doing. Well, at least I'm not doing."

"What's that?"

"Thinking like a wacko."

"Excuse me?" Victoriana asked.

"Thinking like a crazy, like a deranged lunatic who would dream up such a thing."

"I don't think we can think like that," said Sefton.

"No, you can't, guys, but I need to start trying. Thinking like a totally crazed freak. Thinking about the bad side of this. Thinking how, if I was doing it, when and where would I strike!" His eyes were blazing as he tried to take on the look of a psychopath. All the horses leaned back slightly.

"I need to think like Hannibal Lecter, like Osama Bin Laden!"

"You look scary now, Freddy," said Gauntlet.

"Who's A Sodding Bin Liner?" asked Rochester.

"Who's An Animal Licked Her?" asked Yeti.

He ignored them all then snapped his fingers. "Details. I need every detail of the trooping, from beginning to end! If I know all the details there's a damn good chance we can figure out just where they might strike."

"OK, we can do that," said Victoriana, "not a problem; we've all done it enough."

"Good, this is good, something to work on," he said, "so start telling me, everything you can."

"There is an easier way though," replied the black mare.

"What? How? What's easier?"

"Why don't you just come and watch on Thursday morning. You'll see everything then."

"Thursday? Like three days away Thursday?"

"Yes, we told you about it, first khaki rehearsal. Always on a Thursday."

"String band rehearsal," said Gauntlet.

"String band? I thought you had brass bands?"

"We do, but for some reason I've heard it called string band practice too."

"And this is on Thursday?"

"Yes," said Victoriana, "but very early."

"What, like seven or eight o'clock?"

"No, no, we leave barracks more around four o'clock."

"Four o'clock in the morning?"

"Yes, all done and back to barracks before the big traffic starts. Back around seven."

"OK, here's what you need to do. First off, find out exactly what time you leave barracks on Thursday. Second, put everyone one of our contacts around the city to work. And I mean all of them. Pigeons, ducks, swans horses, anyone you can think of. Find even the tiniest bits of information."

Everyone was nodding. Freddy went on. "Any Pegusinni you can contact, we'll use them as well. We have to be positive. We have two weeks to beat this thing! We are not going to let a bunch of bloody nutters win. We can do it!"

Chapter Twenty-one

On Saturday evening after Freddy returned home, Victoriana made the most of her quiet time in the park. She leisurely grazed in the moonlight, rolled on the soft damp grass and occasionally went to the lake for a drink of water. If she suspected any human presence she simply stood motionless in the shadows. A stationary black horse in a shadow is very difficult to notice; any movement at all would immediately draw attention. For a short time she enjoyed the solitude but soon her mind came back to her duty of running the equine regiment. Having missed the senate meeting due to being on guard duty, she'd had a report back from Venetia who had held the chair in Victoriana's absence.

The senate had swiftly dealt with the requirements of the new remounts and other bits of business before coming to the situation of the two geldings who had wilfully misbehaved in riding school. Spartacus had asked the geldings if they had any excuse to offer for their behaviour, only to be told that they had both suffered an attack of IFR.

"Involuntary flight reflex?" Venetia had exclaimed. "Do these two think we were born yesterday?"

"I know, IFR within the walls of the riding school? Ridiculous is what I say." Spartacus and Venetia conferred for some time before reaching a decision for a reprimand. They decided that both geldings would be subject to two full days of solitary, something which both horses would find devastating. But lessons had to be learned and discipline maintained. Victoriana would be informed on her return from guard duty and if she wished to make any changes she would, but for now that was the judgement. Venetia and Spartacus would pass the word through the regiment that anyone not conforming would be dealt with. For the two younger geldings, they now had forty-eight hours of total shut down from the rest of the herd. No one would speak to them, listen to them, look at them or acknowledge their existence. To all intents and purposes they would be outcasts, one of the most devastating punishments that could be given to any equine.

When roaming free in herds, there is as much discipline among equine as there is within the barracks. An alpha mare would have taken the lead position followed by other mares in descending order of authority; the lowest of ranks being the yearling fillies and foals. Young males were only allowed to stay with the herd until they were weaned at around six months and then they are chased off to form small bachelor bands. The herd stallion spends most of his time toward the rear, allowing the alpha mare to take care of the day-to-day running and herd discipline. He is only very active around breeding season or if an outside male attempts to steal his harem. Then, if needed, he will fight to the death. The alpha mare selects the grazing area for the whole herd as well as deciding when everyone should go for water, have play, or rest. Any wilful or bad behaviour is not tolerated and the standard punishment is to be chased off away from the group for a period of time. Being strongly gregarious, one of the most traumatic experiences for any equine is to be alone. Although the military horses are not roaming in fields all day, they have the wonderful security of perpetual equine companionship and leadership and thus are never alone. They thrive on routine and, most importantly for the military horses, they have a job to do which they take extremely seriously. A solitary horse, not working, in a large field with lush grazing, free to roam where he chooses is much more miserable than can be imagined. The troop horses thrive in their huge herd; many of them living longer and healthier lives than their civilian counterparts.

Victoriana had been informed about the disciplinary measures taken by Venetia and Spartacus and had approved. She needed the word to travel through the whole regiment that even in her absence, rigid discipline would be upheld. At her second visit to drink at the lake she had a long conversation with Charles. The two messenger rabbits had settled in well in their new burrow within the Hyde Park community. She asked him to pass on her thanks and to tell them how grateful everyone was for their part in this dangerous business. She brought him up to date with what had transpired at St. James's Park that evening and how, with the help of Freddy, she thought it was all under control. The old swan was intrigued to hear more about the teenage boy. He had heard tales this could happen and indeed it had happened many years previously but he had no personal experience. He would enjoy passing on these tales to the younger members of his group or 'ballet' as it was sometimes called.

As daylight approached on Sunday morning, Victoriana moved over to the fenced riding arena, known as the manage, across from the barracks. She let herself in and closed the gate. Any passing human would see a horse on loose exercise within the confines of the arena, which would be nothing to be alarmed about. A little later Gauntlet arrived and escorted her back across the road after the main gates were opened to allow the civilian riders out into the park. The soldiers hardly ever rode on a Sunday but it was common for officers or their wives and friends to go for a Sunday morning hack.

Later in the day she had been surprised to have a visit from the two Pegusinni Cedric and Falcon and hear their news that Freddy wanted a meeting that evening. Could it be he had dealt with all of the problems and the trouble was over?

Sunday night after Freddy and the others had gone, she gave serious thought to their situation. Despite the best efforts of everyone it looked grim. The items found in the drains appeared not to be dangerous or harmful. There had been no further information or messages passed along and when he left, Freddy had looked slightly deranged. Could this be a good thing? He'd said nothing further about meetings or plans. Only that he wanted to see the first rehearsal on Thursday. She had no idea what he hoped to learn from that as the timing and the routine never changed from one year to the next. Except that the sovereign's escort changed each year. Last year had been the Blues and Royals so this year would be the Life Guards. Meaning they would supply the four out-riding retinue horses and then behind them the mounted massed bands followed by two divisions of Life Guards leading the Royal carriage. The Blues would have two divisions to the rear. Nothing unusual in any of that and she couldn't see how it could help the teenager with any plans.

Her greatest concern was the tremendous responsibility she was feeling for the safety of equine and soldiers. Twenty-five years ago there had been no warning, just a cowardly and brutal attack on a small group of fifteen unarmed horses and men. This time there was a warning, a notification that something could occur with the possibility of hundreds being involved. At least she had the assistance of the fifteen Pegusinni and the strangely talented teenager. His appearance that evening in front of almost the entire regiment of horses on the parade square had caused immense speculation and gossip amongst the equine troops. The next morning she had put about the story that Freddy was a lost boy, stuck between transitions and the Pegusinni were helping him find his way to the right path. This story held up quite well as troop horses had little knowledge of human life, but there were one or two suspicious equine. Spartacus and Venetia had remained sceptical but didn't question her on it at this point. Victoriana would have to face that issue later as deceit was not part of her character.

Monday morning arrived and Victoriana was out on exercise in the park with Webber. Webber, of course, was out to meet Clarissa.

"Ah, it's the pink lady," Nero said as he greeted her.

"Excuse me?"

"Sorry, Victoriana, but it's all over London. The Met nags just couldn't keep quiet."

"Oh, so you know we were out on manoeuvres on Saturday night?"

Nero stifled a chuckle. "Manoeuvres, that's what it's being called? Parading through the park in pink synthetic with a spiky haired teenager?"

"We took the precautions needed to get the job done. And we did get the job done."

Nero's tone turned a little more serious. "What transpired?"

As they hacked down Rotten Row, Victoriana gave him the details of how events had played out on Saturday evening. Nero was impressed to hear how they had discovered the strange items and how Freddy had dealt with the situation. But then she told him about the Sunday evening meeting which was more sobering.

"Are you ruling out the sewers and the drains completely?" he asked.

"No, not completely. Rupert is having the entire underground network looked over today. But Freddy is not optimistic about it at all now."

"I see."

"And when he left yesterday evening he had a very strange look and attitude. I'm not sure what he's up to."

"He's a curious boy to say the least. Did you actually get him to ride without a saddle, at night?"

"Yes, we all played it very low key, as if it were something people did everyday and he wasn't to make a fuss about it."

"Only you could pull off something like that, Victoriana." She accepted his praise graciously but remained quiet.

"And the whole town is still talking about the stunt you pulled off a couple of nights ago."

"Stunt? What stunt?"

"Your mass breakout. The pseudo prison riot."

"It was simply a necessary distraction that was required at the time."

"Well, be warned, I've heard the Kings Troop mob in St. John's Wood are planning their own version, just for the heck of it!"

"Then I need to get word over there today that they are not to, under any circumstances." The King's Troop Royal Horse Artillery or R.H.A. had their own alpha mare leader but the cavalry were an older and more senior regiment so Victoriana's authority ruled the artillery also.

The group moved on steadily westward along Rotten Row, the riders engaged in their own chatter, the equines quiet and thoughtful before Nero spoke again. "Have you informed them, the R.H.A., that there may be a problem at the trooping this year? After all, they do take part."

"No. And nor have we mentioned it to the Buckingham Palace carriage group or the Met nags for that matter and they'll all be there too."

"Don't think you should?"

"Only if we think there will be imminent danger. At this point we have over two weeks to get things sorted. No point in unnecessary panic, is there?"

"I suppose not."

"We haven't even told the regiment here yet, although I believe Venetia and Spartacus suspect something is going on."

"But you will tell them at some point."

"When I have to. Can you imagine the flap those fussy greys will get into when they hear?" she responded, thinking about Whimsy.

"You do have a point. Victoriana, this really is quite serious."

"I know."

"And you will ask old friends for help when needed, and not try to take on the whole world single-handed?"

"Of course."

As they spoke Sefton and Yeti glided in overhead. "We've just seen Freddy at his home," said Yeti.

"He won't be out and about today, said he had things he had to attend to there," from Sefton.

"I see," said the black mare.

"But he had a question."

"Yes?"

"He wanted it confirmed what time the rehearsal would be on Thursday."

"Same as always. Reveille trumpet at three thirty a.m. Saddle up, form up, then leave barracks at four thirty. Usually back by seven."

"That's what we thought but wanted it confirmed. We'll go back and tell him," Yeti said.

"So he's planning on attending?" asked Nero.

"Yes, he appears to think it's very important he understands the full routine," said Victoriana.

"He thinks the big bad thing could be connected to the way the ceremony runs," said Yeti.

"So he's coming to every rehearsal," said Sefton.

"I'll give the boy credit, he takes this very seriously," said Nero.

"He's an odd but dedicated and loyal person," said Victoriana. The hovering Pegusinni nodded in agreement.

"We'll take the message to him now," said Yeti.

"And he did ask that we pass on the results of the second search of the sewers as soon as we know anything," said Sefton.

"Yes, of course," said Victoriana, "but I don't hold much hope of anything there now."

"Wasn't the message something about sewers and toilets?" asked Nero.

"Yes it was, but we have not had chance to look into that part yet," said Victoriana.

"I believe Freddy said he's going to bike over to Horse Guard's early one morning when it's empty and have a look for those, now that all the seating is in place," said Yeti.

Everyone was nodding and discussing these small points when the two riders interrupted things by moving Victoriana and Nero up to trot and heading over to the north side of the park.

"We'll see you back at barracks, after we see Freddy," called the winged messengers as they took flight.

Later that afternoon back in her box stall Victoriana was surprised to see Venetia being led into the colic box.

"Oh my, are you ill?" Victoriana immediately enquired.

"No, not at all," replied the other mare as her soldier closed the door and left. "But I thought we should talk, so I faked it."

"I see."

"They'll have me down here for a couple of hours until they see nothing is wrong."

"What did you have on your mind?"

"Victoriana, it's more what you have on your mind. And perhaps some information on what's been going on around here for the last couple of weeks perhaps?"

"I, er, I'm not sure what you mean," Victoriana fumbled at being caught off guard.

"Let's see now, how about the incredible increase in activity with the Pegusinni? Or your choreographed riot the other night? Or your overnight jaunt into the park? Or your overall distracted and irritable attitude? That should get us going."

"Well, now look here, I really don't have to answer any of this, you know."

"No, no you don't. But we are supposed to be running this regiment together and it's proving darn difficult when secrets are being kept." Venetia said firmly.

Victoriana was completely taken aback.

"I've talked it through with Spartacus and we are in total agreement. We respect your position as alpha, but we don't take kindly to be being kept in the dark about regimental business," Venetia stated.

The alpha mare slowly nodded from across the aisle way.

"Victoriana, we are not fools and one day you are going to be asking for our help."

"I know and I'm sorry. Things have just been adding up more and more each day. You're right; I should have kept the senate informed."

"Indeed," Venetia said.

And so Victoriana drew a deep breath, slowly let out a long sigh and began to talk about everything that had transpired over the last couple of weeks. She left out nothing. Freddy, the fifteen Pegusinni from 1982, the messages, the actions they had taken and where things stood now. After almost thirty minutes of talking Victoriana paused and looked to her second in command. Venetia was stunned to say the least.

"You've been keeping all of this to yourself?"

"Yes, I'm afraid so."

"And you never thought to ask for help or an opinion?"

"No, I suppose not."

"I don't know what to be angrier about. Being kept in the dark. Or you thinking you could cope with this alone," Venetia said.

Victoriana, suitably chastised, said nothing.

Venetia having said her piece was ready to move on, "Well, being angry for any reason won't help so now we all need to think what we are going to do, together."

"Do you agree that my decision not to inform the troops just yet was wise?"

"Absolutely. The last thing we need is rampant speculation and gossiping."

There was a long pause while the two mares thought things through. Then Venetia spoke again. "So when do we get to meet him? The boy, Freddy?"

"He's not keen on visiting barracks since the incident with the night guard."

"I can understand that."

"And also you are in a box stall in a troop barn with more than twenty others. How would we explain his visit there?"

Venetia thought this through before speaking again. "My present officer is not the best of riders. He's asked Corporal Major Varley on the riding staff to give me some further training for him."

"I see."

"Goodness knows why because if he took some extra tuition himself it wouldn't be needed."

"You know officers, not keen on admitting they need help."

"Varley has been taking me to the outdoor manage in the morning for schooling. Spartacus is often around at that time, perhaps you could arrange for the boy to stop by then?"

"I'll have Sefton and Yeti get a message to him tomorrow."

"Good, at least that's a start. When I return upstairs I'll make sure I bring Spartacus in on everything too. Then we can all think this through, as a team."

After Venetia had left for the evening, Victoriana felt a great sense of relief. She hadn't realised how things had been building up or how the pressure was putting such a strain on her. Having unloaded all of the information and shared it with Venetia she felt an overwhelming sense of relief. She was a strong mare but now she felt a huge burden had been lifted. Why on earth had she not thought to share all of this earlier? Of course things would be better with some intelligent input. It was always so much better when things were shared. And if things were going to play out over the next two weeks as she thought they would, Victoriana was going to need all the help she could get.

Chapter Twenty-two

On Monday morning Freddy got himself stuck into his studying, getting ready for his tutorial that afternoon. With all the late night escapades and running backwards and forwards around town he had hardly looked at his books. About mid-morning a light tapping on the window showed Sefton on the fire escape with Yeti close by. Freddy was glad to see them. He wanted to watch Thursday's rehearsal, but he needed to make sure he got to the parade grounds in time. Freddy leaned through the window and asked the two Pegusinni to find out the schedule from Victoriana. The winged horses flew off to find Victoriana and quickly returned with confirmation of the start time for the rehearsal.

He knew he had to think this through. The troops leave barracks at four thirty a.m. So, how was he going to explain that one to Jane? When did a late night become an early morning? Was going out at four a.m. considered night time? No, definitely not. Not if he went to bed at nine and got in seven hours sleep. Definitely not night time, therefore she couldn't complain. Heck, most mothers were always whining that their teens would never get up in a morning. If she got stroppy with him, he'd throw that one at her.

Jane hung around after lunch to meet the new teacher. At two o'clock sharp there was a brisk knock at the door followed by a short red-haired woman striding into the apartment carrying a brief case and a black umbrella.

"How do you do. Jane, Jane Hobbs, Freddy's mother," Jane greeted the woman.

"Good, glad to know he's not entertaining a strange woman," the woman said, shaking Jane's offered hand.

"Oh, she can be strange sometimes," chipped in Freddy.

The teacher turned and glared at him. "Excuse me? But were you spoken to?"

"I, er, just thought…."

"When adults are talking you will wait until you are invited to join in, young man."

Jane tried to hide a smirk behind the woman's back. Freddy glared at his mother. "Great, I get Mary Poppins," he thought.

"So, nice to meet you, Mrs. Hobbs," the woman said, throwing down her tartan jacket and pulling off her gloves.

"You too. Zahra, isn't it?"

"Dupree, Mrs. Hobbs. Ms. Dupree."

This time it was Freddy's turn to smirk.

"I take it you will be leaving now, Mrs. Hobbs? It's very distracting to have the parents around during tutorials."

"Yes, of course, I need to get back to work anyway."

"Good. Good, so we can get on." His new tutor looked back at Freddy. "Don't stand there with your mouth open. Your books, boy, the books. Now."

Jane smiled as she left the room. This looked like it was going to work out well.

Freddy shuffled over to the dining table where his books were arranged. "History? Or English first?" he said as he sat down.

"Who cares, it all has to be covered at some point." She had pulled a chair over near the window, kicked off her brogue shoes and put her stocking feet up on the opposite chair.

"OK, history first I guess," he said finding the appropriate book.

The woman had opened the window and then rummaged in her brief case.

"Smoke?" she asked him offering her pack of unfiltered French cigarettes.

"Are you serious, Ms. Dupree? Or is this some kind of test?"

"Zahra, Freddy, call me Zahra, for God's sake. Leave the Ms. Dupree crap to the parents."

He stared suspiciously at her. She winked, then pulled out a pearl cigarette holder, loaded a smoke, lit up and took a long slow drag. Smoke drifted out of her nostrils and floated out of the open window.

"Bugger, you are serious!"

"Sure as hell am, kiddo. Let the parents think you rule with an iron fist and that leaves us to work to our own rules. You up for that?"

"Heck yes!"

"Be warned, anytime mummsy is around we play the game, got it?"

"Deal."

"So, what sort of crap did they teach you at that school up north?"

He showed her his text books and the work he'd been doing. She blew out some more smoke. "Yeah, figures, usual B.S. that's not going to help you one jot."

"I thought this was the exam course?" he asked.

"It is, but not much use to you in the real world. Let's see if we can give you some help with coping in the real world, eh?"

"Cool, but what about the exams? You know, I need to get good grades."

"Not a problem. My friend Nicole, she's dating one of the education ministers. Let's say we have a little inside knowledge on the annual exam papers, eh?" She raised an eyebrow as she flicked ash out of the window.

"Wow, that's lucky."

"Not for Nicole, he's eighty-two, can you imagine when…"

"Whoa! Stop! Too much information!"

Her face wrinkled as she smiled and gave him another wink.

"Known her long? Nicole?"

"Since the late sixties, met her in California. Although, they do say if you can remember California in the sixties you weren't really there."

This comment went over Freddy's head as he studied her more closely. When she'd smiled he'd noticed a lot more little lines around her bright pink lipstick, and there were grey roots to her spiked red hair.

"So what problems are you dealing with now, kiddo?" she asked.

"Problems like school work?"

"Naw, I mean real life problems. How're you and your mother getting along?"

"Usually OK. She's pretty cool. Sometimes she sticks her nose in where she shouldn't which annoys me."

"Tell me a parent that doesn't."

"Do you have kids?"

"No, never married."

"So how do you know how to get along with them then?"

"Been a teacher for over thirty-five years and I remember what it was like to be a teenager."

"So what do you do differently?"

"Treat them like adults. That's usually what they want."

He stared at her. Wow, a grown-up that gets it.

"Wait a minute," he said, "what's the catch?"

"No catch."

"Not anything?"

"Just if you're treated like an adult then you are expected to behave like one in return. Think you can cope with that?"

"Absolutely."

"So, how have things been going since you moved into London?"

"Yeah, good. You know, good."

"No problems? No issues? Nothing ticking you off?"

"Not really."

"Pity."

"What's a pity?"

"Pity you just failed the adult test."

"Failed? How did I fail anything?"

"Because there isn't a teenager on the planet that's not got some stress and problems going on. Even if it's only facial zits, dandruff, maybe girl problems, maybe lonely, maybe bed wetting. So I don't think you've been totally honest with me."

"I do not wet the bed!"

"Well, you did at some point and I know plenty of teens that still do, so don't get cocky and rule it out." There was a silence between them as he thought this through. Then she continued. "Must be rough, moving away from all your friends, coming to the city, not knowing anyone."

"It's OK, I keep busy. Why do you want to know that anyway?"

"Because I can a learn lot more about you, how you tick, how you learn if I know how you cope with things. What have you been keeping busy with?"

Freddy thought it was time to be a bit more honest. "I go to the park quite a bit. Watch stuff."

"Stuff?"

"Well, mainly the horses." She looked at him with one brow arched again. "I mean I kind of like horses, seem to get on with them, you know?" Freddy said.

"You ride a lot?"

"No. Never. Wait, I did, just one time. It was brilliant."

"So you've only ridden one time but you think you get on well with horses?"

"Yeah, I guess."

"When's your birthday?"

"December. December 7th."

"Sagittarius, not surprising. And you were born in 1990?"

"Yep."

"Hmm, horse year."

"You know about that stuff?"

"A little."

They eyed each other again across the table. How much could he tell her? She rummaged in her bag for another cigarette and at the same time produced a cream coloured candle which she placed on the table.

"We going to have a séance?" he asked.

"Nope. Clove scented candle. It's very Zen. I tell the parents it helps for a good and productive learning environment. Helps your mind to open and you to concentrate."

"It does?"

"Not at all, but it sure as hell covers up the cigarette smoke."

He pushed back in his chair and laughed out loud. This lady was pretty damn cool.

"Tell me more," she said, lighting her second smoke.

"More about what?"

"The horses. Tell me more about the horses."

"Oh, well, I just see them often in the park and going to guard duty."

"Guard duty?"

"Yeah, the cavalry horses from the barracks, they go and come back to guard everyday through the park."

"The same ones? At the same time? Every day?"

"Oh no, they alternate, Life Guards one day, Blues and Royals the next and they rotate the troop horses too so they're often different."

"Sounds like you know quite a bit about them."

"Yeah, Victoriana tells me loads."

"Victoriana?"

"Yeah, she's, er, a friend."

"Now that's not a name you here much these days, is it? Quite unusual."

"I guess."

"And you knew her before you came to London?"

"No, met her here."

"Local girl?"

"Yeah, first saw her in the park."

"And she knows a lot about horses, does she?"

"Oh, like you wouldn't believe."

"How do you know?"

"Know what?"

"That I wouldn't believe."

"Figure of speech."

"Choose your words more carefully; you'd be surprised how much I believe, Freddy."

Again they looked at each other across the table and for the first time he noticed the quite long, narrow pendant on a silver chain around her neck.

"That looks pretty."

She glanced down, looked at the pendant and then lifted it up to the light. "More practical than pretty," she said.

"Is it crystal?"

"Yes," she said, holding it to the window and looking into it. "Tell me more. Tell me more about the horses, Freddy." The light going through the crystal created a small rainbow on the opposite wall.

"I just get on well with them. I like being around them now."

"Now?"

"Yes, more so recently, not so much when I was little."

"And you and Victoriana, you go to the park and watch the horses everyday?"

It was then he realised he'd been drawn into a conversation that was going to be very difficult to get out of without telling any fibs.

"Any other new friends?"

"Yeah, a couple, they knew Vicki before me."

"Local friends then?"

"Yes, they spent most of their life in this area."

"Spent? As in past tense? As in did, but not now?"

He made a decision. It was going to be easier to tell her a few things than try to be evasive. And what harm could it do? She seemed like a good sort. "They're guys. Four of them. Nice guys. They have nick names. Roch, Sef, Gaunty and Yeti."

"They are unusual names."

"I think Yeti's name is because he's big and kind of hairy," he said laughing, "And Sef and Roch are the serious types. Gaunty is a bit flaky. But fun."

"And the guys, they like horses too?"

"Oh yes, definitely."

"Interesting," she mused.

"What? What's interesting?"

"A group of six teenagers, who like to hang around in the park and watch horses. Not really typical, is it?"

"They're not all teenagers, Yeti must be over thirty," he blurted out without thinking.

"Well that makes it even more curious, doesn't it?"

"No, not really."

"Oh come on, Freddy, most teenagers in London like to hang out at the arcade, or the pizza joint, or try to get into bars. You're telling me that your group, some of whom are over thirty, like to hang out in the park watching horses?"

He looked away, avoiding her eye. "Yeah. Not that weird, is it?"

Zahra Dupree stubbed out her cigarette on the window sill. "Freddy, I was born at night, but it wasn't last night." She flipped the butt down into the yard, turned and smiled. He smiled and then the look froze on his face as through the window he saw Gauntlet hovering over the garage roof. Gauntlet was joined by Rochester who landed on the fire escape and went to Freddy's bedroom window.

"What? What are you staring at?" she asked spinning round to look from the window.

"Oh, er, no one."

"It was a person?"

"No, I didn't say that."

"I said what are you looking at and you said no one. That implies a person, Freddy." The woman was gazing at the window; the two Pegusinni only a few metres away from her, looking back. She raised the crystal to the light and peered through it. "Yes, definitely," she said quietly to herself.

Freddy was making hand gestures behind her, trying to get the winged horses to go away. They cocked their heads to one side, realised what he was saying and took flight.

"There! Did you feel it?" she asked spinning around.

"Feel what?" Freddy quickly lowered his hands.

"The presence, the breeze."

"No, I didn't see anything," he said innocently.

"You did it again."

"What?"

"I asked you if you felt something, but you said you didn't see anything. And that look, the look of innocence you have now just screams guilt."

He took the oath of silence.

"Is there something you want to share with me, Freddy?"

He remained silent.

"I knew. I knew when I entered the room. I could feel it. And your aura, it's so vibrant."

Freddy continued his silence as he shrank back in his chair. She walked up and down and then looked again at the silent teenager. "I think I'm in the company of someone rather special," she said.

"No, there's nothing special about me. Honest, there isn't!"

She smiled, "It's OK, it's alright to be a little afraid. You're not alone you know."

"I'm not?"

She reached for her jacket and pulled it on. "I must go. People to see." She quickly gathered up her things and stuffed them into her brief case. She was pulling on her gloves when she said, "Your mother is expecting me Wednesday, correct?"

"Yeah, Mondays Wednesdays and Fridays."

"Change of plan. Tell her I'll be back tomorrow. Two o'clock sharp. Be ready."

"You're leaving? Now?"

"Yes. Must go. People to see. Need to talk to them," she said as she strode to the door.

"But what about my course work?"

"Yes, yes, whatever. Read a few books tonight," she had the door open as she turned, "two o'clock, tomorrow. Be ready." And she was gone.

He sat staring at the closed door. Who the heck was she? What had just happened here? This weird little lady had gotten him talking more in a few minutes than anyone had for years. And what had she seen? What had she felt? Did she know? He sat going over what had just occurred. He'd always been so careful, and now, now it had nearly all come blurting out in a less than an hour. His thoughts finally stopped racing when Jane returned.

"So how did it go?" she asked.

"Fine, yeah fine. Zahra seems pretty cool."

"*Zahra?*"

"Sorry, Ms Dupree. She's, er, a nice lady."

"And your coursework?"

"She knew all about it. She's very clued up."

"Good. Was she a little strict?"

"A little. But she's OK."

"And she'll be back on Wednesday?"

"No, tomorrow. She said to be ready tomorrow."

"So soon?"

"That's what she said."

"You think she's going to help you?"

"Yeah. I do. I really think she will."

Chapter Twenty-three

"You talk like Marlene Dietrich
And you dance like Zizi Jeanmaire.
Your clothes are all made by Balmain
And there's diamonds and pearls in your hair,
yes there are."

The music drifted down the narrow hall to the open door where Freddy and Zahra were standing.

True to her word Zahra had arrived at Freddy's promptly at two o'clock but didn't go into the apartment.

"Are you ready?"

"Yeah, I am," he replied.

"Well, get your coat if you need one. We need to get going." She stood outside waiting for him.

"Where are we going?" he asked, reaching for his jacket and cap.

"Out, to meet people. Now quickly, come along."

"What about mum?"

"She's not coming."

"But she might come back, and we won't be here."

"Leave a note. Tell her we've gone on a field trip. A museum, say we've gone to the museum."

As with so many things recently he decided not to ask questions, just go with the flow. Together they walked briskly to the underground station and rode a couple of stops west to Barron's Court. Out of the underground station she wheeled sharply to the right, along the street and then through a large open gate built into a tall brick wall. To his surprise they were walking through a large cemetery. The path was broad and there were quite a few people walking, cycling, or jogging back and forth.

"Any reason we're in a grave yard, Zahra?"

"Short cut. Everyone uses it. Nearly there."

"I'm guessing not to a museum?"

"No. People. People we need to talk to."

By now they were out of the cemetery and she took a series of left and right turns until they were walking down a quiet street called Gastein Road. They stopped half way down the street, outside a house on the left side, number forty-six. Being close to Fulham Road, this was a very popular and trendy place for young professionals who had been buying up properties and developing them. However, number forty-six did not look like it had seen attention for several decades.

> *"You live in a fancy apartment*
> *Off the Boulevard Saint-Michel*
> *Where you keep your Rolling Stones records*
> *And a friend of Sacha Distel, yes you do."*

The woman holding the door open was swaying to the music. Her colourful full length caftan dress rippled around her broad hour-glass figure as she moved. Much to Freddy's alarm, he noticed a slit in the left side from floor to almost hip height. He tried not to stare.

"At last! Here you are!" She clapped her hands as she greeted them. "And this is him? This is Freddy?"

"Yes, this is Freddy," said Zahra. "Freddy, this is Gloria," she said gesturing.

Freddy gave her a smile and a half wave but that wasn't enough for Gloria who swooped down and gave him an air-kiss on each side of his face. Her long beads and full bosom pushed into him.

"Wow, quite the salad dodger this one," he thought leaning back and trying not to be alarmed.

"In! Come in!" said Gloria leading the way down the hall.

> *"But where do you go to my lovely*
> *When you're alone in your bed*
> *Tell me the thoughts that surround you*
> *I want to look inside your head, yes I do"*

She swung in front of them and pushed through a beaded door curtain into the rear sitting and dining room. The music was coming from a vinyl record spinning on an old turntable. He glanced around taking in the vivid purple and green floral patterned wall paper and the weird lamp on the book case. The lamp was full of red fluid and large lumps of gooey looking stuff kept floating up inside it.

"Sit, everyone sit," said Gloria gesturing to chairs around the aged dining table. As Freddy and Zahra took off their coats and were sitting down, the front doorbell sounded.

"Two ticky wicks!" said Gloria heading back down the hall. Over the music they heard muffled voices from the hall then Gloria returned escorting another guest.

"Freddy, meet Petula," said Gloria.

Freddy stood up and offered his hand to shake, but the tall, willowy lady flipped it over and kissed the back of it. "Charmed, dear boy."

"I've seen all your qualifications
You got from the Sorbonne
And the painting you stole from Picasso
Your loveliness goes on............"

The music ended abruptly as Gloria lifted the arm off the record player.

"Super, everyone's here," she said clapping her hands, "drinks, I think, first."

"Oh, yes, lovely," said Petula opening the jacket of her orange trouser suit and taking her seat. She crossed her leg to show black platform shoes.

"Drinks would be nice, wouldn't they, Freddy?" said Zahra looking to him.

"Er, yeah, sure. Very nice."

"Two ticky wicks," said Gloria moving back to the kitchen area.

"Yes, I see what you mean, Zahra," said Petula looking intently at Freddy, "the aura."

"Quite vivid, isn't it?" said Zahra.

"But how fortuitous that you found him."

"I know, we are so fortunate!"

Freddy was about to object and ask questions, but he didn't. He really was getting used to people talking about him as if he wasn't there.

"Trall-lah!" announced Gloria putting a tray with four glasses and a large green bottle onto the table.

"Oh, heaven," said Petula.

"Gin?" asked Gloria looking to Freddy.

"*Gin?*" he asked, mildly shocked.

"It is Gordon's," said Gloria.

"Er, yeah, but I'm, like, sixteen."

"Oh good heavens, Freddy," said Petula, "When the three of us were sixteen it was more than gin we were enjoying!"

Zahra had stood up and walked over to the teak book case. She returned with a shiny red plastic ice bucket. Gloria looked slightly perturbed for a moment but then, "Tonic! I may have a bottle left over from a party! Two ticky wicks!"

Zahra carefully placed one ice cube into each of the four glasses. Gloria returned with a small bottle of tonic, beaming, showing it to Freddy. "This do you?"

"Yeah, sure, fine. Thanks."

Gloria poured his tonic water and then poured a large measure of gin into each of the other three glasses. Her salt and pepper hair was in a single plait that was so long it swung over her shoulder and dangled between the cleavage of her bosom as she poured. Sitting down, she flicked the braid back over her shoulder. "A toast!" she declared raising her glass, "to Zahra, for finding and bringing Freddy to us!"

"Indeed!" cried Petula, also lifting her tumbler.

"Thank you all," said Zahra smiling and joining the toast.

"I have a question," said Freddy sitting up straighter in his chair. The three women leaned attentively forward. "Why am I here?"

"Well, Freddy, that is because you are a very special boy. And we wanted to meet you and get to know more about you," said Gloria.

"Ok, so what's my aura when it's at home? You all keep going on about it."

"It's all around you, Freddy; sometimes it's mild, but other times it glows very strongly."

"Like a warm soft light," said Petula.

"But yesterday, when Zahra said there was a visitation, she said it was truly vivid. Vibrant!" said Gloria.

"Off the scale," confirmed Petula.

Zahra just sat back and nodded.

"Visitation? What visitation?" he bluffed.

"Late in the afternoon, Freddy, outside the window," said Zahra. The other two nodded intently.

They knew! They bloody well knew. But how? How could these three weird women know about that? Choices. Again he now had choices to make. The last time he'd tried to talk to anyone about what was going on was a very long time ago and back then they were going to put him on Prozac and have him go for psychiatric treatment. For years he'd wanted to talk to someone, to share what was happening in his life and in his head. But he hadn't. He couldn't. He'd become used to it. Used to keeping secrets. Used to the loneliness. And now, these three dingbats were saying they knew all about it.

All three women were quiet, nursing their empty glasses, smiling, waiting. It was then he noticed the crystals. Both Petula and Gloria had identical crystals to the one that hung around Zahra's neck.

"Are you three witches?" he blurted out.

"Good heavens!"

"Good grief!"

"Oh no, no, no," said Zahra.

"We're just open minded Freddy," said Gloria.

"Open to all sorts of possibilities of life," said Petula.

"Or even afterlife," added Zahra.

"Let's just say we are very sensitive to certain things, Freddy," said Gloria.

"We sometimes see and notice things a lot of people might miss," added Petula.

"We like to focus on the spiritual aspect of life, not just physical things."

"We appreciate the stars, the moon, and the Zodiacs," said Gloria.

"And we believe there is not much of a line between myth and reality," said Zahra.

"And we believe you are rather special, Freddy. We believe you have a lot of knowledge that you have never shared with anyone."

"Are you a little lonely?" asked Petula leaning forward and smiling kindly to him.

"If you want to, you can share with us, Freddy," said Zahra patting the top of his hand.

This was it. This was the moment he'd thought about for years. The moment when he could say it all. Tell people what it was like. Tell them all about the craziness. But what was even crazier was that these three would probably believe him.

"You might want to top up your glasses, ladies; this could take a while."

Gloria grabbed for the gin bottle and started pouring. Zahra got out her cigarettes and lit up. And then Freddy started talking. He told them all about what it was like being a kid seeing the little flying horses. All about how he had started to hear voices and then finding out what the voices were. How when he'd moved to London the Pegusinni were there, waiting for him. How he'd met Victoriana. He told them about the evening in the park when he met Troy and the hundreds of Pegusinni. At that point all three women gasped, chugged down more gin and then held hands while he finished. He told them about the fifteen Pegusinni who were still here from 1982. But what he didn't tell them was about the big bad thing. About what he and his friends were now up to their necks in. He wanted to gauge their reaction to the basic facts first.

When he stopped talking, Gloria had her hand on her chest, mouth open, gaping. Petula was quiet, simply running her fingers back through her short, bobbed bleach-blonde hair. Zahra just chain smoked, lighting one cigarette from another. Finally Petula spoke.

"Richard, just so like Richard."

"Indeed," said Zahra. "Absolutely."

"Of course," said Gloria, "but who would have thought it could happen twice during our time!"

"Richard? Who's this Richard bloke?" asked Freddy.

"Richard Adams," said Zahra, "but with him it wasn't horses. It was rabbits."

"Indeed," said Gloria nodded vigorously, causing the necklace of beads resting on her chest to shake, "he had such a connection with rabbits. Talked to them, knew how they were thinking."

"Marvellous man," said Petula, "we all travelled to Newbury to meet him."

"That was back in about '72, wasn't it?" asked Zahra.

"A bloke who could talk to rabbits?" asked Freddy in disbelief.

"Oh yes, wrote a marvellous book all about them. Of course, all the world thought it was total fiction, but we knew better!" exclaimed Gloria.

"Maybe you've seen the book, Freddy?"

"*Watership Down*," said Gloria, became very famous in its time."

"A bloke who talked to rabbits?" repeated Freddy, still in disbelief.

"So you see, you and horses, not so special, eh?" said Petula as she winked at him.

"Freddy, when you were born where were the moons?" asked Gloria.

He was just about to say he had no darn clue when he remembered what Troy had said. "I think there was something about the blue moon and the white moon passing either side of the earth moon."

"And this was December 7th, 1990, correct?" asked Zahra.

He nodded.

"Well, that does explain a lot, same as Richard but when it was Richard's year they were both in retrograde!" exclaimed Petula.

"Which explains the Equus connection for Freddy!" said Gloria.

It made no sense at all to Freddy but he was glad they were happy. "I have to say this is nice to talk to people who don't think I'm a total nutter."

"Don't worry, Freddy, years ago when we talked to people they used to think we were the crazies."

"Or they'd blame it on the mushrooms," said Gloria.

"Mushrooms?" he queried.

"Never mind about that," said Zahra, "the Pegusinni, when do they visit?"

"Well, they just kind of show up. No special time."

"Oh, how we would dearly love to be around when there's the next visitation," said Gloria.

"Yesterday was quite powerful," confirmed Zahra, "so strong but so peaceful."

"I'm so envious!" said Petula, "Freddy, any chance we could be there? To feel them? Near you?"

"Oh, I don't know about that, they just kind of show up, nothing really scheduled, you know?"

"Do they bring messages Freddy? From other people?"

"No, it's not like that. I guess they're just around until they transition to Sagittarius."

"And will they go on the eve of the next new moon?"

"Not sure." Freddy was thinking about what they had to deal with and how they had said they would be staying until it was over. "Nothing is certain."

All three women were now quiet. Looking at him, eyes silently imploring.

"Look, I told you, I don't know, they just show up."

Still quiet, the three sets of wide-open eyes stared.

"Oh, God. Alright, alright, we'll try."

"Yes!" said Gloria jumping up.

"Oh, marvellous, Freddy!" said Petula.

"Well done, kiddo," from Zahra.

"When? Where?" asked Gloria.

"The Park. Hyde Park. I can usually find them around there. If not, they find me."

"At night?"

"Under the cover of darkness?"

"Good Lord, no. No need for that. Don't forget, most people can't even see them. Heck, the swan couldn't even see them."

"The swan?"

"Yeah, well, you know horses can talk to a swan, but a swan can't see a Pegusinni."

"Really?"

"Can you talk to a swan too?"

"No, it doesn't go that far, just equine and Pegusinni for me."

"So, when? What time at the park."

"Mornings are best. How about tomorrow morning, about half past eight or so?"

"Yes, yes," all three nodded showing their excitement.

"I'll drive," said Gloria.

"You know the South Carriage Drive before the barracks?" asked Freddy.

"Off the road from Kensington Gardens?" asked Gloria.

"Yep, that's the one. Meet me there tomorrow morning at that time. We'll see what's going on."

The three women got to their feet; Gloria to get more gin, Petula to get ice, and Zahra to find more cigarettes. Freddy remained seated, looking around, watching his new slightly ditsy friends. But now in a similar way to Victoriana when she had finally shared with Venetia, he didn't feel he was carrying the world on his small shoulders. He was actually relaxed, calmer now it was out in the open. At least a lot of it was out. He'd see how things went tomorrow morning before deciding if he would give them the rest of the information.

The three women stood, raising their glasses of gin.

"To Freddy, for allowing us to share more of the goodness of life."

"I just hope it is goodness," he thought as they chinked glasses.

Chapter Twenty-four

Before Freddy was even out of bed on Wednesday morning he heard clattering on the fire escape. Still in his jammies he went to open the blind and then the window.

"Victoriana has a message for you," said Rochester. Sefton was further back on the garage roof.

"Do you guys ever sleep?"

"No, not really."

"OK, that answers that one. So shoot, what's the message?"

"Can you be at the outdoor manage in the park around nine this morning?"

"Yeah, sure. Actually I had plans to meet some friends there at about eight-thirty so that works ok."

"Very well, we'll tell Venetia."

"Venetia? What's she up to?" He'd heard about the second-in-command from Victoriana.

"She'll be giving Corporal Major Varley some training this morning and she'd like to meet you."

"She knows about me?"

"Victoriana has shared with her and Spartacus. She thought it wise to have some more help with this problem. Are you angry?"

"No, not at all," Freddy said, thinking that he too had shared some of the information with the three women.

"Good, then I shall return with your message." With that Rochester and Sefton formed a neat half section and took to the sky.

Freddy remembered hearing Gloria saying she would drive that morning so he decided to walk and leave the bike; if they decided to go on to somewhere else he wouldn't have the bother of trying to hide it. Just on half past eight, he was walking along the foot path by the South Carriage Drive when he heard the shouts.

"Freddy, dahling!" called Petula from the front passenger seat.

"We're here! We're here!" called Gloria as they pulled alongside him in an ancient open-topped Triumph Herald.

"Morning, Freddy," said Zahra sitting sideways on the rear bench seat, cigarette holder clenched between her teeth.

"Two ticky wicks while I park!" Gloria shunted the small car into a parking spot on the roadside and they all climbed out. Climbed being the word as none of them bothered to open doors. Petula, today in a lemon trouser suit, hugged him first. Followed by Gloria in her purple caftan and finally Zahra in her tartans and tweeds. Freddy looked nervously around to see if anyone was staring yet. When he'd agreed to this it all seemed OK there in the dark little sitting room, but now, out in broad daylight, well, he just hoped they wouldn't cause too much of a stir. Zahra's hair appeared a brighter red in the sunlight, Gloria's caftan was today slit down the right leg and Petula had matching white platforms and a handbag.

"Where to now, kiddo?" asked Zahra as she pushed her smokes into her leather shoulder bag.

"Yes, yes, where now?" Petula was gazing at the sky, slowly looking all around. "Are they here? Can you feel them, Freddy?"

"Look, I don't really feel them. They just show up and we chat. It's not very exciting."

"Oh, but it is for us, dahling!"

"Let's cross over into the park, I have to go to the manage first."

"The **ménage**? As in a **ménage** à trois?" asked a wide-eyed Petula. Zahra slugged her with her shoulder bag. Freddy ignored both of them as they walked briskly to the side of the sand track.

"I mean the outdoor riding arena, there's someone there I have to meet."

"Are you meeting one of the soldiers?" asked Gloria.

"No, the two I.C. second-in-command," he added before they could question him.

"That's impressive, Freddy," said Zahra, "that you know the second highest man at the barracks."

"It's not a man, she's female. And," he paused before saying, "she's equine."

"Your meeting a horse today?" this from Gloria.

"Yes, Victoriana is alpha, Venetia is two I.C."

"And Victoriana is your friend, the leader who you told us about yesterday, correct?"

"Correct."

As they were walking directly across from the barracks, a few yells followed by a long slow wolf whistle came from some of the soldiers looking out of the windows above the parade square.

"Nice to know we still have it, girls," said Petula pulling back her shoulders and trying to push out her rather flat chest. Freddy cringed, put his head down and kept walking. As they approached the manage he could see a man in dark navy remount rider's uniform cantering a refined black horse. The small group gathered on the outside of the rail to watch. Venetia opened and closed her nostrils as she passed by and in turn Freddy repeated the action.

"How good to meet you at last," she said as they cantered a circle.

"And you too," he replied.

"Do you think you could distract him for a while?" she asked indicating back toward Corporal Major Varley, "So we can talk."

"If I can't, I know three willing souls who will."

"Freddy, what's going on? What's happening?" asked Zahra.

"Just talking to Venetia there,"

"What? Now? You just did it?" asked a surprised Gloria.

"We didn't hear a thing!"

"No, you wouldn't, it's all in the nostrils and the eyes. And the mind, of course."

"His uniform is very close fitting," observed Petula eye-balling Varley.

"Petula, why don't you stop him for a chat for a few minutes? Any old rubbish will do, just keep him talking for a while." Varley and Venetia had stopped cantering and now were walking. Petula leaned over the fence, waving and smiling.

"Hello! Good morning, Captain," she said beaming. Varley walked the mare over toward them.

"Actually, I'm not a Captain, ma'am, I'm an N.C.O."

"Well my, you look like you should be a Captain!"

"No, I'm a Corporal Major."

"Shouldn't that be Sergeant Major?"

"No ma'am, there are no Sergeants in the cavalry. The equivalent would be Corporal Of Horse, he has three stripes."

"But why no sergeants?" asked Zahra with genuine interest.

"It's believed to be a slightly derogatory term, like 'servant', and one monarch decided he didn't want them in his personal bodyguard. So, Corporal of Horse it is or in my case, Corporal Major."

With her head tilted to one side and wide eyes, Petula repeated her previous comment. "Well, I still think you should be a Captain."

Venetia and Freddy both rolled their eyes and slightly shook their heads.

"Can you believe they talk like that?"

"Not at all. But it is good to meet you, Freddy. Victoriana has said many good things about you."

"Well thank you, but she's rather a special horse too."

"Indeed, she runs the regiment extremely well."

"And with your assistance, I've heard."

"I do my part," said the black mare.

Zahra and Gloria were intently studying Freddy's face and movements as the dialogue went along. Then both of them raised their crystal pendants and looked through them.

"Look! The energy field!" exclaimed Zahra.

"I see it! Flowing between them!"

Petula stopped schmoozing with Varley and she too raised her crystal to look. Varley looked perplexed as the three women stared through the pieces of glass at the boy and his horse.

"Is there something wrong, ladies?" he asked.

"Looks like we won't have long here," said Venetia to Freddy.

"No, not at all," he replied.

"I hear you are coming to khaki rehearsal tomorrow morning?"

"Yes, we'll have time to talk then, or afterwards."

"Victoriana has told us everything about the trouble; we're all here to help."

"That's good; we're going to need all the help we can get."

Varley raised his riding crop and touched the peak of his hat. "Very nice to meet you ladies, but I need to go now." The trio were still staring open-mouthed through their crystals at the boy and the horse.

"Oh, just a moment, Captain," said Petula, letting go of her crystal and opening her handbag. She rummaged through it until she found a pencil and a scrap of paper and scribbled something on it. "Do stay in touch" she said fluttering her eyes and stuffing the paper into the top of his riding boot. The other two women lowered their pendants.

"Oh, you didn't!" said Zahra.

"Oh, she did," said Gloria.

"Did what?" asked a puzzled Freddy.

"Gave him her mobile phone number!" said Zahra.

"Bye, Freddy," called Venetia as Varley turned to walk her out of the arena.

"See you bright and early tomorrow," he called back.

The ladies busily tucked their pendants away. Zahra lit a cigarette, Petula checked her make up in a compact and Gloria took some chocolate from her bag.

"Where now?" asked Gloria between a mouthful of Cadbury's.

Freddy looked around and noting that, other than some noise from the children in the play area, the park was fairly quiet this morning. "Rose garden. We'll go there next, seems to be a favourite place of theirs."

As they walked away from the manage area, Zahra asked, "The Pegusinni, have you ever been scared by them?"

"Not really, just scared at first that no one else could see them. But never scared of them, even when I was little, they're just so quiet and kind."

"Wonderful. Just wonderful," said Petula.

"Oh, and they really hate shouting, so please, no shouting or raised voices."

"Of course not."

"No."

"Never."

"And you do realise that you won't actually see them?"

"Yes, we do."

"But the energy," said Zahra looking at her colleagues, "we will feel the energy as I did on Monday."

"I don't know about that part, I just see them and talk to them, never really thought about feeling for any energy and stuff."

"And what about the night of the eve of the new moon?" asked Petula, "Were you nervous then?"

"Yeah, that was different, I mean, there were just so many of them and Troy, well, bloody huge. You know, that night I guess I did get a special type of feeling from him."

"But a good feeling?"

"I think so, hard to remember." He paused for a moment then said, "So you three really don't think any of this is just too off the wall then?"

"Not at all."

"No, it just adds to and proves what we already know."

"Remember, Freddy," said Zahra, "you're not the first and you won't be the last."

"So other than the guy with the rabbits, you know of more?" he asked curiously.

"Oh yes," from Gloria, "how many times have you heard about other children who have secret or invisible friends?"

"Or even fairies at the bottom of the garden," said Petula.

"A few, but usually they're thought of as nutters."

"Exactly my point and do you really believe there are truly that many nutters about?"

He thought this one through for a few minutes then said, "So why do you believe this stuff? What's the proof?"

"Let me ask you a question, Freddy," said Zahra, "why would children lie?"

"Well, kids do, don't they? All the time."

"You see, that's our point, children have no reason to lie about things like this and nothing to gain," said Petula.

"And we believe that they have many more visitations than adults because of their innocence and willingness to believe," confirmed Gloria, dabbing chocolate from the corner of her mouth with a paper tissue.

"But I'm not a kid anymore."

"No, but it started when you were very young and we're beginning to wonder if there is a reason for all of this," said Zahra.

Petula had put away her compact and was running a comb through her hair. "I still think there's a connection to Apollo," she said to no one in particular.

"*You* know about Apollo?" asked Freddy stopping in his tracks.

"Of course, keeper of the herds," said Gloria standing next to him.

"So all of that stuff could be true?"

"Of course it's true," said Zahra, "do you know something about it?"

"It's, er, well, been mentioned before."

"Is there more, Freddy?" asked Gloria taking hold of his fore arm, "are there things you have yet to tell us?"

Damn, these three were good! They were onto him. Almost rumbled about the whole business with the big bad thing. He needed to think this bit through some more, maybe talk to Victoriana and the others about it before spilling all the beans to the three odd women.

"Yeah, there could be a bit more, maybe it will come to me," he said vaguely.

He started walking again, picking up the pace and by now they were close to the Rose Garden area, but still no sign of small flying black horses. Freddy stopped on the sand surface of Rotten Row, looking around, checking the skies. The ladies stood behind him, waiting, quiet, hoping that it really would happen.

"See, this is how it goes, when I actually want to catch up with them they're not around and then, when it's like two in the morning they're knocking on my bedroom window." But then he felt the familiar breeze coming from the east blowing softly onto his face. The three behind him looked up as their hair blew around and Gloria's caftan started to sway.

"Ah, here we go," said the teenager shading his eyes and looking skyward. Into his sight came Sefton, Rochester, Yeti and Gauntlet, circling overhead and spiralling down to the ground. The three ladies were looking frantically around searching the trees and the skies, fumbling for their pendants.

"Hi guys, how's you today?" asked Freddy. The four Pegusinni gathered in front of him in a small half circle facing inwards. Zahra, Petula and Gloria were anxiously looking up and around through their crystals. The small horses looked past Freddy and cocked their heads as they watched the women with interest.

"Who're they?" asked Sefton.

"Why are they poking glass in their eyes?" from Yeti.

"What are they looking for in the sky?" asked Rochester.

"Freddy, they look weird," said Gauntlet, now tilting his head the opposite way. Freddy looked over his shoulder.

"Er, ladies, they're not in the sky now. They're in front of me."

Immediately all three women dropped their upward gaze and scanned around the sand as though looking for lost contact lenses. Gloria was bending down almost looking at Freddy's shoes.

"Gloria, they're not that small and like I said, they are in front of me."

This time all three straightened up and looked ahead. Then Zahra let out a small gasp. "See! See the field! Oh my, it's pouring toward Freddy!"

"I see! I see!" shrieked Gloria.

"Me, as well! Oh, this is so special!" said Petula.

By now all four Pegusinni and Freddy were watching the three women.

"Friends of yours?" asked Rochester cautiously.

"Yes, sort of," sighed Freddy, turning back to look at the horses.

"The one in the purple floaty tent thing," said Gauntlet, "did you get the pink head collar off her?"

"No, but I might put it on her before the day is over."

Now the three women had lowered the crystals. They were standing with their feet apart, lower arms away from their bodies, all fingers fanned wide open, leaning slightly backwards with their eyes closed.

"Ah… um," they said in unison.

Two nannies pushing strollers along the near by path way stopped and stared. Then they shook their heads as one said, "Junkies, damn junkies, police should see them off." They both moved on again, picking up speed as they propelled their small charges away from suspected danger.

"Zahra, you're right!" said Petula still with closed eyes.

"It's so strong!" said Gloria.

"Ah… um," all three chanted quietly.

The four Pegusinni tilted their heads left and right trying to make sense of what was going on. Their ears flickered backwards and forwards.

"Freddy, do they have colic?" asked Gauntlet very seriously.

"No, but they're going to give me bloody colic if they keep this up," he muttered. He turned to the three swaying females. "OK, enough! Now stop all that, right now."

They opened their eyes and looked around and then at him.

"Did they leave?" asked Petula.

"Oh, Freddy, that was truly wonderful to feel," said Gloria beaming to him.

"It is such a gift," said Zahra, opening her bag and reaching for a smoke.

"Well, guess we should head back now," said Petula.

"Excuse me," he said, "but they're still here looking at you three like you're the side show."

"Still here?" asked Zahra blowing out smoke.

"But, it normally only lasts for a few seconds, a visitation that is," said Gloria.

"Freddy," said Rochester from behind him, "it's odd being talked about like we're not here, you know."

"Ha!" he said spinning around, laughing and pointing his finger, "so now you guys know how it feels!"

"Yes, it's very odd," said Yeti.

"Look! The energy! It's back all around him again!" said Petula staring at Freddy.

"OK, ladies, keep it down, let's stay calm. Obviously you see or feel the energy field when I'm talking to the guys. It's no big deal."

"Gosh, they really are still here then?" asked Zahra.

"Yes, now give me a minute to catch up with them." He turned back to face the Pegusinni, "any more news, guys? Anybody seen anything else going on?"

"Not really," said Rochester, "Rupert did have the entire drain system checked again but nothing showed up."

"And we do have the whole city on alert looking for anything," from Yeti.

"Did you four know that Victoriana has spoken to Venetia and Spartacus about everything?"

"Yes, and it's probably a good thing."

"Freddy," said Gauntlet who had been quiet up to this point and was now looking around the boy, "have you shared with those three?"

"Oh good grief!" said Freddy turning around. All three women were sitting cross-legged on the sand, hands resting on their knees, palms up, and eyes closed. "Will you three please stand up and act normal!"

The three women looked up and Petula spoke for the group.

"When there's a visitation, Freddy, lotus position is best for total immersion."

"If you don't stand up and act like normal people, I'll be immersing all three of you into the Serpentine!" Freddy turned to the Pegusinni, "Look, guys, I need to get the Spice Girls here out of the park and out of sight. Everything still on for tomorrow morning?"

"Yes, unless anything else comes up we'll see you there."

"OK, bye for now. Ladies, up please, we're done here."

Zahra and Petula stood up and helped Gloria to her feet.

"Freddy, that was wonderful," said Petula, "thank you so much."

"Marvellous, simply marvellous," said Gloria clapping her hands.

"Much appreciated," said Zahra more business like.

The four Pegusinni stared wide-eyed as Freddy strode off, leading the three women who had grains of sand stuck to damp patches on their backsides. They walked directly back to the pathway by the road with the three ladies asking non-stop questions. The chattering continued until Zahra came to an abrupt halt on the pavement. She looked around, but other than a few cars and cabs going by, there was nothing.

"Anyone else feel something?" she asked. Everyone else stopped.

"Oh my," said Petula slowly scanning the surroundings.

Gloria closed her arms across in front of her body. "Definitely," she said quietly. The mood had changed from fun and excitement to deadly serious.

"Freddy, are they back? Are the Pegusinni here again?"

"No, they've gone for now, no one around as far as I can see."

The three women stood close together, shoulder to shoulder.

"It's the darkness."

"So very dark," said Gloria.

"And sadness, do you feel the sadness?" asked Zahra. The other two nodded.

"But there's conflict. I'm feeling conflict," said Gloria softly.

Petula slowly nodded, "Yes, me too, like it's been."

"But coming again?" puzzled Zahra.

"That's it, it's been but I think something is returning."

Freddy was motionless and silent. He was the only one to realise they were standing right next to the discreet, flat memorial to the incident that had occurred on July 20th, 1982.

Chapter Twenty-five

At precisely three-thirty a.m. a bleary-eyed trumpeter sounded reveille on the parade square that was still in darkness. Not long afterwards, bleary-eyed soldiers stomped down the stairs and across to the stables. To the side of the square, bleary-eyed caterers were setting up large tea urns on trestle tables. At about the same time, a bleary-eyed teenager in South Kensington was smacking his alarm clock into silence. It was always a bleary-eyed start to khaki rehearsal.

Most of the soldiers grabbed Styrofoam cups of hot tea and stuffed a few biscuits into their pockets as they made their way to their respective stables to saddle and bridle their allotted horses. As a rule, soldiers stayed with the same horses for guard duty but for occasions such as the Queen's Birthday Parade or a State visit from a foreign dignitary, horses and riders would often be swapped around. A troop horse with good presence who stood up well on parade and had an elegant walk was a popular guard horse. If that same horse also had a stiff jarring trot, he was very unpopular for a long procession. On the other hand, a more heavily boned equine with coarse mane and tail hair may never look as good on guard duty but could have a trot as soft as a cloud on a pillow. Procession time was *his* turn to be top of the popularity stakes amongst the troopers and N.C.O.s

Generally it was worked out that the less experienced riders were paired with the more experienced horses and the younger or nervous equine were ridden by remount staff or experienced N.C.O.s The calmest and most tolerant of equine were used for the mounted band. Band horses had to be totally trustworthy and almost be able to anticipate the musicians' wishes whos riding skills are very limited when holding the four reins of a ceremonial double bridle in one hand and a huge brass tuba in the other.

Dust flew in the barns as horses were quickly brushed and made clean for parade. Drum horse grooms staggered from the tack rooms carrying the huge copper kettle-drums that would be used that morning and at each of the dress rehearsals. The antique priceless solid silver drums were only ever used when Her Majesty the Queen was present. Trumpeters and clarinet players used damp cloths to try and soak the manure stains off the hind quarters of their grey horses. A few soldiers stood out of sight and quickly smoked cigarettes, knowing they would be gone and on parade for several hours. In the same vein, many used the toilets for last minute convenience. By four-fifteen a.m. the regiment was swarming around and forming-up on the parade square, ready for a quick inspection by the Adjutant. At four-thirty, the main gates were opened and the mounted bands from both regiments, followed by two divisions of the Life Guards and two divisions of Blues and Royals, all in perfectly formed sections of four, marched out onto the road. The leaders wheeled to the right behind their police escort and headed for Whitehall. While most of London slept, the Household Cavalry was on parade.

On the other side of the barracks on Knightsbridge Road, Freddy made his own way to Hyde Park Corner, pedalling his bike in the dark. The gates at the Kensington end of the park were still closed and wouldn't be opened until five a.m. so he had arranged to meet up with the four Pegusinni when the regiment crossed over into Green Park. He arrived slightly ahead of them and took a place on the grass to the side of Wellington Arch. Looking up at the huge stone structure, Freddy recalled things he'd read in his guide books. The arch had originally been commissioned by George IV as an outer entrance to the grounds of Buckingham palace. It was completed in 1830, but was moved to this site in 1832. At one time it had housed London's smallest police station. Now as early morning London traffic moved around the island, mounted police officers prepared to completely halt all vehicles and then escort the cavalry over on to Constitution Hill, the road running alongside the wall of the palace gardens.

Constitution Hill, The Mall and various roads directly adjacent to Horse Guard's Parade ground had also been closed to traffic while the rehearsal was underway. Freddy munched on a breakfast cereal bar he'd stuffed into his pocket on the way out of the apartment. He'd also brought a pencil and small note book to jot down anything he thought might be relevant. He hadn't told Jane about his dawn patrol and probably wouldn't unless she asked about it.

The four Pegusinni circled above then came down quietly onto the grass next to him.

"Hey, guys."

"No ladies this morning, Freddy?" Sefton asked.

"Lord, no. I'm only just getting used to them even being around."

"They are definitely interesting to watch," said Yeti.

"Interesting? I spooked," said Gauntlet.

The increasing rattle of several hundred hooves hitting tarmac drew their attention to the gates from Hyde Park as the first of the mounted police appeared, closely followed by the two drum horses leading the mounted bands. The first strands of early dawn were pushing the darkness aside to bring in the new day, giving the whole scene quite a surreal look. Almost two hundred black horses guided by soldiers and musicians moved in regimental lines, with no spoken word, just the relentless clatter of steel shoes on pavement, the rattle of bright chains around the horses necks and the quiet running of car engines, halted to allow the procession past. Once mobilized, nothing got in the path or stopped the movement of the mounted regiment. Cars, buses, pedestrians, cyclists all stopped to give way. A few of the troop horses gave looks of recognition to the Pegusinni and one or two even stared at Freddy with his bike wondering where they might have seen him before. Freddy was used to seeing the troopers in full ceremonial attire when they went to guard each day so it was odd to see the soldiers wearing khaki uniforms topped with their ceremonial brass helmets with either red or white plumes.

"Doesn't this just bring back a few memories?" commented Rochester.

"It does, indeed," said Sefton.

"Good times," from Yeti.

"Do you guys miss all this, then?" Freddy asked looking at them.

"Sometimes, but we still have plenty to do while in this phase," said Rochester.

"And we'll get to do it again if we transition back from Sagittarius."

"Yes, but we may go to another sector," said Sefton.

"Would you want to be a civilian equine?" Gauntlet asked of him.

"Not sure. Life with the regiment is pretty good."

"But civilian life can be really easy, I've heard," said Yeti.

"I did several years with the regiment in Germany, no ceremonial work there at all." said Sefton, "That was rather like being a civilian equine."

"Might be easy, but it looks dreadfully dull," from Rochester.

The other three nodded agreement, watching the river of black horses flowing by in front of them.

"OK, guys, enough of your nostalgia, I need to know what's going on today. Where do they go now? What do they do next?" Freddy asked.

"They'll go along the middle of the road and form up outside the palace gates."

"I haven't seen Victoriana yet," said Freddy.

"Oh, you won't," Yeti said, "she would only be on parade if there was a crisis or shortage of suitable equine."

"Here's the second division."

"How many in a division?"

"Six sections of four," said Rochester.

"And an officer," said Sefton.

"What about the band?"

"Usually twenty for each band, and four greys and a drum horse."

"Each band?"

"Yes, of course, Life Guards and Blues both have bands."

"Wow, it's endless," Freddy said as the equine stream continued to flow by.

"Are you thinking something might happen here, Freddy?" Gauntlet asked.

"No, I shouldn't think so, not much spectacle in doing something on a traffic roundabout. Besides, I don't think this part will be on TV, will it?"

"Actually, Freddy, we've never seen TV," said Sefton.

Freddy looked momentarily embarrassed by his faux pas, "Of course not, sorry, sometimes I forget you're horses."

"Then after they form up outside of the palace, there is the escort down The Mall." Sefton continued.

"Who gets escorted?" Freddy asked.

The four Pegusinni looked at him incredulously.

"The *Queen*, of course. That's why we're all here," from an astonished Sefton.

"Look, it's about half past four in the darn morning, give me a break, guys." The Pegusinni all just shook their heads in a mildly disapproving manner.

"Actually, I've seen a picture of the queen riding at this thing. My Gran has it on an old toffee tin."

"She doesn't ride now, Freddy, she travels in a carriage."

"She was attacked once when she was riding."

"What? Someone actually attacked the queen?"

"Yes, a year before the bad day for the guard here at the park when the bomb went off. A man jumped out in front of the queen on her horse with a gun."

"Her equine is very famous, totally fought I.F.R. and looked after Her Majesty."

"Burmese, that was her name," said Rochester, "that's another story that's passed down to each generation."

"You know, to say you guys are supposed to be only for ceremonial work, you've seen a heck of a lot of action," commented Freddy watching the last of the troops pass by. A strong breeze picked up out of nowhere signalling the arrival of more Pegusinni. They were coming from the east, riding in on the first glimmers of day-break in five pairs of half-sections and a singleton bringing up the rear. They glided down and formed up behind Sefton and Rochester.

Freddy realised these were the other eleven who had been there on the first night he met them all. The eleven who, along with the other four, made up the guard from July 20th 1982.

"Where do you want everyone, Freddy?" Yeti asked.

"Eh? Me? Where do I want people?"

"Yes, everyone is here and needs to know where you want to post them."

"That's the job of the officer in charge, Freddy," said Gauntlet nodding intently.

Freddy thought for a moment before saying, "OK, let's have two go ahead and sit on the roof by the clock tower thingy that overlooks the parade ground. And tell everyone that wherever they are to keep a look out for *anything* weird or unusual. OK?"

Yeti nodded and gave directions to the front two Pegusinni who immediately took to the skies.

"And remember, everyone, I don't know what's supposed to happen or how it all goes. I'm relying on you guys to tell me if anything is not as it should be." The remaining horses all nodded intently.

"What's the name of that big three archway thing at the end of The Mall?" he asked.

"Admiralty Arch, Freddy."

"OK, let's have two guys up on there. They can check out Trafalgar Square behind them as well as watch the whole parade coming down The Mall." Another nod and quick directions to the next two Pegusinni from Yeti and off they went.

"What's the biggest thing at this end of The Mall?"

"That would be Buckingham Palace, Freddy," said Rochester gravely.

"Right, of course. Let's have a couple of guys up on there too. Tell them to look out front and rear."

More directions given and the next pair were airborne.

"And let's have at least four or five guys spaced out on all those buildings on the left side going down The Mall."

Another nod, rapid instruction and the last five took off.

"And that leaves you four to free-lance around and check out anything we think looks a bit iffy."

"And you'll want me next to you, Freddy?" Gauntlet asked.

"Er, will I?"

"Trumpeter's grey is always close to the commanding officer, to give instructions to the troops," said the small grey Pegusinni very seriously.

"Right then, Gauntlet, you stay close to me, matey."

"Yes, sir."

The Cavalry procession was now in the centre of the road on Constitution Hill making its way to the palace. Freddy jumped on his bike. "Let's move it, guys, I want to keep up with them all the way."

Rochester, Yeti and Sefton flew ahead. Gauntlet hovered to the left of the teenager heading down the bike path on the edge of Green Park. Freddy cycled rapidly along next to the sand track he had ridden on with Victoriana on Saturday evening and using the same tactic, stayed behind the tall ornate wall on the perimeter of the road as it curved into The Mall in front of the palace. Freddy wanted to get slightly ahead of the regiment before they started down The Mall to Horse Guard's Parade.

"Hey, isn't that Venetia?" Freddy asked, pausing and resting one foot on the ground. Out in front of everyone was a solitary black horse and rider followed by four Life Guard troopers.

"Yes, she's carrying the Brigade Major, head of the Household Division, and that's the retinue behind him," said Gauntlet.

"Household Division?"

"Yes, made up of the five regiments of foot guards and the two cavalry regiments," said Yeti.

"Foot guards being the guys in the red jackets and tall woolly hats?"

"Bearskins, Freddy," said Rochester.

"Will they be at the parade too then?"

"Freddy, it's their parade! It's their colours or standard that are presented."

"So what's Venetia doing carrying that guy?"

"She's a loaner. Cavalry often supply equine for some of their officers for ceremonies. She'll return to our barracks later today."

"And the four guys directly behind him?"

"Retinue, like his escort."

Freddy and his accompanying Pegusinni stopped about half way down The Mall. He waved to the Pegusinni who were on some of the buildings along the route. The wide road was completely deserted, closed to all traffic at both ends. Steel barriers had been erected and lined the route to control the crowds over the coming weeks but this morning only few pedestrians were on the pavements, night shift workers returning home and others who had to start at dawn. As the full procession headed their way, Freddy turned to the Pegusinni.

"Right guys I am pretty much convinced that nothing is going to happen today. But I am clueless as to what is going on and how it all pans out, so talk me through it."

Rochester started. "Coming first is the Brigade Major followed by the retinue."

"Then there is a gap and the mounted bands are next," said Gauntlet. Freddy propped up the bike and leaned over the railing. Another lone officer rode his black thoroughbred horse in the centre of the road directly in front of the mounted band.

"That's Willamena," Gauntlet said.

"Who's the guy she's carrying?"

"Director of music."

"Gotcha."

The bands were now spread out almost across the full width of The Mall, eight horses wide with a drum horse in front of each band. Bringing up the rear of the bands were the eight greys carrying the clarinet players. They played a rousing march as they approached, causing even the most hardened of London civilians to stop and appreciate the dawn spectacle.

"Now comes the first division of the sovereign's escort," said Yeti, nodding to the first twenty-four Life Guard troopers and their officer.

"And then the second division," added Sefton as the next twenty-four passed by.

"And here's Her Majesty," said Rochester looking at an empty carriage drawn by two grey horses.

"Hi, Daniel!" called an excited Gauntlet to one of the greys. The far side grey pulling the carriage looked surprised at the group of Pegusinni and the teenager on the side of the road.

"Good job you're doing there, McCarthy," Yeti called to the second grey. Both carriage horses now acknowledged the Pegusinni, moved their nostrils and returned the greeting as they passed by.

"That's Daniel and McCarthy, they work at the palace. Windsor greys," Gauntlet informed a bemused Freddy.

"Damn, you guys really all do know each other, eh?"

Following the empty carriage were a few single riders. Sefton indicated to the group. "That will be the Royal Colonels and the field officers and on the actual day, a whole group of very important people." Not too far behind these riders were another four Life Guard troopers who were the rear retinue. Finally the last two cavalry divisions made from the Blues and Royals brought up the rear. From front to back the whole procession took up almost the entire length of The Mall. The leaders at the front were now turning to the right into Horse Guard's Parade, preparing to form up along the perimeter of St. James's Park. Freddy and his colleagues sped along the pathway to catch up, crossed The Mall behind the last division of Blues and Royals and made their way into St James's Park. The mounted band and the whole regiment were lined up facing the parade square, giving Freddy the rear view of two hundred horses.

"Why are we standing here?" he asked the Pegusinni.

"Because we always stand here. Every year we stand here," replied Rochester.

"But guys, you're not on parade now. We could stand anywhere."

"Oh, right."

"Hadn't thought of that."

"Where should we stand then, Freddy?"

"How about somewhere we can actually see?" He quickly tied the bike to some railings and then walked back to the road and up to the north corner, crossed over and stood by the seats on the side of the square. The four Pegusinni followed suit. There were a few uniformed police officers wandering about keeping an eye on things but none of them took any notice of the teenage boy in the baseball cap on his own watching the parade. The bell from the clock on the tower chimed as the empty carriage stopped next to a white podium. The parade ground was almost totally silent now except for noise from distant traffic and a small commuter helicopter passing over head as it left the roof of one of the London skyscrapers. As the clock chimes ended, the band played the national anthem.

"Now it all begins," said Rochester.

Freddy looked across the parade square in the early morning light. In front of the cavalry, several hundred foot soldiers or guardsmen stood in double ranks down one side and along the back of the square. The foot soldiers were in khaki and wore tall, black bearskin hats. Over to the far side stood another small group of foot soldiers. Four of them were holding very long pieces of string forming a huge square shape. A lone drummer stood directly in front of them.

"Is this it? Is this the famous Trooping of the Colour?"

"It's just a rehearsal, Freddy, not the real thing."

"What the heck are those blokes doing with that string?"

"That's the foot guard's band."

"That's the band?"

"Thought we mentioned, it's string band rehearsal. That space represents where all their musicians will stand on Saturday."

Freddy looked incredulously at the sight in front of him. "You mean they don't actually show up for practice?"

"No, not this practice, this is just our practice, said Rochester.

"You mean I got up at half past three in the morning to see four foot guards running around holding bits of string with one guy bashing their drum!"

"String band rehearsal, Freddy," confirmed Sefton. At that point, various officers began yelling orders, and the rehearsal began. The two greys pulling the empty carriage set off followed by the Brigade Commander and his retinue.

"Inspection of the guard now," said Yeti, as the carriage moved up and down between the ranks of soldiers. Freddy was still having a hard time getting his head around the empty carriage and the 'string band'. The carriage returned to its place behind the podium, followed by more yelled orders and then the men holding the square of string started marching forward with their drummer playing solo.

"That's the massed bands doing their slow march," said Sefton.

"Thrilling," said Freddy wryly, wishing he'd brought another snack bar. After more marching and drum banging, the foot soldiers started to do their thing.

"Who's the guy with the flag on the stick?"

"Freddy, that's the colour!" said Rochester, "It's being paraded for their regiment."

Now quite bored with the whole proceedings, Freddy started to look around more. He wondered if they really were out of danger with the drains and sewers directly below where they were standing. He gazed along the roof tops of the surrounding buildings wondering if there was some sort of vantage point a crazy person could be hiding unknown to all the security forces. It hardly seemed possible. There would be police all over this place like flies around a muck heap. For the first time he spotted some portable toilets that were set up below and behind the seating.

"Guys, you keep an eye out for anything weird, I'm just going to nip back here and check this out." He was only gone for a few minutes. "Not much use to us; all locked up. Probably only open them on actual parade day. Makes me think they won't be involved."

"What?"

"Pardon?"

"Sorry, Freddy, missed what you said," from Yeti. All four Pegusinni were staring intently at the parade ground, re-living past memories.

"How long does this thing go on?"

"A while yet, the foot guards still have to do their march past in slow time."

"And then in quick time," added Sefton.

"This is like watching cheese go mouldy. I'm going for another walk about." With that, Freddy walked back up the road that led to The Mall, checking out a large square building covered in ivy on the corner. He reached The Mall which was still closed to traffic and completely deserted. He recalled watching some film where everyone on earth had died except for three people and all of London was empty. It looked like a scene from that movie. He looked up to the right to see the two Pegusinni patiently sitting on top of Admiralty Arch. He waved and they slowly raised and lowered their wings in acknowledgement. Then he saw some pigeons circling higher above the archway. The small group grew in numbers and then swooped down onto the other side of the archways into Trafalgar Square.

"Wait a minute. Didn't this whole thing start with pigeons in Trafalgar Square seeing and hearing something bad?" He ran to the closed metal gates trying to see through the passing traffic on the other side. The pigeons had divided into two groups, a large number on the ground and some in the air. Every bird in the square was located somewhere near the men. Men standing close together, looking over notes, occasionally pointing to The Mall and then sometimes into the air above the buildings.

Men who did not look like business men.

Men who did not look like tourists.

Men who made the hair on the back of Freddy's neck stand on end.

Chapter Twenty-six

He ran as fast as he could back to the parade square. The four Pegusinni were still watching the rehearsal. He was short of breath as he stopped running.

"Guys. We need to talk."

"It will be us soon" said Gauntlet watching the four men holding the rope for the 'string band' and the foot guards doing there last lap around the square.

"The pigeons, I think they're onto something again," Freddy said holding the railing while he caught his breath.

"Pigeons?" queried Rochester.

"Columbaceous?" Sefton asked.

"Yeah, the little damn birds over in the square with the man on the big stick," said Freddy remembering a conversation ages back.

"You mean Nelson's Column in Trafalgar Square?" asked Yeti.

"Yes, yes, all of that. I just saw them swarming around a bunch of blokes. And those blokes did not look like double glazing salesmen."

"What are they? asked Gauntlet.

"Double glazing salesmen?" Freddy asked.

"No, blokes?"

"Oh, guys, men, people. Listen, we need to talk to those pigeons over in Trafalgar Square. Looks like they're onto something else."

"Really?"

"Gosh."

"Oh my."

"So let's get going. Now." Freddy turned to walk away.

"Freddy, one thing," said Rochester.

"What?" turning back to look at them.

"We can't talk to pigeons."

"And they can't see us."

He slapped his forehead with the palm of his hand. "Bummer! Bummer! Bummer!"

"Maybe we won't have to," commented Rochester looking skyward toward a small flock of pigeons descending into St. James's Park directly behind the rows of standing military horses. The four Pegusinni and Freddy were silent as they watched the birds land. The distant sound of the sole drummer for the foot guards beat relentlessly in the back-ground.

"Where are they going now?" asked Freddy breaking the silence.

"I would think to find talpi," from Sefton.

"Right, the mole," said Freddy.

"Who will find lago," said Yeti.

"I know," said Freddy, "the chain of communication. And he'll talk to Rupert, the head swan, right?"

"Yes,"

"Correct,"

"And we'll get the message from Rupert."

"No."

"Incorrect."

"Why? Why the heck not?"

"Swan can only talk to equine, Freddy, not us."

"Well, there's over two hundred bloody equine here this morning!" Freddy said, waving his hand toward the parade ground.

"But how many of them know about the really big bad thing, Freddy? Victoriana isn't on parade today, and Nero won't even be out of his stall yet," said Rochester.

"Didn't Victoriana share with Venetia?" the teenager asked.

"Yes, but she's at the opposite end of the square now. Nowhere near the park."

"But didn't I hear she had shared with the senate, not just Venetia?"

"You're right, she did," said Sefton.

"So who's the rest of the senate?"

"Spartacus and Agatha," confirmed Yeti.

"Then we need Rupert to get any message to one of them!"

"It's our turn now," said Gauntlet staring at the parade ground. The string band moved away to the far side and the hundreds of foot guards were lining back up on the outer edges. The Cavalry mounted band started to move to the centre. They were led by the two drum horses, Achilles and Spartacus.

"And isn't that just perfect timing, there goes Mr. Spartacus so we can't even get near him," said Freddy watching the drum horses move to centre stage on the square.

"Agatha! She's in the rear ranks with the Blues and Royals!" said an excited Gauntlet, "I waved to her when they lined up!"

"And they are the ones still standing by the park?" asked Freddy.

"Yes, yes, she's in the rear."

When the mounted band were in position in the middle of the vast parade square they started to play the first piece of music that would accompany the walk past and salute to the Royal podium. From the very far corner, right on the edge of St. James's Park, came the horses of the Kings Troop Royal Horse Artillery pulling their huge gun carriages.

"Bloody hell! They have cannons at this thing?" Freddy asked in amazement, momentarily forgetting they should be running to see Agatha.

"Only for about ten years, Freddy, they never used to. Not in our time they didn't."

Freddy dragged his attention back to the matter in hand. "You four, fly over there now, tell Agatha to talk to Rupert if he's about. I'll catch you up." The four small winged horses immediately took flight across the corner of the square and came down directly behind the patiently waiting troop horses. Freddy ran to the corner, crossed the road and pulled open a small gap in the metal barriers to get back into St. James's Park. He jogged along behind the standing black troop horses as more of the King's Troop horses poured on to the perimeter of the square. He saw the Pegusinni talking to a heavily boned black mare on the end of the rear ranks. Then a flash of white caught his attention. Rupert. Rupert the head swan, followed by about another dozen of his flock, was waddling slowly across the grass to the horses.

The pigeons who had been swarming all over the lawns now took to the air. Two very small figures were talking in the middle of the acres of empty grass. A mole spoke to a rabbit.

"We need to be quick! The cavalry are about to move off for the march past behind the R.H.A.!" called Yeti now up in a tree top.

"We have a minute or so, the Life Guards have to go first," called back Rochester from another tree top. The first and second divisions of the Life Guards moved forward for their march past.

The rabbit was now sprinting at double bunny speed across to the waddling line of swans. Rupert kept marching resolutely forward as the rabbit caught up and passed along a message. The old swan nodded but never hesitated as he made his way toward the large black mare on the end of the rank.

"Division, walk *maaaarch!*" screamed the officer for the first group of Blues and Royals.

"Come on. Come on!" muttered Freddy to no one as he watched the swan reach Agatha.

"Division, walk *maaaarch!*" screamed the next officer for the last division. The black mare turned her head, spoke momentarily to the head swan but then her soldier used his legs and pressed her forward with the rest of the regiment. And she was gone.

"What happened? What happened?" asked a breathless Freddy running up to the now empty spot where all the horses had just been standing. Sefton and Gauntlet were on the grass.

"She managed to speak to him before she had to move off," said Sefton.

Yeti and Rochester glided down from the tree tops and landed next to them.

"What did the swan say to her?" Freddy asked.

"He didn't have chance, she had to move off," said Gauntlet.

"What? So no message at all?"

"Just one from Agatha to Rupert."

"What was that?"

"She told him to go and talk to Spartacus because he's standing still for a while."

"But he's standing in front of the band! In the middle of the bloody parade square!"

The four Pegusinni were nodding. "Yes, indeed, this will be interesting if he manages it," commented Sefton.

The space in front of them was now completely empty as all horses were on parade.

"Come on; let's go back to the north side. This is never going to work this morning," said Freddy walking away. He slipped back through the gap in the metal barrier and crossed the road to stand in front of the tiered seats on the north side. The sun was up and Freddy shielded his eyes as he looked across the parade ground. "Is that a woman?" he asked pointing to the single rider to the front of the Artillery.

"Yes, they have a female commanding officer now," said Sefton trying to keep a rather prejudiced tone out of his thoughts and voice.

"She'll be OK, Digby will look after her," said Gauntlet.

"Digby?" queried Freddy.

"Digby Snaffles. Actually it's Sir Digby Snaffles. He's a chestnut equine with the R.H.A."

"Gauntlet, is there a horse in this city you don't know?"

"No."

"Didn't think so," muttered Freddy.

The R.H.A. and their gun carriages had completed their walk past and now the first divisions of Life Guards moved around in two perfectly formed lines of twelve abreast. They wheeled effortlessly around the corners of the large square with the inside horses almost at the halt and the flank riders in a brisk trot to maintain the formation.

Now the horses were doing things that Freddy watched with interest. "The regiment keep their lines as straight and in some places better than the foot guards did," he commented.

"I think that's because our troopers are higher up, makes it a bit easier to see," said Yeti, "the foot guards are much lower and have a big chunk of fur hanging in their eyes. Makes it a bit tricky."

The band played on, changing music to suit each regiment as they marched past the podium. As the last of the cavalry divisions completed their walk past, the director of music standing alone out in front of even the drum horses, signalled a change in tempo for the trot past. Dirt and sand flew up into the morning air as hundreds of hooves and wheels from gun carriages moved briskly around the parade ground.

Freddy looked to his right, "I don't believe it!"

"Oh my!" said Rochester.

"Gosh!" from Gauntlet.

"Can't say he's not determined," said Rochester. They were all staring at the head swan of St. James's Park as he pushed his way through the gap Freddy had made in the railing and waddled across the road. And if this wasn't an odd enough sight, he was followed in single file by a dozen members of his white flock. All looking very serious. All waddling along behind each other, almost in step as though they too were on parade.

The first gun carriage for the R.H.A. was thundering toward them in trot down the north side of the square. The music blared. The swans kept very close to the railings but kept moving forward. Freddy and the Pegusinni behind the barriers were speechless as they watched this drama play out. Hooves and guns roared by but the swans were unperturbed. Several of the R.H.A. equine gawked at them in disbelief as they moved past at a spanking trot. Some of the R.H.A. soldiers tried to signal riders behind them as a warning. And still the swans waddled on.

Eventually Rupert stopped half way down the side of the square. All swans behind him promptly stopped too. He was parallel with the front of the mounted band, directly across from Spartacus. The last of the R.H.A. moved past and were followed by the first divisions of the Life Guards, twelve abreast on towering black horses approaching at a brisk trot. And Rupert stepped out in front of them. He moved slowly, still followed by his own loyal troopers. The riders on the front twelve horses saw what was in their path and looked nervously at each other from under their brass helmets. What to do? A dozen swans now lined up side ways directly in front of the advancing division.

"Oh my God," muttered Freddy, "they're going to get splattered!"

The swans stood their ground. The music from the band changed tempo and went off key as musicians saw what was happening. The front rank of cavalry horses slowed to a walk.

"Keep moving!" yelled the officer convinced the wretched swans would move out of his way.

Hundreds of foot guards peered out from underneath their bearskin hats, not believing what they were seeing. And the swans didn't budge. The first division of the Life Guards was now only several yards away, breaking up their straight dressing and the ranks wavering as bewildered troopers wondered what to do. All the front horses were now walking. The officer cantered forward in front of the stationary rank of swans, waving his sword in the air and screaming at them. The band music was more of a pathetic distant whine as more and more musicians lowered their instruments and gaped. The mounted officer stopped, lowered his sword and looked around for the Brigade Major. The front rank of the Life Guards slithered to a halt only a few yards from the line of immobile olor. The horses coming directly up behind skidded to halt behind the front ranks, soldiers and equine wondering what on earth could have stopped the cavalry. The few police officers around the square shielded their eyes as they too looked over, not comprehending what was happening. Within a few moments everything and everyone on the parade square was stationary. The bell from the clock tower chimed soulfully, breaking the silence.

Finally four of the metropolitan police officers reached the line of swans with the intention of chivvying them back to the park. As Rupert made his way steadfastly across the parade ground the remaining twelve turned to face the approaching policemen. With their rears to the cavalry, each swan slowly opened his wings to full span, snaked his neck forward and gave a menacing spit toward the police. In their training the policemen had been taught how to deal with traffic offences. They had been taught how to deal with shoplifters. They had received training on domestic violence and abuse. They knew how to cope with road accidents when people had been hurtled through windshields and splattered across the tarmac. But nowhere in the manual did it say, "this is what to do if you really piss off twelve swans on Horse Guard's Parade." And still Rupert waddled on his own toward Spartacus.

It was at this point that the left flank clarinet player on his grey horse at the rear of the band could no longer contain himself. Slowly he raised his instrument to his lips and as the reed of the clarinet started to vibrate, the haunting sound of *Tchaikovsky*'s most famous piece of music, the theme from Swan Lake, floated across the silent parade ground.

Dee, de de de de dee,
De dee de dee
De de de de dee.

The musicians to his right chuckled, joined in and shortly every one of the eight clarinet players were giving it their all. The shoulders on the foot guards began to shake as they failed to contain their laughter. The four police officers looked hopelessly at each other and then joined in the humour. Tuba and trombone players now were in full swing with the rest of the cheeky musicians as the ballet music gained volume and momentum.

Dah dah dah de de dah de dah.......

The rows of cavalry troopers rested their swords on their shoulders, pushed back their helmets and surrendered to laughter with even the officers joining in. The director of music, recognising that all sense of order was lost, turned his horse around to face the band and yelled, "If you bloody fiddlers and blowers are going to do it, do it right!" With that he raised his baton and started to conduct.

The four police officers in front of the swans were now holding each other up in hysterics, laughing at the hopelessness of the situation. Then two of them stepped to the side and started to perform little ballet steps in their huge shiny police boots and with hands over their heads they went into their own *pas de deux*. As the foolishness continued the twelve swans relaxed their guard, folded their wings and stood demurely and innocently watched the show. The music from the mounted band reached its climax and the police dance came to an end as Rupert finished talking to the drum horse, then made his way back to his own troops. As he waddled past, the swans all turned to their right and in a neat single file followed him back down the side of the square. The music came to a crashing end, musicians rocked with laughter and several hundred foot guards burst into spontaneous applause. The swans reached the railings and as they were about to step through the gap, Rupert turned to give the hundreds of military personal one last look. A look that said "Don't ever think you can mess with me in my park."

Behind the railings in front of the seating Freddy and the four Pegusinni were speechless, shaking their heads in disbelief at what had just happened.

"Guys, I think we better get out of here. Fast," said Freddy looking around as the parade re-grouped and police officers started to look seriously around for anything else unusual. The band was regaining composure and the foot guards were straightening themselves up. Cavalry riders adjusted their dressing by the left and prepared to move off again.

The fair-haired teenager legged it rapidly across the road and over the fence into St. James's Park before anyone started to ask him questions. The four Pegusinni took to the skies and moved up and down The Mall and over the square to bring in all the others from their guard and look-out positions. Freddy had called for a meeting on the empty lawns of the park.

He flopped on the grass and leaned back on his elbows waiting for all fifteen of them to assemble.

"I definitely think Spartacus got his message," said Rochester as the last of the group glided in folded their knees and settled down into resting position.

"What actually happened?" asked Bandit who had been positioned on top of Buckingham Palace and missed the action on the square. Freddy quickly went through the series of events, how the pigeons had seen or heard something and how in turn they had past the message on to the swan.

"So now we have to wait for the regiment to return to barracks to hear what Spartacus knows, right?" Gauntlet asked.

"Yep, we do," said Freddy. "Anyone else see anything weird or unusual out there?" Nearly all the Pegusinni were shaking their heads.

"No."

"Not really."

"Nothing from where I was standing."

"Nothing from the palace end."

One little winged horse was not shaking his head; he was looking thoughtful, pondering something.

"Cedric? Did you see or notice anything?" Freddy asked noting his manner.

"I'm not sure if it's important or not."

"Tell us, anything could be useful at this stage."

"You know, I was the last one at the top of The Mall on the building roof before the turn onto the approach road to Horse Guards?"

"Yes, what happened?"

"Nothing really happened. But the man on the tall stick was acting oddly."

"The tall stick? You mean Nelson's Column in the square? That man?" asked a puzzled Freddy.

"No, the other tall stick close to The Mall." He turned his neck and indicated to what he was talking about. Freddy got to his feet, shielded his eyes and looked in the direction. And looked directly at the monument for the Duke of York. The monument he recalled looking at when he first explored the area. The tall column with the small railed walk-way all around the top.

"You mean there was a real man, not a statue up there?"

"Oh, the statue is still on the top but the man was hiding at the back and then some times peeped out to see what was going on?"

"Oh, my God! You're serious? A guy was up at the top of the tower, sneaking a look at what was going on?"

"Yes, and he did funny things to his eyes."

"Funny things? What funny things?"

All fourteen of the other Pegusinni were silent, locked on to Cedric as he spoke.

"He poked black tubes into his eyes."

"Black tubes? What the hell are,... wait, do you mean binoculars?"

"He poked the tubes in his eyes and sort of stared in them."

"Stared into them when he was facing Horse Guards?"

"Yes. And in particular when Daniel and McCarthy went by."

"Daniel and Mc..?" Freddy couldn't finish his question before Gauntlet jumped up.

"Daniel! Daniel and McCarthy! They were pulling the carriage, Freddy!"

"You mean the empty carriage we saw earlier?"

"Yes, but, Freddy, it won't be empty on trooping day!"

Freddy's jaw dropped as he remembered whose birthday parade it actually was.

"Oh bugger," he said as he realised who would be sitting in that carriage in two weeks time

Chapter Twenty-seven

After the meeting in St. James's Park, Freddy biked back to Kensington and let himself in through the front door. It was about eight a.m.

"Where've you been?" asked his mother from the kitchen area.

"Just out on my bike."

"This early?"

"Yeah, woke up early and I'll probably be in most of the day doing book work."

"Tea?"

"Please," Freddy sat down and kicked off his trainers.

"Zahra coming today?"

"No, shouldn't be, it's Thursday."

"She doesn't seem to pay much attention to what day of the week it is, I've noticed. Just shows up when she likes."

"Well, sometimes she's changed the schedule."

"Where did you two get to on Tuesday then?" Jane asked, pouring him a mug of tea.

"Oh, out and about and we met a couple of her friends."

"What? For school related stuff?"

"Sort of, they're really smart people. We had a discussion about some books."

"Books? What books?"

"One was written back in the seventies about rabbits."

"Watership Down?"

"Yeah, that was it."

"My, I remember buying my own paperback copy of that when I was a kid. Great book."

"Yeah, sounds it."

"So, is it on your list of books for the exams?"

"Think so, might be."

"You feeling OK about the exams then?"

"Zahra's pretty confident about them, so I guess I am."

She put her own mug back onto the table, "OK, I'm off to work, can you do the dishes when you're done?"

"Yep, sure, no problem."

At the same time in Knightsbridge, the regiment had returned to barracks, horses unsaddled, breakfast feeds finally given and tired soldiers headed off for their own food. Doing almost a full day's work before eight a.m. gave a person an appetite. Rochester, Sefton, Yeti and Gauntlet were resting on top of the barrack walls waiting for activity to settle down. When the last of the troopers left the stables area it was quiet, except for the sound of two hundred horses greedily eating. Sefton and Rochester headed up to the Blues and Royals stables to talk to Spartacus and at the same time Yeti and Gauntlet headed to the sick bay area.

"How was it?" asked an anxious Victoriana, "all go smoothly? Any problems? Any signs of trouble?"

Yeti spoke first. "It started out fairly normal and we had to tell Freddy about a lot of things."

"The parade and everything were going smoothly until Freddy and the columbaceous saw some bad men," said Gauntlet.

"Bad men? What bad men? What were they doing? Who were they?"

"We don't know yet, not until the others talk to Spartacus, he has a message."

"A message? Who from?"

"From the birds in the square. We think about the men. They got a message to Rupert."

"And Rupert managed to speak to Spartacus?"

"Yes."

"In the middle of khaki rehearsal for the trooping?"

"Yes, it was, er, different this year," said Yeti.

"Quite different," agreed Gauntlet, nodding.

"Oh, and Cedric saw another man on top of the tall stick."

"Poking things in his eyes."

At that point Sefton and Rochester glided quietly in.

Victoriana asked immediately, "Have you spoken to Spartacus?"

"Yes, we have," said Rochester.

"And you got the message?"

"Yes, but we think he should speak to Freddy."

Victoriana looked perturbed, "why, what's wrong?"

"Spartacus said the message is long, a lot of words, and they don't make much sense to him," said Rochester.

"He would like to pass it on directly to Freddy if he could," from Sefton.

"Yes, of course, if that's what he wants, then he must," said the alpha mare, "can you speak to Freddy today and arrange that?"

"Gauntlet and I will go right away," said Yeti.

"Very well, try to arrange a meeting here in barracks late this evening. That way I can be kept informed." Most years she was rather glad not to have to be involved with the trooping and all the practices but this year was different.

Victoriana was already finding it frustrating not to be out with her regiment when there was the possibility of danger. And this had only been the khaki rehearsal.

At around nine-thirty a.m. Freddy was sprawled on the couch, trying to recover from his three-thirty start. He'd only just closed his eyes when he heard the familiar rattle on the fire escape. Yawning, he got up and pulled back the blind.

"You need to meet Spartacus," said Gauntlet without any hesitation.

"He wants to pass the message directly to you, Freddy," said Yeti.

"He does?"

"Yes, can you come for a late meeting in barracks this evening?"

"Oh guys, you know I really don't like going back in over the wall now, you know, after that close call."

"Yes we can understand that," said Yeti nodding.

"Could you meet him in the park when he's on exercise?" asked Gauntlet.

"Yeah, maybe could do that. Tomorrow is Friday, right? So tell him I'll try to be in the park when he's there."

"Very well, around nine?"

"Freddy, will you be able to distract his rider while you talk to him?"

"No, but I know some people who can. I'll take care of it."

"And you do remember Saturday?"

"What's Saturday?"

"First dress rehearsal, Major General's Review, trooping."

"What time is that one? Not as early I hope?"

"No not at all, parade starts on Horse Guards at eleven."

Freddy was nodding, "OK, we need to be there, see the whole thing in daylight this time. Maybe we'll see something else that might help."

The pair of Pegusinni left and he pulled out his mobile phone.

"Zahra? Hi, it's Freddy."

He took a few minutes to explain that he would like to talk to her and her two friends today, if possible.

"Of course, Freddy, we are all over at the shop."

"Shop?"

She explained that Gloria and Petula ran a clothing shop just off Fulham Palace Road. She told him to get the tube to Baron's Court where he had gone with her on Tuesday and then gave him directions to St. Dunstan's Road just behind Charing Cross hospital where the shop was located.

"So much for a sleepy day on the couch, catching up," he thought, running down the steps from the apartment. The ride to Baron's Court was short and he easily found the street but finding the shop was another matter. He was positive Zahra had said *"Men's Wear By Us,"* but he couldn't see it. He thought it a bit unusual that Gloria and Petula ran a men's clothing shop but on the other hand there was nothing 'usual' about any of them. On his second walk down the street he spotted it on the other side of the road. *"Men Swear Bi Us."*

"OK, catchy," he thought as he dodged traffic crossing the road, then paused to look in the window. "Must be fancy dress or costume hire," as he looked at the ladies ball gowns and models with huge wigs. A bell jangled above the door as he pushed it open.

"Hello?" Looking around the well lit interior he saw several neon wall signs.

"Tiaras from Thailand"
"Boas from Brazil"
"Stilettos size 7 to 13"

"Cooee! Two ticky wicks!" Gloria called from the rear shop behind the counter. Freddy cocked his head to one side looking at a signed framed photo on the wall. It was a man with a beard wearing a sequined ball gown.

"Oh, that's one of our best customers!" exclaimed Gloria bursting through the glass beaded curtain, "Della Catessen!"

"Hi, Gloria."

"Hello, dear boy! A lovely, unexpected visit!"

"So it's a fancy dress shop? Costumes and stuff?"

"Er, yes, sort of. Now, come through. Come through!"

He followed her back through the curtain into a room that was surprisingly spacious. Racks of clothing, shelves stacked with shoes and handbags, and feathers everywhere. In the centre of the room Petula was sitting behind a sewing machine on a large work table.

"Freddy! Lovely surprise," she exclaimed looking up.

"Hi, Petula."

"Hey, kiddo," called Zahra from a chair near the work table.

"Zahra, hi," said Freddy.

"Here, sit, young man!" said Gloria pulling a bag of glittery sequins off a chair. Petula put her head back down and the sewing machine whirred into life as she attached a line of pink frills to a dress.

"Shan't be a minute, but must get this done before I can talk!"

"Who's it for?" asked Zahra.

"Kitten, Kitten Kaboodle, she's opening over at Vauxhall tonight."

Zahra blew out smoke, "solo act?"

"No, she's teamed up with Tequila Mockingbird for a double act. Running all week." She pressed the pedal to release the tension on the pink thread, pulled it through and snipped it off. "Done!"

Freddy had no idea who or what they were talking about. Part of him wanted to ask but a voice from the back of his mind told him to leave well alone. Gloria was standing over a small sink filling the kettle. "We'll have tea in two ticky wicks!"

"Biscuits, Freddy? Or, we have some special brownies," said Zahra lifting a tin box down from a shelf.

"Brownies, dahling?" asked Petula, "it's barely eleven o'clock!"

"A biscuit will be fine," said Freddy. The ladies busied around clearing fabrics off the work table and organising tea cups and milk. "So you all own the shop?" he asked.

"Not me," said Zahra, "these two are business partners now. I teach. Well, you know that."

"I started the shop back in the late seventies," said Gloria swishing back in her floral caftan and putting the tea pot on the table, "then Pet here joined me about ten years ago."

"I used to have a maternity clothing shop over in Bayswater," said Petula pouring milk into cups.

"Girls that go plump in the night," confided Zahra.

Freddy was perplexed. "What?"

"The name of my shop, Girls That Go Plump In The Night," said Petula.

"Oh, gotcha."

"Anyway, being preggy became terribly out of fashion with the city girls in the eighties and nineties so I chucked it in and used the capital to be a partner here."

"It's an excellent business," said Zahra nodding gravely, "customers from all over the country."

"There's one group from Blackpool that hire a mini bus to come for a full day of fittings and shopping," said Gloria proudly.

Freddy remained silent, nodding and sipping the hot tea.

"So, Freddy, why do you want to talk to us?" asked Zahra.

"Oh, but first," said Gloria reaching over and putting her hand on the back of his wrist, "we need to thank you so much for yesterday, such a special time for all of us."

Petula was stirring her tea. "Indeed, you truly are a gifted and special boy, Freddy. So glad we found you."

"Or, did you find us?" asked Zahra with one eyebrow raised.

"Kismet, definitely Kismet," announced Gloria now licking the chocolate from her biscuit.

"Well, whatever it was or is, I need to ask you a favour." Freddy said.

"Us? A favour from us, Freddy?"

"Yes," Freddy put down his tea cup, "something has come up and I decided I need help, if you can."

"Yes, of course, dear boy," Petula said.

"You just name it, kiddo," said his tutor blowing small smoke rings.

Gloria asked, "Is it a big problem?"

"There's kind of two. One immediate one for tomorrow morning, and one that's bigger but happening over the next couple weeks." On the short train ride over Freddy had decided he would tell them everything. Everything about what he thought was going to happen, how he'd become involved, where they were now. All of it.

He leaned forward, knitting his fingers together and resting them on the table. Then he took a deep breath and started his story. As he talked, the three women became more and more engrossed. They didn't even asking questions; they just listened and absorbed all of the details. Of course they already knew about the Pegusinni and how

Freddy could communicate with equine but when he got to the part about who the fifteen little winged horses actually were they couldn't keep silent.

"Oh Lordy, Lordy, Lordy," said Zahra quietly, lighting a fresh smoke from the one in her holder. Gloria had pushed back her chair and her hand was on her ample bosom.

"Oh, the poor little things, I remember the day so well. Horrid. Just horrid."

Petula had stood up and reached for a tissue from her bag. "We were all here, Freddy, in the city that day." She dabbed her eye.

"The poor boys and the beautiful horses," said Gloria slowly nodding as she recalled the events, "three soldiers and nine horses wasn't it?"

"No, four men and seven horses," said Freddy, "but the horses are sort of ok. Those seven transitioned to Pegusinni that day and the rest of the horses transitioned in later years."

"But the soldiers, what about the poor soldiers?" Petula asked from behind her tears.

"I honestly don't know about them, Petula, I think I'm limited to equine and all that goes with them."

"And Freddy, did you know about the poor bandsmen in Regent's Park, on the same day? So many of them died too."

Blowing smoke from the corner of her mouth, Zahra leaned forward, "you know they were playing a selection of music from 'Oliver' that afternoon? And I've heard that to this day their regiment has never played any of that music again."

All three women nodded quietly and then looked back to Freddy, waiting for him to continue. As more details came forward, they became less emotional and more practical with their questions.

"So twenty-five years later, everyone of them is still here?" checked Zahra as she absently twisted her crystal around. "All fifteen of the horses?"

"Yep."

"And now you, with them and the horses at the barracks, are trying to prevent some sort of horrendous disaster?" asked Gloria.

"Yep, I guess." He kept going, telling the women about the messages and the information they had and how they were convinced it was something to do with this years Trooping. He told them about checking the drains and how nothing was there. He told them about the khaki Trooping that morning and what had happened.

"My God!" said Petula, standing and tucking her white blouse into the trousers of today's suit which was sage green, "I told you yesterday, this is Apollo!"

"His name has come up before," Freddy said, "Troy told me about him."

"I know! And I told you about him too," said Petula pacing about, "he's the keeper of the herds. He's made sure that you are here to help them all! That's why the Pegusinni have been around you since you were a child."

Zahra and Gloria were nodding in agreement.

"It all makes sense now," Zahra said.

Freddy was silent, looking very worried. Gloria patted the back of his wrist again.

"What's the matter? We now know why you are gifted, and how you can help them."

He was slowly shaking his head. "But I don't think I can. It's too much. I don't think I can work it out and," he paused then very quietly said, "I get scared, I don't think I'm brave enough."

"Oh dear boy!" said Gloria jumping up, grabbing him and squashing his face into her bosom. "Of course, you are!"

"Look at how brave you've already been," said Zahra between puffs.

Freddy managed to push back from Gloria and return to his seat.

"Brave? Already? I don't think so."

Petula sat back down again at the table. "Freddy, the first night you met the Pegusinni, were you a little nervous? A little afraid, perhaps?"

"Yeah, kind of."

"But you went with them anyway?"

"Yes, I did."

"And then late at night they flew you over a wall into a highly secure barracks to meet an alpha mare, pretty much in darkness. Correct?"

"Yep."

"And were you a little frightened then too?"

Zahra saw where she was going with this so she stepped in. "And in the middle of the night, all alone in Hyde Park on the eve of the new moon you met a huge flying horse that landed on its hind legs, rearing and striking?"

"Oh, yeah, sure. Troy."

"And one night the guards caught you and were going to lock you up but Victoriana and the herd rescued you, correct?"

"Yes."

"And were you a little frightened that night too?"

"Frightened? I was bricking it!"

Gloria then came in. "And did you not ride a huge black horse, without a saddle or bridle, in darkness from the park to Horse Guards and back?"

"Yeah, that was a bit of a trip."

All three ladies were now slowly shaking their heads and smiling.

"And Freddy, you have done all of these things in the last couple of weeks and you think you're not brave?" Petula asked still smiling at him.

"Well, no, I've been terrified at times."

"But Freddy, that's what brave is all about! You were very scared but you still did all these things."

"And it's OK to be scared sometimes," Gloria said, "we're all scared of something at some point."

"And it's OK to be scared and sometimes not do things," said Zahra, "It's not brave, but it's still OK."

Gloria got to her feet again. "So we need to be organised! Here's what I think we should do. First, I'm going to close the shop for the rest of the day."

Everyone else listened and nodded.

"Then we'll get some yummy tofu and watercress sandwiches for lunch and then we will all sit here, go over every detail and come up with a plan!"

"Wow, really?" Freddy asked.

"Of course," said Zahra now on her feet, "you're not alone now, kiddo, you have a team."

"This is really nice of you ladies, but I can only ask you to help out tomorrow morning, you know distracting Spartacus's rider. I can't ask for more, it could be a bit dangerous."

"Dangerous? Bloody dangerous?" asked Petula but not waiting for an answer. "If you're worried there actually might be terrorists involved with this, let me tell you something, my lad." She paused, leaning over the table staring him in the eye. "After the lives we've had, do you actually think the three of us are going to be bothered by a few wimpy terrorists?"

Zahra was aggressively grinding a butt into the ashtray. "Kiddo, let me assure you, any gutless men out there who think they can mess with our boy and his horses had better look out." She gestured to her friends, "these three old broads don't take prisoners."

Freddy stared back at her, wide-eyed, slowly nodding his head. He now wondered if he should warn any terrorists out there what they were about to take on.

Chapter Twenty-eight

They met at eight thirty on Friday morning on the South Carriage Drive where once again Gloria managed to find a parking spot to the west of the barracks. They had spent the previous afternoon discussing every detail they knew about, trying to make more sense of the first message and then deciding which of the ladies would be doing what on Saturday morning at the dress rehearsal. Zahra would be taking notes on everything and anything; Gloria would be taking photographs of locations, people and things anyone else thought they should have a photo of. Because of her photographic memory with men Petula was going to be scanning the crowds, memorising anyone she thought a bit suspicious and telling Gloria to get a picture if possible.

"How do you get a photographic memory?" Freddy had asked.

"It's just a little gift," she'd replied demurely.

"She once dated one of the band members of 'The Kinks'," Gloria stated, "ages before they were famous."

"They were doing a gig at the end of Brighton pier," Zahra had contributed.

"We didn't actually *date*," Petula confided, "but I did wake up next to him in a camper van next morning."

"Anyway, years later they were on TV on Top of the Pops and Pet knew him right away!"

"Oh, right. Quite the gift there," Freddy had said nodding solemnly.

The small group were walking across the grass to the top of The Row. Clouds rolled around overhead; it was a seriously murky and overcast day. There had only been a few warm and sunny days since the incredible summer weather of April. The projected weather forecast was for rain and storms for the foreseeable future. Today's plan was to walk down the pathway alongside the sand riding track and hopefully meet up somewhere with Spartacus. The ladies would engage the rider in light and charming banter while Freddy talked to the horse. A simple plan, nothing could go wrong.

All three ladies were now carrying their shoes and sandals and walking bare foot in the sand. Freddy stuck to the path way, keeping his shoes on.

"You know the good thing about walking barefoot on these sand tracks, Freddy?" Gloria had called over to him.

"Can't say I do."

"No dog poo."

"Oh, right."

"You see all the riff raff let their animals poo on the grass and then pretend to pick it up. But they don't."

"Can't do that on the sand, too easily seen," Zahra added, gleefully feeling the cold sand ooze between her toes.

"Assignation at eleven o'clock!" called Gloria pointing down The Row. Sure enough, head down, walking steadfastly toward them was Spartacus and his rider. The ladies moved to the side of the sand close to the path way with Freddy trying to act casual behind them. As the skewbald drum horse approached, Freddy could see his rider had a thick neck, broad shoulders and a muscular build. There was something vaguely familiar about him but he couldn't put his finger on it.

"How long do you think you'll need, Freddy?" asked Zahra.

"Hopefully, just a few minutes," he was reaching to his back pocket for his note pad and pencil. "Just enough time to write it all down carefully, I guess."

"OK, girls, time to do our bit for Queen and country," said Gloria taking a step forward and waving.

"Helloooo!" called Petula. The rider looked across, smiled and guided the drum horse toward them.

"Isn't he just so handsome!" cooed Zahra clapping her hands and looking like she was auditioning for a teeny bopper in 'Grease'. The soldier tried to look bashful as he brought the horse to a halt next to them. "What's his name?" she asked looking up to the soldier.

"Oh, him?" replied the rider.

"Oh, you too, soldier man," said Petula sidling over.

Freddy discreetly stepped around them to where he was standing almost behind the drum horse.

"G'morning, Spartacus."

"So it is you, young man?" he replied.

"Yep, 'fraid so."

"I've only heard good things. Sefton and the others speak highly of you."

Gloria now had her bag open. "Would it be OK with you if I take some pictures of you with my friends?" she was asking the rider. The ladies were rushing girlishly around, standing either side of the horse. Petula leaned in and rested her hand on the soldier's knee as she smiled for the photo.

Freddy continued his dialogue with Spartacus. "We don't have a lot of time this morning. I hope to meet with you and all of the senate at some point soon though."

"Indeed, very short of time today," came the throaty base voiced reply, "I have the messages for you from Rupert."

"Messages? There was more than one?"

"Indeed, two. And I have kept them in my mind ever since yesterday morning." Freddy had his note book out and started to scribble down as Spartacus spoke to him. At one point Freddy stopped and looked up into the huge dark eyes of the wise horse, "Are you sure about that part?"

"Yes, absolutely. I even questioned Rupert about it myself. That was the second message, clear as water."

"This just gets more and more bizarre," commented Freddy scratching his head and looking at his note pad.

"Hey! You!" called the trooper, turning around in the saddle and looking at the teenager, " I know you!"

"Oh, no, I don't think so, sir," Freddy replied, hastily stuffing his notepad away.

"I don't think so, Kevin; that was your name wasn't it?" Petula asked running her finger tips up and down the rider's leg. Freddy was trying to shuffle behind the two other ladies. "This is my nephew, he's visiting for a few days, you can't possibly know him."

The soldier leaned forward, focussed on Freddy who was walking backwards and realising why the rider looked so familiar.

Trooper Grimshaw's eyes were blazing. "It is you! You little terrorist bugger! You were in the barracks the other night when I was on night guard!"

"Ladies, I have to go. Now!" called Freddy as he spun on his heel and bolted up The Row.

"You won't get away a second time!" Grimshaw called as he grabbed at his reins and gave Spartacus a sharp poke in the ribs with his short spurs.

"That's my nephew! You can't chase him!" yelled Petula.

"Come on! Move, you great lumbering beast!" Grimshaw shouted at his horse.

Spartacus too had weighed up the situation and recalled that it had indeed been Trooper Grimshaw on duty that wet and lively evening. He also thought it would be in everyone's best interest if Grimshaw didn't actually catch Freddy. Not wishing to be a totally disobedient equine, he let out a long low groan and moved up into an ambling trot. Looking ahead, he saw Freddy was easily making ground away from them.

Joggers paused to watch the chase. Freddy was running in front, Spartacus barely jogging after him, carrying a mildly deranged rider, and three oddly dressed women were following the Shire, screaming at the rider. Gloria pulled up her caftan around her knees as she scurried along. No matter how hard he kicked the horse's ribs, Grimshaw could not get Spartacus out of a slow trot. Freddy glanced back over his shoulder to see if they were getting closer and was relieved to see how once again his equine pals were helping out.

His relief was short lived.

Realising the drum horse was never going to move faster than a slow trot today, Grimshaw made a decision. He leapt off the back of the horse and started to run on foot after the fleeing teenager. Spartacus came to a dead stop causing Zahra and Gloria to nearly run right into his rear end. But Petula was having none of it. She tore off the jacket from her maroon trouser suit and then, bare foot in her black and white polka dot blouse, sprinted after the military man. Her arms moved back and forth at her sides like pistons as she kicked into overdrive. Grimshaw was being hampered by his riding kit and tore off his hard helmet and cast it aside as he quickened his pace to close the gap between himself and Freddy. He had no idea he was being pursued by a lady who a few decades back had been a winner of the four hundred metres at county level for Cheltenham Ladies College. Freddy looked back again and saw the soldier closing in, his saliva dripping from the corner of his mouth as he ran. He was only a few metres behind with his arms stretched forward ready to grab the boy. He was almost within grasp and when, with a blood curdling yell, Petula launched herself on to Grimshaw's back.

Still screaming, she locked her arms around his neck, her legs around his waist like a limpet. The soldier fell flat on his face into the sand with Petula on top of him.

"Go, girl!" yelled Gloria from back down The Row.

"Throttle the maniac!" screamed Zahra.

She had him pinned to the sand but for good measure, Petula bit his neck and proceeded to keep pummelling his back. Freddy watched the whole event with his mouth open and then turned to flee again.

"Freddy!" Voices behind him called.

"Arms out, Freddy!"

Sefton and Rochester swooped in, aiming to get the boy out of danger.

Groaning and spitting out mouthfuls of sand, Trooper Grimshaw managed to look up and for the second time in less than a week saw a sixteen year old boy disappear before his eyes. The two Pegusinni, one under each arm scooped up their friend and flew him to safety.

"What the?" mumbled the dazed soldier, now staring at nothing from his position in the dirt.

"How on earth..?" Still straddling her victim, Petula trailed off looking in the same direction.

"Freddy? What happened to Freddy?" asked a panting Zahra as she, Gloria and Spartacus also caught up.

"Gone," Petula said quietly, "just gone."

"What have you done to our boy?" screamed Gloria, kicking the trooper in the ribs with her bare foot. The entire group looked up at the sound of galloping hooves coming toward them as Lance Corporal Webber on Victoriana and Clarissa on Nero approached. Both horses came to a sliding stop next to them.

"What the hell is going on here, Grimshaw?" Webber yelled to the prostrate trooper. The small crowd who had gathered on the pathway looked on with interest at the colourful tableau before them. A short woman in tartans and tweeds, spiky red hair, and no shoes was spinning around as she peered through a piece of crystal the shape of a small icicle. Next to her, a huge brown and white horse stood placidly with his reins hanging around his hooves. Next to him, a well-built woman wearing a torn and sandy covered caftan was also spinning around looking up and down through a crystal. Over to the right, a young soldier lay pinned to the ground by a third barefooted women. A smartly-dressed soldier in a sharp navy blue uniform on a striking black mare looked down on the pinned soldier, while next to him, a blonde girl sat on an older looking horse, shaking her head in disbelief.

Victoriana looked discreetly over at Spartacus. "Do I really want to know what happened here?" she asked quietly.

"Well, no. Probably not," replied the wise drum horse.

"Ladies, I do have to ask you to allow Trooper Grimshaw to stand up," announced Webber.

Petula looked to her friends. "Energy? Did you feel the energy flow too?"

"Indeed, indeed," said Zahra, "but where the hell is he?"

"Must be part of the power he hasn't told us about yet," from Gloria staring across the park through her crystal.

Webber cleared his throat rather loudly, "Ladies?"

"Oh right, sorry," said Petula standing up and brushing sand off her clothes.

Webber again, "Grimshaw, care to explain?"

"This should be killer," said Clarissa with a giggle.

A sweaty and sand-covered Grimshaw slowly got to his feet. "Corporal Webber, you really don't want to know. I've been having a very bad week."

"Yes, I heard about your midnight liberty act on the parade square with about a hundred horses this week. What's going on today?"

Once again for the second time in less than seven days Grimshaw knew it was pointless trying to explain about a teenage yob who could vanish before a person's eyes. He took the oath of silence.

Webber looked to the three women. "Ladies, perhaps you would care to share with me why you were perusing our trooper and then pinned him down?"

The three women looked back and forth to each other.

"OK, here's how it is," said Petula. She paused, then said, "Zahra will explain."

"Eh? I will?"

"Yes, of course, dahling," said a nodding and agreeing Gloria.

Zahra straightened her jacket and brushed down her skirt. "You see it's like this." Everyone stared wondering what she was going to come up with. "Last week when I was walking my poodle, Mr. Bobtail, in the park when a large man ran by and snatched my handbag."

"Yes, Mr. Bobtail," agreed Petula.

"Indeed, handbag," confirmed Gloria.

"And today while walking with my two lady friends, I saw this young man," gesturing to a gobsmacked Grimshaw, "and recognised him as the perpetrator."

"Recognised," again from Gloria.

"Perpetrator," said Petula nodding.

"And being as frail as I am," continued the part-time teacher, "my friends took it upon themselves to help by apprehending my attacker."

Webber stared unbelievably from Grimshaw to Zahra. "You mean this man actually attacked you?"

"Oh, indeed not. My mistake. Upon seeing him close up, he is not, after all, my assailant."

"I see."

"Simple case of mistaken identity," concluded Zahra.

"Simple," said Gloria smiling and nodding.

"Identity," confirmed Petula.

"My attacker was older and not so attractive."

"Older," from Petula.

"Not attractive," from a tutting Gloria.

"We do apologise for any inconvenience," Zahra said looking at a stunned trooper Grimshaw who was also rapidly weighing up the situation. The story from the old bag was certainly more plausible than anything his brain could muster and there was no way he was going to try to explain the truth. They really would lock him up for that story. At least this way he was off the hook. He nodded, resigned, but stayed silent.

"Come along, girls," Gloria said as she hustled other two toward the pathway, "we really need to get going now." She turned to Webber, "We're helping the vicar with flowers for evensong tonight. Bye."

"Flowers," said Zahra.

"Evensong," called Petula they all hurried away.

"Keep walking and don't look back," said Zahra through gritted teeth.

"Bobtail? Mr. bloody Bobtail?" asked an incredulous

Gloria staring straight ahead and striding out. Finally when they were far enough away from the military personnel, they collapsed onto a bench holding each other and laughing.

"My, that poor soldier boy!" said Zahra wiping a tear from the corner of her eye.

"Poor lad had no chance against you!" said Gloria to Petula.

Looking around, Petula said, "Speaking of poor lads, what the devil happened to our boy?"

"Amazing, wasn't it. You both did see what I saw, didn't you?" asked Zahra.

"Yep, I saw the same thing. Looked like he got beamed up back to the mother ship," said Gloria. "There one second and gone the next."

"You don't think he's really gone as in gone, do you?" Petula asked.

All three were quiet again as they gave it some thought.

"I definitely felt the energy surge just before it happened," Gloria said.

"Me too," from Zahra.

"And then he was gone," commented Petula.

"Neat stunt if you can pull it off."

Another moment of silence was interrupted, "Psst, up behind you."

"What?"

"Who?"

"Where?"

"Behind you," called the hoarse whisper, "up behind you."

All three twisted around and looked up into the trees. Dangling from a broad branch, partially covered by foliage was a pair of denim-clad legs and feet with trainers.

"Good grief!"

"Freddy?"

"Is that you?"

"Yeah," came back a rather quiet voice, "thought I should er, disappear for a while."

All three were now standing, shading their eyes and looking into the branches. "You certainly did that, most successfully."

"The coast is clear now, you'll be fine," Zahra said.

"Freddy?"

"Yes, Petula?"

"How and why did you get thirty feet up into a tree? Just call me curious, you know?"

"I got a ride, the guys helped me. Just a minute, I'll come down." The ladies watching saw him hold out his arms, vanish from sight and moments later he was on the sand next to them lowering his arms. "Sorry 'bout that, but I thought better safe than sorry."

"Oh my!" Exclaimed Gloria, "they're here, aren't they? Very close by?"

"Heavens, the energy is tremendous," said Petula looking around, "where are they, Freddy?"

"Just behind you, Sefton and Rochester, but they're leaving now." He raised his hand, "bye, guys, talk to you this evening." Everyone felt a light breeze waft over them as the half section of Pegusinni took flight.

"Going to share this new gift with us, Freddy?" asked Zahra.

"Sure, why not, you know everything else."

The ladies took their seats on the bench, Freddy sat cross-legged on the grass facing them. "It's not much. I found out the first night I went in and over the wall. When I'm in physical contact with the guys I merge with them, sort of."

"You disappear?"

"Just like that?"

"Sort of, I mean, they can still see me and oddly all horses can. But then again they can always see the Pegusinni when no one else does."

"Amazing."

"Outstanding."

"I must become like a Pegu-Freddy or a Fredusinni," he said with a grin. Then, "that soldier, he won't get into trouble, will he? That would be bad if he did. None of it's his fault."

"No, no. Zahra and Mr. Bobtail got him out of that," Gloria told him.

"Mr. Bobtail?"

"Long story." With a more serious tone Gloria asked if it was mission accomplished. He confirmed it was and in fact there were two more messages which he had written down in his note book.

"Come along then, let's hear them," said an impatient Petula. He fumbled for his note book. Zahra loaded her cigarette holder as the others put their shoes back on.

"OK, here is the first. It's a bit strange."

"Can't be more obscure than the first," commented Zahra.

"Let's hear it then," from Petula.

He looked down at his note pad.

"*Plant a copper.*"

"What?"

"Eh?"

"You're not serious?"

"*Plant bees in the flower.*" He looked up at them. "That's the two messages. Plant a copper and plant bees in the flower."

"Plant bees in the flower? What darn flower?" from a perplexed Gloria.

"And how does a person plant a copper?" from Petula.

Zahra was quiet, leaning back on the bench, short legs stuck forward in front of her. Finally, looking up at the sky she asked, "First dress practice is tomorrow, correct?"

"Major General's Review or something like that is what the guys called it," confirmed Freddy from his position on the grass.

Zahra continued, "And we doubt anything serious is going to happen?"

"Not according to the numbers which gave us the date, no."

"So let's totally immerse ourselves into the morning, really see what's going on and then we'll try and link in the messages."

"Always the wise one," said Gloria looking at her friend.

"Sounds like a plan," Petula agreed.

Freddy was nodding but then interjected, "One detail, I can easily get into most of the areas with the guys, you know, now you see me and now you don't. But I believe you need tickets to get into the front area, otherwise you'll be stuck up on the side of the road."

Zahra nipped out her cigarette and put the butt into the small zip lock bag she carried for them, "Shouldn't be a problem, only one phone call."

Petula, Gloria and Freddy looked at her waiting for the solution.

"Nicole. Remember? I'll have her ask her new boyfriend the M.P. He can pull a few strings."

"Oh, excellent," said Petula.

"One last problem then," They all turned to Gloria. "Come on girls, think about it. Trooping the Colour?

What on earth does a lady wear?" The other two grinned as she finished with, "Back to the shop, I'm sure we can pull together a few tasteful outfits"

Freddy shuddered and blocked the vision from his mind.

Chapter Twenty-nine

S partacus had relayed the two new messages to Victoriana and, as with the first one, they made no sense to her whatsoever. It was early Saturday morning and she was completely uneasy in her stall, listening to her regiment preparing for the first full dress rehearsal of the season. Soldiers ran back and forth from the tack rooms, lining up ceremonial saddlery for their horses. On an occasion such as this, there was no extra help for a guardsman getting his horse in full state kit. It was every man for himself. Once his horse was cleaned within an inch of its life, saddled, bridled and left securely tied, the troops ran back to their rooms and lockers to don their ceremonial uniforms. Then it was back to pick up their horses and make their way to join the queue at one of the three mounting blocks on the parade square.

Would it be today, Victoriana wondered? Next week's practice? Or would it be the full occasion in two weeks when her herd could be in serious danger? The Pegusinni were doing their best, Freddy was doing his best and even the three women he had recruited were doing their best. But would it be good enough? She decided she was not going to stand by and allow her horses out into the line of danger without her. She needed to formulate a plan. Until then she would attempt to be calm, patient and supportive to the others.

At the same time Freddy was sitting on the Piccadilly Line, travelling from South Kensington on to Leicester Square where he had arranged to meet the ladies. They knew the city like the back of their hands and with so many roads closed for the morning, Gloria had pointed out that travel by car was pointless. Indeed, travel by bicycle would also be fruitless so they had agreed to meet outside the tube station at nine-thirty on Saturday morning. After their escapade in the park on Friday morning, Zahra had innocently appeared at the apartment at two o'clock in the afternoon, met briefly with Jane and then went over school work with Freddy for a couple of hours. She didn't light up her cigarettes once the whole time she was there. His mother had the afternoon free and hung around resting on the sofa and reading her own book. The problem was Jane's acting skills were not that well-honed and she didn't fool her son for a minute. She was checking to see that school work really was being done and trying to form her opinion of the rather off-beat tutor. Despite Zahra's brisk and business-like manner at their first meeting, Jane suspected there was something else going on and she felt it her duty to figure out what it was.

The train burst out of the darkness into the well-lit station which had surprisingly few passengers waiting around. As he rode the escalator up to ground level, Freddy figured that while Leicester Square was probably packed in the evenings, there wasn't much for tourists to see early on a weekend morning. Outside it was not cold but heavily overcast and looking like rain. He walked up and down outside the station, pausing to look at magazines on the newsstands, and bought some chocolate and chewing gum for later. Gloria had told him this was the best place to meet from the tube as it was only a short walk to Trafalgar Square and the top of The Mall. After hours of agonising discussion with Zahra, Gloria and Petula, he had firmly come to the conclusion that nothing would happen to the regiment on the way from barracks to the palace. If you thought like a crazy person then there would be no point to such an action. There would be few crowds, no press and certainly no TV coverage. If you were going to make a splash and you wanted it to be a *big* splash then whatever you did had to be done where there was maximum people and maximum coverage by the media. It would definitely be something happening either on The Mall as the escort proceeded from Buckingham Palace or, more likely, on the Parade Square when things were in full swing.

Before catching the train, he'd had a short meeting with the Pegusinni. Everyone was to be in the same positions as they had been for the khaki practice, except that Sefton would sit by Cedric so that two of them could keep watch over that darn tower thing. Gauntlet, Yeti and Rochester were to be on mobile patrol over the parade, St. James's Park, and along The Mall. If anything looked even slightly suspicious or out of order, they were to tell him immediately. The Pegusinni were all happy and enthused with these instructions as they certainly wanted to be doing something useful. Unlike Victoriana, who was left behind in a nearly empty barracks with only the occasional chime from the clock above the gate to break the silence.

"Hello! Freddy, we're all here."

He turned around, looked at the three women and his jaw fell open. Zahra was wearing a short black pinstripe jacket with a matching pencil cut skirt and a soft white blouse, open at the collar. Gloria wore a skirt and a chocolate brown jacket pinched in at the waist over a rich creamy-coloured blouse with a matching cream-coloured straw hat, her hair neatly pinned up underneath. To Freddy she looked fifty pounds lighter. She actually had shape. Making up the trio was Petula in a light-weight grey wool trouser suit, coral pink silk blouse and a tiny grey hat perched at a jaunty angle. All three wore a tasteful smattering of jewellery and their handbags and shoes coordinated with their outfits.

"Oh, how sweet! He's shocked!" exclaimed Gloria laughing.

"Thought we couldn't pull it off, eh, kiddo?" from Zahra.

"Bet you thought we'd come in full drag, didn't ya?" asked Petula as she leaned forward and pinched his cheek.

Zahra was in low heels and pulled herself up to full height. "Can't gate crash the Royal enclosure at Ascot if you look like a drag queen."

"You, er, all look really nice. Just different, but nice."

"Well, it's not just dress rehearsal for the troops, you know; we want to check out the competition, make sure we blend right in on the big day."

"You're all coming on the real day?"

"Sure thing."

"You bet."

"Wouldn't miss this party for the world, kiddo."

Petula straightened her well fitting jacket. "Ladies, we need to move. Over a thousand soldiers await our arrival."

"Let's get to them," said Zahra as she strode off down Charing Cross Road with Gloria on one side, Petula on the other and Freddy jogging behind. In just a few minutes they hit St Martin's Place and the top corner of Trafalgar Square where they paused to stare up at Nelson's Column.

"Not the same since old Kenny boy ran his hatchet war on them, is it?" said Zahra as she looked over the historic landmark.

"Kenny boy?" asked a puzzled Freddy.

"Ken Livingstone, our precious Lord Mayor, kiddo. He declared war on our pigeons back in '03, and in the end he pretty much won."

"A bloke declared war on pigeons?"

"Heck yes. You never saw this place before then?"

"No, never before."

"There were thousands back then, usually around four thousand at any one time."

Petula slowly shook her head as she too looked over the square. "He reminded me of that guy in the movie, The Omen, you know, in the last one of the trilogy where he had all the baby boys killed? We called him Damian Livingstone for a while."

Gloria rested her hand on Freddy's shoulder. "You see the couple of dozen birds left here? That's nothing to what it was. It was like walking through a living sea of feathers."

"Remember the sounds? The lovely soft sounds that rang out around here," said Zahra reminiscently.

"How did he get rid of them?" Asked Freddy.

"Had a law passed to make it illegal to feed them. Of course, a lot of us protested, we'd sneak in at all hours and throw grain around."

"Pet even tied herself to one of the stone lions at the base of Nelson," said Gloria indicating the four huge statues, one at each corner of the column.

"Didn't do much good though," said Petula glumly, "except, I did get offered a few parts in some off beat videos being made in Soho."

"Ah, the good old days," sighed Zahra.

"He still Mayor of London, then?" asked Freddy.

"His term's up this year, I seriously doubt he'll get re-elected," said Petula, "heck, I even heard old Boris might have a run at it!"

"Boris Johnson?" asked Gloria, "no way, not a chance. He'd never get it."

The ladies continued their light political banter for a few more minutes before Zahra spoke to Freddy. "Hey, what is it, kiddo? What's up? What are you looking at?"

Freddy slowly raised his arm, pointing across the square. "The birds, the few pigeons over there, see them?"

"Yes, there are still a few that come back," said Gloria.

"I know, but look where they are again."

"Again?"

"Yeah, like on Thursday morning, directly over the top of those four guys."

Everyone stared across to the far corner of the square.

"You're sure it's the same men?" asked Petula.

"Well, it looks like it from here, hard to tell from this distance."

"Then we need to be across this square in two ticky wicks!" stated Gloria as she strode off again.

"Hey, careful Gloria, these could be dangerous buggers!" Freddy warned, catching up to her.

"Nonsense. A few little dark-haired foreigners are not going to dampen my parade."

They all moved quickly down the stone steps into the square and then on behind the fountains. Gloria fumbled with her bag as she strode along, retrieving her camera. "OK, best tourist look, ladies, get close as you can to them while I take your photo. Freddy, stay close to me."

Zahra and Petula moved ahead and then when in front of the men, they turned and made poses for Gloria's camera. They giggled, waved and pointed to the statues of the lions and to Nelson's Column. Freddy was surprised to see how Gloria handled her camera and he noted it wasn't some cheap little piece of junk from the Pound Shop. She focussed, aimed and rattled off a series of shots on speed shutter. As soon as they realised someone had a camera pointing in their general direction, the four men spilt into two pairs and separated. One pair moved quickly toward Whitehall and the other pair went north of The Mall towards Cockspur Street.

"Pet, with me. Freddy, with Zahra, after those two," directed Gloria pointing to the pair moving to Cockspur Street. "All mobile phones turned on?"

"Yes."

"Sure."

"You bet."

The two men heading to Whitehall were caught at the pedestrian crossing giving Gloria and Petula a chance to catch up to them. Not so fortunate were Freddy and Zahra who had to run and dodge traffic to keep up with their quarry.

"It's pretty cool how you trust what I've been telling you," said Freddy as he walked next to his tutor.

"You and the animals, kiddo. We know when something's not right with the birds and the bees."

"Gotcha. Damn, where the heck are these guys going?" Freddy watched them duck down a small quiet street.

"Heck if I know, but let's keep up."

They rounded a corner onto a broad walkway lined with stone walls. Freddy immediately grabbed Zahra's elbow, pulling her back.

"What's up?"

Freddy pressed back against one of the walls and pointed. "That's it. The tower!" In the middle of the walkway, at the top of a long flight of steps, stood the Duke of York memorial. They were looking at the back side of the tall column, and from their vantage point they could see right down to the pavement of The Mall where small crowds were gathering to watch the rehearsal parade. The onlookers stood at the precise point where the band and escort turned right off The Mall and down the approach road to the parade square. Uniformed police lined the road, facing the crowds, watchful for any sign of trouble. Halfway down the steps, the two men leaned against a wall, smoking cigarettes. They occasionally glanced back up to the tower and then back to the street below.

"Hmm, this looks like my call, kiddo. Meet me down on the street when I'm done." With that, Zahra was gone, skipping down the steps toward the suspects. Freddy held his breath wondering how she could be so rash when they really could be dealing with terrorists. He heard her call out, "Hi there boys, got a light for a young lady this fine morning?" She'd opened her bag and retrieved her smokes. Freddy could see her in front of them, waiting for her light. He was too far away to hear anything they might have said. After a minute, cigarette lit, she proceeded daintily down the steps, never once looking back to Freddy. He remained as much out of sight as he could, and watched Zahra blend into the small crowd at the roadside.

Freddy was now separated from everyone and seriously wondering what to do. To meet up with Zahra he'd have to go down past the two spooky characters on the broad steps and they didn't appear to be showing any signs of moving. Then he was jolted from his thoughts by his phone buzzing in his jacket pocket.

"Hello?"

"Hey, kiddo. Can't turn around. They still there?" It was Zahra from the middle of the roadside crowd.

"Yes, still there, showing no signs of moving."

"Anyone actually up on that tower?" she asked.

"Oh, forgot to look! Just a sec." He gazed skyward but saw no one, only Cedric and Sefton on the next building, patiently waiting as they had been told. "Nope, can't see anyone today. But that doesn't mean they're not there."

"When your Pegusinni friend saw them," she asked quietly into the phone, "was it dark or daylight?"

"Still pretty much dark."

"Hmm, figures. So, no one on the ground could possibly have seen them on Thursday morning; just the little flying horses"

"I guess."

"OK, here's the plan. I just had a call from the others. They're walking back this way now. They lost their guys when they jumped into a taxi at the top of Whitehall. "

"OK, so what's going to happen?"

"I'll cross the road and join Pet and Gloria. We do have our tickets. We'll get right into the thick of it."

"OK."

"You stay put, watch those guys and wait to hear from us. That alright?"

"Sure."

"And Freddy."

"Yes?"

"We don't want heroes today. If in doubt, keep away."

"Yep, will do," he said quietly as he snapped off the phone. He glanced at his watch, it was a quarter to eleven. He could hear the massed bands of the foot guards already on parade. There was shouting, drum beats and the sound of hundreds of hobnail boots stomping around on Horse Guard's Parade as everyone got into position. Across on the other side of The Mall, well-dressed members of the public were pouring down the pathway, showing their tickets to the gatekeepers and making their way to their prestigious seats. These people looked like they were dressed for a very up-market garden party. The noise grew from the crowd on the street, some cheering, and some clapping as the first horse of the escort appeared in the centre of The Mall. It was Venetia carrying the Brigade Major. She was closely followed by the four black troop horses of the retinue. Unlike Thursday morning everyone was in full state kit today. The skies were clearing and muted sunlight bounced off the shiny breastplates, swords and helmets worn by the soldiers. As they turned right into Horse Guard's, the two men on the steps moved over to the same side of the passageway as Freddy. He quickly crossed to the opposite side, ducking down behind the tower as he scurried across. Pressed against the stone wall he could hear the sound of the mounted band as they came along The Mall. Behind them would be two divisions of Life Guards and then the carriage drawn by Daniel and McCarthy, the Windsor greys. He looked up again to the top of the tower.

No one was there. Would there be any point to being up there? The only way to find out would be to try it. Of course that would be impossible in broad day light with the public, police and security people everywhere. But what if a person couldn't be seen?

He looked up again; the top of the monument had to be at least a hundred feet up. The furthest he'd done so far was about twenty-five feet up the tree in Hyde Park. Staying pressed against the wall, he silently called to Sefton and Cedric who within seconds were down by his side.

"You alright, Freddy?" asked an anxious Sefton. Victoriana in her capacity as commanding officer had made it very clear to all the Senate and Pegusinni that Freddy was to be looked after and protected at all times. Although, she hadn't mentioned this point to Freddy.

"Yes, yes, I'm fine. Just trying to stay out of sight from those two dubious blokes." Then he told the two waiting Pegusinni his idea. Could they pull it off? Of course, it was not a problem, providing Freddy's grip was secure and held for the trip. He nodded, stepped away from the wall, held out both arms and disappeared from human sight.

Sefton and Cedric went up in a vertical take-off pattern, every muscle and tendon in their necks taut and strained as they carried the teenager. Once they passed twenty feet Freddy closed his eyes, not daring to look down until he had his feet on something solid. The air rushed by his cheeks, his arms in a death hold around the necks of the small flying horses as the trio flew skywards. It seemed like a lifetime but in fact it only took moments before the two small horses carefully lowered the boy onto the railed platform that circled the top of the column.

"Stay close, guys, I can't afford to be seen up here." With a hand still holding each Pegusinni, he slowly turned around and opened his eyes.

"Oh, my god!" He desperately wanted to grab hold of the railings but knew he would be immediately sighted by anyone looking at the tower. The view was like nothing he'd seen before, miles and miles across the city of London. The tower of Big Ben, the Houses of Parliament, the huge white wheel known as The London Eye and the bullet-shaped building called The Gherkin. On the square were hundreds of foot guards in their red tunics; only from here, they really did look like clockwork toys. Determined to remain calm, Freddy took some slow breaths as he steadied himself and leaned against the base of the statue. Sefton and Cedric looked curiously at him as they couldn't understand why anyone would be frightened or nervous up here.

"You alright, Freddy?"

"Yeah, sure. Just need a minute to catch my breath."

"Here's the second division," said Cedric looking down as the Queen's escort passed below them. They watched as the Life Guards turned right towards the parade ground, followed by the open carriage pulled by the Windsor greys. Freddy leaned forward. From where he was standing he had a clear view of the carriage and anyone riding in it. All the soldiers, all the police and probably any security were looking over the crowds on the ground. Hardly anyone appeared to be looking up. He looked down to his left and the two suspicious blokes had stepped away from the wall and were staring down the steps and pointing as the escort and carriage passed. Finally, the last division of the Blues and Royals passed and Freddy could see all the cavalry forming up on the parade next to the mounted band, with their backs to St. James's Park.

It all looked so surreal from this position. The carriage was halfway across the parade square, followed by a few officers on horses. Freddy pulled his stare upwards again and out across London. He saw two more Pegusinni circling high above the square. Pigeons and other city birds zigzagged back and forth. The carriage came to a halt by the podium exactly as the clock tower at Horse Guards began to chime eleven o'clock. Two planes circled in the distance, probably waiting for a landing spot at Heathrow. The chimes rang out as an old soldier guy mounted the podium. A city helicopter lifted off from a high rooftop across the Thames. It was a completely different world from up here.

Then, still staring ahead, Freddy's eyes glazed over. In the distance the clock reached its eleventh chime and stopped. The old guy on the podium was saluting. He had to be the Major General or somebody who was in charge today. Through blurred vision Freddy saw all the things on the ground, the parade and the London landmarks and then all things in the air. The planes, the birds, the helicopter, the Pegusinni. All silently moving. And out of the silence from the back of his mind he heard the first message. Coming from a pigeon, to a mole, to a rabbit, to a swan, to a horse and finally to a teenage boy. Over and over the message ran through his brain, but now taking on the dialect and accent of each creature it had passed through. He almost lost hold of Sefton as he realised what it was. What he and everyone had been missing. Then the second and third message came into his mind and echoed again and again. From pigeons, to a mole, to a rabbit, to a swan and to a drum horse. And eventually, to Freddy Hobbs.

"Oh bloody hell!"

"What? What is it?" asked an alarmed Sefton.

"It's ok, it's not going to happen today. But now, now I know what it is and exactly when it's going to happen!"

Chapter Thirty

"Checked out all the ladies' loos near the seating area. Nothing. Nothing at all." Gloria sipped her tea as she spoke.

"We even looked in the tanks and cisterns," said Petula as she checked her hair in her compact. "Nothing. Did anyone else notice how young the foot guards look these days?"

"Darling, you were probably coming up from an air raid shelter during World War Two last time you saw that many soldiers so close up," replied Gloria, nibbling on peanuts.

"You ok, kiddo?" asked Zahra looking over her coffee cup at Freddy. They were sitting in the Rockwell bar in the Trafalgar Hilton, just off the top of The Mall. After they left Trafalgar Square, Gloria and Petula lost track of the two men they had tailed when they jumped into a cab and headed down Whitehall toward Westminster. The ladies then watched the event from the main seating area. They'd snooped around, checked everything and everyone they could possibly think of but hadn't noticed anything unusual. Zahra joined the two in the seating area and told them about the two lurking up near the Duke of York memorial. Not a lot really to tell, though. Foreign by the look and clothing, but as they hadn't spoken a word to her, just gave her a light, she had no idea whether they had accents. It had been Petula's idea to meet at the tucked away bar, to allow the crowds time to disperse and for them to have beverages and swap notes.

"Yes, I'm fine," Freddy answered Zahra's question, "I just think I have a bit of news for everyone." After his epiphany at the top of the tower, he had been stunned by the realisation of what was going to happen. Sefton and Cedric had noticed the change in him and immediately asked if they could help or do anything. No, nothing they could do for now. In fact there was nothing anyone could do for now. He'd told them to round up everyone else who was stationed around the area, have them follow and escort the regiment back to barracks and to let Victoriana know that they would have to arrange a meeting for that night. This time he had something really big to share.

Gloria reached over and put her hand on top of his, "What is it, sweetie? We old broads have been gabbing since we got here, haven't given you a chance."

"Were you ok after I left you, with those two chaps still lurking on the steps?" Zahra asked?

"Yes, yes, I was ok. I actually took a little trip."

"A trip? Where to?"

He pointed with his index finger. "Upward. Up, up and almost away."

"What?"

"Explain, dear boy."

"The tower, I figured it had to be important in this whole deal, so I took a trip up and had a look from the viewing platform."

"You did what?"

"Oh, my God! Freddy! What were you thinking? If your mother ever found out..." Zahra trailed off as he broke in.

"Well, she won't and it did prove more than useful. And I was well looked after."

"Was the little door open? Did you climb up all those inside stairs?"

"No, not at all. My, er, friends gave me a ride."

"Friends?"

"Ride?"

"Yep, you know, Sefton and Cedric," he lowered his voice as a waiter dressed in all black put more hot water for the tea on the table. When he left, Freddy continued, "like in the park the other day. Up in the tree."

"You mean the Pegusinni flew you up to the top of the tower?"

"Yep, why not?"

Gloria was wide-eyed as she said, "You know, back when it was first built, people could pay something like a sixpence to climb all the stairs to get to that viewing platform."

"Really?"

"Oh yes, but they closed it to the public after a short time." Everyone looked at her, waiting for her to finish. She lowered her voice, "they closed it because too many people were jumping off to commit suicide!"

"Are you totally serious?" Freddy asked.

"Yes! Of course, I am. Freddy, that was so dangerous to do!"

"Well, I'm ok and it was worth it."

Petula now had her lipstick out. "You know, the entire British army each gave up a day's pay to cover the cost of building that thing." She dabbed her mouth with a folded tissue.

Zahra looked at her, "The Duke of York must have been very popular with his troops back then for them to do that for him."

"A hell of a lot more popular than the present Duke of York, that's for sure."

"Oh, be nice," said Gloria, "I find Prince Andrew rather fetching."

Petula looked at her friend. "Fetching? Darling he's chunky! The Duke of Pork! That's what you like."

Zahra tapped her spoon against her coffee cup. "Enough, isn't anyone interested in what Freddy has to say?"

"Yes, absolutely."

"Of course, darling."

All three were then silent as they looked to Freddy who was pushed back in his chair.

"Well, kiddo? Going to share with us?" asked his tutor.

Still pressed back in his chair, he spoke very quietly and very slowly.

"I know what they are going to do."

"What!"

"You do?"

"Good grief!"

"I know what they are going to do and I know when they are going to do it."

Zahra grappled with her bag as she rummaged for a cigarette.

"Can you smoke in here?" asked Petula.

"Damn smoking ban doesn't start till July; this is a bar, not the Sistine Chapel. Yes, I'm going to bloody well smoke!"

"You're absolutely sure, sweetie?" asked Gloria, looking at Freddy.

"Yes, I worked out the messages, as well, which confirms it all."

Petula was on her feet snapping her fingers. "Waiter! Three large very dry gin martinis. And extra olives. Now!" Across the room the waiter nodded and made his way to the bar. Zahra found her lighter and pearl holder, then took a deep drag as she sat back in her chair. "OK, spill the beans, kiddo."

"It was when I was at the top of the tower, just before the parade started; it was, like, really quiet up there but I could also hear loads of things." His face was expressionless as he continued. "And I could see things I hadn't noticed before. And then I saw things I had seen before, and it all made sense."

"And the messages, you worked out the messages? Gloria asked tentatively.

"Yes, that too."

"That's amazing," from Petula.

"Not really, I just thought about it. And I remembered my birthday parties at the Rectory in Spinkhill."

"Birthday party?"

"Spinkhill?"

Everyone fell silent as the waiter arrived with the tray of martinis. As he leaned forward and placed glasses on the table in front of the ladies, Freddy tried to count the number of gold studs he had in his left ear. There were so many studs all around the edge it reminded him of the Chesterfield sofa in Maurice's library.

With the waiter gone Zahra cleared her throat. "So, going to share with us, kiddo?"

"What does it have to do with birthday parties?"

"Eleanor, she used to organise all the games at my birthday party. And she played the piano for musical chairs."

"So you worked out the meaning of the messages from musical chairs?" Petula asked.

He gave her a withering look. "Don't be silly. We used to play Chinese Whisper. We'd sit in a circle and Eleanor would write down a message on a piece of paper and the first kid had a few seconds to read it, then whisper the message to the next kid until it went all around the group."

"Oh well, we know that game."

"Exactly, and by the time the last person whispered it to Eleanor she would hoot with giggles and tell us what it was to start with."

The others swigged at their martinis and waited for him to go on.

"And I figured that's what happened to our messages. By the time it had gone from a pigeon, to a mole, to a rabbit, to a swan and eventually to a horse and then us, there was just a small chance it had gotten a little mixed up along the way."

"Oh my goodness, so all the words were wrong."

"Not at all, they just sounded like the words we got at the end."

"Go on."

"So with what I saw and heard this morning, it all fell into place."

"And that is?"

"Remember the first message? The one that's had us running all over the city looking for things we couldn't find?"

"Yes."

"Absolutely."

Freddy repeated the first message as they all thought it had been. They nodded, waited. Then in a quiet voice he said it again, with a different accent and the emphasis on different syllables.

"Oh, my God!"

"You can't be serious!"

"Dear Lord!"

"Totally serious and what I saw on Thursday morning at the khaki practice and saw today just proves it."

"And the other messages from Spartacus?" asked Gloria anxiously.

376

"Same thing." He repeated both of them as they thought they had heard them. Then he did the same thing only with a different accent and different stress on the words.

The whole group was silent. Smoke curled up from a slightly shaking cigarette holder, and then simultaneously all three ladies grabbed their glasses, drained them and sat back. Without needing direction, the waiter saw the empty glasses, swept them away and went to get fresh drinks.

Freddy reminded them of what he had seen on both days, of what the Pegusinni had seen on the Thursday morning, and the timing of everything. The waiter returned with the next round of drinks.

"This is big Freddy. We must go to the authorities with this," Gloria said, still rather shaken.

"And tell them what? That I can talk to horses, I see little flying ones and, oh yeah, I can disappear when they pick me up?"

"No, no, tell them about all the terrorist parts. We must tell someone!"

"And do you actually think they'll believe a word of it? Coming from a teenage kid and three doped-up old hippies?"

There was a stunned silence at his last comment.

"Sorry, sorry, I didn't mean the last part. I mean that's what the police will think, not me. I think you're all really nice. I like you a lot." Freddy fidgeted uncomfortably as all three looked at him through lowered lids over the top of their drink glasses. The silence continued for what seemed like an age before Gloria slowly put her glass on the table.

"Yes, well, I suppose we have been called worse things in the past."

Zahra concurred, "I believe we peaked with The Witches of Eastwick"

"Oh, I almost forgot that one," said Petula, "but I do remember *Psychedelic Pot Heads.*"

"Do you remember the Marijuana Mediums?"

"And the Merlot Madams?"

"Ah, happy days."

"So, Freddy, no harm done. And you believe that's what the police will think?"

"Yes," he said nodding slowly, "I mean come on, you three believe me, well, because it's your type of thing. But do you think real people will?"

"Real people?"

"Sorry, bad choice of words."

"No worry, kiddo, we know what people think and say about us. No harm done," from Zahra.

Petula was biting her lower lip. "So, what to do? You think you know the plot, the what, the when and the where. But you think there's nothing you or we can do about it?"

"Freddy looked at her. "Yep, and the whole thing scares the crap out of me. Don't forget, my mum, my Gran and my aunt Sharon are planning on being there too."

"Oh my, almost forgot that part."

Gloria, who had been quietly thinking, spoke up. "Freddy, I don't think you are discussing this with the best people. You know, like the people who could really help."

"Who's left? You're the only people I know."

"No, dear boy, think. Think how you became involved."

Petula was nodding, "Yes, Apollo knows what he's doing."

"And it was him that led you to your new best friends," Zahra added.

"The horses, Freddy, the horses and the Pegusinni; they are the people who you should be talking to. They are the ones you're helping, and they are ones who could actually do something about it."

"How many horses are with the cavalry?" asked Petula.

"About two hundred."

"And how many with the King's Troop?"

"Around a hundred and thirty."

"And police horses in London?"

"About a hundred and twenty, I think."

"And Pegusinni?"

"At least fifteen that I know of."

"So, you have about four hundred and fifty horses as well as fifteen Pegusinni. That's quite an army, Freddy."

Gloria clasped her hands on her lap, "And at the moment they are all looking to you as their leader. Even Victoriana, correct?"

"I guess that's how it's turned out."

"Guess? It most certainly is, young man," said Petula, "Now, you need to go and rally your troops. Discuss, plan, organise. They must all be wondering where you are right now."

"I said I would try to meet with Victoriana tonight, but I'm really worried about getting caught again."

"Freddy, last time you got caught you were all alone, you hadn't told anyone, not even your mother, right?"

"Right."

"And that big guard was probably terrifying to you."

"Yep."

"So," continued Gloria, "what's the worse thing that could happen to you? You might get caught, but what will they do? I'll tell you what they'll do."

"Shoot me?"

"Oh, don't be so dramatic! This is Knightsbridge in 2007, not Russia in war time!" She paused a moment to let that sink in. "They'll probably take you to that little guard room on the Knightsbridge side of the barracks and keep you there till they find out who you are."

"Is that the guard room where you get asked in by the soldiers to see the horse with the green tail?" queried Petula.

"No, darling, that happened to you down at Horse Guards. And you were in there for quite some time, if I recall," Zahra said. "By the way, did you ever see the green tail?"

"No, I don't think I did, but I did see…"

"Enough!" Gloria held up her hand, "young minds present!"

Petula stared off into the distance recalling her evening of company with Queen's Life Guard.

"Anyway, Freddy," continued Gloria, "they will ask who you are and who your parents are and will want to contact them before any police."

"And at that point," said Zahra, "you will give them my name and my mobile phone number and I will come and collect you. We'll write it off as a teenage prank."

"Will you go this evening?" Gloria asked.

"Yes, probably. That's what I told the guys this morning."

"Well, you just keep in mind that you are now not alone. We'll all wait up till we hear from you that you got safely home, ok?"

"OK."

"Right, young man, you need to be getting home and getting some rest. You have a big meeting with your officers and troops tonight."

"And we really should get back to the shop and open for a few hours. You know how we always get repairs in after Friday night stag and hen parties."

"Crowds should have gone and roads will be open now," said Zahra, "we could all share a cab."

"I think I'll walk if that's ok with you. I need some air and time to think a bit," said Freddy, standing up and pulling on his jacket.

"OK, kiddo," said Zahra patting him on the head, "you just let us know when you need us. And don't forget to call tonight, no matter how late it is. Right?"

He smiled and nodded, "Right."

Outside the over-cast weather had cleared, leaving warm May sunshine as he walked down The Mall toward Buckingham Palace. A couple of weeks ago this had been all a vast and strange place. Now it felt as familiar as his old back garden up at The Rectory. Hands in pockets, St James's Park on his right, he walked steadily on. He mulled over the messages as he walked. He thought about what they had to really mean.

And he and four hundred and fifty horses were the ones who were going to stop this?

Chapter Thirty-one

Victoriana stared silently at Freddy from her open stall door as he explained what he thought was going to happen. Rochester, Sefton, Yeti and Gauntlet were gathered behind Freddy in the dim light of the stabling. They had met with him in the park and escorted him into barracks without any hitch. Because Freddy was apprehensive about being inside again they also had Cedric on guard by the foot of the ramps to give plenty of warning should the night guard be patrolling.

"So you see, we have quite a problem," concluded Freddy.

"Problem?" exclaimed the black mare, "this could be complete and utter disaster!"

"Freddy, I know we asked before, but why would someone do this?" enquired Gauntlet in a small voice.

Freddy turned to him. "Look, mate, I've figured out what, I've figured out where and I've figured out when, but don't ask me why. I have no clue why. These are crazy people, off-the-wall total dingbats! I don't know how they think."

"Oh, ok. You see, we don't have horses like that. That's why we don't understand."

Victoriana drew herself up to full height, took a deep breath and then spoke again. "A plan, Freddy; we are military and we always work from a detailed plan."

"OK, I'm cool with that. What's the plan?"

"Actually, I was hoping you would have one worked out."

"Sorry, Vics, this has got me beat."

There was a short pause as they all thought, "We still have two weeks left and one more dress rehearsal, we will work something out," said Victoriana.

"You're not even going to be there, at the practice or the real thing."

She drew back her head and looked down her nostrils at him from the upper part of her eye, "Well, we'll see about that."

"OK, we'll use this week and next Saturday's rehearsal to check things out and confirm I'm right. And if I am, we will have six days left to come up with a plan," Freddy said

"Very good. Now, all of you, be gone, get Freddy out safely. If anyone needs to talk we will try to do it in the park."

Everyone nodded, Victoriana stepped back and closed her door while the others, under the cover of darkness headed quietly for the ramp. In a few moments they had Freddy safely back in the park and he was soon jogging westward to home. He stopped by the railings in Kensington gardens to call Zahra and confirm he was ok. Then quietly into the apartment and to bed where he slept for almost nine hours.

"Hmm, so not totally in a coma?" queried Jane, looking up from her Sunday paper.

"Umm, Hi. Any tea?"

"You slept like Rip Van Winkle, what were you doing all day yesterday?"

"Had a day out downtown, near Westminster, Whitehall, the parks, those areas."

"Anything else?"

"Well, I was home later in the afternoon, but you were out."

"Yes, they had an ambassador and his wife for dinner; it was a late shift for me. You must have been well gone when I got in. Did you go out at all last night?"

Freddy eyed her suspiciously. Damn, had she checked in his room? Had she found jeans smelling of horse poo again? He'd been pretty careful about all of that stuff. He went for the full bluff. "No, stayed home, pretty tired, did some school work. Early bed."

"Not seen that group of friends in the park? The ones you told me you were helping? From Ireland, I think you said."

"Not so much. They seem to be doing better. You want some toast while I'm making some?"

"No, I'll be starting Sunday lunch in about an hour." They both gave each other a neutral, non-committal smile.

"Yeah, didn't realise how late it is."

"And will you be out today too?"

"Er, nope. No plans. Should be staying home all of today."

"My, isn't that a change?"

"No need for the 'tone'."

"No tone, just pleasantly surprised." She broadened her grin, then went back to the colour supplement.

And that was Sunday. He showered, she made Sunday lunch, they ate together, she went shopping, he did some school work and tried to catch up with some rest. It was unbelievable how tired he felt after the last couple of weeks. In fact, he felt totally exhausted. Like most teens, he was clueless of the meaning of the term 'stress' and he had no idea what had hit him. This was the first day for weeks when nothing actually happened. He checked in with Zahra and she would be around tomorrow afternoon to do school work with him.

When Jane came home they had sandwiches while watching TV. At one point she casually enquired about how things were going with his new friend, Vicky. The one with the pony tail, she reminded him.

Yes, he'd seen her a couple of times. Nothing serious going on. They had a short chat about the oncoming visit of Gran and Aunt Sharon. Maybe Freddy needed to go shopping and get a spiffy outfit for the trooping day, she'd suggested. Now she was on a fairly good income they could afford to splurge a little. No need, he'd said. He'd wear something he already had. Something that wouldn't cause her any embarrassment. Preferably something bullet proof, he thought to himself.

Monday morning and Victoriana was hacking around the park with Nero. They kept up a steady working trot pace for their riders as she told him what had transpired over the weekend. When they came back down to a walk and Webber lit up a sneaky cigarette, Nero finally spoke up.

"Well, I can certainly understand now why Freddy is here. There is no way on earth that equine and a group of Pegusinni could have worked all this out." The black mare completely agreed with him. Then Nero asked, "Does he have a plan? A plan to solve all of this?"

"Unfortunately, not yet. But I personally plan to be there, in case last minute decisions need to be made and orders given."

"I see, and are you just going to casually stroll saddle-less and rider-less down The Mall alongside the regiment?"

"Sarcasm doesn't suit you, you old fool."

"Old I may be, my dear lady, but fool? No, not really. Seriously, how on earth are you going to pull that off?"

She turned her head and neck slightly toward him, wrinkled her left nostril, gave him an equine wink and said nothing.

Monday afternoon and Zahra arrived punctually at the apartment. While Jane was still at work she and Freddy gave each other updates. He on how the meeting with the horses had gone on Saturday evening and she with what the ladies had talked about and how to approach next Saturday's dress rehearsal.

"We need to approach it differently this week, from a different angle."

"Like what?" asked Freddy.

"If everything is like you think it is and, by the way, we do think you have it right, then we won't bother with all the faffing about getting into the stands again."

"I see."

"We've done it once and it's not going to help one bit, is it?"

"Not really."

"So, what do you think?"

"I think we should meet in the park and walk with the mounted band and the regiment from barracks to the palace and then down The Mall. That way we can check on everything we didn't see last time and maybe notice anything else."

"Not bad thinking, kiddo. Plus, we'll end up in the right places to confirm everything one more time."

"And if we stand on the top corner by St. James's park and The Mall, we can see just about the whole thing. The Mall and the tower will be across the road in front of us and we'll be behind the regiment looking over Horse Guards."

"And maybe then we'll come up with a plan."

"Heck, I hope so."

"Last resort, kiddo, we do go to the police, MI5, Scotland Yard, F.B.I., C.I.A., heck, the Kremlin for that matter, or Gordon Ramsay, but we sure as hell can't let this happen. Not again, not after 1982."

He remained silent and just nodded his agreement.

And so the week crept slowly by. A few brief meetings with the Pegusinni on the fire escape and in the yard, short talks with Victoriana and Nero as they rode by in the park and Thursday afternoon over at *'Men Swear Bi Us'* for tea, planning and generally moral support. Everyone desperately trying to come up with a plan. And everyone definitely coming up with nothing.

Saturday morning he met the ladies in the park across from the gates of the barracks. They were dressed more casually today. Zahra had on blue and white striped shorts that went from a high waist to mid calf, open sandals and she carried a light weight jacket. Gloria wore a navy bib and brace set over a red shirt, her long hair tied back in a single braid.. The bib put up a good fight to keep her bosom under control. Petula was wearing a lime green and black floral top over pale ice blue flared jeans that were frayed at the hems. Unlike the other two, she opted for low white heels instead of sandals. Freddy felt positively and safely dull in his t-shirt, jacket and jeans. The South Carriage Drive was closed to traffic and the mounted officers from the Met. waited patiently on the road, ready to clear the way for the regiment. The huge double gates were closed but standing in the park, the four could hear plenty of shouted orders as the band and two squadrons were forming up and being inspected. Sefton and Rochester stood calmly on top of the high brick wall watching the activity on the parade square. Yeti and Gauntlet waited with Freddy and his friends. As with the two previous rehearsals, the remaining Pegusinni had positioned themselves along the route.

Eventually, after much yelling of orders from behind the walls, the huge gates slowly opened and horses and riders poured out onto the road. First, the retinue of Life Guards, closely followed by Willamena carrying the director of music, the two drum horses and the mounted band. Behind them, the four divisions of the Queen's escort.

"Time to get moving," said Freddy to the ladies as he strode off, keeping up with the lead horses.

"Freddy, why don't we wait, spread ourselves out a little, in case something occurs further back?" suggested Zahra.

He looked back over his shoulder, "OK, meet me at the top of The Mall like we planned. See you there."

Gauntlet and Yeti hovered above Freddy, while to the entertainment of the troop horses, Sefton and Rochester slowly cruised back and forth along the full length of the moving regiment. At one point, Freddy saw Spartacus give him a nod and a wink as he carried the drummer for the Blues and Royals.

The walk from barracks, through the park, across Hyde Park corner and on to Buckingham Palace was completely uneventful. While the regiment took their places outside the palace gates, the four pedestrians took the opportunity to cross over into St. James's Park and move down the pathway alongside The Mall. The dress rehearsals were not as broadly advertised as the official trooping so again the crowds were light along the route. They were mainly made up of tourists who were there purely by chance. Venetia was at the front, carrying the Brigade Major, as she strode elegantly and purposefully down the centre of The Mall. The mounted band struck up a lively tune, the light crowds lining the route cheered and everyone was happy. Happy, except for three mediums and one teenage boy who were tight-lipped and anxious as they made their way to the top of the park.

Freddy paused at the top of The Mall directly across the road from the Duke of York's memorial tower. Venetia and the retinue were turning right down to the parade square as Freddy shaded his eyes and looked up to the top of the tower. Nothing. Only Cedric and Sefton circling slowly around the top, trying to see any signs of life. The mounted band passed and then the two divisions of Life Guards escorting the carriage drawn by the Windsor greys, Daniel and McCarthy. Looking lower down to the bottom of the tower he saw the same two men standing in exactly the same position as they had been last Saturday. Standing, smoking and occasionally pointing, but doing nothing illegal. As the two divisions of Blues and Royals rattled by on the tarmac, he heard a voice call from behind.

"Hey, kiddo. Anything going on?" Zahra was striding along, flanked by the other two women.

"Not really. Well, just the things we suspected," Freddy nodded towards the characters across the road at the top of the steps.

"Hmm, our little smoking foreign friends are back, eh?"

Freddy glanced at his watch. "Yep, and any second now we'll see if I'm right about the other parts as well."

Most of the crowd was trying to get closer to the Horse Guards. The tiered seating looked much fuller this week and there was more yelling of orders coming from the square. Finally there was silence, broken only by the chime of the eleven o'clock bells from the archway leading to the guard area.

"Some guy will be on the podium now, taking the salute thing, like she will next week," said Freddy. And then in the distance another sound became apparent.

"Oh my God," Gloria said very quietly.

"It just can't be," from Petula.

"Looks like you were bang on, kiddo," said Zahra resting her hand on Freddy's shoulder. He was silent, just nodding and looking with wide eyes. Then he spun around to look up to the steps by the tower. Petula followed his stare. "Hey, they've gone," she commented.

"They'll be back," he said, "and I know exactly when too."

"What do we do now? Asked Gloria.

"We wait. We just wait till they've done their parade and are leaving. Then we'll see if the second part is right."

Having no desire to sit through the whole parade business again the four walked over to an empty bench on the grass in the park. True to form, Zahra lit up, Gloria removed her sandals and rubbed her feet and Petula checked her makeup and hair. They sat in relative silence for a few minutes.

"I can't stand this doing nothing and if we do figure something out, having to wait another week before we can do anything," said Freddy to no one in particular.

"Why don't we try group?" suggested Zahra.

"Why not, couldn't do any harm" Gloria said.

"Maybe we'll see a face, or a sign."

"OK, on the grass, small circle," directed Petula.

"Mind if I ask what exactly group is?" Freddy asked.

"Just join us in the circle, feet slightly apart and join hands with us."

"Head back, eyes closed," directed Gloria across from where Freddy was holding hands between Zahra and Petula.

"Lord, I must look a right prat," he thought as he joined in. But after his tactless comment last week to the ladies about being aging hippies, he was trying to make things right again.

"Oh my! Something's very strong," said Gloria with her eyes still closed.

"Yes, I feel it. Strong and close," Zahra said, head also thrown right back. "But it doesn't feel bad or evil," commented Petula, shaking her head.

"Settle down, ladies, no big deal," said Freddy, looking at the grass in the centre of the circle, "when did you land, mate?"

"Just a moment ago," said Gauntlet. "Sefton was watching you from the top of the tower; he thought you might be going to have colic."

Freddy released his hand hold from the two ladies and knelt down on the grass. He reached forward and scratched Gauntlet under the chin. "Well, thanks for checking, little guy, but I'm fine. Just waiting till the parade finishes."

"And will you have a plan then, Freddy?" asked the small winged horse.

"Maybe, we'll see," sounding more confident than he really felt. He got to his feet and brushed bits of grass off the knee of his jeans. Gauntlet smiled, nodded, then lowered his haunches, tucked his fore legs and took flight to let the others know that their commanding officer was alright. The three ladies looked at Freddy.

"Pegusinni, I take it?" Zahra asked.

"Yes, just one of the boys checking that things were ok."

"You're going to miss those little friends when this is all over, Freddy," said Gloria smiling at him.

"Yeah, I guess so." He hadn't thought that far ahead. It all being over and the Pegusinni gone to wherever they went.

Petula was looking at her watch. "Time for a short stroll before they're done with trooping their things. We could go over to the lake for a few minutes." The other three joined her as she walked across the grass. Zahra was looking in her bag.

"Oh dear, I don't have anything for the ducks and swans."

"Don't worry, they won't be around for long," said Freddy dryly. Sure enough as they approached the side of the lake, the birds started to squawk and take flight. Several swans opened their wings and snaked their necks forward, hissing from the back of their throats.

"Well, you got that one right, Freddy," said Gloria watching the frightened and angry birds.

Zahra had stopped. "Wait, isn't that the tune for the last trot on the parade?"

"Does sound like it, we should get back to the corner then," said Freddy turning from the lake and striding along. As they reached the corner, they saw the mounted band and all four divisions of cavalry turning left down The Mall. They were followed by several groups of foot guards in their red tunics and tall furry hats. Sandwiched between all of these guards was the carriage drawn by the greys. As the carriage went up the short road toward the top of The Mall, Freddy pointed up to the steps under the tower.

"Bingo. Or, game, set and match. Or whatever the heck you say when something is so horribly right." The two men were back, standing at the base of the tower in front of the small wooden door.

"But you say they were only seen once, up at the top, Freddy?"

"Yes, on the khaki rehearsal, when it was dark, when they knew no one could see them."

"No one except a sharp eyed Pegusinni, that is," said Zahra.

"One thing really puzzles me," she continued very quietly, "how on earth did they get to the top of the tower, and worse, will they pull it off next week?"

Chapter Thirty-two

At three thirty a.m. on Sunday morning of April 29th 2007, three men poured petrol over the wooden door at the base of the Duke of York's memorial tower. As they moved back, one of them casually flicked a lit match toward the soaked area. They retreated back into the shadows as the fumes ignited into a mini explosion. Within seconds the old door was ablaze. Waiting calmly and patiently in the darkness the three men watched as the fire drew attention from late night pedestrians on the lower steps near The Mall. They observed as several grappled with mobile phones to call the police and fire brigade. The fire burned on, sending up plumes of black smoke and throwing out a surprising amount of heat. Within minutes the sirens could be heard as police and firemen scrambled to the scene. Hoses were unravelled and connected and water quickly extinguished the blaze.

While policemen kept the few people back from the scene, the officer in charge made a series of quick phone calls. As the flames subsided and murky water flowed from the base of the monument down the stone steps to The Mall, firemen scratched their heads and talked.

"Who would start such a stupid fire?"

It made no sense whatsoever. The door was so old and thick there was no way a fire like this would have burnt all the way through. Stupid, pointless vandalism was the conclusion. And still the three dark haired men waited calmly and quietly out of sight. An hour later, after the firemen had all but cleared away the mess, an old Renault car pulled up on The Mall. The police officer in charge went forward and spoke to the old man climbing out of the driver's seat.

"Now this has to be the most ludicrous thing I ever 'eard of in all my time in this job," said Wilfred Henderson as he climbed up the steps toward the memorial.

Wilfred had worked for the city of Westminster for over thirty years as a generic caretaker and keeper of the keys for many historical buildings and monuments across the London. Shaking water off his boot by the old door, he rested a battered briefcase on his knee. He opened it and sorted through a collection of large keys. The senior police officer waited patiently for Wilfred to look the door over. It appeared there was no damage other than the charring of the wood but protocol called for the officer to have the place inspected by the correct person. So, he had called Wilfred Henderson from his bed at four a.m. to come to the scene and carry out his inspection. Wilfred stuck his head through the open door and slowly swung the light from his torch from left to right.

"I can't see nuffin wrong in 'ere," he muttered.

"What about up the stairs at the top of the tower?" asked the young police officer, "Shouldn't you check up there?"

"Look, sunshine, I'm twice your age, I've got old bunions and a new verruca started. You think I'm going to climb to the top of this old thing and poke around in the dark?"

The officer remained silent and smiled patiently. Wilfred passed him the torch. "Alrighty, you're so keen, you go up. I'll wait here with the fire lads."

The police officer took the torch and started up the inside of the tower two steps at a time. Wilfred and the firemen enjoyed a smoke as they waited. No one noticed that the three dark-haired men were now gone from their hiding place. No one noticed a dark blue car with blacked out windows pulling up a hundred feet behind Wilfred's Renault.

The young policeman emerged from the tower, closed and locked the door behind him. "Couldn't see anything wrong at all. But this is just too weird for words."

Wilfred nodded his head in agreement as he put the large old keys back into his briefcase. "I blames the schools. They should never have done away with the cane. Give some of these cocky little sods six of the best and they'd soon be running home to their ma's." Everyone was muttering and nodding as Wilfred got into his old car, fastened his seat belt and started the engine. "And if you get a bloody rocket up the arse of Nelson's Column, don't call me out in the middle of the night!" He slammed his door and slowly pulled away from the kerb. The police and firemen chuckled at the antics of the old guy. No one noticed the dark blue car now quietly following Wilfred.

And the dark blue car with the dark windows followed old Wilfred all the way out to the east end of London where he had lived all his life. As the two cars reached smaller and darker streets, the dark blue car accelerated passed the Renault, slowed and finally stopped at an angle virtually blocking Wilfred's route. The old caretaker wound down his window and peered out. A dark-haired man stepped out from the driver's side of the blue car, smiled and waved to Wilfred and walked toward him.

"So what the 'ell is going on 'ere, sunshine?"

Wilfred's attention was now caught by the dark-haired man extracting his wallet and opening it to pull out a large handful of notes. You simply can't beat a large display of money to grab someone's attention. And the caretaker was so distracted he didn't see or hear the passenger door of his own vehicle quietly opening and another man sliding in. In one practised move, the visitor to Wilfred's car swung his arm forward and covered the older man's face with a thick white cloth. Much later, all Wilfred could recall was seeing a man with a lot of money in his hand standing in the road and several hours later waking up with a blinding headache, still in his car. When he looked around, there was no sign of robbery, no damage, nothing. His car was fine, he was fine and his briefcase was exactly where he'd tossed it on the passenger seat. He checked his own pockets and wallet. All present and correct.

"Bloody hell," he thought through a thumping head, "I must have passed out. Is this the first sign of dementia?" He rubbed sleep from the corner of his eye, started up the car and drove slowly home.

What Wilfred didn't know was that while he was sedated from the fumes, his briefcase containing all the precious keys had been taken away by the man who had driven the dark car. The second man had carefully pushed the old Renault to the side of the road so it looked neatly parked and wouldn't attract attention and then sat in the passenger seat keeping the sleeping caretaker company. Ready to let any curious passersby know that his friend had had one too many whiskeys and was sleeping it off. Within an hour the dark car had returned, the briefcase was placed back on the seat and then the two men drove quietly away into the first light of day. Placed carefully on the back seat of their car was a small case containing a full duplicate set of keys matching those in Wilfred's possession. This small group of men now had total access to the tower, to come and go as they pleased, knowing full well that no one would be looking for them. No one would suspect anything. And no one would see anything before Saturday the 17th of June. No one except a sharp-eyed Pegusinni known as Cedric.

Now it was several months later and Cedric was as anxious as the rest of his group about what was happening in the city. The week before the second dress rehearsal had dragged on, but now, the week after was flying by. The days were ticking away as Freddy, three middle-aged mediums, a group of Pegusinni and several key equine at the barracks all tried frantically to come up with some sort of plan to counter what was about to happen. Toward the end of the week the daily mounting of Queen's Life Guard changed to Long Guard when the royal family returned to London in readiness for the weekend. About the same time, another 'royal family' arrived in London Freddy's Gran and his Aunt Sharon. On Thursday afternoon Jane and Freddy rode the underground over to St. Pancras station to meet the train coming in from Chesterfield. St Pancras was still in relative chaos as building work was nearing completion for the new Euro Star rail link from London to Paris. Workmen with loud drills and other machines virtually drowned out any noise from people or trains. After group hugs and family kisses at the gate by the platform, Gran commented that Freddy had grown in the time she hadn't seen him. He pointed out it was only about five or six weeks but she replied it seemed like a year so he must have grown. Dragging small suitcases on little wheels they took the underground back to Kensington, with Gran and Sharon commenting on all things 'London'. Fred kept quiet, marvelling at the fact that only a few weeks earlier he'd felt the same way.

After a quick look around the small apartment, Jane took her mother and sister over to the main house for a guided tour. With Caroline and Paul away on official business, the large diplomatic home was empty. There was much 'Ooohing' and 'awing' from Gran and Sharon as they wandered from room to room. At one point Gran gripped Jane's arm and said, "Eee, you've done right well fer yer self, me duck." Jane pointed out that she didn't actually live in this house but it made no difference to her mother who was already planning on what she'd tell all of her friends at bingo. As they were about to leave by the back door, Jane paused, turned around and invited her sister Sharon to open her handbag. To Freddy's amusement, Aunt Sharon attempted to be offended but quickly gave in and opened her bag. Jane then suggested Sharon return the small items back to their places around the house. Ornaments, small pieces of silver, a tiny gold-framed photo all went back to where they belonged. Jane simply rolled her eyes upward as she walked past Freddy and to the apartment.

That evening they walked down Kensington High Street to eat at a small Italian place Jane favoured. With her bosses were away, she planned on doing as little cooking as possible. Back at the apartment the three ladies had a night cap glass of wine and made plans for shopping on Friday. Freddy excused himself under the pretext of going to the rear yard to make sure his bike was chained and covered. The truth was he realised that with Gran sleeping in his room and him on the sofa, the Pegusinni would not be able to contact him from the fire escape and he couldn't sneak out that way. He looked quickly up and down the street, checked the yard and fire escape and even on the garage roof but there were no little flying horses anywhere.

"Oh, well, let's hope there's no crisis tonight," he thought as he made his way back inside via the front door. He spent the night in a turbulent sleep, tossing and twisting, visions of the scene at Horse Guard's playing out before him and totally clueless as to how to stop things. How to protect his friends. And now, how to protect his family. At around three a.m. he sat bolt upright on the sofa, kicked off his blanket and paced up and down around the small sitting room. He'd been looking at it from the wrong angle. He'd been trying to figure out how he could stop this horrendous scene from happening. What if there was no way he could stop it from happening? But what if there was a way to prevent harm and injury to all of the horses and the mounted soldiers? That had to be worth trying. The most complicated problems sometimes had the simplest of answers. It was so obvious he hardly even dare mention it to Victoriana and Zahra. Hundreds of horses and soldiers could be safe. But what about his mother and family? That was another issue. Another issue unless he could prevent them from attending in the first place.

One small snag with the plan was he would need a meeting with Victoriana and once again he definitely did not like the idea of going in over the walls to the barracks. On the other hand, it was a small price to pay if he could keep so many people from harm. What he was about to propose was so radical it would need full approval and co-operation from Victoriana. There was no way he could send a message about this to her through the Pegusinni. He would have to face her himself and present the idea. In the darkness of the kitchen he made himself a cup of hot chocolate, returned to the couch and eventually dozed off into a light fitful sleep.

Friday morning he declined the invite to accompany his family on the shopping trip. He assured them he would be fine and wouldn't venture too far and he reminded his mother that Zahra would be around for Friday afternoon class. Did she really want him to skip that too? It was the master stroke that left him alone for most of the day. Straight after breakfast he was in the park and cycling down the pathway next to Rotten Row, having a brief conversation with Victoriana as Webber trotted along next to Clarissa. Tension between the black mare and the teenager was high. Less than twenty-four hours before the regiment left barracks for the trooping and heaven only knew how many would return safely.

"We have to talk, soon," he called over to her as he pedalled along.

"I doubt we'll be stopping today," she called back, "apparently Webber has a busy schedule and we are due back in barracks shortly."

"Maybe I could be of help?" offered Nero as he huffed along next to the smartly moving mare.

"Thanks, Nero, but I really need to talk to the boss lady about this," Freddy answered. With a resigned sigh he continued. "I'll try to come to barracks this evening with the guys. We really need to talk before tomorrow."

"Very well, but you will need to be there before midnight. I have another small venture planned this evening."

"You do? What are you up to?"

"If you wait around after we talk tonight, you'll see."

He slowed his bike as the riders moved the horses up to canter. "Okie dokie, see you tonight," he yelled as the horses pulled away from him. He brought the bike to a standstill and watched the rear ends of the horses growing smaller as they cantered away. "And please, just maybe this will be the last time I have to break into property belonging to the Ministry of Defence."

That afternoon over the dining table he slowly explained his idea to Zahra.

"Well, that's great kiddo. Sometimes answers are so obvious." She reached over and patted the back of his hand. "Just one problem though. What about all the foot soldiers and all the spectators? If these crack-pots do what we think, well, there will still be a lot of harm done, eh?"

"For God's sake give me a break, Zahra!" He pushed his chair back as he jumped up. "You think I hadn't thought about that? You think I'm not frantic with worry? As far as I know, I'm here to help the horses and the mounted soldiers and I'm doing that!"

She just looked at him, staying quiet as he let go of his anger and frustrations. She watched as he screwed up his face, fighting back emotions and tears that were welling.

"Damn it! My own mother and family are going to be there if I can't stop them from going! You think I'm not aware of that too?" He was shaking as Zahra stood up, calmly walked around the table and gave him a warm hug.

"We know. We know you're trying, kiddo. And we're all trying with you." He slowly calmed as she hugged him. "And, you've figured out half of the problem. You just watch. You just see. We know you'll figure out the rest."

He pulled back from her. "You think so? You really think so?"

"Of course, me and the girls have talked about it endlessly. You are a special boy, Freddy. We know you can do it."

"Thanks for the support, Zahra, but I'm not so confident."

"And," she continued as she opened her bag looking for a smoke, "the girls and I may have figured out a way to help keep your family safe."

"You serious?"

"Yep. You concentrate on the horses and the soldiers; let the old broads look after your family."

That night at around eleven-thirty he met the Pegusinni in the park outside of the barracks.

"So you have a plan, Freddy?" Sefton asked.

"A plan to stop the bad men?" from an anxious Gauntlet.

"Yes, I have an idea that you could call a plan. No, I haven't thought of how to stop the bad guys."

The group of four small winged horses looked puzzled.

"Just wait till we're inside, I'll explain it clearly when we are with the boss. Let's just hope she approves." After Yeti had gone ahead to check that the coast was clear, Sefton and Rochester 'escorted' Freddy up and over the wall. Gauntlet brought up the rear. Standing in the shadows in front of her box stall Freddy wondered for the last time if it was such a good plan after all. He quietly pulled back the bolt and swung the door open so Victoriana was properly part of the group. All eyes were now on him.

Freddy cleared his throat. "OK, you know how our main thing is to keep equine and soldiers safe?"

They all nodded. "This is what I think we should do."

After he had explained his idea there was a stunned silence, broken by Rochester.

"No. Oh no, Freddy. Not possible."

"Indeed, that must be out of the question," Sefton agreed.

"You want us to involve about two hundred troop horses and soldiers in this type of thing?" Yeti was amazed.

"Freddy, equine could never do such a thing," very quietly from Gauntlet.

"Well, does anyone else have any other ideas?" the frustrated teenager said.

Victoriana had been silent to this point. Finally she spoke, giving her opinion.

"I agree with Freddy, we have to do it."

"Really?"

"Oh my."

"Never heard of such a thing!"

She continued. "I've considered it and the consequences are a small price to pay."

Now all were silent as the alpha mare spoke. "If this prevents harm to equine and soldiers, then we do it. And I will take full responsibility if there are repercussions. It is my duty to make sure no harm comes to this herd, therefore we will do as Freddy suggests."

After more silence Rochester ventured, "Do we inform the troop horses tonight? In the morning? Or when you say it happens?"

"No, we don't tell them this evening. Too many of them will get silly ideas and some will start to fret and worry." Victoriana was thinking of equine such as the nervous grey mare, Whimsy. "We tell them tomorrow, just before we take action."

Freddy was amazed and pleased that she agreed with his plan. "If we do this, we will need the help of all fifteen Pegusinni. We won't get a second chance to pull this off properly. We'll need really good communication with everyone."

The clock above the archway to the barracks chimed twelve. Victoriana pricked her ears at the sound.

"Very well, I now have another plan to carry out."

"What are you up to, Vics?" asked Freddy.

"No time to explain, we agreed to shortly after midnight. Now, all of you out of here. Actually, if you sit on the barrack wall you could watch the fun."

"Who agreed to what?" persisted Freddy.

"No time. Now, move! Out of here please!"

With that, the four Pegusinni and Freddy hurried up the ramp and quietly sailed to the top of the wall. Keeping a firm hold on Rochester's neck, Freddy sat with his legs dangling and looked over the dimly lit parade square.

"What the hell is that old nag up to," he wondered as they sat in silence.

Within a few minutes they heard the clatter of large steel shoes on tarmac and then in the moonlight Spartacus appeared at the top of the ramp for the Blues stables. He paused, looked around, then to everyone's surprise, let out a long, extremely loud whinny. The noise resounded around the empty space, bringing anyone within earshot to attention. He then trotted briskly down the ramp, paused as he reached the doors to the forge, stretched his neck up and forward and let out another piercing scream. Then he jogged to the centre of the square, his hooves the size of dinner plates making a great racket. The night guard for the Blue's stables came running down the ramp.

"Oh bloody hell! How did you get out?" He continued running only to see to his dismay the old drum horse trot diagonally across the square heading for the ramp to the riding school. The guard ran after him but no sooner had he reached the ramp then Spartacus shot back up past him and back onto the square. This was going to be a moonlight game of 'chase', and the guard needed help. He called to the night guard from the Life Guard stables who quickly appeared.

As the jolly chase continued, the five spectators on top of the wall were shocked to see a sleek black horse moving quickly and quietly down the ramp from the Blues stables. Within seconds another black mare was seen heading up the ramp from the Life Guards barns. The two mares nodded to each other as they keep moving and disappeared into the darkness of their opposite stables.

"Well, the smart old queen bee," said Sefton to no one in particular.

"So that's how she's pulling it off," commented Yeti.

"She's too smart for her own good that one," from Rochester.

"Would someone please tell me what the heck is going on?" hissed Freddy in the dark. In the distance they could still hear the night guards trying to catch a loose Spartacus.

"Freddy, you remember how Victoriana said she wouldn't let her regiment out into danger without her?"

"Yeah, she said that."

"Well, now she'll be there. Tomorrow morning."

"How the hell has she pulled that off?"

"The distraction with Spartacus, now I see that was part of her plan."

"Victoriana just moved into Venetia's stall."

"She did what?"

"And if my guess is correct, Venetia will now be in Willamena's stall."

"And Willamena will be where Victoriana should be," interjected Yeti.

"Three identical black equine," said Gauntlet, "very difficult for the grooms to notice when they are in a hurry tomorrow morning."

"And once more I say, you are kidding me!" an amazed Freddy said.

"Not at all. Tomorrow Willamena will be left here, in Victoriana's stall. Venetia will be carrying the director of music. Who of course will be following the horse carrying the Brigade Major at the front, Victoriana, leading her regiment."

Chapter Thirty-three

By seven thirty a.m. on Saturday morning the small apartment was buzzing with activity as Jane, Sharon and Gran hurried around having baths, ironing best clothes, drying hair and choosing makeup. Freddy had hardly slept again. With nothing much happening before nine a.m., he went for his breakfast at the café on Kensington High Street. As he wolfed down a couple of bacon sandwiches and a mug of tea he thought things through for one last time. He felt much more comfortable knowing that Victoriana was going to be there. He really did admire her guile and cunning. And with her agreeing to his plan, at least hopefully, the regiment would be safe. His worry about his family had been lifted when Gloria and Petula confirmed they would 'take care of things'. When he'd spoken to them the previous day, Petula had given him one small task to do for her. An odd task, at that, but she had hushed him up and told him all would become clear on Saturday. They had agreed it was better for him to go along with the pretence that all was normal and he would be attending with his family without objection. Zahra was to meet Freddy on the top corner of The Mall at the right turn down to Horse Guard's parade grounds. The spot directly across from the Duke of York's memorial tower.

Glancing at his watch, Freddy realised he needed to get back to change. He was hoping and praying Gloria and Petula were good for their promise about his mum and family. At one point he had thought of hiding their tickets but that would not have been a big obstacle for Jane and his royalty-obsessed Gran. Their names would be on an official list somewhere and they would have got themselves in, regardless. No, it would take something bigger than that to stop them. All three women were crowded in Jane's bedroom putting finishing touches to hair and makeup.

"That you, Freddy?" his mother called as he walked into the hall way.

"No, it's Prince William, decided to dodge the show today and hide in a strange woman's flat in Kensington."

"Don't have a smart mouth with me, young man. Now, get yourself ready; the car will be here soon."

In his room he pulled on the fresh white shirt that had been ironed and laid out for him, made an attempt at doing up the tie neatly and pulled on his sport jacket just back from the cleaners. He looked in the mirror. "Gawd, think I was going to some farty wedding, not to a bloody war zone." He desperately wanted to walk with the regiment from barracks down to the palace and on to the parade ground but that was not going to happen. Still, Victoriana had coped for years without him so no doubt, she'd be coping now. Albeit in the guise of Venetia.

"Car's here! Come on, everyone," Jane was calling from the door. In the hall way he saw Gran in her new outfit. A powder blue short jacket, matching skirt with a white blouse, pearl necklace and a frilly hat in the same shade of blue. She was beaming at her grandson.

"Eee, int' this just too exciting, our Fred, eh?"

"Yes, Gran, really exciting. Do you know you look like the queen mother today?"

"Oo, er! I 'ope not. She's dead!" She cackled with laughter, picked up her blue handbag and set off to the car. She was followed by Aunty Sharon who was in a gold shiny mini dress with a black, broad plastic belt, black broad brimmed hat, black high heeled shoes and bag. Gold hooped earrings swung around her neck. Posh Beckham need not feel threatened. Jane was the most subtle and tasteful of the three in a floral print burgundy summer dress, a short light jacket hung over shoulders, narrow cream belt, soft straw sun hat and cream shoes. She eyed him up as he walked slowly down the hall.

"Hmm, not really Prince William, but you'll do. Now, into that big black car. Driver's waiting."

"Yes, mum, he's waiting for us. That's the whole point of a chauffeur, you know."

She glared. "I've warned you, no smart mouth today. This is going to be a nice family day out. One to remember."

"Yep, mum, I think it will."

As the clock over the main gates chimed six a.m. and the duty trumpeter blew reveille, Victoriana stood in Venetia's box, trying to be patient. Today she had more than a risen clench to worry about. During the night, she had gone over the plan Freddy had put forward. Something like this had never even been heard of before, let alone carried out. It would need the strictest leadership, control and discipline to work correctly. Again she worried about the nervous ones such as Whimsy and the new young remounts who would be at the official trooping for the first time. They had gone through the three rehearsals without incident but today was the real thing. The atmosphere and feeling would be different and equine were very sensitive to such changes.

She heard the groom coming to prepare who he thought was Venetia for the big day. Her tail was shampooed, hooves scrubbed, dried and carefully covered with black boot polish. The groom put on the ceremonial leather bridle and breastplate so highly polished some people actually thought it was plastic. At the last minute when she was out of the sawdust of the stall, her hooves would be brushed with oil so they would glisten as she walked down The Mall. Just like the two previous Saturdays but with more intensity, the Household Cavalry prepared for its biggest event of the year. For today's event, the huge solid silver kettle-drums to be carried by Spartacus and Achilles had been brought out of storage. The priceless silver drums were only ever used in the presence of the reigning monarch. On all other occasions, copper kettle-drums were used.

Because Victoriana was carrying the Brigade Major she was ready before the regiment and ridden on her own to the side of Buckingham Palace. There she and the Major would wait for the regiment and the royal procession. Like Freddy, she also had wanted to walk with her troops but they were all assured no harm would come to anyone between the Knightsbridge barracks and Buckingham Palace. It was after the move off from Buckingham Palace that mattered.

The N.C.O. taking her to the palace for the Brigade Major took the usual route through the park, across Hyde Park Corner and down Constitution Hill. But today was different. Today the route was lined with steel barriers and traffic was stopped or completely blocked in many places. Huge flags swung from tall white poles, moving slightly in the occasional breeze. And crowds of people, growing thicker by the minute. Some would have been at the kerb side waiting all night to make sure they had a front row seat. Families, groups of teenagers, and thousands of foreign tourists lined the royal route, all determined to watch up close and personal this globally famous event. The Metropolitan Police Division was out in force. Hundreds of uniformed officers were everywhere, from Hyde Park all the way to Whitehall. When the royal procession left the palace, dozens of them would be lining the kerb side facing the crowds. Dotted along the route were television vans and crews, and down by the Palace and The Mall special platforms had been set up for their cameras to broadcast the event to the world. Nervous commentators and announcers were going over their scripts, checking to make sure they could pronounce any unusual names or military ranks.

At the same time Victoriana reached the palace and Freddy was on his way in a large black car, three women were meeting up at Admiralty Arch. Three women who each wore a long narrow crystal on a thin chain around her neck. Dressed in the same smart outfits they had worn for the first rehearsal morning, they were ready to blend in with the crowd who would be going down to the seating area around the parade ground.

"OK, ladies, this is when we part company for a while," said Zahra looking at her watch, "coming up to ten o'clock"

"Two ticky wicks," Gloria said as she leaned over and dabbed a tissue at some smudged lipstick on the corner of Zahra's lip. "There, much better, you don't look like The Riddler now."

"That would be The Joker, he was the one with the face, in the Batman flick," said Petula.

"Really? I thought he was the one in the white tie and tail coat?"

"No, that was The Penguin."

"Enough with damn Batman, we have our boy and a few thousand soldiers to think about!" Zahra's tension and nerves were frayed this morning. "Girls, I'm going over to the park. We don't want Freddy's mum spotting me. She knows the sight of me far too well."

"Yes, off you go. H hopefully we'll see you later this morning."

"Of course, you'll see me!"

"Just make sure you and our boy stay out of harm's way, ok?"

"I promise, we will. And we'll do our level best to darn well stop anything too."

Zahra had turned to walk away but now stopped and turned back to look to her friends. "Heavens, I hope they don't keep you too long. Try to make it back by about eleven-thirty and then meet us in the park."

Petula looked rather pensive as she replied, "We will if there is still a park left to meet you in."

"Go on now, scoot before you're spotted," called Gloria. Zahra disappeared into the crowd and made her way across the road at the official crossing hosted by the police. A steady stream of well-dressed people was making its way under a tented archway to have their tickets scrutinised. The massed bands on the square were already playing rousing tunes. The atmosphere was like that of a grand street carnival, but without alcohol, kebabs, drugs and sex.

On the other side of Admiralty Arch a large black limo with a family from Derbyshire pulled over to the kerb and four people stepped out into Trafalgar Square. Jane, Gran and Sharon moved excitedly along the pavement under the arch towards the top of The Mall. Freddy followed at a slower pace, dragging his heels. He was more than apprehensive about what was going to happen in the next few minutes.

"Come on, Freddy! Don't dawdle! We want to get to our seats and see everything!" His mother called over her shoulder. The crowd was thicker now, all moving in the same direction at a steady pace under the tall arch and along toward the parade ground. People were smiling, some laughing and everyone generally having a good time. As the three ladies from Derbyshire in their best clothes linked arms and stepped forward, smiling, grinning and loving the moment, two more women stepped out from the side and walked toward them. Heads turned, talking loudly to each other, Gloria and Petula walked slap bang into Jane, Gran and Sharon.

"Oh my!"

"Oh, dahlings, so sorry!"

Petula had dropped her bag by Sharon who picked it up and handed it to her.

"Thank you soooo much, just so clumsy of us not to look where we were going."

"No problem," said Jane, smiling and nodding, "it happens. So many people." She moved off to catch up with her mother and sister who were walking on again. Then it happened. Petula looked into her bag, rummaged around and looked up and screamed, "Hey! Stop! Stop them. Thieves!"

People stared and moved back as Petula and Gloria gave chase to the three ladies.

"Stop those women!" called Gloria, "they mugged us!"

"What on earth…?" said Jane looking around.

Petula grabbed Sharon by the shoulder. "You! Thief! Give it back!"

Sharon shook herself free. "Get off me, you crazed cow! I haven't got anything!"

"You leave my lass alone!" yelled Gran, swinging her hand bag and managing to land a clout on Petula's arm.

"Help! Police! Now! Police!" Gloria, red-faced and screaming, waved to some of the uniformed officers standing nearby. Freddy tried to blend back into the crowd, staying far away from the screaming women and twirling handbags.

Jane planted herself between Sharon and a yelling Petula.

"You are out of your mind, woman! You bumped into us!"

By now, two police officers were at the scene.

"Now, ladies, let's all be calm. What seems to be the trouble here?" asked the male officer.

"Calm? Bloody calm?" Sharon's eyes blazed as she glared at Petula. "That crazy heifer is accusing me of theft!"

The female officer stepped forward and put herself between the two angry women. "Now, madam, no need to get excited, let's all stay calm."

"Don't patronise me, you trumped-up uniformed piece of butch! I din't do nothing!" Sharon was now pulling, trying to get at Petula to land her one.

"Thieves! Thieves! They stole from us!" Gloria was causing as much chaos as she could. Gran stepped up and swung her bag at her.

"You watch your gob! You fat, loud mouthed London-lump!" Two more uniformed police joined the fray.

"Ladies! Quiet please!" yelled one of the constables. The crowd had formed a large circle on the pavement around the action. They were thrilled to have a roadside cabaret while they waited for access to their seats.

"Now, you," called the constable pointing to a red faced Petula, "You tell me what's going on here."

"Certainly, constable." Petula ran her hands back through her blonde hair as she continued. "My lady friend and I were making our way to our seats when this group shoved and mugged us."

"You lying trollop!" Sharon pulled against the female officer who was restraining her.

"You weren't going to your seats! You were walking toward us," said an indignant Jane. She was the only one trying to remain calm. Petula chose to ignore that comment and went on.

"They bumped into us, forcing me to drop my bag," she paused for effect, "then stole from me!"

"We din't steal nowt! Ya skinny, southern twig!" Sharon was nearly foaming at the mouth. Freddy pressed back further into the crowd, partially hiding behind two nuns in black habits. One of the constables looked to Sharon. "Is this true, madam? You took something?"

"Is it hell true! I'd rather put wasps up my bum than steal from a cheap-looking old tart like that!"

"Tell her to open her bag then!" challenged Petula.

"Oh dear God, this really isn't happening. Not today. Not today of all days," Jane muttered.

"Yes, search her bag!" Gloria yelled.

"Hey!" called Gran poking Gloria in the mid-riff, "you stay out of it, ya lard arse!"

"Here! I'll empty my freakin bag! I don't care! I have nowt to hide!" Sharon bent down about to tip her bag on the pavement. The male officers tried not to look at her underwear showing from under her mini dress.

"Madam, you are not obliged by law to empty your bag at this point."

"Make her do it! You'll see she has my gold compact in there! It was given to me by my great grandmother!" Petula looked around to the assembled masses and added for good measure, "She was a maid to Queen Victoria, my great grandmother, that is."

Several people in the crowd nodded and were impressed.

"For god's sake, Sharon, just empty your bag and let's get this over with, eh?" said Jane through clenched teeth.

Sharon ceremoniously tipped her bag upside down and the few contents fell to the pavement. Her purse, some lipstick, tissues, keys, an address book and a delicate gold compact. The same one Freddy had placed there the night before.

"There!" shrieked Petula, "and look on the back, it has my initials! P.A.D. Petula Andromeda DeVere."

The whole group was silent, everyone staring at the gold compact on the pavement.

"No, no. I didn't. I didn't take this," said Sharon shaking her head and looking up at them all.

"Oh hell, Sharon, just for today couldn't you have behaved? Just for once?" Jane's tone was bitter as her eyes blazed, burning holes into her younger sister.

"Eh up me duck. You just couldn't 'elp yourself, could you?" said Gran with arms folded and a disapproving tutting.

"Lock her up!" Gloria was yelling again, "lock them all up! Darn thieves and pickpockets! Coming to London to steal from the residents!"

"Officers, I wish to press charges. I want to go to the police station right now and have reports filed and charges brought against these women." Petula was standing tall, arms folded, determined and defiant.

"No! No, we can't, not today. Today's our big day," Jane looked at the officer who appeared to be in charge. "My mother and sister have come all the way from Stavely for today, please, let's just drop everything?" The female officer was helping Sharon to put items back into her bag.

"No, not the compact, madam, I'll keep that, till we get this sorted out at the station."

"Throw the book at them!" Gloria stood shoulder to shoulder with Petula, arms folded rigidly under her bosom. The four police officers talked briefly, deciding who would go with the first of the day's trouble makers to the station.

One of them made a call on his radio and within minutes a patrol car arrived, ready to take the group away.

"This won't take long, ladies, we'll have it all sorted within a couple of hours."

"A couple of hours? It'll all be over. We'll miss everything," said an incredulous Jane.

"Tough. You shouldn't bring your thieving relatives to town then should you?" said a tight-lipped Petula as she walked to the police car.

From his position back in the crowd Freddy saw another police car pull up and Petula and Gloria get into the back. His mother stopped, looking around. "Wait! Freddy! Where the heck is Freddy now?"

"Who's that then, madam?"

"My son, my boy. He's here, somewhere, with us!"

"Missing child? Oh, that's all we need," the police man said. "How old is this lad?"

"Nearly seventeen."

"Well, I think he can be looking after himself, eh? Now, why don't you get into the back of the car with your sister and we'll get this all sorted."

And as Freddy watched the cars pull away, he raised a finger to his forehead in a small salute.

"Enjoy the trooping, mum. See you later."

Then he heard the clock over Horse guard's strike ten fifteen. The regiment would be nearing Buckingham Palace, ready for the walk down The Mall.

Chapter Thirty-four

Freddy crossed the road at the official crossing and looked around the park for Zahra.

"Over here, kiddo." She was standing by a tree, pearl cigarette holder clenched tightly in the corner of her mouth. "How did it go? I saw a bit of chaos from here."

"Well, they're out of the way for some time, but I'm not sure my mum will ever forgive me if she finds out."

"Let's hope she won't, eh?"

Freddy looked over to the other side of the street. "Oh, that's all we need."

Zahra followed his gaze to see about one hundred school children dressed in navy and black uniforms walking in pairs, holding hands and being escorted by nuns down to the parade square.

"Kids? Little kids here? Today?"

"Guess so, must be a big school day out for them."

Sefton glided in and landed softly on the grass next to Freddy.

"Lots of children, and then the other extreme." He nodded with his long dark face with the broad white strip to indicate more arrivals. At least a dozen wheel chairs with elderly and handicapped ex soldiers were being assisted to the parade ground.

"And, they all get front row seats. The children, the handicapped, the Chelsea Pensioners and older senior members of the British Legion."

"Front row? In wheel chairs?"

"Well, they're not in the seating. All of the children and the others, they will have special places all along the front at ground level. We used to see them every year. They sit so close to the rope that they get dust in their eyes when we do the trot past."

Freddy quickly explained to Zahra what Sefton had said. She and Freddy looked at each other in grim silence.

"Not too much we can do about it just now, kiddo. At least your family and the regiment should be safe."

"But little kids? And the old folks? This is bloody awful, Zahra. What if these crazies pull it off?"

Zahra pursed her mouth tightly. "Well, any more ideas?"

Freddy turned to Sefton, "Everyone else in position?"

"Indeed, most are down on the palace roof waiting for the move off and then the word from Victoriana or from you"

"Cedric? Yeti?"

"On watch up near the tower. Have been for most of the night."

"And?"

"One man. Arrived about four o'clock in the morning. Used a key to get into the tower. Hasn't been seen since."

"But still in there?"

"Definitely."

"And he had a key?"

"Yes."

Freddy turned to Zahra. "Cedric and Yeti said that there's a guy in the tower. Now. Waiting. He had a damn key to get in."

"How on earth did they manage that?"

"God knows, but some wacko is definitely in there."

The small winged black horse, Zahra and Freddy turned and looked towards the top of the tower across the road. Of course, there was nothing to see. Not now. Not on the outside. Not yet.

The parade square clock cheerfully chimed ten thirty a.m. Gauntlet glided in and took his place next to Freddy.

"Officer's grey, ready to help with orders, Freddy."

"I don't think I'll be giving many orders, little guy. Vics knows the plan, she'll be the one telling the troops."

Suddenly, the crowd lining both sides of The Mall exploded into cheers and clapping. Looking over, Freddy saw everyone waving flags, parents hoisting small children up onto shoulders, all eyes fixed on the road way.

"What the heck's that? The regiment isn't due for about another fifteen minutes or more!"

Sefton and Gauntlet nodded knowingly.

"Junior royals and their chaperones," explained Sefton.

"Usually two or three carriages," added Gauntlet.

"Junior Royals?"

"Yes, this year it will be the two young princes and close family members."

"But they weren't at any of the rehearsals!"

"No, they don't rehearse; they just show up on the day."

Zahra and Freddy could see the tops of the carriages pass by and make the right turn down to Horse Guard's.

"Wills and Harry?" guessed Zahra.

"Yep, just a few more to add to the possible carnage."

From behind the trees they heard the massed bands strike up the national anthem as the carriages entered the parade ground. The music stopped abruptly after only a few moments.

"What happened there?" asked Freddy, looking at Sefton.

"Usual thing. Junior Royals don't get the full piece. Just six bars of music. Only the monarch gets the full version."

Freddy took a few minutes to talk to Sefton and Gauntlet about the plan for the regiment. Now that they were all formed up outside of Buckingham Palace, word would be spread through the regiment by the Pegusinni. First to the four retinue equine, then to the mounted band horses and finally to the troop horses. Gauntlet had visited the royal mews that morning and explained to Daniel and McCarthy about the danger and how they would need to participate in the plan with the regiment. They had nodded and agreed to the orders. Being older and wiser carriage horses, the greys recognised the importance of their personal co-operation. Both confirmed they had suspected something like this would eventually happen. Their personal worry was for head coachman, Mark Hargreaves. 2007 was to be his first year as coachman for the monarch. He would be mounted on McCarthy, with Daniel to his right. How would he cope with the action of the regiment and all other equine? Sefton took flight to join his colleagues down at the palace and to assist in keeping the troop horses calm and organised. Meanwhile back on the parade square, the bands of the foot guards struck up another lively tune. Out of sight, the sound of the pleasant music floated across the park and the treetops. Zahra and Freddy, with Gauntlet close to his side, made their way to the rear of the crowds at the top of The Mall. The road was lined with dozens of straight-faced foot guards in their red tunics and tall, black bearskin hats, ready to present arms when the royal carriage approached. Dozens of uniformed police lined the road as well, but they were facing outwards, looking to the crowd and checking for any sign of trouble or disturbance. Excitement was building as the minutes and seconds ticked away before eleven o'clock.

Eleven o'clock when the bell over the archway would chime.

Eleven o'clock, exactly when the queen would step onto the podium as she always did.

The one thing the crazy people could rely on. Military precision. The *exact* time. Every time.

Eleven o'clock, exactly when a small helicopter would lift off from the roof of a city building.

It never had been: S*ewers to the side. Toilets.* It had always been: *Suicide Pilots.*

It had never been: *Plant a copper.*

It had always been: *Plan A: Chopper.*

It had never been *Plant bees in the flower.*

It had always been: *Plan B: The Tower.*

Freddy predicted that moments after eleven o'clock a helicopter loaded with explosives would crash-land into the centre of Horse Guard's parade ground. The parade ground overflowing with soldiers, bandsmen, royalty, horses and thousands of men, women, and children. An event being broadcast around the world on television.

The open spaces of St. James's Park were practically deserted. Deserted except for a few dozen swans and a collection of rabbits and moles. Dozens of pigeons fluttered from treetop to treetop. All the small animals were out to help their equine friends if they could.

A roar from the crowd rolled down The Mall. Cheering, clapping, frenzied flag-waving signalled the approach of the mounted bands of the Household Cavalry, the two front divisions, the royal carriage, half a dozen individually mounted dignitaries and, bringing up the rear, two more divisions of the royal escort. Today the band was wearing their gold brocade frock coats, only ever to be worn on parade when the Monarch was present.

Zahra gripped Freddy's arm. "Any last thoughts, kiddo? You think it's really going to happen like you said?"

Freddy, white faced and silent, stared down The Mall as he watched Victoriana stepping out at the very front of the parade, carrying the Brigade Major. Sunlight bounced off her polished ebony coat. Her neck arched, her poll flexed, she proudly lead her regiment toward the parade ground. Up above, a dozen Pegusinni soared back and forth along the length of the route, calling instructions to the band and troop horses below. Step by step the procession edged its way along road. The Director of Music, carried by Venetia, raised his baton, and to the delight of the crowds, the mounted musicians struck up a traditional marching tune. Led on one side by Spartacus and on the other by Achilles, the band was eight horses wide and took up the full width of the road. The drummers pounded the silver kettle drums in unison. The crowd cheered while some of the police officers sneaked a quick glance back over their shoulder.

Victoriana stepped resolutely forward. The entire parade was less than one hundred yards from the top of the Mall. The point where they would turn to the right to the access road that led to the square where thousands were waiting, television cameras were rolling, and soldiers stood rigidly to attention.

The blare of the music grew louder as the mounted band approached. Fifty yards now before the turn.

Zahra was on tip toe, neck craned. "Will they do it, Freddy? Will they really do it?"

"Dear God, I hope so. At least we can hope to save all of them out there now, if not the poor souls already on parade."

Twenty-five yards to go before the turn. Sefton, Yeti, Rochester and all of the other Pegusinni were now tearing up and down overhead getting everyone ready.

Fifteen yards.

"This is it," muttered Freddy, "I hope she really can pull this off."

Ten yards.

The alpha mare suddenly raised her head and neck and in a voice that was incredibly loud to Freddy and all the horses on parade, she bellowed, "Regiment *halt!*"

She stopped herself so abruptly that the unsuspecting Brigade Major tipped forward and fell unceremoniously onto her neck before quickly correcting his position. The four retinue troopers of the Life Guards directly behind him also tipped forward and braced themselves with their sword hand as their mounts simultaneously planted their hooves into a square and dead halt. Like a long line of dominoes falling against each other, the action of horses halting rippled rapidly backwards down The Mall. Venetia carrying the Director of Music, Spartacus, Achilles and then the entire mounted band. Each horse squared up their hooves and came to a full halt.

"Now! Now! Halt! Halt!" The Pegusinni zoomed up and down the line, blaring Victoriana's order to the dozens of troop horses in the first and second divisions of the escort. Directly behind the two divisions, on Gauntlet's order, the Windsor greys brought themselves and the royal carriage into a smooth halt. Within fifteen seconds the entire Royal Procession for the Queen's birthday parade was immobile. Along the length of The Mall and, where the mounted band had stopped, across its full width, two hundred military equine stood stock still.

Up at the front, the Brigade Major tapped and dug his heels into Victoriana's sides, trying discreetly to urge her forward again. But there was no reaction from Victoriana. Even her head and neck were motionless. The mounted band nervously played a few bars of music while trying to get their horses to move off. The two drummers attempted to keep the rhythm while they too struggled with the large pair of parked Shire horses. "Good grief, she did it," muttered Zahra to Freddy.

"Yep, she's done it. No going back now," replied the Freddy, all colour drained from his face.

The crowd continued their cheering and clapping, relishing the moment that the parade had stopped directly in front of them, offering them a close up view of the horses, the soldiers and all of their highly polished equipment. The Brigade Major now was really agitated, using the small sharp wheel of his spurs on Victoriana's sides. Behind him the four troopers of the retinue didn't even attempt to get their horses moving, as there was no way they could pass the Brigade Major. Further back, the Director of Music also realised he couldn't move, even if he did manage to get his steed into motion. The two mounted drummers glanced at each other, shrugging their shoulders. They did the only thing they could think of and that was to keep on drumming. Because the drummers kept going, so did the rest of the mounted band. The music played, the crowds cheered and the parade went nowhere.

Head coachman Mark Hargreaves, mounted on McCarthy, was now standing up in his stirrups, craning his neck to see what the momentary hold up was. It was his personal duty to ensure he got the queen to the podium exactly as the clock chimed eleven o'clock. He could only think there was something up ahead causing the problem which was why no one at all was moving. No one, that is, except for a few anxious plainclothes police officers on security detail who moved tensely about on foot, glancing to each other. One used his radio to call to the mounted police at the very top of The Mall. He got a very odd reply. The mounted police were having difficulty with their horses. None of them would move. Every one of them was stationary. The mounted patrol was temporarily out of service. Police officers on foot were walking back and forth across the top of The Mall trying to see what had halted the escort. They looked to the Brigade Major for a reason, but he was too busy wiggling in his saddle, pushing with his seat, and kicking with his heels, desperately trying to get his mount to move. Not a chance. Victoriana had mentally zoned out her rider. Finally, as the act of a desperate man, he lowered his sword and gave her a quick tap on the right flank. In response, she promptly pinned her ears, humped her back and sharply lifted her haunches six inches off the ground, threatening to buck him off if he tried that again. Some of the spectators behind the railings clapped and cheered, thinking it was part of the show.

The clock ticked relentlessly on. By now the parade should have been entering Horse Guard's, taking the royal carriage to the podium. But it wasn't. The parade was spread out motionless all down The Mall.

The Pegusinni continued to cruise at a low height up and down the road, calling encouragement to the troop and band horses below.

"Stationary! No movement now! Commanding officer's direct orders! Not one hoof to move!"

Most of the senior equine thought actually being told to blatantly disobey their rider's commands was unusual, to say the least. Such a thing had never been heard of. Not in their time. But this order had come directly from Victoriana and no one was going to argue. Some of the younger remounts were starting to lose their nerve. They fidgeted and tossed their heads and necks up and down anxiously. The older Pegusinni stayed close to them offering words of support and calmness. Full co-operation of all equine on parade was necessary.

Suddenly a four year-old remount in the last section of the first division of Life Guards could contain himself no longer and started to shuffle rapidly backwards and side ways out of the ranks. Immediately Yeti and Rochester dropped down behind to encourage him back into position again. The moment the young horse was back in line, the two senior horses on either side of him swung their haunches inwards to block another rearward bolt.

Whimsy, who today was carrying a clarinet player in the mounted band, had her head and neck as high in the air as she could, rather resembling a white periscope. Desperate to see what was happening, she asked, "What's going on? We've never practised this! We should be formed up on parade now! Oh dear! There'll be such trouble!"

The horses on either side told her to remain calm and stand still. This was all part of a plan from Victoriana and everyone had to obey.

"But we are totally disobeying riders! We can't do this! Not ever!"

Uniformed police officers were running up and down The Mall trying to see why on earth the entire parade, on no one's orders, had come to this unscheduled halt. One of the mounted officers had dismounted and was unsuccessfully attempting to get his horse to move. His horse did not respond and quietly looked into the distance with glazed-over eyes. The plainclothes officers casually surrounded the Royal carriage, asking the coachman why his horses weren't moving. No one had an answer and now even the crowds realized this was not going according to plan. Gradually the cheering stopped. Flag waving ceased. Children and parents looked puzzled. Progressively an eerie silence rolled down the sides of The Mall just as the earlier robust shouting and cheering had done.

From the very rear of the parade came the sound of two police officers on motorcycles, slowly making their way forward. They passed the two stationary rear divisions of Blues and Royals, the group of the Royal Colonels, the Crown Equerry and the other dignitaries all mounted on individual, motionless horses. The motorcycles moved slowly past the Royal Carriage with the pair of Windsor greys who looked frozen in time. On past the two divisions of Life Guard's and finally up to the rear of the mounted band. And here the two police officers stopped and looked across the road at each other. The divisions of the mounted escort were each one section, or four horses wide, leaving plenty of room on either side for the motorcycles to pass. But the mounted band was eight horses wide and spread completely across the full width of the road, effectively blocking the way for the police officers. One of the officers called to a musician at the rear.

"Hey, move your horse over, we need to get past!"

On hearing this, Sefton immediately dropped in next to the grey horse in question and gave him an order. Promptly the white horse pinned his ears, swished his tail and flexed his left hind leg in a very threatening manner.

"You want to try to make this bugger move today, mate?" called the clarinet player nervously, holding the reins and his instrument.

"Er, no, maybe not," replied the policeman as he moved his motorcycle back away from the threatening horse.

Policemen were up close to the Brigade Major and the Director of music asking why they weren't moving on. Across the city, controllers behind the CCTV cameras jumped from screen to screen trying to see what was causing such a disruption to one of the biggest events on the London calendar. The police were fully trained in how to deal with trouble makers, disturbances, vandalism, and threats of terrorism but they needed to be able to see what or who was causing the problem. In this case, there was nothing to see except two hundred horses standing rigidly still on The Mall. Security personnel discreetly positioned on roof tops all along the parade route worriedly scanned back and forth with their binoculars. They searched the crowds lining the route. They looked for any vehicles that shouldn't be there. They would have been happy to see at least a bicycle in the wrong place, but there was nothing. Only thousands of quiet people staring curiously at the statue-like horses.

Chapter Thirty-five

The massed bands on the parade square were silent as they had no more music planned to play. They knew at this point they should have been playing the National Anthem as the Queen approached the podium but she wasn't there. Of course, the entire royal procession wasn't there. Silence swept across the square as bandsmen, foot guards, police officers and thousands of spectators all curiously waited for the late arrival of the sovereign and her escort. And then came the sound Freddy, his friends, Victoriana and the Pegusinni had not wanted to hear. Resounding across the uncanny silence of the parade square, the clock above the archway began to chime eleven o'clock. Zahra's fingernails dug deeply into Freddy's arm as they both tried to ignore the clock, ignore the stationary parade, ignore the stillness and silence from the square and lock their eyes onto the rooftop of the tall building in the distance. The roof-top where a small helicopter was lifting off and starting its short journey toward them.

Freddy and Zahra moved quickly back away from the crowd and went further into St. James's Park. The clock continued its doleful chimes. The Household Cavalry regiment remained motionless on The Mall away from direct danger. Crowds seated around the square were quiet, confused by the late start to the event. The military personnel on parade were almost frantic with the change in timing and the routine. The buzz of the small helicopter grew steadily louder.

"Oh Freddy, I really and truly hoped you were wrong about all of this!"

Freddy was speechless, slowly shaking his head wishing he had been wrong.

"The police, Freddy! Perhaps it's not too late! They may believe you!"

"And do what? We have about ninety seconds before that flying bomb makes contact!"

"But what can we do about all the people on the square? There are hundreds of small children and elderly people there!"

"Damn it, Zahra, I *know* who's down there! You forgot to mention the nuns and two princes! What the hell did you expect me to do?" His eyes blazed as he clenched his fists and shook from anger and frustration. "We've got the regiment safe; that was the main job! Apparently *that's* why I'm here."

Plump pearl-shaped tears slowly ran down Zahra's face as she stared to the sky and then to Horse Guard's, watching the distance between the small aircraft and the parade ground grow shorter. Any police around were still on The Mall still trying to spot the problem that had halted the royal escort. No one was bothered by the lack of activity on the parade square.

From the corner of his eye Freddy caught sight of movement across the empty acres of the park lawns. The swans, the rabbits, the moles and circling pigeons were still there. But his eye was drawn to a small white winged

Pegusinni gliding softly down to land. For a moment he didn't see it as his friend Gauntlet, the trumpeter's grey. He saw a flying white horse. Sunlight flickered off Gauntlet's wings and for an instant it looked like star dust. In a distant part of his mind he heard a deep, baritone masculine voice.

"Do what you can, and let me know if you need help."

"How will I get hold of you?"

"You know my name, yes?"

"Er, well, yeah, Troy, I guess."

"Then use that."

Freddy broke away from Zahra. Running. Sprinting. Tearing at full speed to the centre of the empty grass area, his eyes searching the skies.

"Troy! Troy, I need you *now!"* His calls were silent only heard by the nearby Pegusinni and the horses at the top of The Mall. Victoriana immediately looked over in his direction. She couldn't see him behind the thick crowd but she could hear his yells clear as day.

"Troy! For God's sake where are you? We need you!"

Victoriana called to Freddy over the heads of the crowd.

"Freddy! Are you calling for *him?"*

Freddy was running in circles waving his arms to the sky, screaming, "Troy! Oh damn it, I need you now!"

Victoriana raised her volume again. "Freddy! Are you calling for him?"

This time Freddy heard her and quickly called back, "Yes!" We need him now!"

"Then we will help," responded the alpha mare in her usual calm and authoritative manner. She raised her head and neck and silently bellowed a name Freddy had never heard and probably couldn't even pronounce. It sounded very similar to the noise he'd heard whales and dolphins using when they communicated under water. He stopped dead in his tracks as he saw most of the black Pegusinni coming toward him and landing in half sections.

"We heard Victoriana calling. You need him?" asked Rochester anxiously.

Freddy pointed to the helicopter getting closer by the second. "Yes, we all bloody well need him!"

Sefton turned to the others, nodded and immediately all Pegusinni were making the same sound as Victoriana. Necks extended, nostrils raised, their eyes locked on the skies. Gauntlet, acting as commanding officer's grey, leapt into action and took flight toward the stationary horses on The Mall.

"We need him! Everyone call for him! Colonel Freddy's order! Now! Call!"

Without any of them moving a single hoof, all horses on parade extended their necks, raised their nostrils, locked their eyes on the skies and made the same silent equine call Victoriana had made only moments earlier. To Freddy in the park the sound was deafening. He couldn't believe no one else could hear the strange and eerie calling of two hundred horses and fifteen Pegusinni. On Gauntlet's command, every equine repeated the call. Freddy dropped to his knees, hands over his ears, his eyes still searching the skies. He almost fell out of his skin when Zahra placed her hand on his shoulder.

"Freddy! Are you ok? What is going on?"

"Help," he replied hoarsely, "we're trying to get help!" He was now back on his feet, again running in circles, ears ringing with the sound of the calling. The noise of the helicopter was getting closer.

"Troy!"

"Freddy! Oh Lordy! Freddy! What's happening?"

He stopped running, turned and saw that Zahra had now fallen to her knees and was clutching her pendant. A pendant that glowed with a small but brilliant light. She held it away from her body up toward the sky. Zahra was shaking as the pendant blazed and shook in her grasp.

"Who is it? Who's coming?" she called to Freddy.

Then the wind came up out of the east, blowing Freddy's hair back, lifting the manes of the small Pegusinni and gently shaking the plants and low bushes around the park. And Freddy finally saw, floating in on the wind, the languid vertical motion of huge white wings rising and falling, and enormous black hooves thrashing the air and glinting in the sunlight.

"Freddy! The force! The power! It's so strong! Are we safe?" Zahra gamely held on to her pendant and looked desperately to the teenager.

Freddy was standing head thrown back, arms away from his body, staring to the east. "We're fine! It's ok, Zahra! It's a good thing!"

Zahra frantically looked all around but she couldn't see the Pegusinni. She couldn't see the great white horse landing on his hind legs only yards away from herself and Freddy. She could only see the glowing crystal and feel the energy of something immensely powerful.

Troy's hind legs touched down on to the grass as lightly as snow onto a rose petal and then he slowly lowered his forehand. He stood motionless, his neck arched with star dust falling from his mane, tail and wings. Eyes reminiscent of huge dark rock pools looked calmly at Freddy. He said nothing, giving an enquiring look at the dishevelled, sweating teen and a curious glance at the woman on her knees who was sobbing and clutching a crystal.

At that point all two hundred horses on The Mall and all Pegusinni slowly lowered their necks.

Freddy didn't waste time with formalities; he ran up to the great leader, cupped his hands around his mouth and started yelling.

"Now, calmly, Freddy," said the wise white horse, "calmly and in equine please."

Zahra felt a fabulous sense of tranquillity settling around the area. In the midst of the panic and the chaos came a tremendous wave of calm and serenity. She saw Freddy jumping up and down as though he was talking to a very tall person. She watched as he pointed frantically to the sky above Horse Guard's and towards the approaching helicopter. Then he rapidly nodded his head as though agreeing with someone and finally stepped backwards and looked at her. He ran to her and explained who was there and what was happening.

There was a strong back draft of wind as Troy took flight. So strong it rocked Zahra back on her heels and dislodged her hat. Freddy helped her to her feet. All the Pegusinni and every equine stared at the skies, watching the great white horse approach the helicopter.

He soared toward the aircraft which was dropping lower over the roof tops of Whitehall and Horse Guard's. The crowds on the ground stared up at the helicopter, some pointing, curious as to what was happening now. With wings maintaining a slow rhythmical beat, Troy positioned himself directly in the path of the helicopter, his fore legs striking the air. To any equine this was threatening behaviour and it would be a brave or foolish animal that didn't retreat. But the pilots were on a suicide mission and even if Troy had been visible, they would not have wavered from their course. They were prepared to die and take hundreds of innocent people and horses with them.

Zahra was gripping Freddy's arm so sharply if he had not been in a numb state of shock, it would have been painful.

"Freddy! The helicopter's still coming! What's happening?"

"He's up there, challenging them! But I don't think they see him!"

Realising his threatening posture was not going to have the effect he wanted, the great white horse abruptly changed position. Rearing, fore leg striking and biting are all *aggressive* equine signals, but now he needed to change tactics. Hundreds of his followers were on the ground. He needed to defend his herd. This needed *defensive* action. The helicopter pilots, oblivious to what was only yards in front of them, kept the helicopter steadily moving. With wings still beating their relentless slow rhythm, Troy faced away from the menace. Giving no warning, he dropped his head and neck down between his forelegs and with precise split-second timing, raised his haunches and thrashed up, out and back with both hind legs. With a power that knew no limit from a horse the size of two drum horses, both hooves pounded into the side of the small helicopter as it tried to pass him. There was a deafening, piercing crash as hooves crumpled metal and glass and sent the aircraft completely off course.

On the ground the crowds gasped as they saw the helicopter suddenly rise and twist crazily into the air. A few started to clap and cheer, thinking it was an extra part of the military show they didn't know about. The foreign pilots never knew what hit them as they urgently struggled for some sort of control, madly pulling and wrenching on controls. The engine whined as the helicopter bucked and careened through the air. The falling helicopter would miss the centre of the square but was dangerously close to crashing into the small courtyard on Whitehall where the Queen's Life Guard were standing on duty. Realising the aircraft was coming down quickly, Troy manoeuvred for a second strike. With immaculate timing he turned, dropped his head and neck and struck again. This time with even more power, he catapulted the wrecked helicopter back up into the air and to the south. Resembling a football that had been struck for a winning goal, the now useless piece of machinery sailed up over the buildings of Whitehall and the Victoria Embankment. To the thousands gathered on Horse Guard's Parade it fell from sight. But the hundreds gathered in the Jubilee Gardens watched a falling, twisting, tumbling mass of oddly shaped metal crash down into the centre of the river Thames. Like a rock the size of a large car, it hit the water, sending spray high above the river before sinking out of sight.

The stunned silence that followed was shattered by an underwater explosion that sent water funnels into the air. The funnels were visible to the crowds in St James's Park and on The Mall who cheered and clapped, incredulous at the lengths the military seemed to have gone to to put on a good show. Troy hovered above Whitehall, watching the river surface as the water gradually calmed. Hundreds of people and some police were running along the river bank trying to understand what had just happened. In St. James's Park, Freddy leapt off the ground, punching the air with his fists.

"He did it! Oh god! He did it!"

Zahra pulled her skirt above her grass stained knees and danced an Irish jig across the turf, tears of laughter glistened in her eyes. Then Freddy grabbed her hands with both of his and leaning backwards they both spun in circles, laughing, crying and repeatedly saying, "Yes! Yes! Yes!"

Out of breath, they finally stopped spinning and flopped on the grass. It was only then Freddy realised that a group of black Pegusinni and one small grey to the side were all watching him silently and intently. Sefton cleared his throat, cocked his head to one side and spoke.

"Is it over, Freddy?"

"Is it gone now?" asked Yeti.

Gauntlet stepped forward and quietly asked, "Are horses safe now, Freddy?"

"Yes, little guy, I think we can say horses are safe now," replied the grinning teenager.

"Freddy!" Victoriana's voice rang out over the crowds. "Is it gone? Is the bad thing done?"

He jumped to his feet and ran to the roadside, followed by Zahra. He pushed his way through the crowd to the railing.

"Yes! It's done! Everyone should be safe now!"

The alpha mare looked carefully to her right, eyed the teenager by the kerb side before saying, "Very well then, we shall now troop the colour."

She brought herself to full height, raised and arched her neck

"Regiment! Prepare to move! Walk *march!*"

Chapter Thirty-six

The noise of police and fire engine sirens whined in the distance.

"You did it, kiddo. You saved the horses and all the people." Zahra said.

"Me? Not just me. Me with all the help from you and Gloria and Petula and every horse on parade. We did it."

They were both laying flat on their backs, arms and legs spread wide as though trying to make snow angels in the short warm grass of the park. They both gazed at the empty blue sky, unable to stop smiling.

"Actually," said Freddy propping himself up on one elbow to look over at Zahra, "I wonder how they'll report this on the news tonight? You know, horses frozen on parade, random helicopters crashing inexplicably into the river. Trooping the Colour starting late. Quite the lead story, eh?"

Zahra sat up and hugged her knees. "Not half the story it would have been if the crazies had got their way."

"They must have died," Freddy said.

"Who must have died?"

"The crazies. The guys in the helicopter. They must be dead after that."

"No great loss to the world is what I say."

"Maybe. But I don't like this death and killing stuff."

"There would have been a lot more killing if they weren't dead by now."

"Possibly, but that doesn't mean I'll get used to it."

"Freddy, they were going to die anyway. Don't forget they planned to die and take hundreds of innocent people with them."

Freddy sat upright and looked across the empty lawns of the park.

"What are you staring at?"

He raised his arm and pointed with his index finger. "Troy. Troy and all the guys. Looks like they are having a meeting of some sort."

The great white horse stood calmly on the grass, wings folded, neck lowered as he communicated with the Pegusinni gathered around him. In the distance, music from the massed bands drifted over the trees occasionally interrupted by an officer calling commands to the troops. Oblivious to what had almost happened and albeit later than scheduled, the military and the members of the royal household were proceeding as planned. Behind the music, the crunching of hundreds of pairs of boots hitting gravel could be heard as the foot guards trooped their colour.

Zahra looked down at the crystal hanging around her neck. It was still glowing brightly but had stopped shaking. Freddy glanced at it.

"That thing looks like something from Dr. Who. Like a sonic screw driver, the way it lights up and glows."

"Ha! David Tennant should be so lucky to have one of these," she replied smugly.

"Yeah, I never did ask you about those things. All three of you have them, where did you get them?" Freddy asked, but before Zahra could reply,

"Cooee!"

"Dahlings! Dahlings! We're here!"

Gloria and Petula hurried across the grass toward them. Breathless and beaming, they were hanging onto their hats, clutching hand-bags and trying to run in their smart outfits. Zahra and Freddy leapt to their feet and ran toward them, arms out-stretched. As they met, everyone fell into big hugs, laughing, yelling and slapping each other on the back.

"We were running back down toward Whitehall when we heard the explosion! But it was from the river! Is everyone here safe?" asked an excited Petula.

"Oh yes! Yes! Everyone is safe now!" said Zahra tearfully as she hugged her friends again.

"Oh, two ticky wicks!" exclaimed Gloria as she retrieved her hanky to dab at her own damp eyes. "This is so thrilling! Everyone safe!"

"It's crazy over on Whitehall and along the embankment! Police, fire engines, ambulances, news crews showing up!" exclaimed Petula.

"Was anyone hurt?" asked Freddy anxiously.

"Not that we saw or heard about. But I guess there are a few wet people along the embankment and in the Jubilee gardens," said Gloria, "that water funnel was huge!

"And all thanks to our boy!" said Petula hugging Freddy again as tightly as a hungry python. The 'boy' gasped for breath until she released him.

As he stepped back from her, he said, "It's like I just said to Zahra, it was everyone, not just me."

After another brief group hug Freddy asked, "What about my mum? And Gran and Sharon?"

Petula opened her bag to find her comb and ran it through her hair. "They're fine. A little angry, to say the least. But all fine."

"What happened at the police station?"

"Oh, nothing much. Once we got them there and out of danger, we told the police it was a terrible mistake and we wouldn't be bringing charges."

"Although your Aunt Sharon nearly charged Petula like a crazed bull," confided Gloria.

"And the younger officer was definitely interested in taking down my particulars," said Petula, trying but once more failing to look demure.

"Lord! My mum and the other two must be livid!"

"Yes, not too happy. But we ran ahead of them and directly back here. I heard them saying something about going back to The Mall and at least seeing some of the parade."

"Good grief, what is that?" exclaimed Gloria as she looked down at her crystal glowing brightly.

"Oh, my! I see what you mean!" Petula was looking at her own slender shaped pendant as it glowed with an intense white light.

"Troy," said Freddy casually, "he's still here. He's the one that really saved the day."

"The energy is so strong! He must be incredibly powerful," said Petula.

"Oh, you have no idea just how powerful," Freddy replied, thinking how the huge winged horse had kicked a small helicopter out of sight and into the river.

"Is he still with the Pegusinni, Freddy?" Zahra asked.

"Yeah, dunno what they're talking about."

"Talking about you I would imagine!"

"I doubt it, but I guess he'll be leaving shortly."

The ladies continued to go over the events of the morning. Freddy was puzzled as he watched Troy and the Pegusinni.

"There's something different," he mumbled, "can't figure out what it is though."

"What's that, Freddy?" asked Zahra breaking away from her friends, "What's the problem?"

"I don't know, just something looks slightly odd over there." He continued looking for a few moments and then suddenly snapped his fingers. "That's it. It's Gauntlet."

"What about Gauntlet?" asked Zahra who couldn't see the Pegusinni anyway.

"He's not standing on his own."

"So? Why is that odd?"

"When they're all together, they always stand in half sections. Together, lined up in pairs. Because there are fifteen of them, one of them stands on his own and that's Gauntlet the grey."

"But why is that odd?"

"Because they are all in pairs. Gauntlet's standing with Sefton, which means there are only thirteen black ones here, not fourteen. There's always fourteen black and one grey."

"One is missing?"

"Missing. Or somewhere else."

Hearing the talk between Zahra and Freddy, the other two joined them.

"Who's missing?" asked Petula.

Zahra glanced to her friend, "Apparently one of the Pegusinni."

Freddy spun on his heels to look at them. "No. No he's not missing! He's where he's been all morning! It's Cedric! He's still up there! Watching the damn tower!"

"What?"

"Oh my!"

"Exactly!" called Freddy as he strode off across the grass, "we still have a lunatic in the tower!"

"Oh, good grief!"

"Wait! We're with you!" called Zahra and Gloria as they scooped up their bags and hats and ran after the teenager who was now jogging toward the top corner of the park. He glanced back over his shoulder as he ran.

"*Plant bees in the flower!* Plan B. The tower!"

"Freddy! The police! We must get the police this time!"

"Yes! They'll believe you. Heck, after all the crazy stuff they've seen today they'll believe anything!" called Petula.

Freddy stopped running and spun on his heels to face the three ladies.

"OK. Ok, but you tell the police. They are not going to believe some kid with a Derbyshire accent!"

"They'll get keys," said Zahra excitedly, "they'll find keys and get the crackpot down from there!"

"Heavens! What type of harm can a weird guy up a tower do anyway?" Petula asked.

Freddy took a deep breath. "He was there at the early morning khaki rehearsal. Out on the walk way. Looking at the end of the parade."

"But that's not dangerous," said Gloria.

"Cedric said he was poking black tubes in his eyes."

"Tubes?"

"Binoculars. I figured it had to be binoculars."

"Still a long way off to do any damage."

Freddy looked Zahra directly in the eye. "He was leaning over the railing, right at the end of the parade. Paying particular attention when Daniel and McCarthy passed directly in front of the tower."

Zahra kept his gaze. "Daniel and McCarthy?"

"Yes. The two greys who pull the royal carriage."

"But the queen will be safe inside her carriage, Freddy!" stated Petula.

"She would be, if it was a covered carriage. But it's not. She uses a very informal, totally open carriage for this gig."

"Oh, my God!"

"Exactly. What if this freak up in the tower has something like a rifle with one of those telescopic lens things? Like on James Bond or something?"

Petula was striding toward the back of the crowd still lining The Mall. "Police! We tell the police now!"

The others ran behind her, Freddy scanned the buildings and roof tops by the tower until he spotted Cedric. A solitary, small, black winged horse who never for a moment would think of leaving his guard position. Calmly carrying out his duty, he was on guard and would remain on guard until he received orders to 'stand down'. Freddy raised his arm and signalled, calling to Cedric.

Petula was now pushing her way through the throng to get to the front. "Hey! You! Police person!" Petula bawled to one of the uniformed constables facing the crowd. She leaned over the metal barrier. "I have something to report! We think there's a crazy person over there!" She pointed across the road to the base of the tower. The policeman stepped forward toward her and a look of recognition passed over his face.

"I see, madam. And would this be another crazy person who has robbed you today?"

"Oh damn! Just my luck," she muttered as she backed away from the railing. "Thousands of coppers in this city and I meet the same one twice on the same day. Terrific."

"Tell him!" called Zahra, "Tell the police, now!"

"Hmm, it will have to be you, dahling. P.C. Plod and I are already on intimate terms." She backed into the crowd and tried to blend out of sight.

"What? You've dated that copper?" exclaimed her friend.

"Let's just say, we had an encounter. Now, let's try another one."

Cedric saw Freddy's signal and landed on the turf next to him.

"Is he still up there, Cedric? The crazy man, did you see him?"

The Pegusinni flicked his ears and said, "Not since early morning. That's when I saw him go in the small door."

"But you haven't seen him come out either?"

"Oh no, definitely not. No one has come out since I started my guard duty."

"So as far as you know, he is definitely still in there?"

"Certainly."

"Damn. Damn. Damn."

"Anything else I should do?" enquired Cedric.

"Yes, go and get Sefton. I want both of you up there; keep a really good look out. Tell me if anything happens in or around that tower."

"Do you want to go back up today, Freddy? Like you did at the first rehearsal?"

"Hell no! Not if you think that guy is still in there!"

"Very well, I'll call Sefton and return to guard duty." Within moments both small black horses flew across The Mall and soared up to the rooftop next to the tower. Gauntlet took his place at Freddy's side, waiting to give orders to the troops if needed. Looking back to the crowd, Freddy could see that Zahra had pushed her way to the front and was yelling to a policeman. This one actually appeared to be taking notice of what she was saying. He listened and asked her a couple of questions. He turned to speak to one of his colleagues and then both of them sprinted across the top of the empty Mall and climbed over the crowd barrier.

"What's happening? What's going on, Zahra?" Freddy called from behind the crowd.

"I think they believed me! I think they believe something is wrong! Look! They're checking now!"

"After all the madness that's gone on this morning, they have to believe you!"

The two uniformed police men had pushed their way through the small crowd on the other side of the road and were now running up the steps to the foot of the tower. One ran completely around the stone base while the second one was inspecting the charred wooden door. Across the road in the park, Freddy and the ladies waited anxiously to see what would transpire.

Nothing.

Nothing happened except that the officers stepped back, scratched their heads, gave the door another look and then started to walk back down the steps.

"They're not doing anything!" muttered a tense Petula.

"Oh, crap," said Gloria.

Within a few moments the police were back to Zahra, explaining that everything looked fine. There was no sign of a break-in so no one could possibly be in the tower.

"But they have keys. They have keys!" The small, red-haired woman was jumping up and down in frustration behind the railings. "That's why there's no sign of a break-in!"

"And how would you know they have keys?" enquired the officer.

Zahra paused, thought for a moment and said, "Indeed, how would I know? Yes, of course, officers, I couldn't possibly know, now could I? Not unless a little bird told me." A bird or a winged horse she thought as she moved back toward her friends.

When she re-joined the group she explained what had happened.

"See! I knew no one would believe us!" Freddy said angrily, "it's all too crazy for normal people to believe!"

"Yes, but we know it's true, Freddy!"

"Fat lot of good that will do the queen when she comes up off Horse Guard's and around that corner in her open cart!"

"Oh good grief, that's all we need," said Gloria very quietly.

"What? What do we need?" asked Freddy looking around.

Gloria silently raised her arm and pointed across the road.

"Oh, no," from Petula.

"Crikey, who would have thought?" from Zahra.

Freddy was speechless as he stared across the road and watched his mother, his Gran and his Aunt Sharon standing on the steps right below the base of the tower. His mother had her mobile phone in her hand obviously trying to make a call. Freddy pulled his phone from his pocket. It was on silent mode but the message flashed that he had missed nine calls from Jane. His Gran had pulled a small flag out of her bag and Aunt Sharon lit a cigarette. They stood shoulder-to-shoulder. This time no one was going to rain on their parade. They were determined to get a good view of the queen in her carriage, even if it killed them.

Chapter Thirty-seven

"Freddy, we need help again," said Zahra quietly. He had his hand over his eyes as he looked through the crowd and across the road to his family. He slowly turned and looked at the ladies.

"Help? Who can help now?"

"What about Troy?"

"What? You expect him to fly up there and kick the crap out of the top of the tower?"

"Well no, but he might do something."

"Oh sure, I'll ask him to fly up and do a giant poo and have it land on the guy!"

"No need for sarcasm."

"What about the Pegusinni?" asked Gloria anxiously, "perhaps they can help."

"They're little, timid flying horses that no one can see! What do you think they could do?"

"I don't know! I'm just trying to be helpful!"

"Well, try harder!"

"Freddy always gets irritable when things are difficult," Zahra confided to the other two.

"Do you mind? I'm standing right here!"

"Yes, I see what you mean," Petula said, looking at the teenager.

Freddy walked off across the grass feeling angry, frustrated and useless. He stopped by the Pegusinni.

"Well done, Freddy."

"What? What for?"

Yeti, Rochester and Gauntlet gathered in front of him.

"For solving the messages."

"For coming up with a plan."

"For keeping all horses safe."

"Oh, that. Yeah, right. Sorry, thinking about something else right now."

Gauntlet raised his head and pricked his ears forward, locking on to the sounds coming from Horse Guard's.

"It's the Keel Row. My favourite piece."

Freddy looked down at the grey listening to the music from the band.

"The Keel Row?"

"Yes, it's for the equine trot past for the salute. Means the parade is nearly over."

"The foot guard's march past in slow and then in quick time, but we do it in walk and then trot," added Yeti

Rochester was nodding. "Yes, after the trot past we all form up again and the Kings Troop leave by the approach road."

"And then it's all over?"

"Rochester stepped forward and spoke again. "Not quite. The massed band plays the anthem one more time and then the mounted band follows the Kings Troop."

"And we, the mounted regiment follow the band," added Yeti.

"The queen? Remind me when she leaves?"

"After the last division of the mounted regiment has left, the foot guard's band follow, then Daniel and McCarthy bring the carriage."

"And hundreds of foot guards follow on to bring up the rear," added Gauntlet.

The Keel Row's lively tune came to an abrupt end.

"Oh, that's it, soon be done now," said Gauntlet casually, "then everyone back to barracks."

"So we don't have much time now? Before everyone is heading up the approach road to The Mall?" Freddy asked tensely.

"Correct."

"Freddy! Freddy!" The three ladies were jogging toward him.

"We have a plan! Well, an idea!"

"What? What plan? We don't much damn time!"

Zahra was now up next to him again. "You said Cedric, the Pegusinni, was on the roof top near by. Yes?"

"Yes. So what?"

"Well, if the police had a marksman up there he could nail the crazy man if he comes out of the door!"

"Great plan!"

"Oh, gosh you think so?"

"No! Not at all!" Freddy gave Zahra a withering look. "We don't have time to persuade the police about this! The parade is nearly over!"

"My, he does get irritable doesn't he," commented Gloria as she listened to the exchange.

"My mother is standing directly below a tower where some crazy person is going to come out and try and knock off the queen!" He was yelling now. "Don't you think I just might be a little irritable?"

The stunned silence was broken by Gauntlet. "Freddy," he said quietly.

"What?"

"You're shouting again."

"Aggh!" Freddy strode away punching his clenched fists into the top of his legs. He took a few deep breaths, calmed himself and returned to the group. He was about to speak as Sefton glided down and landed in front of him.

"Freddy, you wanted to know if there was any movement, correct?"

"Yes! Yes, what's happened?"

"There was."

"Was what?"

"Some movement."

"Who moved? What moved?"

"Oh, sorry. The small door on the walk-way opened, a man stepped out and briefly looked at the parade square and then went back in."

"Is that it? Nothing else?"

"No, nothing else."

"So he's still in there?"

"Yes."

"Wait. Was he armed?"

"No."

"No gun? No nothing?"

"Ah, I see. I thought you meant sword. He was not carrying a sword."

"A sword is not bloody-well armed!"

"Well, our soldiers all carry them when they escort and protect the queen."

All four Pegusinni stared up at Freddy as he became more and more agitated. A small pulse was visibly throbbing at his right temple. Then he knelt down so he could look Sefton in the eye.

"Sefton, think carefully. Was the man carrying *anything?*"

"Yes."

"What? What was he carrying?"

"A gun."

"A gun?"

"I think it's called a rifle. Something like the ones the foot guard's carry. But not the cavalry."

"And he definitely went back in?"

"Yes."

"Why? Why would he come out and go back in?"

"The timing is off, Freddy."

"Of course!"

"The parade is running several minutes late due to the equine action ordered by you and Victoriana."

Freddy slowly stood back up. "Terrific. In less than a few minutes, the queen riding in her open carriage is coming up the road off Horse Guard's and some nutter is in the tower with a rifle."

"What's he going to do?" asked Yeti.

"Well, to hazard a guess, I think I can safely say he's going to have a go at assassination."

All four Pegusinni looked puzzled. Gauntlet spoke first.

"That's a really big word, Freddy."

"It's a really big act!"

Rochester wrinkled and scratched his muzzle before asking, "What does it mean, Freddy?"

"Shoot. Kill. Murder. Death. Destroy!"

"Someone is going to shoot *the queen?*"

"Yes!"

"Oh my."

"Good grief."

"That's terrible."

"I know it's bloody terrible!" Freddy exclaimed.

"Well, the cavalry are the queen's personal body guards. We must stop this. That's our job!" exclaimed Rochester, showing the smallest amount of anxiety.

"We must tell Victoriana, she'll know what to do," said Yeti confidently. The others all nodded.

"Yes."

"Indeed."

"Of course"

Freddy stared at them, "Victoriana? What can *she* do now? She's on bloody parade in the middle of Horse Guard's!"

There was another moment of total silence broken again by Gauntlet speaking very quietly.

"Freddy, this man has to be stopped."

"I know that, Gauntlet. But who can stop him now?"

"A hunter could stop him."

"Yes."

"Of course."

"Indeed."

"A *hunter?* Where the hell are we going to find a …?" Freddy's voice trailed off as he saw them looking at him. Nodding. Knowing exactly who they meant.

"Oh, no way. Not a chance! Not me. I've told you before; I don't want to be a hunter!"

The group of small winged horses remained silent as they listened to his protests.

"No! It's beyond my scope!"

Still no comment from the Pegusinni, just quiet confident stares.

"I don't have any weapon!"

The Pegusinni moved their heads slightly, but said nothing.

"It's too far! I couldn't reach!"

"You could reach if you were very close when he comes back out again."

"How? How can I be very close when he comes back out? He's over a hundred feet up there!"

Sefton stepped forward out of the line up and indicated to the grass behind Freddy. He spun around and he saw Troy standing motionless, stardust falling from his mane and tail, looking at him with his huge dark eyes. Freddy stared back. Finally he let out a long slow sigh. "Why do I do things?" he muttered to himself as he walked across the grass toward the equine leader. The great white horse towered above him as he stopped in front of the massive black hooves.

"OK, boss man, we have a problem."

"Really?" came the baritone reply, "and what would that be?"

Freddy quickly explained what he thought was going to happen.

"So this time it is human danger, not equine?"

"Correct. But like some really important human."

"Are some humans more important than others?"

"No, no, not really. But this one is special. And if these bad guys pull it off, well, they'll get most of what they wanted."

"What is that?"

"Publicity. Fame. World notoriety. That stuff."

"As they did twenty-five of your years ago?"

"Yes, but this would be even bigger. Well, no horses hurt now. But a huge act of cowardice."

"Then we must do everything we can to stop this. How can I help?" He lowered his head and neck and listened carefully as Freddy hurriedly spoke.

"Freddy! What's going on? Who are you talking to now?" Zahra called from the group of three ladies.

He called back and quickly explained what the Pegusinni had seen and the action they suggested. When he'd finished all three women were speechless.

"You can't be serious!"

"Oh no, Freddy, that is far too dangerous!"

The sound of several hundred hooves clattering on the approach road signalled that the King's Troop was moving off the parade ground. As they halted at the top of The Mall, the massed bands struck up 'God Save the Queen', signalling the end of the Trooping of the Colour for 2007.

"We have four or five minutes! Anyone got any better ideas?"

Petula spoke quietly but firmly. "You know, Apollo got him this far. I say let him do it. *Someone* is looking after this kid."

The three women simultaneously clutched their crystals and watched as Freddy turned, took three or four steps forward, reached up with his arms and disappeared into thin air.

In reality he walked toward Troy and the great white horse dropped to his knees and slowly lowered his enormous left wing, allowing Freddy to reach up with both hands and grab a firm hold. Troy raised the wing until it was parallel to the ground permitting Freddy to crawl along it and slide into a sitting position on top of the immense white shoulders. His thin legs dangled on either side as he wrapped handfuls of white mane around his fists.

"Oh, Jesus!" he yelled as Troy straightened his legs and once more stood to full height.

"It's ok, Freddy," called Gauntlet hovering nearby, "we'll be with you. You won't be alone."

"No! Tell Cedric to stay up there!" Tell everyone else to position themselves down The Mall and across the parks so they can keep us informed!"

By now the great winged horse was walking resolutely across the grass, the petrified teenager hanging grimly to the white mane.

"Oh, good grief! This is nothing like sitting on Victoriana!"

Over on the square, the band played the last note of the National anthem, followed by the sound of cheering and clapping from the crowds around the sides. The trooping was officially over.

"We must go now, Freddy," called the deep voice from below him. Eyes tightly closed, Freddy gripped the white main with white knuckles, his knees clamping inwards with all his strength.

"OK! Ready! Do it!"

Three long effortless canter strides across the short grass, the extensive wings opened to full width and the pair was air-born. Climbing over the park, they crossed over the small lake and turned right toward Buckingham Palace. As Troy flew higher still, the wind whipped against Freddy's pale cheeks, so terrified he couldn't open his eyes. Troy increased his wing beats to gather more speed and flew higher yet over the rear gardens of Buckingham Palace and on to Hyde Park Corner.

"Details, Freddy! I need details. Where exactly do you need to go?"

"Kensington! My house!"

There was a short pause as they soared over Hyde Park Corner. Hundreds of vehicles and pedestrians directly below the flying pair continued about their Saturday business, oblivious to the aerobatics above.

Then Troy said, "Freddy, I don't know street names in your cities."

"Well, I'm not opening my eyes!" screamed back the terrified teen.

They were now speeding along above Rotten Row, Freddy's hair spiked up on end, partially from the wind and partially from fright.

"Freddy! Commanding officers grey! Right beside you, Sir!" called Gauntlet into Freddy's ear.

"Gauntlet! Show Troy my house!"

"Certainly, Sir!"

Gauntlet dropped his neck, pinned his ears and his wings and dived into position below and in front of Troy. Once there, his small wings opened to full span as he took the lead toward Kensington. No words passed between the small Pegusinni and the equine leader as they covered the last part of the journey at breakneck speed. They passed the deserted cavalry barracks on their left as they raced on toward the Royal Albert Hall and finally Kensington. Freddy felt the g-forces against his cheeks slacken as they slowed and went into a downward spiral over the Prince Albert memorial. Then Gauntlet straightened and glided along a side street with Troy directly behind him. Gauntlet landed softly on to the garage roof watching as Troy saw a break in the light traffic on the small road and touched down. Freddy sat frozen from the speed of the wind and from sheer fright.

"Quickly now, Freddy. Not much time."

Feeling no movement, Freddy popped his eyes open.

"Oh, dear Lord! We're here! I'm not dead!"

A small black Pegusinni flew in behind them.

"Parade moving off the square!" called Yeti. "Word just came down the line!"

"I'm moving! I'm moving!" Freddy yelled back as he shook his numb fingers and legs and slithered off the feathered wing to the pavement. He saw vehicles coming toward him on the road.

"Troy. Go to the park by the Albert memorial! I'll be there in one minute!"

The white horse took flight as Freddy raced to the side gate, ripped it open, ran up the steps of the fire escape and dived through the open bedroom window. He fell to the floor and groped frantically under his bed. Where? Where the heck was it? Finally his fingers curled around the slender piece of wood. The bow. The bow that had remained unused since Maurice Kinghorn had given it to him on his twelfth birthday.

It wasn't one of the modern style bows used in archery competitions. This was a traditional long-bow, beautifully made from yew wood, with six arrows. He dragged the bow out across the carpet and reached back under the bed and grabbed two arrows. Then back to the window and down the fire escape with bow in one hand, arrows gripped in the other. He raced through the gate and sprinted up the street toward Kensington gardens.

"Cavalry mounted bands about to leave the square now!" called Yeti hovering above.

He saw the traffic bumper to bumper moving slowly along the road toward Kensington High Street. No time to use the crossing. Jumping and diving between cars with angry drivers cursing and blowing their horns, he dodged his way across to the pedestrian gate into the park. Seeing Freddy running toward him, Troy flexed his knees down to the grass and lowered his left wing for the boy to mount. Gauntlet flew in small anxious circles above them.

"Quickly now, Freddy! Mounted regiment about to move off the square!"

"I'm trying, damn it!"

He slung the bow across his back and tucked the two arrows under his left armpit and then frantically wrapped the long white mane around his hands.

"Ok! Ready. Let's do it again!"

Within seconds they were air born, heading back to Horse Guard's Parade where Her Majesty the Queen was now leaving her birthday parade in an open carriage.

Chapter Thirty-eight

They streaked across the sky of west London and as they passed each hovering Pegusinni, the small black horses joined in arrowhead formation behind their leader. Silvery white mane and tail flying out behind him with stardust showering the ground below, Troy accelerated as they reached Buckingham Palace and the start of The Mall.

"Holy mother of God!" screamed Freddy, feeling he was about to go into orbit without a space suit.

"Nearly there, Freddy!" Gauntlet called into his left ear.

"Queen is in her carriage about to leave Horse Guard's!" called Rochester coming in from the front and then swiftly changing course to bring up the rear of the Pegusinni. Below them, the King's Troop Royal Horse Artillery was making their way down the centre of The Mall, heading to Green Park where they would set up their gun carriages and fire a forty-one gun salute. Some of the equine pulling the gun carriages looked up to see the spectacle above them.

"Hi, Digby!" called Gauntlet as he shot overhead passing the chestnut gelding carrying the Commanding officer for the R.H.A.

"This is not a bloody social mission, Gauntlet!" Freddy croaked in a very hoarse voice.

"Oh, sorry. Hey, look! That's Cedric coming toward us!"

Freddy dared to open his eyes and squinted to see Cedric flying straight to him.

"Man out of the door, Freddy! He's bending down poking a stick or a rifle through the bars!"

"Almost there!" called Troy in his calm and assuring manner.

Below the crowds were cheering as the mounted bands of the cavalry regiment played and made their way down the road toward Buckingham Palace. Behind them came Victoriana leading the Sovereign's escort. She twisted her neck as she walked to see what was going on above her. Rochester dropped out of formation and swooped down to give her the latest news.

"Steps to the tower on the left, Freddy!" called Gauntlet in the teen's ear.

"Royal Carriage entering the approach road!" screamed Yeti.

They could hear the crowd going into a mild frenzy of cheering and flag waving as their beloved queen approached.

"Troy! Slow down! I can't do anything at this speed!"

The white horse adjusted the angle of his wings and went into a slow circling pattern around the top of the tower. Freddy nervously let his hold go with one hand to get one of the arrows. As he looked down he caught sight of his mother, his Gran and aunt standing on the steps looking upwards to see what was causing such a wind. Jane had her hands at her sides holding down her skirt. The pale blue hat his Gran was wearing gently floated off and rolled down the steps. The little old lady didn't hesitate and sprinted forward to follow it, heading directly into the line between the tower and the approaching royal carriage.

"Gran! No! Get back!" He used his loudest voice and without thinking started to raise his arms to wave, losing his hold on the two arrows tucked under his armpit.

"Shit!"

He lunged to the left and managed to grab one arrow as it fell but lost his grip on the broad white shoulders and began to slide straight off into what was a one hundred foot fall onto concrete. No sound came from his throat; he closed his eyes and expected death. But within seconds he felt himself being pushed roughly back upright by Gauntlet and Sefton.

"You really do need more riding lessons," said Sefton quietly.

"Man raising his gun!" called Cedric.

"Troy! Get me lower, around in front of the tower. Now!"

The clatter of hooves from Daniel and McCarthy below grew louder as they proudly pulled the queen's carriage forward.

Troy had dropped down almost to the ground and was now ready for a last vertical launch on Freddy's command. Palms running with sweat, fingers shaking, he placed the back of the last arrow into the string of the bow. Then, holding the bow down on his left side, he called,

"Now Troy! Up!"

His brain was going to mush. "Come on. Just like in the garden. Don't think about it. Don't aim. Just do it naturally," he muttered through clenched teeth as he was propelled vertically by Troy's powerful body. And then he was there. Face to face with an eerie dark-haired man holding a rifle.

He paused, his mind clearing. In one smooth movement, he drew back the string, swept the bow up and released the arrow. It was done.

Time stood still for Freddy and the hovering Pegusinni as the arrow flew straight into the left shoulder of the man with the gun. It took him a second to realise that he had a large arrow piercing his body. Eyes wide, looking for an assailant, he staggered backwards, dropping the rifle and screaming in pain as he held his bleeding shoulder. The rifle plummeted silently to the ground directly toward the spot where Freddy's family was standing, cheering and waving their flags.

"Noooooo!" Freddy managed to gasp just as he saw Rochester swoop in and flick the falling weapon with his neck, sending it clattering to the ground behind the tower. At the same time, Queen Elizabeth II gave her royal wave to the crowd as her carriage turned onto The Mall and from the base of the tower three loyal subjects from Stavely waved back.

Across the road on the corner of St. James's Park three middle-aged women leapt up and down and screamed with joy as they watched the man falling wounded onto the walk way of the tower. And even more cheers when they saw the falling rifle strangely change course and land safely behind everyone.

"Police!" Now! Over there!"

"There's a terrorist up in that tower!"

This time the police officers saw there was indeed a person in the tower. One officer called into his radio and within moments uniformed and plain-clothed police and security forces were all around the tower.

Zahra, Gloria and Petula were holding hands and jumping up and down with total abandon when they felt the strong breeze. Turning quickly, they saw a rather dishevelled Freddy rolling across the turf as he slithered off the invisible winged horse.

"Freddy!"

"Dahling boy!"

"Our hero! Our true hero!"

The darling boy braced himself as he was smothered by the three females. Petula was off the ground and hanging onto his neck from behind. At the front, Gloria was pressing his face into her bosom, her eyes moist with joy and excitement. Zahra had dropped down and had her arms tightly around his legs.

"I think we did it, ladies," he said between gasps of air. Finally all three let go and stood back.

"You did it Freddy!"

"You and the wonderful Pegusinni!"

Catching his breath, Freddy allowed himself a small grin as he realized everything was going to be ok.

"Can you believe that? The way everything happened? It was crazy! All those coincidences in my life? Coming together today? It's totally freaking me out."

"Pwah! No coincidences," said Petula regaining her composure and looking for her comb.

"Indeed not," added Zahra lighting a much needed smoke.

"Not at all, Freddy," said Gloria leaning forward and pinching his cheek, "it was all meant to be."

A quiet noise behind him caused Freddy to turn. All fourteen black Pegusinni were standing smartly in half sections with Gauntlet on his own to the left.

"Is it over now, Freddy?" asked Sefton from the front pair.

"Are people safe now?" asked Rochester standing next to him.

"Are all horses safe now?" asked Gauntlet quietly from his lone position.

Freddy let out a long slow sigh, looked at his small equine friends and said, "Yes, I think everyone is safe now."

"Very well," said the small grey, "should I dismiss the troops now, sir?"

Freddy threw back his head and laughed.

"Yes, why not? Do that!"

"Troops! Dismissed!" called Gauntlet in his loudest Pegusinni voice.

Hearing the order the group of small winged horses broke ranks and started nibbling grass and rolling on the turf; one pair began mutual grooming.

"Hey! You! Kid with the damn bow!"

A uniformed policeman strode past the three ladies and toward Freddy who had a beautifully made English bow slung across his back.

"We're looking for some lunatic with a bow and arrow. Stand right there!"

"Oh, bugger, time to disappear." He looked to where Troy was patiently waiting. "Any chance of one last ride, boss man?"

"Certainly, Freddy, I think we can manage that."

The police man was only yards away when Freddy called to the ladies.

"Sorry, girls! I have to fly! See you by the rose garden!" He had no idea why he'd suggested that place; it was just the first thing that came to his mind.

Troy had his left wing lowered as Freddy walked up. This time the teenager grabbed it much more confidently and hoisted himself aboard, disappearing from sight in front of the perplexed policeman.

For the third time that morning Freddy settled into his position on top of the broad shoulders.

"And where to?" enquired Troy.

"East end of Hyde park, please. By Rotten Row will be great."

464

"Certainly."

"And, Troy."

"Yes?"

"Don't spare the horses."

"Excuse me?" said the great equine to the chuckling teenager.

"Aw, Gawd, some days I just crack myself up!"

"I'm sure you do," was the only droll reply.

"But could we go, like, really slowly this time, please, and not too high. Heck, I might even open my eyes."

As Troy cantered forward and took flight, Gauntlet called from behind.

"Troops re-forming and following, Freddy!"

"Ok, guys! Enjoy the trip!"

He let out a long slow sigh, relaxed his grip on the white mane and actually did open his eyes. They were gliding slowly and silently across the park toward Buckingham Palace when Freddy called out again.

"Any chance of going up really close to that flag pole thing on the top there?"

"Certainly."

Atop the tall white flag pole in the centre of the Palace roof, the gold Royal Standard flapped back and forth in the breeze. Troy spiralled down and around the flag as Freddy leaned his left.

"Closer!" called an exhilarated Freddy.

"No problem."

As Troy glided nearer, Freddy leaned over and with his fingers, brushed the edge of the golden fabric.

"OK! Done! Woo Hoo!"

Troy straightened out and took a course again toward Hyde Park.

"Why did you do that?" called Gauntlet into Freddy's left ear as he cruised alongside.

Yelling against the wind, Freddy called back. "Because one day I want to tell my mum I've been to a place with really high standards!" His voice tailed off into gales of youthful laughter as Gauntlet looked curiously at him, not at all comprehending what had been said. Gauntlet had no idea the boy was practically drunk on the release of emotions, adrenalin and relief.

Within moments they touched down onto the soft sand of The Row. Freddy immediately slithered down to the ground. The first thing he did was to yank the bow off his shoulders, spin it around his head several times and hurl it up into the branches of a tree.

"Hope I never have to see that thing again," he muttered staring upwards.

"I have to leave you now, Freddy," came the quiet deep voice next to him.

"What? Oh. Well, will I see you again?"

"Oh, indeed. I'm sure you will. But for now, I have to leave and attend to other matters of the galaxy."

"Wow. Well, ok then." Freddy raised his hand and gave a slow wave. "You sure I'll see you again sometime?"

The huge white winged horse turned to the boy and gave him a slow equine wink, "I'm quite sure. And, you know my name."

"Yes, I know your name. And you know, thanks for all your help and stuff."

"No, Freddy, it is we who should say thank *you.*" And then he took flight to the west.

"Bye," said Freddy softly still holding his hand in the air.

"Everything ok?" asked Gauntlet, standing quietly next to him.

"What? Oh yeah, I just need a minute to think. You know, get my head around all of this." Suddenly feeling all of his energy had been drained from his body, Freddy slowly lowered himself to the ground and sat cross-legged on the sand, staring into the skyline to the west where Troy had disappeared from sight. Sensing it was a time for calm and quiet, the assembled Pegusinni all moved to graze on the short sweet grass while they waited for him to gather his thoughts.

"You're everywhere and nowhere, baby,
that's where you're at.
Going down the bumpy hillside, in your hippie hat.
Flying across the country and getting fat
Saying everything is groovy
when your tyres are flat!"

He snapped back to reality at the sound of the raucous singing. He had no idea how long he'd been sitting there, totally zoned out to the world but the off-key chorus certainly woke him up.

Zahra, Gloria and Petula were bearing down on him, skipping barefoot in the sand, swinging their shoes over their heads.

"And it's hi-ho silver lining
anywhere you go now, baby!
I see your sun is shining but I will make a fuss
Though it's obvious!"

"Come on, Freddy!"

"On your feet!"

"Get with it, kiddo!"

They were now dancing a circle around him as they hummed their tune.

"And shoes off this time!"

"No backing out!"

"Time to celebrate!"

He grinned, shook his head, not believing he was going to do it. Then he bent down, pulled off his sneakers and socks and joined in with his slightly crackpot friends.

"One more chorus, girls!" Gloria shrieked as she danced across the sand toward the rose garden.

"And it's hi-ho silver lining
anywhere you go now, baby!
I see your sun is shining but I will make a fuss
Though it's obvious!"

In single file behind her, snaking from side to side, skipped Zahra, Petula and for once a rather uninhibited Freddy, toes tickled by the sand and swinging his shoes around his head.

"You three made good time!" He called to the dancing trio as he finally stood still to watch them again.

"Caught a cab from Trafalgar Square right after you left us!"

"Only took two ticky wicks!"

He used the palm of his hand to brush sand from his feet before pulling his trainers back on. He didn't bother with the socks, just stuffed them into a pocket of his jeans. The ladies stopped their singing and dancing and were sitting on the sand in their smart outfits, chattering to each other and attempting to pull on their own shoes. Brushing the sand off his hands on the side of his jeans, he glanced up toward the rose garden. He tilted his head slightly to one side as he stared.

Sitting on one of the green park benches were four men. Three of them were not much more than twenty years old and the fourth was possibly in his middle thirties. At first no one said anything, they just smiled and nodded, watching Freddy and the ladies on the sand. All four had smart cropped hair and were wearing very clean white shirts with button-down collars casually open at the neck, trim black belts, neatly pressed light-coloured denim jeans, and very clean white tennis shoes. They looked like four young men who might be on their way to the tennis or cricket club. There was no one else in the close vicinity, just the ladies giggling on the sand, the teenage boy standing motionless, and the four smiling young men on the bench.

"Do I know you?" asked Freddy very softly.

"No, don't think so."

"Not really."

"Probably not."

"But it's nice to meet you, Freddy."

He was surprised one of them knew his name but he didn't panic. He just continued to stare at them, sensing calmness and a feeling that the men were somehow familiar to him.

Still smiling, the four young men stood up and walked toward him. The one on the very left held out his hand. "Hi, Freddy. I'm Simon."

Freddy stepped forward and shook the young man's hand, realizing that the guy was only a few years older than himself.

"I'm Roy," said the one in his middle thirties, holding out his hand.

"Hello, Roy," Freddy said, slowly returning his handshake.

"Jeffery," said the third.

"Hi Jeffery, nice to meet you," Freddy exchanged another handshake.

Finally, "Hello, old chap, Anthony, or, Tony actually."

"Hello, Anthony or Tony Actually," said Freddy smiling back at the young man.

"Old chap! Old Chap?" The one called Simon laughed and pointed his finger at Anthony. Then he looked at

Freddy, "All this time hanging around with us and he still has that la-di-dah Sandhurst accent!"

The others joined in the laughter and good-natured ribbing of their friend.

"Why do I feel I know you?" Freddy asked again.

"Well, we may be familiar. You know, we've been keen to meet you."

"And great job today, Freddy," said Roy, giving him a thumbs up.

"Today? You know about today?"

"And a neat piece of trick riding there, up near the top of that tower," Jeffery said.

"Indeed, remount staff would have been proud of you," added Anthony.

"Wait! You saw? You know…..? Freddy's voice trailed off as a great sense of realisation swept over him.

Simon leaned slightly forward and said in a conspiratorial voice, "And don't let that Rochester intimidate you, he can be a grumpy old nag when he wants to be."

"No. No way. You can't mean? I mean," Freddy fumbled for words, "I mean, like, you guys are…?"

The young men threw back their heads and laughed kindly at Freddy's confusion and then his recognition and realisation. As they smiled, a round white light appeared a short distance behind them. Initially it was no bigger than a tennis ball, floating, hovering in mid-air. It glowed with an implausible intensity but not in any way glaring or harmful to the eye. The hanging disc started to grow in size and in a matter of moments, spread from the size of a tennis ball to almost six feet across.

Roy looked over his shoulder.

"Hey, guys, looks like our ride's here."

The shining bright white disc continued to grow in diameter until it was almost twelve feet across.

"It was good to meet you, Freddy."

"And you make sure you look after everyone for us."

"Wait, where? Why? You have to go?"

"Indeed we do. We'll leave for now, but, Freddy, you do know we'll always be here, don't you?" said Roy. He raised his hand to wave and then walked toward the glowing circle.

"Bye, Freddy", called Simon, following Roy.

"Take care of everyone, now," said Jeffery walking behind Simon.

As Anthony reached the shining circle of brightness he stopped, turned and raised his right hand to his forehead in an extremely smart salute.

"A little insider information, Freddy," smiling, he paused, still with his hand raised, "Blues and Royals are the only regiment who are allowed to salute when they are not wearing a hat." With a final wink and a wave, he stepped through the circle into the dazzling light.

Within a split second the entire light vanished and Freddy was left staring at the shrubbery around the rose garden. White-faced and trembling, he turned around to see the three ladies sitting cross-legged in lotus position; tears were streaming down their cheeks, their make up streaked and their hair damp. The pendants around their necks were filled with flashes of light and sparkles. Eyes closed, palms of hands facing upwards, the three women were smiling and sobbing at the same time. And this time Freddy didn't get angry with them. He didn't make fun of them. He walked over and stood between Zahra and Gloria and gently rested his hands on each of their shoulders. None of them spoke.

Their shared moment of unity and calm was broken by the clatter of steel horse shoes on the South Carriage Drive. The regiment was returning safely to barracks from the Trooping of the Colour 2007.

"Come on, ladies," said Freddy wiping his nose with the back of his hand, "Let's go over and cheer on our soldiers, eh?"

With streaked faces, dishevelled hair, and damp sand stuck all over, they made their way across the Row to the grass near the roadside. They stood under the trees behind the round, flat stone memorial.

Victoriana was at the front, ridden by the N.C.O. who had taken her out that morning. Directly behind her was Venetia with the Director of Music, closely followed by Spartacus, Achilles and the mounted bands.

"Eyes right!" called the Director of Music to the mounted musicians as they passed the memorial.

But then came a second command.

"Regiment! Eyes *right!*" called Victoriana to every equine present. On her order, two hundred horses, including the alpha mare, turned their heads to the right and lowered their necks as they marched past the teenage boy with the three odd-looking women standing behind him.

Freddy gulped, fought back the dampness in his eyes and then did his best version of the military salute he had seen Anthony do only moments earlier. He kept it until the last of the regiment clattered by, making their way back to the comfort of the barracks.

"Freddy," said a small equine voice behind him, "we have to go now too." It was Gauntlet, looking up at him. All fourteen of the black Pegusinni were standing in neat half sections, with Sefton and Rochester the front pair.

"Where? Where are you going, guys?"

"We need to get ready for our transition now, Freddy," said Rochester.

"We have to head to the west," added Sefton.

"What? Just like that? You'll be gone? Forever?"

"Oh, I don't think forever," replied Sefton, "but yes, some have been here a long time, we need to move on."

"It's been a privilege to have had you as our commanding officer," said Gauntlet and he slowly lowered his neck. The other fourteen joined Gauntlet and lowered their necks toward Freddy.

And this time he couldn't stop it. Freddy Hobbs who was sixteen and a half years old, from Stavely, North Derbyshire, let the tears run down his cheeks. As the fourteen black Pegusinni in their neat half sections moved off down Rotten Row for the last time, he waved and cried. The small winged horses tucked their forelegs, lowered their haunches and silently took flight. At first to the east, and then banking sharply, they turned toward the west, led by the grey.

Dedication

I wrote this story to honour and perpetuate the memory of the men and horses who were murdered In Hyde Park and Regents Park on July 20th, 1982.

You will not be forgotten.

Peter DeCosemo

To all members of the Household Cavalry Mounted Regiment past and present.

As you were reading the story you probably at some point yelled out,

"That's not true! He's got that wrong!"

Well, you are probably right. As an ex serving member and remount rider for the regiment, (from a *long* time ago), I based most things around my memory but, to benefit the story I took the occasional liberty with a few facts. In particular with certain aspects of the layout of the equine sick bay area and some of the security in place throughout the barracks. So please don't feel the need to write to me or to argue on bulletin boards about the liberties I took. It is all in the spirit of the story which I hope you enjoyed reading as much as I did creating.

My best wishes,

Peter DeCosemo

Acknowledgements

To Pip Wheatcroft for her input, suggestions and making the mistake of saying, *"Well Peter, if you are going to write a book, make it a really good big book."*

To Anne Pilgrim and Mal Magson for encouraging me to keep going as I was churning out the chapters and for their enthusiasm when I got the first copy finished.

To Dave Elsdon, the first non-horseman to read the manuscript. He gave it a great review and went on to help with the technical side of the document and spent a massive amount of time on the photos for the cover and created the website.

To Cathi Pool, from York Publishing, who as an industry professional gave the book a big thumbs up, and was instrumental in getting it to print.

A thank you to Warrant Officer II Richard Castelow, Master Saddler for the regiment, the first military chap to read the manuscript and give it a green light. Thanks, you miserable old Yorkshire ***** !

And huge thanks to Becky Holmes in Helena Montana. She came for a visit to the U.K. and when acting as her tour guide, I took her Hyde Park, to the barracks, to the memorial in the park and to Horse guard's Parade. It was during this day the idea for the story arrived in my head. Becky then went on to do the first proof-read of each and every chapter as I emailed them to her and was driving force in me getting to the finish line.

"Damn well hurry up, I want to know if all the horses are safe!"